THE SEX CLUB

L.J. SELLERS

THE SEX CLUB

ISBN 978-0-9795182-0-1
Published in the USA
Library of Congress Control Number: 2007903440

 spellbinderpress.com

This book is for women around the world who have been denied reproductive choices and services. I wish to express deep appreciation for all the individuals who provide those services and/or work to change the laws that deny them.

I also thank my family members and friends who have supported my writing over the years. Special thanks to Detective Michael Quakenbush for providing background information for this story, to editors Judy Sawyer and Cher Mikkola for their professionalism and encouragement, and to graphic designer Gwen Rhoads for her provocative cover.

‹ **1** ›

Tuesday, October 19, 9:32 a.m.

"You can put your clothes back on, then we'll talk some more."

Kera gave the girl a quick smile and stepped out of the examining room. Jessie, if that was her real name, claimed to be sixteen. But Kera suspected she was younger, maybe all of thirteen or fourteen. The girl was slender, with the small breasts and flawless skin of someone who hadn't grown into her adult body yet.

Kera lingered in the clinic hallway and jotted some notes on Jessie's chart. Genital warts (HPV) on the inner labia treated with liquid nitrogen. Clearly, her client was sexually active, but there was no sign of bruising or abuse. Yet her tender age made Kera wonder if the sex was truly consensual. Sometimes she walked a fine line between respecting a client's sexual privacy and ignoring a potentially abusive situation. She would ask a few probing questions just to make sure Jessie was in a mutually consenting relationship.

Kera gave the girl enough time to get dressed, then knocked lightly and stepped back into the windowless room. Crammed into the eight-by-ten space was an examining table, a cabinet–sink combination, a wheeled stool, and a simple black-cushioned chair. The pale cream walls failed to make the room seem bigger.

"How long have you been sexually active, Jessie?" Kera took a seat on the stool.

"For a while." The girl flipped her waffle-iron-straight, blond hair off her shoulders and stared defiantly. "Why?"

"Is someone forcing or pressuring you to have inter-course?"

"No." Jessie rolled her eyes.

"This is a safe place to talk about your sexual situation. Everything you say here is confidential."

The girl's gray eyes flashed with irritation. "I said there's no pressure. I like hooking up."

"Do you use contraception?" Sometimes her questions were so routine, Kera felt more like a waitress than a health-care worker.

The girl shrugged. "Sometimes we use condoms."

The way she used the word "we" gave Kera pause. "Have you had more than one partner?"

Now Jessie hesitated. "Nicole said I didn't have to tell about them."

Kera noted the plural use of "them," but the reference to "Nicole" also caught her attention. She had treated another young girl with genital warts last week, and her name may have been Nicole. It bothered Kera that she didn't remem-ber for sure. But she saw so many young women, and often only once, for about twenty minutes. They came, picked up their pills or antibiotics, and went on their way. Kera knew the work she did was important in a big-picture way, but she wished she saw more proof of it in the everyday details.

"You don't have to tell me about your partners, but you do have to tell them about the genital warts. It's very im-portant that they get treatment, so they don't spread it to others."

"Okay. I'll tell 'em."

"Where do you go to school?"

Again Jessie hesitated. "Spencer High."

Kera was doubtful. But Spencer was only a block away from Kincaid Middle School, which suddenly seemed more likely. And a little disturbing. The girl she had seen last week was a student at Kincaid. And two months earlier, a fourteen-year-old girl from the school had come in for emergency contraception.

Kera made a mental note to look back through the files to see how many kids from Kincaid had visited the clinic in the past six months. And how many of them reported having unprotected sex. Maybe she needed to call the school, find out what kind of sex education they were teaching—if any. Perhaps even conduct an outreach program there, if the school's administrators would let her. Even if young teenagers thought they were ready for sex, they certainly weren't ready to be parents. And nobody was ever prepared to find out they were HIV positive.

"Are you aware that the HIV virus is sexually transmitted?" Kera asked, expecting more eye rolling.

Instead, Jessie seemed to deflate, then spent a long moment looking at her fingernails. When she looked up, she had the same expression Kera used to see on her son's face when he wanted to tell her something, but couldn't. On impulse, Kera pulled a business card out of her jacket pocket and wrote her home e-mail address and cell phone number on the back.

"This is my personal contact information. You can e-mail me if you have questions or concerns that you feel you can't discuss face to face."

Jessie took the card, then quickly looked away.

"I'd like to talk to you about birth control options." Kera handed her a pamphlet from the rack of educational materials on the wall.

"I can't." Jessie shook her head. "You don't know what it's like in our church. If my mother ever found the pills, my life would be ruined." Her distress was palpable.

"It doesn't have to be pills, there are other—"

The girl jumped up and grabbed her backpack. "I gotta go. Thanks for the medicine."

"Wait," Kera called after her.

But Jessie was already out the door, blond hair swinging as she turned into the hall. Disappointed by her failure, Kera finished writing notes on Jessie's chart. Perhaps the girl would come back. She flipped the manila folder closed and scooted off the stool. As Kera moved toward the door, she noticed a tiny pink cell phone on the examining table next to the discarded birth control pamphlet. Jessie must have left it.

Kera grabbed the phone and headed toward the front of the building, hoping to catch Jessie at the front desk. She turned left in the middle of the building where the two main hallways intersected under a giant skylight.

The clinic staff had moved into the new building a few months ago, and Kera loved everything about it. The creamy yellow walls were freshly painted, the stainless steel shined, and nothing was scratched or dingy, yet. Compared to the metal sheds and mud huts she'd worked in during her years in Africa with the International Red Cross, the building was a dream. And compared to the chaos and heartache of the years she spent working in the ER, her time at the clinic felt stress free.

Near the front, the walkway opened on the left into a small reception area where daylight filtered in through opaque floor-to-ceiling windows. Directly in front of her stood the building's entrance, a small enclosed plexiglass foyer with a camera and a locked inner door. Nobody came in without telling the receptionist their name and their business at the clinic. Security was a top priority. Behind the wall to the right was the surgical area where two non-staff physicians performed abortions on Tuesday and Friday mornings.

Beyond the entrance and across the grass, a small group of protestors gathered on the sidewalk. Kera had counted seven as she hurried into work this morning. Now they were lowering their signs and preparing to leave. Like clockwork, they showed up every Tuesday and Friday before 7 a.m. with signs that said things like "Choose Life" and "Don't Murder Your Baby." The group was mostly female, although occasionally a middle-aged man joined in. Kera had come to recognize two of the protestors who participated every week: a young woman of around twenty who looked half starved and always wore red—a symbol of blood, Kera thought—and a tiny middle-aged woman with close-cropped hair who often carried a Bible in addition to her homemade sign. The anti-abortionists called out with cries of "We can help," hoping to attract the attention of the women who entered the clinic in the early hours.

But those activities were over for the day. The protestors were getting into their cars and heading home, and the clinic was unusually quiet. Two young mothers with babies on their hips stood at the counter, where Roselyn, the young Hispanic receptionist, silently stared at the computer screen, searching for information. Another young woman waited in a chair near the front windows. Jessie seemed to be long gone.

As Kera spun around, intending to place Jessie's chart in the to-file basket, thunder boomed, the building shook, and the glass in the front windows blew out. Stunned by the blast, she lost her footing and went down. As she fell, Kera hit her head on the corner of the reception counter and, for a minute, her world went dark.

‹ 2 ›

Tuesday, October 19, 9:45 a.m.

She woke to wailing babies and the sulfur stink of burnt gunpowder. Kera's temple pulsed with pain, but she ignored it. She pushed herself up, felt a cool October breeze blowing through the lobby, and promptly became so dizzy she had to lie back down. What the hell had happened?

Pounding footsteps charged down the hall. Most were muffled, the soft thud of work shoes. Only the director's pumps made sharp staccato sounds as they approached. In the background, the babies kept crying.

"Kera. Are you hurt?" Sheila Brentwood kneeled next to her, the tall woman's voice sounding far away. Lavender-scented hands touched Kera's forehead.

"I don't know." Her own voice seemed distant. "I think I hit my head."

"You did." Sheila turned to someone and said, "Bring some gauze and some ice."

"Has anyone called 911?"

"I am right now."

The excited voices jumbled together, and footsteps thundered in from the reception area. "A client is hurt."

Kera desperately wanted to sit up, to rush to the aid of the injured, but she knew she wasn't ready. "Am I bleeding?" The fog in her brain began to clear, replaced with a sharp sting at her temple.

"Just a little."

Sheila still had the bedside manner of a nurse, but with her black blazer and auburn hair pulled tightly into a bun, she looked like the administrator that she had become.

"Was that a bomb?" Kera asked.

"It blew out the front windows." Andrea, the clinic manager, pressed gauze to Kera's forehead. Andrea's perfectly balanced Japanese features showed worry for the first time since Kera had known her. Kera reached up and tried to push Andrea's hand away. "I'm okay. Go help the others."

"Only one young woman is injured, and both Janine and Julie are with her."

"How badly?"

"There's a three-inch chunk of glass sticking out of her neck." Andrea's voice was soft, but her enunciation was always perfect.

Sirens sounded in the distance. Sheila and Andrea breathed a collective sigh of relief, and Kera willed their young client to hang onto her life. If the girl made it into the emergency room, the ER doctors would save her. Kera had witnessed that miracle many times.

She shuddered to think how many people could have been hurt if this had been a busy Friday afternoon instead of a quiet Tuesday morning. Who could have done such a horrible thing? What were they thinking?

THE WOMAN blinked as the windows blew, and she missed seeing the full effect of the explosion. But the sound was overwhelming. Even from across the street, the noise was bigger than she had expected. It was only her second pipe bomb. The first one—for practice—had been a bit of a dud, so she'd apparently over-corrected this time. But bigger was better. It was the only way to get through to these people. The political channels were too slow, and hundreds of babies' lives were at stake every day.

Accessing the clinic had been quite a challenge. It was new and built with security in mind. There was a camera mounted on each side of the building and not much in the way of shrubbery to hide behind. She had cased the clinic during its first few months from the safety of a group of regular protesters. After methodically planning her moves, she had stopped coming with the group. Today, the navy-blue hooded sweatshirt, jeans, and backpack she had worn made her look like a kid—if the camera even caught her.

Now the sweatshirt and backpack were stuffed under the car seat, and she was just another middle-aged woman in the parking lot at the shopping center across the street. She knew she should get moving, but the sight of women and girls running from the building transfixed her. Upending their ordered little world where they encouraged promiscuity and discarded life was immensely satisfying. She could feel God's approval.

Out of the chaos, a young girl emerged, moving quickly across the parking lot and up the sidewalk toward Commerce Street. For a moment, she thought it might be Jessie Davenport, a young church member and close friend of her daughter. But it couldn't be. Not Jessie, not here. Just someone who looked like her.

The wail of a siren sent a bolt of anxiety through her, and she almost lost control of her bladder. She put the Tahoe in reverse and sped away from the shopping center. She had to hurry home and change before her volunteer shift at the hospital.

DETECTIVE WADE JACKSON turned down Commerce Street and was relieved to see the clinic still standing at the end of the block. The report of a bomb had stunned him. He had lived in Eugene, Oregon, his whole life and had been on the police force for half of it, but had never dealt with a sizable explosion. A few years back, a young male ecoterrorist had set fire to a car lot full of SUVs down near the university, but overall, Eugene was a safe, mid-sized town with a hundred and forty thousand people, many of whom drove around with bumper stickers that said "Visualize World Peace."

As the most experienced detective in a group of sixteen, Jackson typically investigated homicides rather than sex or property crimes. But he didn't have an active investigation at the moment, and the supervising sergeant had asked him to take the lead. A wave of guilt hit the pit of his stomach. Now that he was a single father, every time he took on a new case, for the first few days he effectively abandoned his daughter. And Katie was still struggling with her parents' separation and the fact that her mother chose to continue drinking rather than be part of their family. If this bomb case turned out to be long and complicated, he'd have to give up the lead to another detective.

Jackson pulled into the long narrow parking lot, where he passed a group of women—assorted sizes and ages—huddled on the sidewalk near the street. Two young girls each held a baby on their hips. One wept openly, shoulders heaving, but no one in the group looked bloody. Tension drained from his shoulders. Maybe this would not be as awful as he'd expected. The nightly news for the last three years had led him to associate bombs with body parts scraped off the pavement.

Only a dozen cars, including a black-and-white police unit, were scattered throughout the lot. Jackson slammed into the first open space. He felt for his Sig Sauer and evidence collection bag, then jumped out of the car.

He jogged up the sidewalk toward the main entrance. The intentionally nondescript gray brick building sat on the back curve of the street and sported good visibility on all sides. Its one vulnerability, the windows in the reception area, had been blown out, and a gaping hole exposed its soft yellow inside. A twenty-something Asian woman in light blue scrubs ran out the front door, spotted him immediately, and sprinted down the sidewalk.

She grabbed his arm. "We need an ambulance. Someone's hurt badly."

Jackson started to reach for his cell phone, but in the distance he could hear the wail of the ambulance screaming up West 11th Avenue. Another patrol unit careened into the parking lot and almost hit a blue Toyota pulling out of its space. Jackson motioned for the officer behind the wheel to roll down his window.

"Secure the perimeter," he yelled. " Don't let that car leave. And don't let anyone in that group near the sidewalk leave."

As he looked over at the huddled clinic workers, his eye caught a group of protestors across the street, at the edge of the shopping center. Their signs hung limply at their sides as they stared back at the clinic. "And bring those protestors back over here for questioning."

Then it hit him. This bomb seemed almost inevitable. A few months earlier, one of Portland's abortion clinics had been rocked by violent protests, followed by several pipe bomb explosions. The statewide group that sponsored the Portland protests had a chapter here in town. In hindsight, it was only a matter of time before they turned their attention to Eugene's new clinic. Jackson was glad that his daughter was only fourteen and that he didn't have to worry about her coming to Planned Parenthood for many years.

He turned back to the clinic and started up the front walkway. Shards of white-tinted glass and mangled azalea branches covered the narrow lawn and spilled onto the cement path. The smell of gunpowder wafted past on a warm gust of wind. The combination reminded him of summer afternoons at the firing range.

Once inside, Jackson found himself in a small glass-walled foyer with a camera mounted above the door. But the security system was unmanned at the moment, and he pushed through the unlocked door into the waiting area. Near the massive hole in the front wall, two clinic workers huddled over a young female client, who, from where he stood, looked lifeless. Blood pooled in the area around her head. Jackson rushed over, past the twisted chairs and scattered debris, desperately trying to recall his first aid training. The women weren't wearing white, so Jackson asked, "Is either of you a nurse or doctor?"

The older of the two looked up quickly and said, "I'm a nurse." She wore her hair pulled into a ponytail and her makeup-less face was drained of color. "But I can't do much here."

Jackson was close enough to see the injured girl now, with her Goth-black hair, delicate features, and Green Day T-shirt. A chunk of glass thrust out of her neck and the blood flowed freely around it. The nurse pressed white strips of cloth to both sides of the wound. The injured girl's eyes fluttered open, then closed again. She didn't look much older than his daughter.

"I'm afraid to remove it," the nurse said, her voice almost a whisper. "If I do, she could bleed to death."

They all heard the ambulance then, its siren cutting off as it entered the parking lot. For a moment, silence settled over the room. Then a sparrow burst through the opening in the wall and began chirping wildly as it swooped around looking for an exit. For a second, the bird drew their attention away from the bleeding girl. A moment later, paramedics charged through the foyer door, and Jackson gladly stepped back.

"Is anyone else hurt?" he asked the nurse.

"One of our staff is down in the hallway."

Jackson moved quickly to the end of the counter, around the corner, and into the wide hall.

Another female lay prone on the crème-and-gray tile floor, attended to by a tall woman in a tailored black blazer. Jackson recognized her as the clinic's director, Sheila Brentwood. He had met her at a fundraiser last year, an event his soon-to-be-ex wife had dragged him to. Sheila nodded to him but didn't speak.

"Is she all right?"

The prone woman sat up. Through the skylight, the sun lit up her copper-colored hair, which fell in a braid nearly to her waist. Even seated on the floor with a bloodied forehead, she looked strong and athletic.

"I felt dizzy for a few minutes. But really, I'm all right." She tried to smile, but didn't make it. Her wide-set hazel eyes held a sadness that went deeper than this incident.

"The paramedics will be right with you. I'm going to check out the rest of the building."

Sheila stood and said, "I think it's empty now. I asked everyone to stay outside and speak with the police when they got here, but I'm afraid a few of our younger patients may have left. And who could blame them?" She gave him a thin, determined smile.

"Once we've secured the building, I'll need a place to conduct interviews," Jackson said. "And a list of everyone that was here at the time of the explosion. And anyone in the parking lot, if they're still here."

Jackson moved off and began to search the rooms—for more injured victims or even the bomber, who could be hiding somewhere. But he knew that was wishful thinking. The Portland police had failed to identify their bomber, even with the help of the FBI. Meanwhile, they had beefed up security around all the clinics, but one had eventually closed. Jackson made a mental note to suggest to Sheila that she hire a full-time security guard. If this was the work of the same person or group, there was more to come.

OVER HER PROTESTS, two good-sized paramedics hauled Kera outside on a canvas stretcher. She was relieved to be outside and back in touch with fresh air and blue sky, but she would rather have walked. The ambulance carrying the injured client pulled away from the clinic as the medics transferred Kera to a metal gurney on wheels. They were near the back end of a second ambulance, but she had no intention of getting in and riding to the hospital. After they checked her vital statistics, Kera pushed to her feet.

"I'm fine, really. In fact, I'd like to walk around for a moment."

"Doctors and nurses make the worst patients." The young man in the dark blue uniform grinned, then said somberly, "I think you need a CAT scan for your head."

Kera smiled back. "Thanks, but I'm fine."

Without thinking, she moved toward the street and away from the building. Her legs trembled with a cellular memory of the blast. It had been so unexpected. So otherworldly and overpowering. Then it hit her like a punch in the gut. Nathan must have experienced something very similar during the moment his convoy was hit. Her son had not survived, though. The car bombs in Iraq were intended to do much more damage than what had happened in the lobby here.

Not now, she told herself. With all her mental discipline, Kera pulled her thoughts away from Nathan. She had to stay focused on what was happening to the clinic, to help her co-workers get through this, to help them find the courage to come back to work. As the chaos around her escalated—with more police cars arriving and a ring of onlookers gathering across the street—Kera stood on the grass and took long slow pulls of oxygen, breathing from deep in her abdomen. She had learned the technique from a grief counselor, and it had become part of the fabric of her life.

As Kera turned back toward the clinic, a white news van lurched to a stop on the pavement a few feet away. A young blond woman jumped out, followed by a middle-aged man with an oversized video camera. The reporter, who looked like a high school girl on career day, rushed up to Kera and asked breathlessly, "Do you work at the clinic?"

"Yes. But you should speak with our director for a comment."

"We'll never get past the cops in the parking lot," she gushed. Her bright blue eyes sparked with excitement. Behind her, the cameraman was setting up his equipment on a tripod.

"Please give me a quick statement. I'm Trina Waterman with KRSL TV."

Kera shrugged. "Okay, a quick one. I need to get back in there and see how I can help."

"First, who are you and what do you do here?" Trina held out her microphone.

"Kera Kollmorgan. I'm a registered nurse and the clinic's Youth Outreach Coordinator."

"I notice you have a bandage on your head. Were you near the bomb when it went off?"

The camera was rolling now, but Kera was at ease. As the clinic's outreach person, she'd given on-air interviews before. "Not really. The repercussion made me lose my footing though, and I fell."

"Was anyone else hurt?"

"A young girl is on her way to the hospital now. She has a chunk of glass sticking out of her neck."

"Who do you think did this?" Trina cranked up her intensity for the camera.

"A fanatic with no regard for human life."

"Will the clinic shut down?"

"Of course not," Kera said. "Our services are vital to women in this community." Just then, a patrol cop in a dark blue uniform rushed up and shouted at the news crews to get back. Kera took the opportunity to terminate the interview and head back toward the building.

As she weaved through the half dozen patrol cars choking the parking lot, Andrea rushed up to her. "Where were you?

Are you all right?"

"I'm fine. How's the girl who was hurt?"

"The paramedics said it nicked her carotid artery."

Kera bit her lip. "What's her name?"

"Rebecca Dunn."

Kera didn't think she had ever met her. "What now?"

Andrea shrugged. "The detective wants to speak with you. He's in Sheila's office."

DETECTIVE JACKSON looked up quickly from the desk. "You're feeling better?" Sheila's office was up-scale by non-profit standards: It had carpeting and a small window.

"I am. Thanks."

"Kera Kollmorgan, right?"

"Yes." She couldn't read his dark eyes. Was he irritated? Had she kept him waiting? Kera took a seat on the other side of her boss' desk and looked him over. She decided he looked like a typical cop with his navy blue slacks and al-most matching suit jacket. The white shirt underneath was open at the collar, and his face was pleasant with a strong jaw and full lips. A small white scar tugged at the corner of his left eye.

"Where were you when the bomb went off?"

"Right there in the hallway where you saw me. I lost my balance and fell." Kera looked down at her shoes. "My Birkenstocks have lost all their tread."

"Did you see anyone or anything suspicious before the explosion?"

"No. I was with a patient." The scent of Sheila's lavender perfume hung in the air. Kera thought she might sneeze.

"Have you seen anyone unusual around the clinic lately? Someone who doesn't look like they belong? Or who has been here too often?" He bounced his pen on the desk as he fired off questions.

Kera gave it some thought. "There was a young man in

the lobby yesterday afternoon. Of course, we get some guys in here, but not many. He was just waiting for his girlfriend, but the tattoo caught my eye."

"Can you describe it?"

"Thick dark triangles along his neck." She gestured with her hands. "But he was just sitting in the chairs, not acting suspicious in any way. I shouldn't have mentioned him. Tattoos are pretty mainstream these days." She had a small bronze-and-turquoise sun on her left shoulder, a present to herself from Thailand twenty years ago.

"Have you received any threatening calls or letters lately?'

Kera shook her head. Not unless she counted the "I'm not coming back" letter her husband had sent from Iraq last week.

"Have any of your patients made any threats or said anything disturbing recently?"

"About five months ago, a patient's mother called and said she would 'bitch slap me silly' if I ever gave birth control to her daughter again."

He raised one eyebrow. "And did you?"

"The patient has not been back."

"What's her name?"

"I can't divulge patient information."

Those dark eyes tried to intimidate her. "I can get a search warrant."

"You'll have to." She smiled to show it wasn't personal.

"Okay. That's it for now. You should go home and rest. Ms. Brentwood said you hit your head hard enough to black out."

"I'm fine. I come from a long line of thick-skulled Dutch people. You know that song that was popular a few years back? I get knocked down, but I get up again… That's me."

"You don't look thick skulled." He smiled, and his eyes

finally lit up. Kera decided he was okay. "Take care, Ms. Kollmorgan."

"Thanks. I will."

Kera had no desire to go home. But staying at the damaged clinic made no sense either. Most of the staff had gone, and they certainly weren't taking any clients this afternoon. Kera gathered her sweater and purse and walked out with Andrea.

"Do you want to stop at Taylor's with me and have a glass of wine?" Kera asked when they reached the parking lot.

"Thanks, but I can't. I've got to pick up the kids."

Police officers were still searching the property and questioning some of the protestors as Kera drove away. A wave of despair washed over her. She still found it hard to come home to an empty house, and today would be more difficult than most.

‹ **3** ›

Kera hung her sweater in the front closet, then walked through the living areas and stood gazing out her back windows, which had a partial view of the city below. She was grateful for her bright sunlit home and comfortable furnishings. Five years in Uganda witnessing soul-crushing poverty had taught her not to take anything for granted. The simple act of turning on a faucet and having hot water come out still made her smile.

But she was not used to the silence and sterility—no radio playing in the background, no lingering smell of burnt toast. Sometimes it felt more like a plush hotel suite than a home. Looking down at the busy streets only served to remind her that she was alone. But she had not ended up that way overnight, and so she'd had some time to adjust.

Soon after high school, Nathan had joined the Army, leaving a vacuum that had once been filled by young laughter and loud music. Kera had fought his decision with every piece of logic she could muster, but Nathan was an independent and patriotic young man who wanted to make his own way in the world. At first, he'd been stationed at Fort Wainwright in Alaska, and Kera had been so relieved, she'd refused to let herself feel sad about his absence. Two months later, 9/11 happened, and her life, as she knew it, began to slide into the abyss.

First, her husband Daniel had started to drift—working late, keeping to himself, and talking about finding a new purpose in life. That plateau of uncertainty—married but feeling more and more alone—had gone on for nearly a year. Then in August, Nathan had shipped out to Iraq, and a week later, the men in uniform had come to her door. Kera had been alone then too, and she began to weep even before they opened their mouths. Nathan, who had trained as a medic—following in his parents' footsteps—had been killed on his second day in Iraq while transporting wounded soldiers to an airfield.

Kera felt the tears spring hot and bitter to her cheeks. Her son and best friend was gone forever, and there was a hole in her life that could never be healed. Daniel, inconsolable in his grief, had deserted her two weeks after Nathan's funeral, heading for Iraq "to find purpose in his life."

Kera wiped away her tears. She had to stop letting it pull her down. There were millions of people in worse shape—people who were not only lonely, but cold, hungry, and homeless too.

She changed out of her work clothes into some baggy cotton tie-dyes, then grabbed a can of Diet Dr Pepper from the fridge and sat down in front of her computer. The Internet was her refuge. It connected her to people everywhere. Some were silly and self-involved, but most were reaching out in a passionate and generous embrace of the world around them.

Kera logged on to www.1stheadlines.com. She needed to know what had changed in the world while she was at work. She had been a news junkie since college, but in the last three years, the news had become an obsession. The wars, the terrorists, the right-wing fanatics; it was critical to keep track of the things that threatened her.

She scanned the headlines, noting that her husband had not been killed or kidnapped in Iraq. Kera suspected that on some grief-stricken level, Daniel wanted to die and that his stay in the war zone was really a suicide mission.

Impulsively, Kera popped out of her chair and began to

pace. She couldn't get today's explosion out of her mind. Had they really meant to hurt someone or was it a scare tactic gone wrong? She thought of the bomber as "they" because of the clinic's protestors and the extremist group they belonged to, the Conservative Culture Alliance.

Kera hurried into the kitchen and used the wall phone to call the patient information line at North McKenzie Hospital. "This is Kera Kollmorgan, a nurse from Planned Parenthood. I'm calling about Rebecca Dunn. She was brought into the emergency room this afternoon. I'd like to know how she's doing."

"Let me check for you." After a moment, the receptionist said, "She's still in intensive care. I can put you through to the charge nurse there."

"Please do."

The nurse took a long time to come to the phone. "What's your relationship to the patient?" she asked.

"I'm a nurse at Planned Parenthood. Rebecca was a client in our clinic when she was injured."

"I'm sorry to report that Rebecca is in a coma."

Kera bit down on the inside of her mouth. She had worked in emergency rooms and knew what that meant. "What's her prognosis?"

"I can't tell you that. But she lost a lot of blood."

"Has her family been contacted?"

"They're here now."

"Thanks." Kera clicked off the phone and pressed her hand to her mouth. She could taste blood on her tongue.

She slammed her fist against the phone book. How dare they kill an innocent young woman! She paced the kitchen, swearing out loud at the bomber. Her heart pounded until the rage felt like it would consume her.

Tuesday, October 19, 5:27 p.m.
JACKSON COULD BARELY keep his attention on the video

footage. He was starving and had been staring at the television screen for hours. Nothing on the tape had moved for twenty minutes.

After spending the afternoon at the bomb scene, he and Rob Schakowski, another veteran detective he often partnered with, had come back to the department with a box load of videotapes from the clinic's surveillance cameras. Armed with coffee and notepads, they had set up a VCR in the "kids" interview room with the overstuffed brown couches. First, they had watched the tape of Planned Parenthood's inner foyer, jotting down names and reactions as people came into the clinic and announced themselves. No one stood out as unusual. Now they were watching the tape from the camera mounted outside the front of the building, and after an hour of staring at landscaping, Jackson was restless and hungry.

"We should send out for pizza," Schak announced suddenly.

Jackson paused the tape. "Can we do Chinese instead? I'm trying to lose a few pounds."

"Great. You find out you have high cholesterol, so now I get to eat vegetables instead of real food."

"Shut up about it, Schak. I never should have told you." After separating from his wife—kicking her out, actually—Jackson hadn't discussed anything personal with another adult for about six months. Then one day, he started telling Schak some of the things he used to share with Renee, when she was sober. Now he regretted it.

"I'm just messing with you. Don't be so sensitive." Schakowski, with his crew-cut hair and barrel-shaped torso, would never be mistaken for the sensitive type.

"Chinese or not?"

"Fine. But no fucking broccoli."

Jackson went back to his desk where he had the number for the Grand China restaurant handy. As he reached for his phone, it rang on an internal line.

The dispatcher sounded a little worked up. "Detective Jackson, a call just came in reporting a body in a dumpster behind the Regency Apartments. The 1700 block of Patterson Street."

Shit. That was his neighborhood. "Any other information?" he asked.

"A young man named Trevor Michelson made the call. I asked him to wait by the dumpster and not let anyone near the body until you got there."

"Call the medical examiner and the DA's office. Get Mc-Cray and Evans down there too. I'm on my way."

Tuesday, October 19, 6:05 p.m.

KERA LOOKED AROUND for a project, something that would distract her and use up her negative energy. After the letter she'd received from Daniel two days ago, she knew just what would make her feel better.

She made a quick trip to Safeway for large plastic bags and picked up a dozen empty produce boxes while she was at it.

Determined to take charge of some part of her life, Kera hauled some of the empty boxes into the master bedroom and began to pack up Daniel's stuff. To hell with him, she thought. Their marriage had been half dead before he left for Iraq, and she would never forgive him for abandoning her during her grief.

Suit jackets, slacks, shoes, and drawers full of jogging clothes; Kera filled the three boxes quickly and went back to the living room for more. Tennis rackets, CDs, his family photos—she tucked all of it into the brown cardboard containers and sealed them with clear tape.

She carried the first box out to the garage but found no place to set it down. The space was crammed with more of Daniel's stuff: power tools, snow skis, water skis, model planes, woodworking machines—most of it unmarred by actual use. Her husband's interests had shifted quickly.

Kera grabbed her keys and backed her car out of the garage and into the driveway to make room for the boxes and bags she'd filled. If she didn't hear from Daniel in the next two weeks, she'd hire a mover and put all his junk in storage. She refused to play the role of crap keeper, the one left behind to safeguard the stuff he no longer wanted but couldn't let go.

Back in the house, Kera looked down the hall toward Nathan's room. She had to tackle it sooner or later. With a burst of courage, she grabbed some boxes, charged down the hall, and pushed open Nathan's door. Then she froze. His scent—Old Spice deodorant mixed with sun-kissed skin and rubber basketball—lingered in the air. Kera's chest tightened until she couldn't breathe. She backed out and closed the door. Okay. Not yet. Not tonight, anyway.

Later, feeling emotionally exhausted, she sat down at her iMac and opened her e-mail account.

She read a quick note from her sister in Bend and another message from a charity called Food for Lane County that she volunteered with on Saturdays. Then she spotted a file from a hotmail sender called *blowgirl_jd*. Kera almost deleted it. But curiosity got the better of her. It had been sent at 12:15 that day. She clicked it open.

Kera
Here's a question for you. How do you say no to some kinds of sex? I mean, I like regular hooking up a lot. Even some nasty stuff. But not everything. I like to make "Mike" happy but sometimes he has strange…

That was it. Not even a signature. As if the writer had accidentally sent the e-mail before she intended. Or maybe she had been interrupted. Kera intuitively knew it was Jessie. The message had been sent an hour after Kera gave Jessie Davenport her contact information.

Kera hit reply, typed "jd" at the top of the screen, then hesitated. This was such a fine line. To keep the communication open, she had to accept Jessie's sexuality on its own terms and try to help with her concern. Yet, given the opportunity, Kera would discourage any girl that age from starting a physical relationship. For her, it was not so much a question of morality but one of emotion and consequence. But Jessie was already in a relationship and obviously needed her help.

Kera kept her response brief:

This is a problem in many relationships. When your partner suggests something you don't want to do, suggest (and start) something else instead. If he pressures you, say "no" and end the encounter. You don't have to do anything you're not comfortable with. And don't forget to use birth control. —KK

After sending the e-mail, Kera wondered for a moment about Jessie's boyfriend. She thought that he might be older than Jessie, probably in high school. But the idea that he wanted "strange stuff" bothered Kera a bit. Most adolescent males were not very imaginative about sex. They didn't have the patience. Or at least, that had been her experience as a teenager. But now some kids—in a misguided effort to stay virgins—engaged in oral and anal sex rather than vaginal. But they typically didn't consider those activities strange. What did Jessie's boyfriend want from her?

Kera tried to put Jessie out of her mind. She would probably never hear from or see the girl again.

Tuesday, October 19, 6:27 p.m.
JACKSON AND SCHAKOWSKI headed for their city-issued cars in the underground parking area and neither mentioned the missed dinner. The department, located in city hall, had outgrown its space years ago, but local taxpayers had turned down three requests for the money to build new

headquarters. Yet that was the least of Eugene's law enforcement financial troubles.

"You said you were tired of investigating scumbag-on-scumbag homicides," his partner commented as they reached the garage.

"I was thinking more along the lines of a promotion."

As Jackson pulled the Impala into traffic, the evening sun broke through the clouds and illuminated the thin sheen of rainwater scattered over the downtown area. The hodge-podge of old buildings had no theme, except that none were over four stories tall. Many were empty—thanks to a misguided city council decision two decades ago—and almost none contained the same business enterprise for more than a few years. The eight-block downtown core reinvented itself continuously, to the delight of some and disgust of others. Only the kids and transients who hung out around the bus station stayed the same.

Jackson headed south on Pearl Street and used speed dial to call his daughter, Katie. When she didn't answer the house phone, he tried her cell phone number. She picked up after three rings, sounding impatient.

"Hey kiddo. It's Dad. Where are you? I thought we agreed that you would be home by six o'clock."

"I'm on my way. Emily's mother is giving me a ride."

Hmm. Jackson liked Emily, but he had never met her mother. Still, he couldn't deal with any of it right now. "I'm not going to make it for dinner. I just got called out on a homicide, and I'll be working very late. Sorry honey." Jackson paused, but his daughter didn't comment. "I'm going to call your Aunt Jan and have her pick you up. I want you to stay there overnight."

Katie let out an exasperated sigh. "So first you rag me for not being home, then you tell me I can't stay home."

"I like to keep you on your toes."

"Nice."

"I'll call Jan now, and I'll check in with you tomorrow." Jackson turned right on Patterson. "I love you."

"Same." Katie hung up. Jackson pushed aside the guilt. He didn't work late that often. And it wasn't his fault that Katie's mother refused to get sober.

A white Explorer on his right suddenly cut him off. Jackson leaned on the horn. Idiot.

In a few blocks, Jackson passed the familiar laundromat and health food store he jogged by on occasion. Then eased his car through a narrow parking lot in front of the Regency Apartments, a two-story building with a dull-white paint job and terra cotta doors. He counted eight units on the street side, four on each level. Massive oak trees stood on each end of the complex as if guarding it—or holding it up. Built in the forties, as were most of the homes in the neighborhood, the apartment building looked dingy, even though the landscaping was neatly tended.

As Jackson drove into the back parking area, the setting sun cast an eerie pink light over the scene. Hesitant shadows peeked out between the cars. A tall, scrawny teenage boy shivered next to a gray dumpster at the rear of the lot. Dressed in knee-length shorts and a T-shirt, he rubbed his arms against the chill. Jackson figured his body heat was escaping through his buzz-cut scalp.

As he pulled up near the boy, Jackson appraised the layout. A half-sized basketball court separated the back lot of this apartment complex from the back lot of the apartments on the next street over. An alley lined with chain-link fences and overgrown weeds stretched behind the open area of the court. Quick mental math told Jackson they would have fewer than thirty doors to knock on to cover both apartment buildings, plus a few single-family homes on the next block. Not a worst-case scenario. Unless they had to canvass the whole neighborhood between here and the schools—one of which Katie attended.

The sky's pink glow faded and the shadows grew. He cursed the outdoor crime scene and loss of daylight. Schakowski pulled in behind him and left his car partially blocking the exit. Reflexively, Jackson felt for his Sig Sauer, then grabbed a black gym bag from the back seat floor. It contained, among other things, two cameras, extra film, a flashlight, crime scene tape, paper booties, an assortment of brown paper bags, and a box of latex gloves.

He and his partner hesitated. There was no rushing to save a body. And once the image was burned into the brain, it never faded.

"I'll take photos," Schak offered.

"Use film."

Jackson preferred the convenience of a digital camera, but the district attorney's office had instructed law enforcement officials not to use them for evidence collection in violent crimes. They feared that a defense lawyer would claim a digital image had been altered.

The open dumpster called to them, the scent of rotting produce permeating the crisp fall air. Jackson found himself wishing for a fresh corpse, one that had not been dead long enough to stiffen and stink. Jackson also wished for the body to be male. Most men who were murdered asked for it some way: a drug deal gone bad, an earlier act of violence, an infidelity with another man's wife or girlfriend. But women were almost always innocent victims.

Jackson dug out a pair of latex gloves, pulled them on, and motioned the shivering young man to step away. The air stood still, silencing the rattle of the tree leaves. A sense of dread washed over him as he stepped up to the looming black hole. At six-two, Jackson was tall enough to look down into the container.

A lumpy black plastic trash bag lay on top of several crates loaded with brown heads of lettuce. The bag's contents spilled out the opening, revealing the ghastly secret it had tried to hide. Jackson's empty stomach heaved. He held his breath and pushed the girl's hair away from her face.

It was a face he knew well.

4

Tuesday, October 19, 6:47 p.m.

Jessie Davenport and Jackson's daughter had been insepa-
rable through most of the sixth and seventh grades. Jessie
had spent countless hours in his home, although she had
not spoken more than twenty words to him in those two
years. The girls were a study in contrast: Jessie, tall for her
age, blond and lean, a model in the making, while Katie was
short, a little plump, with wavy brown hair and freckles. But
they had laughed at the same jokes, hated the same teachers, and loved the same boy bands.

Then abruptly last spring, the overnighters and marathon phone calls had come to an end. Jackson still didn't
know what had happened. Katie refused to talk about it. He
groaned inwardly at the thought of telling his daughter that
Jessie was dead.

Schakowski stepped up and looked into the dark canister.
"Ah. Jesus. Poor girl." He began to snap pictures. The angle
of her head, the stillness of her chest, the lack of color in her
cheeks—every detail said she was dead—but Jackson felt for
a pulse anyway. Had her skin started to cool? Through the
latex, he couldn't be sure. His arms ached to pull Jessie out
of the plastic and the dumpster. It was a revolting place for
any human being to end up, and he hated that her parents
would have to think of her like this. If it had been Katie…he
could think of no words to describe such despair.

Jackson wanted a closer look at everything right now, her
clothes, her wounds—which he could not see—the bag she
had been stuffed into. Every detail mattered.

Every moment mattered.

He stepped back from the dumpster and spoke to the teenage boy for the first time. "I'll be with you in a minute." He located his cell phone and used speed dial to call the county medical examiner's cellular line.

The ME answered on the second ring. "Gunderson here." Radio and traffic noise muted his voice.

"It's Jackson. You're on the way?"

"Yep."

"I want to take her out of the dumpster."

"Don't. I'll be there in five minutes."

"I need to see her wounds before I talk to the kid who found her."

"Leave her. I'll be right there."

They both hung up. Jackson turned back to the young man, who seemed to be on the verge of tears.

"Name?"

"Trevor Michelson."

"You live around here?"

"About five blocks away. I come here to shoot hoops."

"Where's your ball?"

"My friends took off with it after the homeless guy started shouting."

The kid was visibly shaking. Was he upset or just cold?

"Tell me about him."

"He rode up to the dumpster on a bike. After a couple minutes, he started yelling at us to come over. My friends thought it was pretty funny, but then they had to take off. I decided to go see what he was yelling about. I wish I hadn't. I feel kinda sick."

"What did the guy look like?"

The kid shrugged and his teeth chattered. "Like an old homeless guy. Dirty jeans. Dark blue jacket that looked like it came from the Mission. Bad teeth. Shoulder length dirty brown hair."

"Why did he leave?"

"He said he couldn't deal with cops. Something about a warrant."

Jackson jotted down the transient's full description. A patrol officer might know who he was and why he had an arrest warrant. Jackson hoped he would be able to read his notes later. The sun was completely gone now and the dull yellow from the pole light in the parking lot didn't illuminate much.

"Do you know the girl?"

Trevor shook his head.

"Let me see your hands."

The kid held them out. Jackson used his flashlight for a decent look. Trevor had long narrow fingers with the swollen knuckles of someone who liked to pop them.

"Over."

The kid's left palm had a slight bloody scrape.

"Explain that."

"I fell on the court." He lifted his leg to display a matching scrape on his shin. "Can I go now? I'm freezing and I haven't eaten all day."

Jackson's gut feeling was that he was telling the truth. But until he could corroborate the kid's story, he was a suspect. He jotted down Trevor's phone number and address as well as the names of his friends who had been there earlier.

Headlights came around the corner of the building, and Gunderson pulled up in the body van.

Jackson turned to the kid. "You can go, but I want you available for further questioning tomorrow. That means you and your friends don't go anywhere except to school. Are you a student at Spencer High?"

"Yeah. We have an away game in Salem tomorrow." The idea of missing a basketball game seemed to cause him physical pain.

"We'll try to talk to you again in the morning."

Jackson turned toward the medical examiner's van, and the kid hurried off into the darkness.

The ME's bald forehead glistened in the lamplight, and his ponytail was held back with a beaded black band. In his mid-fifties, Gunderson had been on the job for seventeen years, and Jackson had witnessed his many hairstyles over the years. The white lab coat over a black turtleneck and black slacks never changed though.

In a few quick movements, the county ME had retrieved battery powered flood lights from the vehicle and set them up near the dumpster. They looked like vehicle headlights on yellow spider legs.

"Any idea who she is?" Gunderson asked.

"Jessie Davenport. Lives about eight blocks from here and was a good friend of my daughter's."

"Shit. I'm sorry to hear that."

Standing at the end of the dumpster, Jackson watched as Gunderson analyzed the girl where she lay, turning her head, lifting her shoulders, and mumbling to himself. The rest of her body remained inside the plastic bag. While the ME clicked off about ten pictures, Jackson's thoughts kept returning to his own daughter. What if Katie had still been friends with Jessie? Would Katie be dead now too? The idea was unbearable, so he shut it down.

After another minute, they carefully lifted Jessie, still mostly covered by the black plastic, out of the foulness and set her down on a body bag Gunderson had laid out. The ME carefully cut open the plastic and exposed the rest of its contents. Under the glare of work lights, Jessie was nude, but stunningly unblemished. No blood, no bruises, no abrasions. Not even a freckle.

"Who's going in?" Schakowski asked in response to the unspoken question: Where are her clothes?

"You know you are. There's coveralls in the back of my car and booties in my bag."

"Thanks." More sarcasm than appreciation.

While Schakowski dug through the garbage, Gunderson examined the body, talking out loud for Jackson's benefit. "Lack of rigor mortis, except for in the small muscles of the hands." Then a little later: "Body temperature is 95.5, and it's 64 degrees right now, but it was warmer earlier. Most likely, she's been dead for three hours, maybe a little longer. I'd say she most likely died between 4 and 5 p.m. today."

"Do you see any sign of trauma? A blow to the head maybe?" Jackson wanted to know what had killed her, and so far, her body wasn't giving it away.

"Not yet." Gunderson began to probe around the girl's genitals. Jackson involuntarily looked away. The ME's voice was unaffected. "Swelling around the inner labia indicates recent sexual activity, but no real sign of rape."

Sexual activity? Jackson was stunned. Jessie was only thirteen, or maybe fourteen by now. He turned back to the ME. "How do you know it wasn't rape?"

"There's no bruising, tearing, or blood," Gunderson responded. "And the swabs I just took show semen in the anus."

"What are you saying?" Jackson knew, but he did not believe.

"She had vaginal and anal sex, most likely consensual, sometime today. We'll see how viable the sperm are under a microscope."

Jackson struggled to set aside his personal feelings. He had to forget that he knew this girl, that she was his daughter's friend. He had to be objective and focus on the facts. She was probably sexually abused by someone she knew.

"There's trace evidence," Gunderson said, using tweezers to lift something from Jessie's pubic area. "A short dark hair, definitely not hers, most likely pubic."

Excellent, Jackson thought. Now all he needed was someone to match it to.

After a few minutes, Gunderson noted that there were faint red marks around the girl's wrists, indicating she may have been bound. In this case, Jackson had no idea what that meant. If she wasn't raped, he couldn't assume she had been forcibly abducted or held against her will.

But like every other person in this county who had died under suspicious circumstances, Jessie would be sent to the state medical examiner's office in Portland for a full autopsy. Like every other death he'd investigated, Jackson would attend. The trace evidence would be couriered separately to the lab for DNA testing, which could take a week or longer. First thing tomorrow, Jackson would call the lab's supervisor, a woman named Debbie he'd known for years, and ask her to prioritize the work. This case was more important than any drug-related homicide.

"Any idea on cause of death?" She didn't just die, he thought.

Gunderson's permanent frown line puckered a little deeper. "If I had to guess, I'd say either drug overdose or suffocation. And that's all I can do here. Let's get her into the van and on her way to the morgue for an ID."

As they were loading the body, Lara Evans drove up. At thirty-two, she was the youngest detective in the unit and still single. She wore her ash-brown hair short and feathered, emphasizing her heart-shaped face and bright blue eyes. Her expressions were as changeable as a chameleon—sweet one minute, inscrutable the next. She reminded Jackson of the actress Ashley Judd. Evans wore her standard on-the-job combo of black slacks and a pastel blazer.

Jackson quickly briefed her. Evans had been a detective for less than a year, but her first response reminded him why he had picked her for the investigation.

"Consensual sex doesn't mean she wasn't the victim of a sexual predator. We need to pull in all the known perverts in this area, registered or not."

"You're right. We will."

Schakowski, who now smelled like cold pizza grease and cat litter, joined them. "I haven't found a single thing that looks like it might belong to a young girl," he said. "I'm going to pull the top layer of garbage out and use the spotlight."

"Great. We'll check the other dumpsters and cans in the area too." Jackson turned to Evans. "When McCray gets here, I want you guys to split these units," he gestured at the two apartment buildings separated by the basketball court, "and knock on every door. Move quickly. Our priority is to find a witness or get a description of anyone who may have been seen in the area this afternoon. We'll go back tomorrow with photos of the girl and get more specific."

Jackson watched the body wagon pull onto the street and heaved a sigh.

"I'll go see her mother."

Judy Davenport frowned when she first saw him, then looked confused. The last time they'd spoken, Jackson had been upset with her—maybe yelled a little—because she had let Katie and Jessie stay overnight somewhere else when he had been told that the girls would be in the Davenport home.

This time, she did not know why he was here and was not prepared for what he would tell her. Jackson didn't feel ready either. This was the first time he'd ever had to tell a parent that their young child had been murdered. In the other homicides he'd investigated involving children, the parent or guardian had reported—and committed—the crime.

"Mrs. Davenport?"

She opened the screen door. "What can I do for you?" Judy was mid-aged, mid-sized, and would have been attractive if she had not been stuck in the eighties. The pile of teased gray-blond hair made her face look small, and the padded shoulders of her blouse made her seem insecure.

"Is your husband here?"

"Not any more. Why?" Her eyes darted from Jackson to his car, then down the street. She was starting to panic.

"I'm afraid I have some bad news. Can I come in?"

Judy stepped back, letting the screen door bounce. Jackson followed her into the living room. In all those times he'd picked Katie up here, he'd never come inside. The barrage of color and clutter made him want to run. Mrs. Davenport stood at the end of a maroon-and-green floral couch, facing him. Her hands pressed against her chest, as if to protect her heart from a blow.

Her lips began to tremble. "It's Jessie, isn't it?"

"Yes. I'm very sorry to have to tell you that she's dead."

For a few seconds, she was absolutely still, as though her brain had shut down. Then a floodwater of tears built up behind her eyes until the pupils looked as if they would drown. Judy Davenport sank onto the couch and began to pray and cry in a cacophony of sounds. She rocked back and forth, begging for Jesus to help her.

"Is there anyone I can call who can come over and stay with you?"

She ignored him, rocking and wailing on her bright floral couch. Jackson moved away, taking a moment to look around at the house. The living room and dining area were cluttered but clean, and totally feminine. Pink and red throw pillows, wall hangings with embroidered poems and prayers, and shelves full of porcelain figures. But nothing, on the surface, to explain how the girl who had lived here had ended up dead.

Jessie's mother took several gulping breaths, then looked up. "How did it happen?"

Jackson moved to the couch and sat next to her. "We don't know yet. Someone found her body. But there's no evidence of any trauma."

"What are you saying? She just died?"

"She was naked and in a dumpster. We're treating it like a homicide."

A wounded animal sound burst from her throat. Davenport closed her eyes and began to pray again, her lips moving in a whispery singsong.

"I know this is very difficult," Jackson prodded, "but I need to ask you some questions. Maybe some tough questions about Jessie's social life."

Suddenly, she sprang off the couch. "You think this is my fault, don't you? You think I'm a bad mother. You always did." The outburst was followed by more weeping.

Jackson gave her a minute. "You're a fine mother. I just need to figure out what happened. And I need your help. Will you please sit down and answer some questions?"

She sat, but she would not look at him.

Jackson took out his notepad. "When was the last time you saw Jessie?"

"This morning before school."

"What was she wearing?"

She whipped her head around. "Why? Do you think the way she was dressed was responsible for whatever happened to her?"

Jackson fought to keep his cool. "A detective is standing in a dumpster right now looking for your daughter's clothes, in case those clothes have evidence on them that can help us. I'd like to tell him exactly what he's looking for."

She pressed her lips together, looking chagrined, then said, "A denim skirt and a pink and blue striped pullover."

"What about shoes or a backpack?"

"I don't know about the shoes, but she always carried a backpack. This year it was one of those clear plastic ones. I only saw her briefly before I left for work. I had an early shift at the nursing home this morning."

Jackson used his cell phone to relay the information to Schakowski, who had not found anything yet. Mrs. Davenport went to the kitchen and came back with a glass of water for herself. Jackson had more questions.

"Did Jessie have any plans to go somewhere after school today?"

"She had Teen Talk."

"What's that?"

"A group of Christian kids who get together after school once a week." This was new to Jackson. He didn't remember the activity from when Katie and Jessie had been friends.

"Where do they meet and what do they do?"

"It's a Bible study. They meet at Angel's. She has a big rec room with a pool table."

"Angel Strickland?" When Katie had been friends with Jessie, Angel's name had come up a few times. Jackson may have met her once but couldn't remember for sure. He often got Katie's friends mixed up.

Mrs. Davenport nodded.

Jackson asked, "Do you know if Jessie was at Angel's today?"

"She would have called me if she went anywhere else."

"Did she carry a cell phone?"

"Yes."

Jackson made a note to subpoena the records. "Did she have a boyfriend?"

The mother scowled. "Of course not. She's only thirteen. Well, almost fourteen." Davenport began to cry again. Through sobs, she choked out, "Her birthday is next week."

"Do you know anyone who would want to harm Jessie?" If Jessie had been an adult victim, he would have asked that first.

"No. Of course not."

"Do you have a current photo?"

"I've got her school photo from last year." Mrs. Davenport pulled a tissue from her smock and wiped at her face.

"I'd like to release Jessie's name and photo to the media and ask for the public's help."

She nodded and pulled herself off the couch.

Jackson asked if he could see Jessie's room. Davenport hesitated, then sighed and led him down a short hallway, her too-tight jeans rubbing noisily. She opened the door at the end and stepped back to let him pass. Behind him, Jackson felt her move into place in the doorway, intent on keeping watch over Jessie's things.

Pale apricot walls, topped with fringed shawls hanging from the corners gave the room a cocoon fairytale feel. Posters of clean-cut boy bands lined the wall behind the bed, which was topped with an orange and white comforter that reminded him of the Fruit Striped gum he'd chewed as a kid. The furniture was a mixed assortment: the wooden desk looked old and scarred, as if it had been purchased secondhand, but the white bed frame looked new and possibly expensive. A pile of clothes and shoes had been pushed up against the closed closet, and a small painting of Jesus hung above the desk. Jackson didn't remember Jessie being religious. But the truth was, they hadn't chatted much.

From his bag, he removed his camera and took several photos of the general layout. Then he pulled on some gloves and began to search her dresser. Nothing of great interest, except a collection of panties that filled a whole drawer. Did all young girls have this much underwear? Jackson rifled through her desk drawers next, finding old homework reports, religious booklets, and a few innocuous notes addressed to Jess and signed May-May. He put the notes in a brown paper evidence bag.

"Hey, what are you doing?" Judy Davenport rushed into the room.

"Collecting evidence. Please step back and let me do my job."

"You're not taking anything out of here." Judy Davenport was on the verge of tears again.

Jackson's heart went out to the woman. "Why don't you go call someone to come over and stay with you?"

"I'm not leaving you in here alone."

Time to switch tactics. "Is there a computer in the house?" He was surprised that Jessie's room didn't have one. According to Katie, every kid in her school had their own computer, cell phone, and television.

"Not any more. It was just a portal to pornography and violence and a multitude of other evil influences."

"Didn't Jessie need a computer for school work sometimes?"

"They have them at the school, at the library, at Starbucks. All her friends have them. She didn't need one of her own."

Back to square one. Jackson moved over to the bed and lifted a corner of the mattress.

"What are you doing now?"

"Looking for a diary."

Jackson spotted a book in the center of the box springs and pulled it free. The paperback was titled Road Trip, and the cover sported a naked couple on a motorcycle. Mrs. Davenport grabbed it out of his hands. Then she gasped and dropped it like it was a snake. Clearly, she had not known her daughter all that well, and Jessie had been a conflicted young girl.

5

Wednesday, October 20, 6:10 a.m.

KERA HEATED WATER in the microwave, then poured it over her freshly ground coffee. While it seeped into the cup, she stepped outside to get the newspaper. Even though most afternoons were still warm and sunny, mornings now were dark and cold. Knowing the season could change abruptly, Kera decided it was time to dig her winter clothes out of the back of the bedroom closet just to be prepared.

Coffee and paper in hand, she sat down at the kitchen table and glanced at the headlines. A photo of the bombed clinic took up half the front page. Eugene had never experienced anything like this before, and the photo alone would sell out news stands. Trina Waterman of KRSL had broken the story last night, and the newspaper account didn't add much detail, except to speculate about the bomber's possible motives.

Kera got up to scramble eggs and turned on the small TV she kept in the kitchen to catch some national news. As she opened the refrigerator, the KRSL morning anchor—a big man named Thaddeus Brown— announced a "breaking story." Kera turned to the TV, stunned by the news that followed:

"The body of 13-year-old Jessie Davenport, a student at Kincaid Middle School, was found in a dumpster late yesterday afternoon behind the Regency Apartments in South Eugene. The police have not released any information about the crime but have asked for the public's help. If you saw Jessie Davenport yesterday or saw anything sus-

picious near the Regency Apartments at 17th and Patterson, please call 686-0505."

They cut to a picture of Jessie, looking younger and happier than she had yesterday, then showed the Regency complex, then cut to a dark gray dumpster surrounded by yellow crime tape. *"We will have more on this story at six."*

Kera sank back into her chair. The girl she had treated in the clinic yesterday—who had e-mailed her immediately afterward—had been killed and dumped like trash. The coffee soured in her stomach, and the little tremor she had been experiencing in her hands came back.

Kera laid her forehead against the cool rosewood table. Why was this world so messed up? Why did so many young people have to die? First Nathan, now Jessie. Even though she hadn't really known Jessie, the girl had reached out to her. Jessie's death felt like another loss, a personal failure. Kera breathed deeply into her abdomen and empty her mind. She could not afford another layer of grief and guilt. She had to function. She had a job to do, people who counted on her.

In a few minutes, she forced herself to get up, brush her teeth, and dress for work. As she grabbed a container of yogurt for her lunch, Kera thought she heard a faint musical sound. But her cell phone was right there on the kitchen counter, quiet as usual. She heard the sound again. Kera followed the tone into the living room and realized it was coming from the front closet. Puzzled, she opened the closet door. The next ring was much louder. She reached for the sweater she'd worn yesterday and pulled a pink cell phone out of the pocket.

In a flash, she remembered that she had picked up Jessie's phone from the exam table and tried to return it to her. Kera had no idea how it ended up in her pocket. It had been in her hand when she fell. Perhaps one of her co-workers thought it was hers and put it in her pocket. Or maybe she had done it herself. Her memory of the events right before and after the explosion was fuzzy.

But who would be calling Jessie's phone now? Someone who didn't know she was dead? What if the police were calling the phone trying to locate it?

Kera flipped it open. "Hello."

"Who is this?" The young girl on the other end sounded surprised and confused. "Where's Jessie?"

Kera mentally kicked herself for answering the phone. "My name's Kera. I found this phone yesterday after Jessie dropped it." This is so awkward. "I tried to get the phone back to Jessie, then a series of unexpected events prevented me from doing so." She could not even mention the clinic without violating Jessie's privacy.

"Hmm. I guess I'll call Jessie at home. Should I tell her you have her phone?"

"You can't call her at home." Kera struggled for the right thing to say. "What's your name?"

"Nicole."

The friend Jessie had mentioned during her appointment? "Nicole, I'm afraid I have some very bad news for you. Another unexpected thing that happened yesterday is that Jessie…Jessie is dead."

"Oh my God."

"I'm very sorry for your loss. I just heard it on the news this morning."

"Oh my God."

Kera winced. The girl was not taking it well. "I'm very sorry to tell you like this over the phone, Nicole. Is there someone there who can comfort you?"

"I knew God would punish us! I knew it. We're all going to hell." Nicole hung up.

On the drive to work, Kera became painfully aware of the difficult position she was in. The police wanted to know where Jessie had been yesterday. Under any other circumstances, Kera would have gladly cooperated with an investigation. But she worked for Planned Parenthood, and Jessie had come in for STD treatment. That information was strictly confidential. Kera could not reveal it to anyone, even the police. And she could not turn the phone over to the police without indirectly revealing that Jessie had come into the clinic. Unless she lied about where she found it, and Kera could not do that. Maybe she should mail the phone to the department anonymously.

What if Jessie's clinic appointment was important to the investigation? What if knowing that piece of information would help the police find her killer?

Kera was so preoccupied, she missed her turn off Chambers. Damn. Now she would be a few minutes late. Nobody at the clinic would care, but it bothered her. She made a risky left turn against traffic and whipped around in a QuickMart parking lot. Back on the road, she tried to reason her way through the dilemma. How could Jessie's appointment be related to her death? It seemed unlikely that a stalker or serial killer had followed the girl from the clinic.

Oh shit. Maybe they had. Jessie had been in the clinic at the time of the explosion. What if the bomber was also a psychopath? Kera's heart raced at the thought. In the greater scheme of things, keeping Jessie's confidence might not be the right thing to do. By the time Kera parked her Saturn at the clinic, she was deeply troubled.

Seeing the plywood boarding up the clinic's front window made her chest muscles tighten. Some of her co-workers might not show up at all today. Kera wouldn't blame them for that.

Roselyn buzzed her in and greeted her with a cheerful "Good morning." Roselyn's chunky cheeks bunched up in a bright smile, and Kera was glad to see their young receptionist was still her usual upbeat self.

"Hi Rosie. You seem to be taking this whole thing pretty well."

"I grew up in Compton." Rosie waved it away. "That little pipe bomb was nothing."

Kera smiled. "It's good to keep your perspective."

"Staff meeting at 7:45 sharp," the receptionist called after her as she walked back to the break room. The aroma of fresh-brewed coffee filled the small space. After hanging her purse and sweater in her locker, Kera poured herself a cup, knowing the freeze-dried taste would disappoint her. It didn't matter. Holding a cup of coffee was comforting, even if she only sipped it.

She checked for morning appointments on the computer in the shared office next to the break room. Nothing for her until 8:30. Kera wandered into the windowless meeting room, where Andrea was busy reading charts.

The manager looked up. "Thanks for coming in."

"Sure."

When the day's staff of ten had assembled—minus only one lab assistant who'd called in sick—the clinic director gave a short speech about how important it was to maintain a business-as-usual attitude.

"Naturally, our clients will ask us about what happened yesterday," Sheila said. "But let's keep those conversations short. I've hired a security guard, for now. It's not in the budget, and we'll have to make cuts somewhere down the line, but I think it's necessary. Are there any questions or comments?"

"We'll have to revise our employee handbook again," Kera said. "The section on dealing with activists doesn't cover bombs." A few of her co-workers laughed, and everyone else smiled. Kera was glad no one had lost their sense of humor.

Sheila quickly charged back into leadership mode. "We all

have to be hyper observant. Pay attention to anything suspicious left lying around: purses, backpacks, even coats. As long as we have the security guard, we'll have him inspect backpacks before they come in." She paused and looked around. "Thanks for showing up today, all of you. Other people, in other lines of work, might not have. It took a lot of courage, and we'll do our best to keep everyone safe. You're a great group of people, doing great work."

A moment of silence. They needed to hear that, and yet, it made them uncomfortable.

"One more thing. Please don't talk to the press, even if they approach you outside of work." She glanced in Kera's direction. "I'm not telling you that you can't. I'm just asking you to refer them to Andrea, so that she can speak in one voice for all of us."

"Have you heard from the police?" Kera asked. "Do they have any leads?"

"Not yet. But they're going to coordinate with the Portland detectives who handled their bomb cases. I'll keep everyone posted if I hear anything. So back to business."

For a second, no one moved. Then, almost in unison, they rose and began to file out. But their steps lacked spring. Kera stayed and caught Sheila's eye. The director stuck around until everyone was gone.

"What's on your mind?" Sheila tapped a fingernail on the table.

"Did you hear the news this morning on KRSL about the dead girl?"

The director looked alarmed. "What dead girl?"

"Her name's Jessie Davenport. She was in here yesterday at the time of the explosion. I treated her for genital warts. Now she's dead. They found her body in a dumpster."

"Dear God." Sheila dropped back into her chair.

"The police want people who saw her yesterday to come forward."

Sheila shook her head before Kera finished her sentence. "You can't. It's that simple. If the police discover on their own that she was here and get a search warrant for our files, then we'll cooperate. We cannot divulge client information under any other circumstances." Sheila reached over and patted Kera's hand. "I know you want to help, but it's like when a reporter won't reveal her sources even to help solve a crime. We have to protect the greater, long-term good of what we do."

"I hope they get the guy very soon."

"Me too."

Wednesday, October 20, 7:55 a.m.
RUTH DROPPED THE KIDS off at school, then cut over to West 11th Avenue and headed west. She was anxious to see the results of her work. To see the building all boarded up and empty. The sluts driven from their house of horror.

The clinic bombing story had dominated the local news last night and made the front page of the paper this morning. Ruth had inhaled every word. It was thrilling to finally be making things happen instead of sitting on the sidelines complaining and praying. The only disturbing part of the news was from that clinic whore, Kera Kollmorgan, who had called Ruth "a fanatic with no regard for human life." How dare she? She was the abortionist!

Ruth reminded herself not to care what others thought of her. This was God's work. And God was pleased. Ruth was certain. When she opened her Bible this morning—choosing a page at random—it had opened to Matthew Chapter 3. Then Ruth had closed her eyes and pointed to a line on the page. It was 3:17. *Suddenly a voice came from heaven saying, "This is my beloved Son, in whom I am well pleased."*

It was a sign. God was well pleased with her efforts.

Ruth hummed to herself as she drove. Not even the heinous traffic on West 11th tested her good mood. Rather than drive right past the clinic, she pulled into the Target parking lot and drove through it to the far exit. She sat in the exit and stared at the gray brick building across the street. The lights were on, the parking lot was half full of cars, and a young woman hurried up the sidewalk as if late for an appointment.

Business as usual.

Ruth's jaw clenched, and for a moment, she was too upset even to pray. How was this possible? She had shaken their building with the wrath of God. Yet, they were still going on—dispensing birth control to young harlots and scheduling more baby killings — as if nothing had happened. Ruth shook her head. She had been too conservative. The devil was a tenacious and treacherous enemy.

She would show them. The next bomb would be much bigger. They would not bounce back so easily.

6

Wednesday, October 20, 8:07 a.m.

KERA BARELY HAD TIME to pull files and stock the exam rooms before the first clients arrived. She had been worried that women would skip their appointments this morning—out of fear for their safety or concern that their privacy would be violated by reporters or cops hanging around. Which, of course, was the point of the bomb. But clearly, women were willing to risk their lives for birth control.

They only had two no-shows that morning—one less than average. The walk-in traffic was a little lighter than usual, but the vehicle traffic on the street was constant. The front-page newspaper story about the explosion was drawing plenty of gawkers driving by to take a look at the damage. Kera was grateful for the break from walk-in clients. She had twenty minutes until her next scheduled appointment, and she planned to spend it searching through the charts for Nicole and any other Kincaid students who had come into the clinic recently.

The last twelve months of client folders were filed alphabetically in a wall of shallow cabinets in the front office. The folders were tagged and color-coded by last names and dates. When the twelve-month expiration period passed with no new visits, folders were moved to the back filing room where they kept inactive charts for three years. Once a client had been gone for three years, the staff moved those charts to a storage unit, where they stayed for another seven years. Every January, they shredded all the charts older than ten years.

Fortunately, they had moved from a previous site downtown into this building only a few months ago, and they had carted a load of folders off to storage early. The clinic was also blessed with volunteers who helped out with everything from stuffing envelopes for fundraising drives to shuffling the files from one place to another. Of course, all volunteers went through a background check and rigorous screening process to weed out any potential saboteurs.

But it wasn't a foolproof system, Kera realized. Had a volunteer planted the bomb?

She called out to Roselyn at the front desk a few feet away. "Were there any volunteers in the building yesterday?"

The girl finished her task on the computer and turned to face her. "Not that I know of. But Sheila gave a list of volunteers to the cops yesterday."

Of course, the director had already thought of that. Kera went back to the charts, hoping that Roselyn wouldn't ask what she was looking for. With a sinking feeling, she realized that the project would take hours and that she would have to stay quite late to get through all the charts. And what would she really accomplish? Many clients, especially the young ones, didn't bother to fill out the questionnaires completely. So if any of the Kincaid students had skipped the optional line for where they attended school or had made something up, they would slip through her screening process. But then, the kids who came into the clinic knew their information would never be shared, so most of them were not afraid to be truthful.

Kera shook off her doubts and decided to follow through. Jessie's death—followed by Nicole's outburst of guilt and fear of God's punishment—made Kera anxious to see if there was a pattern of unsafe sexual activity among students at Kincaid Middle School. She was head of the clinic's teen outreach program. This was her job. Lives could be at stake.

Fifteen minutes later—starting in the A's and working through the C's—she found Nicole Clarke. The thirteen-year-old Kincaid student had been treated with liquid nitrogen for genital warts on September 12th. She had come in for condoms a month before that. Obviously, the supply hadn't lasted long enough, or she hadn't bothered to use them. Julie had seen Nicole that first time and had noted in the chart that she had encouraged the client to consider a more reliable form of birth control.

Kera jotted down Nicole's basic information and returned the file. She paused for a moment, feeling ill at ease. Was she violating clinic policy? Not if she didn't take the information out of the building. And she had no intention of sharing the names with anyone. She was just gathering data and looking for a pattern—in essence, conducting her own micro-epidemiological study.

Her concern went beyond a group of adolescent kids having unprotected sex. One of those girls was dead. Because so many murdered women died at the hands of their lovers or ex-lovers, Kera thought it very likely that Jessie's sex life was connected to her death. She would learn everything she could, then find a way to share what she could anonymously with the police. Detective Jackson came to mind, and she wondered if he was handling Jessie's case.

Wednesday, October 20, 8:03 a.m.
JACKSON PICKED UP a breakfast burrito from one of the portable kiosk vendors on the downtown mall and a tall cup of house coffee from Full City. A group of middle-aged male joggers in shorts trotted past him as he walked back to the department. Jackson felt a pang of guilt. His doctor was bugging him to exercise more, in addition to taking the cholesterol medicine, but so far, he hadn't worked it into his schedule.

A damp gray cloud hung over the downtown area,

but Jackson could feel the heat of the sun trying to burn through. Morning traffic picked up speed as he hurried in to city hall.

He had worked out of the white-brick building for nearly twenty years, and passing by the ugly fountain felt like coming home. Warm meat and coffee smells from his purchases drifted into his nostrils as he clipped into headquarters and down the hallway that opened into the investigations area.

Not even feng shui could help this setting. The only saving grace in the large room was the bank of windows along the outside wall. But the vertical wooden beams that surrounded the building ruined the view, and the blinds were often closed anyway. There were no dividers between the crowded group of desks and no plants in the corners. The work stations were grouped according to units: property crimes, financial crimes, violent crimes, and vice/narcotics. Narrow walkways lined with filing cabinets separated the clusters. Violent crimes had the largest area, with eight of the sixteen detectives. Everyone in the room reported to Sergeant Denise Lammers.

Jackson moved toward his desk in the rear right corner. Detective Michael Quince, who had been assigned the bomb case when Jackson was pulled off, looked up as he passed. "The Portland police think we should get the FBI involved in the bombing case."

"Ask Lammers," Jackson responded. "It's her call. "

Jackson plopped in his chair and washed down a Vivarin tablet with a gulp of coffee. On the first few days of a homicide he couldn't consume enough caffeine. He had been up for more than twenty-four hours now, and this was only round one. The burrito disappeared in six bites. His stomach, which hadn't encountered food since yesterday lunch, rumbled in surprise.

Last night after leaving the Davenport home, he'd met with an assistant district attorney and together they had written up half a dozen search warrants, including paper for a complete search of the Davenport home and vehicles—the vehicle search was valid because Jessie had been transported—phone records (land and mobile) for both Jessie and her mother, and a list of tenants for both apartment buildings. Judge Cranston, a great friend of law enforcement, had gotten out of bed at 10:30 last night and signed them all.

Before picking up breakfast this morning, Jackson had met with Sergeant Lammers to update her on the Jessie investigation. And earlier, in the middle of the night, he had entered the few details of the crime that he had into NCIC, a national homicide database run by the FBI—in case they were dealing with a sexual predator or serial killer.

A few partial hits had surfaced, but nothing solid. In two other killings, in Idaho and Illinois, the young women (eighteen and nineteen) had been raped before being left in a dumpster and a landfill, respectively. And another case, in which the victim had been suffocated, involved a thirty-three year old woman who had been raped and beaten first. Neither was a good match. The lack of obvious violence in Jessie's case was an anomaly.

Sipping his coffee and hoping the Vivarin would hit soon, Jackson typed all his handwritten notes into a Word document, then made lists of leads to follow up and people to interview. The typing skills had come to him slowly, grudgingly, over the years. His thick fingers were too big for the keypads and he had to look at the numbers every time, but the skill was invaluable. It allowed him to expand his fractional descriptions and thoughts into a detailed and highly readable document.

Finally, he hit print, picked up his paperwork, and headed for the small conference room where the Jessie task force was scheduled to meet at 9 a.m.

The room was claustrophobically small but uncluttered, containing only a dozen folding chairs and a single podium. A five-foot-long, dry-erase board ran across one wall. It would be used to map everything and everyone connected to the case.

Evans was the first to arrive. She looked surprisingly good for someone who had probably slept less than three hours. But then Evans took good care of herself. She was lean and muscular and worked out regularly.

"Anything on the background checks?" Jackson asked as Evans settled into a chair, tall premium coffee in hand.

"Nothing noteworthy." She shook her head. "One tenant, Louis Frank, has a long history of theft and drug possession, but nothing for the last two years and no sex or violent crimes ever. Lives with his girlfriend and works at a door-making factory."

McCray and Schakowski hustled in, both also cradling tall coffee cups from one of the dozens of vendors that had sprung up on every corner in town. Jackson wondered how much money the four of them spent on caffeine every day.

"Schak, you showered. Nice." Evans teased him about spending half the night picking through garbage.

The big guy flopped into a chair, his barrel-shaped body hanging over the sides. "Trash digging pays. I found her clothes and backpack in the dumpster behind the dry cleaners at the end of the alley."

The update was for the benefit of Evans and McCray. Jackson had seen the evidence in the predawn hours when Schak brought it in. The denim skirt, striped sweater, and pink flip-flops were on their way to the state crime lab in Springfield. The backpack's contents were still in the department, awaiting fingerprint analysis, but unfortunately, the girl's cell phone was not in the mix.

"Anything, McCray?"

The older detective was lean and gray and had a pleasant but well-lived-in face. He was also fond of brown corduroy.

McCray was tenacious but not competitive, a rare combination in law enforcement.

"Jose Sanchez, age thirty-one in unit twelve of the Oakwood Apartments, has two assault charges and recently finished a ten-month stretch in the county jail," he reported. "Both his assault victims were males around his age. Bar fights is my guess. He also had a warrant for failure to report to his parole officer. I sent a patrol to pick him up."

Sanchez didn't sound like a solid suspect. Jackson told the group, "I've got Pete Casaway compiling a list of known sex offenders who live within a five-mile radius of Jessie's home and/or the dump site, which are less than two miles apart." He turned to Evans. "Did you get the prints made?"

"Yep." She handed each of them a stack of four-by-five headshots of Jessie. Jackson was surprised to see how grown up Jessie looked in the photos. Was it the effect of makeup? Or had she changed that much in six months?

"Let's go back to the apartments and show everyone the photos. Start with the units where you didn't find anyone home last night. After that, we interview friends and family. I made lists." After Judy Davenport's sister had come over, the grieving mother had calmed down and become more cooperative. With prodding, she had provided a list of people who knew her daughter.

Jackson handed out the paperwork as he spoke. "Evans, I want you to talk to Jessie's teachers and family. McCray, you hit all the neighbors, and Schak, you talk to the church members." Jackson flipped through his notebook for the search warrants. "I'll interview Jessie's close friends: Angel Strickland, Rachel Greiner, and Nicole Clarke. They all attend Kincaid Middle School." Jackson wondered if he should assign Evans to interview his daughter. Did Katie know anything? Probably not. Katie and Jessie hadn't hung out in six months. An eternity in teen time.

"Let's meet back here at 5 p.m. sharp."

7

Wednesday, October 20, 11:13 a.m.

Jackson's first stop was the Cricket store near the Gateway Mall. The mall was a busy retail development just across the line that divided Eugene from Springfield, its blue-collar sister city. The Cricket store manager, a pregnant woman who seemed young for the job, was flustered by the court order and called her district supervisor.

"There's a cop here with a subpoena," she whined, "and I don't know what to do." After a moment, she handed the phone to Jackson. He explained what he needed and extracted a promise from the supervisor that the records would be faxed to him within twenty-four hours.

As Jackson drove down Coburg Road, the late morning sun burned through the clouds. Another day of Indian summer, he thought, grateful for the change-of-season delay. He was happier and more productive when the sun was out.

Kincaid Middle School sat in the center of a busy southside neighborhood with a mix of commercial and residential buildings. The school had a gray utilitarian look, with grass-only landscaping around the buildings. Not much had changed since Jackson had attended there almost thirty years ago. As a kid, what he'd liked best was the school's proximity to the minor league baseball field where he'd watched the Ems play.

This morning, the school was quiet. No children were milling around and no cars were coming or going. Jackson felt a little guilty about pulling students out of class for a police interview; he knew how sensitive kids this age were about what their peers thought. But he needed to talk to Jessie's friends now, without their parents around. It was the only way to get useful information.

Kincaid's office had been remodeled and expanded, but the secretary, although new, seemed the same: middle-aged, a little pretty, a little plump, friendly on the surface, but instinctively wary. She looked at his badge closely when he offered it. Jackson respected that.

After looking up the girls' schedules in the computer, she said, "Angel Strickland and Rachel Greiner are in biology class with Mrs. Berg, and Nicole Clarke is in advanced math with Mr. Abrams. I'll bring them here to the office and find a place for you to talk."

"Thanks."

She used the intercom to summon the students, then led Jackson through a maze of filing cabinets to a short hallway. The secretary opened the first door on the left and said, "This is our vice-principal's office. Mr. Ferguson is at a district meeting today, so you can borrow it."

After five minutes in the small windowless office, the three girls appeared together at the open door. The thin one in front said, "You wanted to see us?"

Jackson's first thought was how somber they seemed, then he remembered that they had just lost a friend. His second thought was that all three appeared conservative in comparison to current fads. No bellies showing. No cleavage. No unconventional piercings.

Jackson didn't intend to interview them together, but he wanted to get a quick sense of the group dynamic, so he waved them all in.

"Thanks for coming. I'm Detective Jackson. I'm very sorry for the loss of your friend Jessie. She was a friend of my daughter too."

No one responded.

"Please introduce yourselves."

The same girl who had spoken before said, "I'm Rachel Greiner."

She wore no makeup but had intense aqua eyes and high arched eyebrows that gave her an exotic look. Her ash blond hair was pulled back into a ponytail, and she seemed a little thin and small for her age. Despite her size, he pegged her for the leader.

Jackson nodded, then looked at the girl who stood a step behind her. Her lips trembled as she said, "Angel Strickland."

Judy Davenport had told him Angel had flunked fifth grade and was a year older than her friends. So he was not surprised that she was taller and more filled out than the other two. But her strawberry blond hair, freckles, and heart-shaped face made her look younger. She blushed and looked away. The shy one.

The third girl stood a little to the side, expressing an independence from the group. "I'm Nicole Clarke."

Her bright orange sweater contrasted with her long, almost-black hair and delicate features. Nicole's brown eyes were smudged with mascara. She had been crying and looked like she could burst into tears again at any moment.

Jackson smiled gently at the group. "It's important that I talk to each of you alone. So Angel and Nicole, please go back out to the front office. I'll call you back in a few minutes."

The two seemed glad to leave. He motioned for Rachel to sit.

"Rachel, I know it's difficult to talk about Jessie now, but I need your help to find out what happened to her."

"I don't see how I can help." She spoke distinctly without the typical teenage rush and mumble.

"How long had you know Jessie?"

"Since fourth grade."

"What was she like?"

Rachel gave a half shrug, half smile. "Fun. Smart. Generous."

"In what way was she generous?"

"The usual. She didn't mind sharing her stuff. And she wanted to be a social worker. To help homeless people. Not many people knew that about her."

"Did Jessie have a lot of friends?"

"Oh yes."

"Was she popular with the boys?"

"Of course. Maybe the most popular girl in our class." Rachel sat very still for a fourteen-year-old.

"Did she have a steady boyfriend?"

She scowled a bit. "No."

"Do you think Jessie could have had a boyfriend you didn't know about?"

"No. She told me everything."

Jackson countered, "I believe Jessie was sexually active."

"That's not possible." Rachel shook her head. "Everyone in Teen Talk took an abstinence vow."

Jackson decided it was time to press. "The state official who examined her body said she was sexually active. Who was she involved with?"

Rachel looked him right in the eye. "I have no idea."

Jackson didn't believe her. "This is important. It could help us find her killer."

"I really don't know."

"Did Jessie ever talk about being sexually abused by an adult?"

"No."

"Did you see Jessie yesterday?"

"Of course. I saw her at school, then again after school at Teen Talk."

"Is that a club?" Jackson had heard about the group from

Jessie's mother, but he wanted to see what Rachel would tell him independently.

"Just a small group of Christian kids who get together once a week."

"What do you do and where do you meet?"

"We meet at Angel's house. It's supposed to be a Bible study, but mostly we talk about our faith and how to be good Christians, especially in such an evil world."

This is a very serious young girl, Jackson thought. "What time did Jessie leave the Bible study?"

Rachel hesitated for the first time. "Around 4:30, I think."

"Do you know where she was headed?"

Rachel shrugged. "Home, I assume."

"Did she have a ride?"

"No. She walked. Or maybe caught a bus. She had a bus pass."

"Did you see or speak to her again?"

"No." Rachel pressed her lips together, and her eyes teared up. "I can't believe she's dead."

Jackson handed her his business card. "If you think of anything important that I should know, please call me."

She nodded, took the card, and left. He thought he heard her sob as she stepped out the door. He braced himself for more grief as the next girl came in.

After an hour at the school, Jackson headed back to the department. The other two interviews had been more emotional than the first and almost as unproductive. Both Angel and Nicole had insisted that Jessie did not have a boyfriend. They also seemed upset to hear that their friend had been sexually involved.

From Angel, Jackson heard that Jessie's parents had split up the year before and that her younger sister had drowned two years ago. It made him realize that he had not learned much about Jessie when she and Katie had been friends. He had been oblivious to the grief Jessie had gone through.

Nicole had been a little more forthcoming about Jessie's habits. She told him that "sometimes Jessie left Teen Talk a little early" and that Jessie had "a special friend she saw sometimes."

The special friend intrigued him, but when Jackson had pressed for information, Nicole retreated. But she gave him the names of the boys who attended Teen Talk: Greg Miller, Tyler Jahn, and Adam Walsh.

Jackson decided he would have Evans interview the guys. They might open up more with a woman.

As he neared the downtown area, his cell phone rang.

"It's Casaway. There's a sex offender named Oscar Grady. A teacher who did time for statutory rape of one of his students. He's only been out for three months. He lives on Patterson about four blocks from where the body was found."

"Good work. What's the address?"

"2817 Patterson. It's a halfway house run by the Real Recovery Center."

"Thanks. I'm on it."

Jackson felt a little surge of energy. Grady could be Jessie's "special friend." Sex offenders had the highest recidivism rate of all convicts. And, as an ex-teacher, Grady would know how to get close to a young person.

Jackson made a left on 8th and headed back to the south side. Using speed dial, he called the Parole and Probation office and tracked down Grady's PO. Barstow wasn't in, so he left him a message. Parole officers liked to be kept in the loop when their charges were picked up.

The two-story house desperately needed a new coat of paint, but the yard was free of debris. A collection of decrepit bicycles cluttered the front porch, and a giant coffee can filled with sand served as a front-porch ashtray. Jackson rang the bell and waited a long time for someone to come to the door.

Rusty, as he introduced himself, was fifty going on seventy, with skinny legs, a soft belly, and hollowed-out eyes. Jackson guessed alcohol to be his poison of choice.

"Oscar's at work," Rusty said. "Over at Cartell's Lumber. At least that's where he's supposed to be."

"Does Oscar skip work often?" Jackson asked. "And when he does, where does he go?"

"I didn't say that." Rusty scratched his dirty hair. "Check the lumber yard."

Cartell's wasn't much of a business. The yard was an open, mud-splattered mill that cranked out dog-eared boards for picket fences. The tiny front office was housed inside a rust-streaked trailer that smelled of mildew. And the morbidly obese owner was squeezed behind a desk that was two sizes too small for him.

"What can I do for you, officer?" he asked with little enthusiasm after Jackson introduced himself.

"I'm looking for Oscar Grady."

"He's here. Like most days. Want me to go get him?"

"Not yet. Was he here yesterday?"

"Yep. Clocked out at three with everyone else."

That left Grady with plenty of time to meet up with Jessie, Jackson thought. "Did you ever see him with anybody? A girlfriend? A kid?"

"Nope. He came and went on the bus just like all the other ex-cons who work for me. I don't know a damn thing about his personal life, and I don't care. He's dependable, but a little slow-moving. That's all I can tell you."

"Thanks. Will you show me who he is?"

The big man sighed and heaved up from the desk.

Grady was about thirty-five with a thin build that suggested vulnerability. His delicate features said "trust me." Jackson could see how female students would find him approachable.

"Can you make this quick?" he asked before Jackson could speak. "I'm on the clock here, and I don't want to lose my job."

"Why don't you clock out? This may take a while."

Jackson followed him to the time clock near the front office, then suggested they talk in the car.

"I don't think I can help you much." Grady flashed Jackson a power smile.

They climbed into the Impala, and Jackson slammed the car door shut.

"I'm one of the good guys," Grady offered. "I go to work. I go to meetings. I see my PO once a week. That's my life."

"Where did you go after work yesterday?"

"Home." Grady smiled sadly. "If you can call that place home."

"Did anyone see you there? Did you make any calls?"

"I don't remember. Why? What is this about?"

"Just answer the question. Did anyone see you after work yesterday?"

"Not right away. I went straight to my room and slept for a while. Then I went to a meeting later. People saw me there." A drop of sweat started down Grady's forehead.

"What meeting? When and where?"

"AA meeting. At the Baker Building near campus. It started at six."

"You're an alcoholic?"

"No. But I have to attend two meetings a week to live at the Recovery House."

"Why do you live in a Recovery House if you're not an alcoholic?" Jackson asked.

Grady shrugged. "It's cheap. And the residents make no judgments."

Time to mix it up, he thought. "How well do you know Jessie Davenport?"

Grady blinked. "Who?"

"Jessie. You know. The girl you've been seeing."

"No." Grady shook his head emphatically. "You've got the wrong sex offender. Whatever happened to her, it wasn't me."

Jackson forced Grady to make eye contact. "What makes you think something happened to her?"

"Because you're here, asking me questions." Grady's cool charm started to frazzle.

"Tell me about the girl you had sex with before you went to prison."

"No. That's the past. You can't do this to me." Grady rocked forward in the seat.

Jackson put the keys in the ignition. "Let's go down to the station and get a DNA swab. I'll call Barstow and see if your PO can join us for a chat."

"Oh shit." Grady grabbed the door handle and pushed out of the car. Jackson, a step behind, paralleled his move. Free of the car, Grady ran for the railroad tracks. Jackson raced after him, the Sig Sauer jamming into the ribs under his arm. Mud sucked at his shoes, and his heart pounded heavily. Jackson couldn't remember the last time he'd had to chase a suspect.

It was a short chase. Grady lost his footing on the muddy railroad embankment and went down. Jackson slid into him and landed on Grady's stomach with both knees. Grady was cuffed before he could get his feet under him.

The Hyster driver watched from his perch on the big yellow machine as Jackson led Grady to the Impala.

"Don't do this to me," Grady pleaded again.

8

Wednesday, October 20, 10:15 a.m.

RUTH WAS CAREFULLY packing potassium nitrate into a four-inch metal cylinder when the doorbell rang. It startled her so badly she almost dropped the device. She tried to ignore the intrusion, but whoever it was rang several more times. Then she remembered the radio was on in the living room and realized her visitor must feel certain she was home. She set the would-be pipe bomb down on the laundry table, stepped out into the hall, and closed the laundry room door. She hurried into the kitchen and peeked out the corner window. The car in the driveway was a dark blue sedan she didn't recognize. Probably a salesman who was ignoring her No Solicitors sign. It was best to answer the door and send him on his way.

Ruth yanked off her apron—which reeked of chemicals—stuffed it under the kitchen sink, and hurried across the dining room and into the foyer. She reached over and touched the Bible on the credenza and took a moment to compose herself. Then she opened the door a few inches. "Whatever you're selling, I'm not interested."

The bulky man in the ill-fitting suit held up a badge and said, "I'm Officer Schakowski of the Eugene Police. Can I come in?"

Ruth almost had a heart attack. They knew! But how?

"What's this about?" Ruth asked, praying to sound casual.

"I'm investigating the death of Jessie Davenport. I understand you and your daughter were close to her."

Jessie was dead? How? When? Ruth was stunned. Then relief washed over her. The cop was not here about the bomb at the clinic. Her brain scrambled to find the right words. "How in the Lord's name did it happen?"

"That's what we're trying to find out. I'd like to ask you a few questions."

"Let's sit out on the deck." Ruth stepped outside, closed the door behind her, and led him over to the Adirondack chairs. The bright sun failed to warm the morning air, and Ruth wished she had a sweater. She noticed the cop giving her a thorough appraisal. What did he see, she wondered? A petite, Christian woman in her mid-forties who dressed nicely even at home by herself? Or did he see a nervous Nellie who did not want him in her home for some suspicious reason? Ruth perched on the front edge of a chair and prayed it was the former. She had to get this over quickly, so she could finish her task and put away her materials before picking the kids up from school. Silently, she asked God to keep her secrets safe.

There was still much work to do.

"When was the last time you saw Jessie?" The detective had a notepad in hand.

"Last Sunday at church." Unless that was Jessie at the clinic yesterday. "Why are you questioning me?"

"Her mother said she spent a lot of time here." He made it sound like a question.

"She had dinner with us every once in a while."

"Do you know why anyone would want to harm her?"

"Was she murdered?"

"Yes. You haven't seen it on the news?"

"We try not to watch that liberal propaganda." Ruth tried to keep her face from telegraphing her disgust.

"Back to my question," the detective said with a little impatience. "Do you know of any reason why someone would want to harm Jessie?"

"Of course not. Jessie was a sweet girl."

"Did she have a boyfriend?"

"She was friends with other Christian boys in the Teen Talk club, but they're all too young to date."

"Did she know anyone who lived in the Regency or Oakwood Apartments between Hilyard and Patterson?"

Ruth shrugged. "I don't know. She was a good Christian girl. If someone killed her, it had to be some psychopath. I told Judy not to let her dress that way."

The detective jotted something down. "How did she dress?"

"I probably shouldn't have said anything," Ruth backtracked. "She wasn't trashy like some girls, but her skirts were a little short, and she wore too much makeup for a thirteen-year-old."

"What hobbies or activities did she have?"

"I really can't help you. Just because she went to our church doesn't mean I knew her that well." Ruth stood up. Jessie's death was a shame, but she had nothing else to say, and she really needed to get the cop out of there. She would make a point to counsel and pray with Judy Davenport later this week.

"What church is that?"

"The First Bible Baptist."

The detective jotted it down. "Is your daughter Rachel here?"

"She's in school, but I'm sure there's nothing she can tell you either."

The detective handed her a card. "Call me if you think of anything that might help us find Jessie's killer."

When he was gone, Ruth thanked God for getting her through the ordeal. It was one more sign that she was doing the right thing and that God would protect her.

She returned to the laundry room and went back to work on the device. Her training as a chemist had been largely wasted in the ShopKo pharmacy where she'd worked before marrying Sam. Filling pill bottles had been tedious, mindless work. Then one day at a CCA meeting in Portland, she'd mentioned her chemistry degree to Josiah Stahl, a soft-spoken man from the Beaverton chapter. His eyes had lit up, and he'd leaned in and asked her what she thought about Eric Rudolph. Ruth had replied, "He should have stuck to abortion clinics."

After that Josiah had invited her to join him in a private Bible study. He had quoted her many moving passages, such as Matthew Chapter 18, in which Jesus said, *"See that you do not despise one of these little ones, for I say to you that their angels in heaven always look upon the face of my heavenly Father."* During the prayer session that followed, God had revealed to Ruth why she'd spent all that time studying chemistry. With a little coaching from Josiah, she developed the skills to make bombs. Tactical intimidation bombs that would help close the abortion clinics that allowed young women to evade the consequences of their sins.

Ruth smiled to herself. Actually, anyone could make an explosive device. It was not complicated. But a little knowledge of chemistry could keep you from blowing your fingers off. Speaking of which, she was rushing this too much, trying to make up for the lost time spent with the detective.

Ruth stepped back from her worktable and centered herself. She had to finish this today, but every move had to be deliberate. A cleansing breath, followed by a brief prayer. Please Lord, if this mission is your will, keep me safe. Ruth had decided that morning to set off another bomb at the clinic right away. Then they would have to take her seriously.

If she skipped lunch, she would still have time to complete the device, put all her materials away, shower and change her clothes. Then she would gather up Caleb's baseball gear so she could pick him up and take him straight from school to baseball practice. While he was out in left field, she would visit Judy Davenport and counsel her about spending more time on CCA's missions. Maybe Jessie's death would be the wake-up call that would get Judy right with God again.

Wednesday, October 20, 3:35 p.m.

KERA HAD ANOTHER opportunity to peruse the files late in the afternoon when one of her scheduled appointments didn't show. She checked the clinic lobby and found it empty. No surprise. The extensive media coverage of the bomb incident would probably keep some clients away for at least a few days. And anyone who hadn't seen the news might still be intimidated by the boarded up front window and yellow crime-scene tape roping off a big chunk of the landscaping. Kera didn't have much confidence the police would catch the bomber. A different detective, Michael Quince, had come by the clinic this morning and started over with the questions. That was not a good sign. He had also said the FBI would soon take over the case. Another bad sign. Federal investigators were notoriously poor communicators.

Meanwhile, the clinic's lab assistant who had called in sick yesterday had called in and quit this morning. And Bria, another nurse, had called in with a family emergency. Kera wondered if she would ever see her again. Now the lobby, which had seemed business-as-usual that morning, was empty of clients.

Kera pushed those thoughts aside and dove into the files. Investigating the "sex club"—as she had come to think of it—would help keep her mind busy, giving her less time to worry. She started at the end of the C section where she had left off this morning and began thumbing through charts. Patients' birthdates were listed on the file tab, so it was easy to skip everybody older than sixteen.

In a short while, she found a second client who matched the profile. Rachel Greiner, also a student at Kincaid, had made an unscheduled visit to the clinic on July 7 and asked for emergency contraception. Andrea, who was a nurse as well as the clinic manager, had discussed several birth control options with Rachel, but the girl had declined everything but some condoms to take with her. Andrea's notes indicated that Rachel believed birth control pills were an abortifacient.

Kera shook her head. The notion that hormonal contraception could keep a newly formed oocyte from adhering to the uterine wall had no scientific basis. The pharmaceutical company that had first marketed "the pill" in the fifties had made the claim—without any scientific data—because they thought it would help sell the product. Now a growing number of anti-abortion activists, including some doctors, believed it to be factual. Marketing was the glue that held myths together.

Kera jotted Rachel's information on her notepad and hoped the girl would come back in for condoms. So far, she had not.

The next hit came quickly: Katie Jackson had listed her age as fifteen, but the client also noted her school as Kincaid. Unless the girl had flunked a few grades, she was probably fourteen or under. Her last visit had been more than six months ago in late February, when she'd left with condoms and a three-month supply of pills. Katie had not been back.

"Can I get in there for a second?" Julie was suddenly at her side.

"Of course." Kera stepped back and let her co-worker pull a chart.

"Doing your own file moving?" Julie asked. The dark circles under her eyes seemed more prominent today.

"That's how slow it is. Do you think it'll be like this all week?"

"We could never get that lucky." Julie closed the drawer. "That's it for me. Don't work too late."

"See you tomorrow."

Julie moved off and Kera continued her search. Because she wasn't sure yet what she would do with her findings, she didn't feel ready to share her investigation with her co-workers.

The clinic was nearly silent, the only sounds the hum of computers and an occasional clunk of a drawer being closed. Most of the staff had gone home, and for the next hour, Kera didn't hear anyone announce themselves in the foyer. She could feel the daylight fading and her hunger growing, but she pushed on, eager to get through the files.

Eventually she found two partial matches in the M section. Savannah Montgomery, fourteen, had left the school line blank. And Greg Miller had listed his age as thirteen but his school as Spencer High School, which did not match up—unless he attended the middle school next door. Greg had been treated for genital warts six weeks ago.

Kera checked her watch. It was 6:15 and her shift was over, but the clinic would be open until 8 p.m. She decided to take a quick dinner break, then come back and finish searching the files.

Wednesday, October 20, 4:57 p.m.
EVANS AND MCCRAY were already in the room, writing lists of suspects on the case board when Jackson arrived.

"Nice penmanship, Evans. On the other hand, McCray, you write like a cranked-up second grader."

McCray had the good humor to laugh, despite the fact that he'd been on the job for nearly thirty-six hours with only a few winks of sleep. They all had. Jackson was looking forward to dinner with his daughter and maybe a short nap too. Having a suspect in custody made him feel like he could afford to take a short break. The team needed to hear about Grady, but not until he'd heard their reports first. He didn't want anyone censoring their findings. Everyone connected to the case was still a suspect.

"Are these the tenant lists?

McCray nodded. "I've contacted everyone at the Regency Apartments at least once, most of them twice. Only one reacted to Jessie's photo. Bettina Rajnek in unit twelve. She saw Jessie crossing the basketball court once recently."

"When?"

"A week or so ago. But she's not certain."

"Jessie must know someone in the apartments." Jackson brightened a little. "Anybody you haven't shown the photo to?"

"These two." McCray underlined two names, then let go of the marker and slipped into a chair. The relief was obvious on the older man's face. Jackson felt guilty about calling him out on this case. It could go on like this for days, maybe a week.

"Hey, what did I miss?" Schakowski hustled in carrying a thermos and wearing a red stain on his shirt.

"Your face?" Evans laughed at her own joke.

Schak looked down and cursed.

Jackson brought the focus back to Jessie. "One of the tenants thinks she might have seen Jessie outside the apartments a couple weeks ago."

"So what's the theory?"

"We're not there yet." Jackson turned to Evans, who was in a chair now, with her long legs stretched out. "What about your renters?"

"No one admitted recognizing the photo. But I swear the guy in unit three reacted like he did, then denied it. That's Louis Frank by the way, with the theft and drug record."

"What's your take on him?"

"I think he's seen the girl around but doesn't want to draw any attention to himself. Maybe for good reason."

"Let's bring him in."

Jackson had lost all patience with cagey ex-cons.

"I'd like a chance to talk to his girlfriend first, without him around." Evans sat up and looked at her notes.

"Okay. What else?"

"I've interviewed almost everyone at the complex twice now. But there are still two units where no one has been home either time I've been there." She pointed at the names on the board underlined in yellow: Joseph Orte and Mariska Harrison.

"Have you asked the manager about them?"

"He wasn't home either."

"What's his name?"

"Ray Bondioli. He's in unit two. I'll go back in an hour or so and try again."

"I'll go," Jackson offered, jotting the name down. "I want you to interview Mrs. Davenport instead. I'm hoping you'll get more out of her than I did."

"What's she like?" Evans flipped her notepad to a fresh page.

"Religious. Defensive about her parenting. Maybe bitter and lonely too. Her husband left about six months ago. By the way, let's find out where he is. And if Jessie had any contact with him." Jackson wrote down the Davenport address and handed it to Evans.

"Schak, what have you got to report?"

"Ruth Greiner, friend of the Davenports, seems a little squirrelly." He tapped his note pad with a pen. "First, she wouldn't let me into her house. We talked outside on the deck. Then she couldn't get it over fast enough. But whatever her problem is, it doesn't seem to be connected to Jessie. Greiner seemed genuinely surprised to learn of the girl's death."

"Maybe she just didn't want you to see her dirty house," Evans said.

"I saw her talking to herself," Schak said. "Not out loud.

She was just moving her lips."

Jackson thought about Judy Davenport's reaction to Jessie's death. "Was Greiner praying?"

Schak touched his forehead. "Of course. I should have realized that. She mentioned that they all went to the same church."

Nobody said anything for a moment.

Jackson looked at Evans. "I'd like you to talk to Greg Miller and Adam Walsh next. I missed them when I was at the school." To Schak, he said, "Follow up on the legitimate public call-in leads. Casaway has been screening them for us."

He addressed the group. "Casaway also gave me a lead from the sex offender database. I picked him up this afternoon. Oscar Grady has a history of statutory rape. The girl was fifteen. I'm holding him until I get a warrant for a DNA swab, but I'll have to release him after that if we don't come up with something else."

He looked at McCray. "Take his life apart. Talk to everyone Grady associates with. Find something on this guy."

Jackson stood. "Meanwhile, the rest of us keep looking. Church seems to be the common denominator in this social circle. Jessie and her friends met on Tuesdays after school for a Bible study called Teen Talk. And sometimes Jessie left early. If someone saw her at the apartments, then we have to assume the girl started using her free time to do something more exciting than Bible study."

9

Wednesday, October 20, 6:33 p.m.

Jackson's bungalow on the corner of 25th and Harris was dwarfed by giant oak and birch trees that had already begun to shed their leaves. As he hurried up the walk, he wondered how long he could let the yard go before he absolutely had to get out the rake. So far, October had been dry and warm, so the leaves hadn't started to decay and stink yet.

A memory from when he was ten years old bubbled. He and his older brother Derrick had a yard care service—right here in this neighborhood—that included mowing, weeding, and raking. Once, being stupid kids, they had dumped leaves in the trash can of the crazy old woman next door, and she'd called the police. The sight of a cop standing in his living room wanting to talk to him had made Jackson's knees tremble. But the officer had been kind and had even complimented him and Derrick for having their own business. Jackson's fear quickly turned to awe. He was captivated by the crisp uniform, the gun, the authority—and the compassion. At that moment, he had decided to become a cop. And never wavered from that dream.

Jackson stepped in the front door and called out, "Katie. Are you home?"

She yelled from her bedroom, "Give me a minute."

The tension in his shoulders eased just from being home. He'd lived in this house since he was eight years old, buying it from his parents when they divorced during his first year as a patrol officer. The furnishings were old, but they were quality pieces that were well cared for. And Katie was a neat freak too, so the place actually looked better than it had when Renee had been there. Organization had not been his wife's strong point.

Jackson took off his jacket and his weapon holster and hung them both over the back of a kitchen chair, the jacket covering the Sig Sauer. Katie hated even the sight of it. He made a pot of coffee and searched the freezer for possible dinner items. A frozen lasagna looked like the best bet. He popped it in the microwave, then stepped back into the hallway.

"Katie, I don't have much time here."

After a minute, his daughter appeared. He was happy to see that she was wearing baggy track-style pants and a plain T-shirt that covered her stomach. They'd had a few battles lately about how much belly she could show.

Katie's eyes were red and her sweet face was puffy from crying.

"Why didn't you tell me?" she demanded.

She was upset about Jessie. Of course. Jackson mentally kicked himself. "Honey, yesterday when I called you, I didn't know it was Jessie."

"But you knew this morning. You could have called me before I went to school. But instead, I had to hear it from my friends."

Jackson tried to read her emotions. Clearly, she was upset because a friend, or ex-friend, had died, but she also seemed to be embarrassed that as a cop's daughter she was the last to know. This was a new one.

"I'm sorry. I was busy doing my job, tracking down leads, trying to find her killer."

They stood in the hall, staring at each other, as they had so many times in the past. Katie, hands on short hips, Jackson with his arms out in an open, pleading gesture. After a moment, she stepped forward and Jackson pulled her in for a hug. Katie had been through a lot over the years with

Renee's drinking, then sudden departure. Jessie's death was yet another blow. He was glad she had not lost her current best friend.

Katie was the first to pull back. She wiped away tears and said, "You will get the guy, won't you?"

"I will."

They ate the lasagna, cool in places, tongue-burning hot in others, without complaining. Katie had put celery sticks on the table so they could tell themselves they'd had a vegetable. Neither cared for greens unless they were in a salad smothered in ranch dressing.

Jackson turned on the TV to catch up on the local news, then quickly shut it back off. The lead story was Jessie's death.

"Did they have grief counselors at your school today?" Jackson asked between bites.

"There were two people from the district office, but I didn't talk to either of them."

"Are you doing all right? I feel bad that I can't be here for you."

"I'm fine." Katie gave him a sad, brave smile that broke his heart.

After a few minutes, Jackson said, "I have to take you back over to Aunt Jan's tonight. You know I have to work straight through for another day or so. It's the only way to break a homicide case."

"It's okay. I want you to find the guy that killed her."

"I know you haven't been hanging out with Jessie lately." Jackson paused. "But is there anything you can tell me about her friends, or boyfriend, anything that might help?" Like who she was having sex with.

"After she joined Teen Talk, she didn't have time for me." Katie put down her fork and wouldn't look at him. "I really can't help you."

She jumped up and rushed to the sink to rinse her plate.

"I know she was sexually active." Jackson turned in his chair so he could see her reaction, but his daughter was still facing the sink.

"Then you know more about her than I do." Katie dried her hands and bolted toward the hallway. "I've gotta pack some stuff."

Jackson let it go for now. He knew better than to push. His daughter could be incredibly stubborn, and she came by the trait naturally.

Ray Bondioli was home when Jackson showed up after dropping Katie off at her aunt's. Thirty-something and sporting a mullet, Bondioli had the nervous twitch and rotten teeth that Jackson associated with meth use. The manager invited him in and offered him a seat at a stained Formica table near a kitchen that reeked of days-old garbage. Jackson passed a living room couch covered with two sleeping kids. With some Pine-Sol and new carpet, the apartment could have been okay. It was bigger than he'd expected.

"You want something to drink? I've only got beer and water."

"No thanks." Jackson didn't drink from glasses handed to him by strangers, and he didn't drink alcohol when he was working.

"What can I do for you?" Bondioli sat, but didn't relax.

"We're interviewing the building's tenants in connection with a homicide investigation."

Bondioli cut in. "Yeah. I know. I talked to that other cop yesterday. The woman."

"I want to know about two of your tenants who have not been home in the last few days." Jackson glanced at his notes. "Joseph Orte and Mariska Harrison."

The manager breathed a quick sigh of relief. "Joe's gone on business. He left last Friday. Travels all the time. But

Mariska Harrison," Bondioli shook his head. "I haven't seen her since she rented the place. Other people use the apartment sometimes, though."

"What other people?"

"A guy in a business suit. And I saw an older couple coming out of it once too."

"You're okay with that?"

"She pays the rent on time, doesn't draw any complaints from her neighbors, and never needs anything from me." Bondioli grinned. "Hell yes, I'm okay with that. She's my favorite tenant."

"You have a phone number for her?"

"Sure." The manager went over to the narrow computer desk in the dining room and opened a drawer. He took out the file, copied down two numbers on the back of a grocery receipt, and handed the paper to Jackson.

"Thanks."

Jackson pulled out a photo of Jessie from the back of his case-file and held it up. "Have you ever seen her before?"

Bondioli shook his head. "Is that the dead girl?"

"Yeah."

They both took a moment to reflect on that.

"How old are your kids?" Jackson asked.

"Seven and ten. But they're my sister's kids. I'm just baby-sitting while she works the dinner shift at Sheri's."

"Thanks for your help."

Back in his car, Jackson called Mariska Harrison. She didn't answer, so he left a message and tried the other number. After two rings, she picked up. He could hear the chatter and clang of a restaurant in the background.

"This is Detective Wade Jackson of the Eugene police. I need to talk to you about your Oakwood apartment."

"May I ask what this is about?" A clipped and cool voice.

"A homicide investigation. Can we meet right now?"

"I'm having dinner with friends. I can meet you in about an hour at Adam's Place."

"Downtown mall?"

"Yes. I'll be at the bar. In black pants and a maroon sweater."

"See you then."

Mariska Harrison was younger than her businesslike voice had led him to believe. She was stocky, in her late twenties, and had curly dark hair that molded to her scalp. Her light brown skin and mixed-race features made Jackson think she might be Puerto Rican.

Harrison shook his hand firmly and offered to buy him a drink. Jackson ordered a Diet Pepsi and put two dollars on the bar. Mariska asked for a glass of dry white wine, then turned to him and asked, "So who's dead?"

"Let's get our drinks and go to a table where it will be quieter."

The upscale bar was small, appointed with dark-toned wood, and crowded with Eugene's better-dressed citizens, which meant no tie-dye, hemp, or sandals. Jackson picked a booth that was not right under a speaker. The piped-in jazz set his teeth on edge.

When they had settled in, Jackson pulled out his notepad. There was barely enough light to see what was on the page. "Tell me about the Oakwood apartment you rent on Patterson Street. The manager says you don't really live there."

Harrison scowled. "He really didn't have any business telling you that. But first, tell me who's dead."

Jackson gave her his best don't-fuck-with-me stare. He was tempted to take her over to the department for questioning, just to show her who was in charge of this conversation. But it would be a colossal consumption of time. And time was running out.

Jessie had been dead for more than twenty-four hours

now, and they still didn't have a viable suspect.

He held up Jessie's photo. "This girl was found in a dumpster between the Regency and Oakwood Apartments. Do you know her?"

"No." A little bravado went out of Harrison's tone.

"Tell me about your apartment there."

"I rent it for the mayor. I'm his personal assistant."

Jackson tried not to show his surprise. "Why does the mayor need a small, low-rent apartment? Doesn't he have a nice home in the south hills?"

"He works very long hours and sometimes, when he has a break during the day, he goes there to nap or listen to music. His parents stay there when they come into town to visit too. They don't like hotels and they don't like his wife."

"Did the mayor take a break there yesterday?" Jackson tried to picture Miles Fieldstone—tall, lanky, and ridiculously good looking—stretched out on a couch in an apartment similar to Bondioli's. He couldn't make the image work.

"Not that I know of." Harrison shrugged and sipped her wine.

The mayor's secret-apartment scenario intrigued Jackson—always good to see tax dollars hard at work—but did it have any bearing on this case?

"So you've never stayed in the apartment?"

"No."

"But you pay the rent?"

"The mayor reimburses me."

"With city money? Or out of his personal account?"

"I don't know. He gives me cash."

"I need to talk with Mr. Fieldstone. Get me on his calendar tomorrow."

"I can't. He's in meetings all day."

"This is important. I'd like to clear the mayor from this investigation as quickly as possible. Especially before the press gets wind of the connection."

Mariska sneered at his clumsy threat. "I'll do what I can."

Jackson handed her a business card. "Call me with a meet time."

He left the bar and drove the six blocks back to the police department. Judge Cranston had likely signed the warrant for Grady's DNA and sent it over by now. Jackson would swab him, then interrogate him again. Casaway had also brought in two other sex offenders who still needed to be questioned. Jessie's crime scene photos had been processed, and Jackson would use them in the interrogations. Maybe he would catch a break. Sex offenders sometimes had more guilt than your average criminal and would confess their sins when confronted with the visual reminder of what they had done.

Wednesday, October 20, 8:17 p.m.

AS RUTH WASHED the dinner dishes, she strategized about how to add another level of pressure on the abortion clinic workers. Something personal in addition to the explosives.

Ruth fed the cat and decided to start with some motivational letters. Nothing like the fear of God delivered directly to your doorstep.

She wiped the kitchen table, dried her hands, and started down the hall toward her husband's office. Out of the corner of her eye, she saw Rachel in the den at the family's computer. Ruth worried about the time her children spent on the Internet. She had suggested canceling their service, but Sam wouldn't hear of it. He stayed up late every night posting on his CCA blog.

Ruth stepped into the den. "Hey, sweetie. Is your homework done?"

"Not yet. But I don't have much, so it won't take long."

"Homework first. You know the rules."

Ruth started to move away, then realized Rachel was making no move to leave the computer. Her daughter was completely ignoring Ruth's request to do her homework first. She marched over to the desk, grabbed her daughter's ear, and yanked.

"Owww!" Rachel shot out of the chair. Ruth moved toward the door, pulling Rachel behind her.

"You can let go now," Rachel said through clenched teeth.

Ruth pinched harder. "Don't take that tone with me. Are you ready for another whipping?"

Rachel didn't respond. In a moment, Ruth released her grip. Rachel hurried into her bedroom without looking back. Ruth and Sam had had to re-educate their daughter recently about not arguing with them. It was a lesson both kids had learned early, but shortly after her thirteenth birthday, Rachel had decided to test the policy. Apparently, she was still pushing the boundaries. Ruth would not let her guard down. The Bible was clear about parents' disciplinary responsibilities to their children. But she was careful to never draw blood or leave scars, the way her parents had.

Ruth considered going back to the den and using the family computer but decided against it. She needed privacy. Sam didn't like anyone to use his computer, but he would be gone for hours at his men's Bible study.

Ruth made some peppermint tea and took it into Sam's office. Crowded bookshelves lined two of the four walls, and a map of the western states covered most of a third. Hundreds of pushpins identified where abortion clinics were located. The ones they knew about, anyway. Abortionists were getting craftier about keeping their whereabouts and identities hidden.

She perched on the edge of her husband's desk chair and booted up his PC. Ruth opened up a letter template but left the salutation blank, for now. She had the list of recipients in her head, but she wanted to craft the body of the message first.

Dear Sinner,
Planned Parenthood is the work of the devil and you are
his pawn. You must repent your sins and stop murdering
unborn babies. It is the worst transgression against God.
Teaching God's children to fornicate freely is the second
worst transgression. You must stop or God will punish
you. This is a promise. And God does not break His prom-
ises.
—*God's Messenger*

Ruth reread her letter, made one minor correction, and printed three copies. Then she printed envelope labels for Sheila Brentwood, the director, Andrea Drake, the manager, and Kera Kollmorgan, the hypocrite who had called her a "fanatic with no regard for human life." The nerve! From a woman who assisted with abortions and reached out to corrupt children into sexual deviancy.

At the last moment, Ruth remembered about fingerprints. "Damn." The curse slipped out. She pinched the skin on the back of her hand and apologized to God for swearing.

She shredded the envelopes and went to the laundry room for latex gloves. Back in the office, she pulled on the gloves and started over with the envelopes. When she finished, she deleted the electronic files and opened ten of Sam's Word documents to erase her files from the software program's history. She didn't want Sam to know about this activity. He was president of Eugene's CCA chapter and an advocate of legal intimidation of abortion clinic staff and clients. But he did not support breaking the law. So Ruth kept her activities to herself.

She hurried the stamped envelopes out to her car and shoved them under the driver's seat. McMillan Street was dark and silent under a blanket of stars, and the sound of a car door closing rang out into the night. Ruth cringed at the noise and hurried back inside. Rachel stood in the foyer, her face blank, her hands in her pants pockets. Ruth knew the expression well. Rachel was still angry but would not show it. Good. The girl was learning some self-control. Just as motherhood had taught Ruth to master her own impulses.

"Did you finish your homework?"

"Yes. May I use the computer now?"

"For an hour." Ruth checked her watch.

Rachel turned away without another word. Ruth squared her shoulders. Her daughter would come back around. She always did.

‹ **10** ›

KERA CHANGED OUT of her work clothes, made a cup of decaf, and listened to her voice mail. Three reporters had called asking for interviews about the clinic bombing. Sophie Speranza of the Willamette News had promised her anonymity, but the TV reporters wanted her to go on camera. Kera decided to ignore them all. She should never have done the first interview on the morning of the bombing. Now they saw her as an easy source.

She sat down at the kitchen table to pay bills. The mortgage statement, sitting on top of the stack of mail, made her dread the legal complications she faced now that Daniel had decided to stay in Iraq. Would she have to sell the house? Did he expect her to file for divorce?

Kera picked through the mail, looking for more bills. Most of the stack was junk. Credit card companies wanting to loan her money and charities wanting her to give them money. Kera dropped most of it into the paper recycling.

One letter stopped her short. It was addressed to Nathan at a base camp outside of Baghdad, and the handwriting looked feminine. It had been among her son's possessions that the Army had finally returned to her. Kera had placed it on the table, thinking that she would open it later.

Weeks had passed, but still she could not bring herself to face the letter's contents. She considered simply tossing the letter in the recycling so she wouldn't have to think about it again. Stabbing the back of her hand with the letter opener would have been less painful than reading the last communication written to her son.

Kera set the letter aside for another time. Some day she would have to take the plunge and sort through Nathan's stuff. She would try again this weekend. If she succeeded, she would call St. Vincent DePaul's and ask them to come pick up everything of Daniel's too. It would be a clean start. Then she could move her car out of the driveway and back into the garage.

After putting stamps on the bills, Kera headed for the den to get online. She checked a couple of news sites, then went straight to militaryfamilies.com. The website hosted a chat room where she could converse with and draw comfort from other parents who had lost their children in the war.

But as soon as she typed in her screen name, kikoll, Kera thought about the e-mail she had received from *blowgirl_jd*. She was sure it had come from Jessie. And if Jessie was like other kids, she spent plenty of time on the Internet. Out of curiosity, Kera opened up another browser and typed in *blowgirl_jd*.

A full page of search listings came up. Kera clicked open the top link and landed on a chat room page called Girl2-Girl at girlsjustwanttohavefun.com. The site was clearly the work of an amateur, but what it lacked in design finesse, it made up for in color and enthusiasm. Bright lime green and pink lettering punctuated with exclamation marks shouted at her to come on in. Kera hesitated briefly, then logged in as *blowgirl_jd*. The unsophisticated site did not require a password but probably limited its access to certain user names.

Kera had no desire to engage anyone in chat, especially using a dead girl's screen ID, but she thought it might be informative to read some of Jessie's postings. In a moment, a menu of chat subjects presented itself in the middle of the screen.

From a list that also included Dirty Gossip, Disgusting

Guys, Hot Guys, and Parties, Kera clicked a button that said Sex Talk. She searched around until she found an exchange, dated October 5, between chatters named *blowgirl_jd*, *perfectass*, and *freakjob37*. Kera scanned through it, hoping to find a reference to Jessie's sex partners. The postings started out with a catty conversation about a girl who had missed a lot of school recently, then abruptly turned sexual.

freakjob37: My dad has a new video called Candy Strippers. It's really hot. Lots of butt sex.

blowgirl_jd: Cool. I like it up the ass, I mean, if I'm ready for it. And no worries about pregnancy.

perfectass: Despite my screen name, I'm not that crazy about anal encounters, but neither is TJ so we'll hook and let you guys do the nasty stuff.

blowgirl_jd: Like you can get through a "meeting" only doing one guy. Hah!

freakjob37: I think it's time for little miss *perfectass* to start doing girls too.

perfectass: I'm working up to it. I made out with RG last time. The guys got really hard for that session.

blowgirl_jd: Talk about hard. My new guy "on the side" can stay up forever! He wears me out. Seriously. He is a fuck machine.

perfectass: Why won't you tell us who he is? It kills me not to know!

blowgirl_jd: I can't. It's too unreal. Too dangerous for him. But I will tell you what we did last time.

And she did, in graphic detail. At first, Kera was compelled to read, in the same way she couldn't turn away from news stories that shocked and sickened her. But then she quickly felt overwhelmed and voyeuristic and had to click off the site.

It wasn't the sex that bothered her. She had heard it all and done much of it herself at least once. But never in a group. And never with another female. And these girls were still in middle school. Her biggest concern, though, was that they weren't using condoms or birth control with any consistency. At least according to the charts she'd seen at the clinic. One of these girls would end up pregnant. And even though Kera supported a woman's choice to have an abortion, she wouldn't wish the experience on anyone.

Then it hit her again. Jessie was dead. Found naked in a dumpster. Had her sexual fun and games gone too far? And who was Jessie's "guy on the side"? Jessie had called him Mike in the e-mail she sent, and her reference to his sustained erections made Kera wonder if Mike was older—maybe old enough to have access to Viagra.

Had Jessie ever told her friends who he was? Kera wondered if she would be able to figure out who he was by reading other chat room conversations. She realized that she could probably identify most of the kids once she finished sorting through the files. Kera jotted down the screen names and initials mentioned. GM could be Greg Miller, and RG could be Rachel Greiner. Was Nicole either *freak-job37* or *perfectass*?

It didn't matter. Kera was not going to contact them personally or name them to anyone. But she would schedule some time tomorrow afternoon to visit Kincaid Middle School. She would talk to the principal, ask about the sex ed curriculum, and suggest they set up an outreach program. The sex club needed an intervention before anyone else got hurt.

Wednesday, October 20, 8:10 p.m.
THE INTERROGATION ROOM at the jail was even smaller than the one at the police department. After twenty minutes of back and forth with Grady, the gray-green walls started closing in on Jackson.

"I'll be back in a few minutes. Would you like a Pepsi?"

"Sure." Grady looked grateful.

Jackson headed for the vending machine in the sheriff's lounge and bought two cans of soda, with and without sugar. He carried the drinks back to the interrogation room, which was not far from where wives, mothers, and girlfriends visited the worthless men in their lives through plexiglass windows.

"Did you like being a teacher?" Jackson asked when he sat down.

Grady looked wary. He'd given up on being charming. "Yeah. I did."

"What did you like about it?"

"I liked working with kids. All right? Isn't that what you want me to say?"

"Did you know you were sexually attracted to children when you started teaching? Or did you become sexually attracted to kids while you were on the job?"

"It's not like that." Grady shook his head.

"What is it like?"

"You wouldn't understand."

"I might." Jackson took a drink of soda. "Tell me about it."

Grady leaned forward. "I'm not sexually attracted to children. I became attracted to one girl. A young woman." His eyes misted as he spoke. "We had a connection. Whenever Amy and I were near each other, the energy just sparked. We smiled at the same things. We knew what each other was thinking. I never meant any of it to happen. It just did."

"How does Amy feel about you now?"

Bitterness flew out of Grady's mouth. "I don't know. I'm not allowed to see her."

"Have you found a girlfriend since you got out?"

"No." Grady's eyes jumped around.

"Bullshit." Jackson slammed the table and stood up. "Guys like you always have someone. I think you're working a new girl right now. Just like the way you worked Jessie. Poor Jessie wandered by the Recovery House one day after school and caught your eye. You befriended her, then seduced her. When things got out of hand, you killed her because you're afraid of going back to jail."

"No. No. No." Now Grady's leg thumped wildly under the table.

"I have your DNA swab." Jackson leaned down into Grady's face. "When it matches the trace evidence we found on Jessie, you'll go away for homicide. The only chance you have of making a deal is to tell me what happened right now."

"I don't hurt girls. I love them." Grady's lips started to tremble. "And they love me."

Jackson laughed. "They don't love you. They just need attention. And when they grow up and learn to love themselves, they start to hate you. Don't they? I'm sure Amy finds you revolting now."

Grady begged, "Don't say that. Please don't say that."

"Did Jessie try to break it off? Is that why you killed her?"

A tear rolled down the ex-con's face. "Don't do this to me. Please. Just leave me alone."

Thursday, October 21, 7:38 a.m.

Jackson hated the first half of the drive to Portland. It was flat and straight and crawling with huge trucks. But at eighty miles an hour, it went quickly. The sky was dark and all the commuters had their headlights on, but the clouds were expected to burn off again today. The last twenty miles of the trip were even worse as traffic congealed and slowed near the Portland metro area. But for every homicide on which he was lead investigator, he made the trip. This time he was headed to the new state medical examiner's building on 82nd Street near the Clackamas Town Center.

Jessie's autopsy was scheduled for 9:45 a.m. in unit C, and he had only a few minutes to spare. Inside the pale green room with the stainless steel countertops and harsh florescent light, the medical examiner was gowned and waiting for him. Jackson had called ahead to let Hillary Ainsworth know he was coming. It would be their seventeenth autopsy together, but Jackson had seen her only once without a surgical mask and goggles. He had been surprised at how soft she seemed. Her fuzzy gray-blond hair and pink chubby cheeks didn't match the woman with nerves of steel who cut open bodies and picked glass out of smashed-in skulls.

"You're cutting it close, Jackson." Today, the mask and goggles obscured Ainsworth's expression and he couldn't tell if she was teasing. He suspected not. Her small crew processed dozens of bodies a week, and she liked to keep things moving. Jackson grabbed a mask from the shelf by the door. The gown was optional, and he didn't usually stand close enough to get bloody.

This time was even more difficult than his very first autopsy. Jessie's young body on the table made him think of his daughter, and the emotions he normally kept locked up tight during homicide investigations threatened to break loose. Jackson focused on Ainsworth's hands and voice.

The ME started near the top of Jessie's head with a visual exam that included trace evidence collection. The first point of interest was that Jessie had fibers in her nose. Ainsworth extracted them with a long pair of tweezers and bagged them for the lab to analyze.

"My guess is cotton, similar to that used in sheets and pillowcases." Ainsworth turned back to the body.

After a few minutes, she noted the marks on the girl's wrists, which had deepened into thin postmortem bruises. "I'd say they were most likely caused by restraints made of fabric. Metal or plastic would have caused lacerations."

After noting an old scar on her knee and a tiny fresh scratch on her left big toe, Ainsworth finally began an examination of Jessie's genitals. After a moment she said, "This is interesting. See these small red, burn-like marks?"

Jackson nodded but did not look.

"I believe they were made from cryosurgery, the application of liquid nitrogen. It's commonly used to treat genital warts."

"A sexually transmitted disease?" Jackson wondered if Grady, his suspect, had any sign of it.

"Yep. They're caused by HPV or human papillomavirus. The most common form of STD. There's something like five million new cases every year just in this country. We'll test her blood for it."

"She was definitely sexually active?"

"Yes. But at her age, it could have been an abusive situation."

"Any indication of rape?"

"There is no bruising or tearing around the vagina or anus, although there are signs of recent sexual activity in both orifices. No bruising on the inner thighs or anywhere, for that matter. No semen in the vagina, but a fair amount in the anus. And a vaginal discharge, indicating orgasm. I won't know for sure until I get it under a microscope."

The orgasm threw his sexual abuse theory off base. Jackson tried to wrap his mind around the idea that this almost fourteen-year-old girl had been having consensual, satisfying sex. Maybe with Oscar Grady. Was Grady's perception realistic? Were his victims really more like sexual partners?

The ME took multiple swabs of Jessie's genital area, vagina, and anus, then bagged and labeled each.

She reached for her scalpel. "Ready?"

Twenty minutes later, Jackson finally had a cause of death: asphyxiation, or lack of oxygen to the brain.

"Considering the fibers in her nose, it's most likely she suffocated," Ainsworth said.

"Suffocated? Or was suffocated?" The distinction was critical.

"I'm not certain yet. Very few people over the age of five suffocate accidentally. It does happen, but it's not common."

"Are you ruling it a homicide?"

"Don't rush me. Of course, you should treat it as such for now, but I can't make a final determination until I see the lab results."

"When do I get them?"

"We'll prioritize. That's all I can promise."

Jackson could feel a serious headache coming on. Very little sleep, too much caffeine, and now a squishy death ruling. It was obvious that this was not the work of a stranger–

rapist. But still, sometime after consensual sex, the girl had been suffocated and dumped in the trash.

On the way out of the autopsy, Jackson called the Lane County jail and asked to speak to the nurse.

"Detective Jackson here. I need you to check Oscar Grady for genital warts. He's in C-block on an investigative hold."

"Do you want just a visual check or should I get a blood sample?"

"Both please."

Halfway down the Willamette Valley corridor on Interstate 5, a connection occurred to him. Where would a young girl get liquid nitrogen treatment for genital warts? She couldn't go to her family doctor without her mother finding out. Either Judy Davenport knew about Jessie's sex life or the girl had gone somewhere like a Planned Parenthood clinic.

‹ 12 ›

Thursday, October 21, 12:35 p.m.

Cranston was in court for the day, so Jackson went down the hall to Judge Marlee Volcansek. She was a lifelong Democrat, a member of the ACLU, and not fond of small talk. Jackson was not optimistic.

The judge looked up from her computer without smiling. "What can I do for you, Detective Jackson?" Her razor-straight black hair was pulled back from a face that could have been thirty-eight or fifty-eight; the Botox made it impossible to tell. Without the robe, she seemed smaller than he remembered from court.

"I just witnessed the autopsy of Jessie Davenport, a young girl who was found dead in a dumpster. The medical examiner says Jessie was recently treated for genital warts. I need to confirm that with medical records." Jackson presented the search warrant he'd crafted.

The judge didn't even look at it. "How exactly is this relevant to finding her killer?" Her dark eyebrows arched even higher.

"If we can prove she had genital warts, and later, if we arrest someone who also has the disease, it's one more connection."

"Circumstantial evidence at best. Not good enough."

"The clinic may also have a record of the girl's sexual partners."

"And if it does?"

"One out of three female homicide victims is killed by someone they've had sex with."

Volcansek gave that some thought, then said, "Can't you find out who she's slept with by simply interviewing her friends and family?"

"Not this time. Everyone says Jessie didn't have a boyfriend, that she was a good Christian girl. But the autopsy says she was sexually active. So either they're all lying to me or Jessie was very secretive about this guy. I have to find him. And connect her to him. This is the only way I have."

The judge shook her head. "I don't want to set a precedent. With medical records, there's the overriding issue of protecting the patient's privacy." Her argument lacked passion.

"She's dead," Jackson reminded her. "Jessie's privacy is less important than bringing her justice."

Volcansek pressed her lips together. She scanned the paperwork. Finally, she made a small notation, then signed the document.

"This is a very limited search. You can access only the parts of her file that refer to the recent treatment of genital warts and any record of her partners' names. You will not go browsing around in personal medical information that is irrelevant."

"Thank you, ma'am."

Jackson thought about stopping for lunch on the way over to the clinic, but he was too keyed up. The heavy noon traffic on West 11th nearly drove him crazy. He needed a break in this case. Now. And he needed the old people in the car in front of him to get the hell out of his way.

By the time he reached Commerce Street, his heart was pounding with anxiety and caffeine overload. He had to settle himself down before entering the clinic or he would scare someone. Jackson stepped out of the car and paused for a moment to watch the construction workers rebuilding the wall around the clinic's front window. Then he strode into the foyer, flashed his badge to the receptionist, and marched down to Sheila Brentwood's office. The door was open, so he stepped in without knocking. The director had a deli sandwich in her hands.

"Ms. Brentwood. I'm sorry to interrupt your lunch, but I'm investigating the death of Jessie Davenport." Jackson handed her the paperwork. "I have a search warrant that entitles me to see the record of Jessie's last visit here."

Sheila's shoulders sagged. "What makes you certain she was a client here?"

"I'm guessing. Now you can either bring me that particular paperwork or let me search for it."

"Please wait here."

Brentwood moved quickly, giving him a look as she went.

Six minutes later, she was back. "I made a copy of the chart for her visit on Tuesday, October 19." She passed him a single sheet of paper. "She was treated with liquid nitrogen for genital warts and offered birth control. She left without the birth control and without paying for the service."

Jackson looked up from the file. "I thought you guys were free."

Sheila stifled a sigh. "We offer services on a sliding scale. We do not refuse services to anyone for lack of money. But we bill everyone and hope that they pay. It costs money to run this place."

"Of course. Uh, I don't see a reference to her sexual partners."

"There isn't one. We don't ask for names."

"Even with sexually transmitted diseases?"

"No. The county requires us to report cases of chlamydia and gonorrhea, which are bacterial infections. County health agencies then sometimes contact those patients and request partner names if they think it's part of a major outbreak."

"But you don't get partner names?"

"No."

Jackson's energy deflated. He itched to peruse Jessie's entire file, but his search warrant didn't give him permission, and he knew there was no point in asking.

"Thanks for your cooperation."

"You're welcome."

After leaving the clinic, Jackson drove across the street to the Mongolian Grill. He figured he had time for one trip through the pick-your-own-stir-fry line. Sizzling meat smells greeted him at the door and made his empty stomach growl. He loved everything about this place except the mustard yellow walls.

In compliance with his doctor's orders to cut back on fat, he loaded up on noodles and chicken and threw in just enough mushrooms and onions to satisfy the vegetable police. A few minutes later, cooked food in hand, he headed for his table. On the way, he spotted Kera Kollmorgan, the nurse who'd taken a fall the day of the bombing, sitting at a window table by herself. He wondered if—outside the clinic—she would loosen up and give him some information he could use.

Jackson stepped over to her table. "Hello. Kera, right?"

"Yes. Hello, Officer Jackson." She gave him a warm smile.

Encouraged, Jackson said, "How are you holding up? I mean, after the bomb."

Reflexively, she reached up and touched the small abrasion on her forehead. "I'm fine. Thanks for asking."

A moment of silence.

"Would you like to join me? Your food's getting cold."

Jackson shrugged. "Sure. Thanks." He slipped into the chair across from her and dug into his stir-fry.

They ate in silence for a moment, Jackson gulping noodles and Kera picking slowly at vegetables.

"Are you a vegetarian?" He had to start somewhere.

"Oh no." She laughed at the idea. "I just ate all the beef first. I'm a protein burner."

He liked her uninhibited laugh and the way her big hazel eyes lit up. "If I worked nearby like you do, I'd probably come here every day."

"I'm a frequent flyer, for sure. The secret is to load the bowl properly the first time—meaning meat on the bottom—so you don't have to go back through a second time."

"Good strategy."

She poured both of them some tea, and he noticed a faint white line on her left hand where a wedding ring used to reside.

"Detective Quince was asking questions at the clinic yesterday, and now you're here today," she commented. "Are you still investigating the bombing?"

"No. A homicide occurred, and that's my main jurisdiction."

"Jessie Davenport?" She put down her fork.

"Yes. Do you know her?"

"I've seen the news stories."

"Your initials were on her chart. You treated her for genital warts."

Kera leaned back. "So that's why you were at the clinic. Did you get what you wanted?"

"Not exactly. I still want to know who her sex partner was."

"Do you think he killed her?" Her eyes were intense, but Jackson didn't sense that she was angry with him.

"He's our number-one suspect, until we learn otherwise."

"Any leads?"

"I couldn't tell you if I did have one."

She pushed her plate away, and Jackson dug back into

his. In a minute, he would probe some more. He could tell she wanted to help. He just had to earn her trust. And he thought he knew how. "My daughter Katie loves this place," he said between bites. "She'd be jealous if she knew I came here without her."

HE WASN'T WEARING a wedding ring, so the mention of the daughter surprised Kera. "How old is she?"

"Thirteen. Middle school. Oh boy." Jackson gave her a pained smile.

"It's a tough age." Kera didn't want him to inquire about her child. Nor did she want to be rude and change the subject, so she asked, "How does your daughter feel about your being a police officer?"

"She's okay with it. In fact, I think she's kind of proud of me," Jackson said.

Names and ages suddenly slammed together in her head. A thirteen-year-old girl named Katie Jackson was one of the students on her sex club list. Kera fought to keep the information off her face and out of her voice. "Where does Katie go to school?"

"Kincaid."

Kera took a gulp of tea. Maybe his daughter's last name wasn't Jackson. Maybe it wasn't the same girl. But she knew it had to be. Eugene was not that big. And Kincaid Middle School didn't have two Katie Jacksons.

Oh great. Now she not only had information about a murdered girl that she couldn't share with the detective, but she also had inside information about his daughter. Kera decided it was time to leave. She reached into her purse for her wallet and found Jessie's cell phone instead. It occurred to her that she could give it to him now. He already knew that Jessie had been to Planned Parenthood.

She held out the phone to Jackson. "This is Jessie's. She left it at the clinic."

Jackson seemed stunned. Then angry. "You've had it since Tuesday?"

"I didn't find it until yesterday morning," Kera said, feeling defensive. "I planned to put it in the mail to you today, but I just now realized that I could give it to you without violating Jessie's confidence. I mean, now that you already know she was treated at the clinic."

His face softened, but he didn't smile. "Thanks. This reminds me that I'm expecting a fax from the phone company, and it should be here by now. I need to get back to the department." He looked around for his waitress.

Kera felt inexplicably sad and guilty. "I'm sorry about the delay in getting the phone to you. But we promise our clients confidentiality, and we honor that promise."

"I understand." He signaled the waitress to bring his check.

Kera didn't think he really did understand. "In states where minors need a parent's permission to get birth control, teenage pregnancy rates are nearly double what they are here."

"I can see why." Jackson stared at her. "Do you know who Jessie was having sex with? She may have been the victim of abuse. And he may have killed her."

"I don't know. We never ask our clients for that information. But I did ask her if the sex was consensual, and she insisted that it was."

"Good. I'm glad to know you ask about that."

Kera grabbed her purse and stood to leave. "Good luck with your investigation."

"Thanks." He didn't smile.

AS HE DROVE BACK to the department downtown, Jackson regretted the way he'd acted. Kera was a nice woman. And he could tell by the compassion in her eyes that she cared about Jessie. About all her clients.

Nice woman. He let out a short laugh. Kera was more than nice. She was also smart and attractive and under different circumstances, he would have considered asking her out. But his divorce was still a fresh wound, his daughter was not ready for him to be a swinging single, and he had a killer to track down.

The fax of the phone records had come in, and someone had put it on Jackson's desk. Its arrival saved him the hassle of scrolling back through Jessie's call history one number at a time. Jackson labeled Jessie's phone and took it to the fingerprint techs in the department's small lab. Maybe the killer had handled it.

Back at his desk, he rummaged around for the cheap reading glasses he kept handy, then began to scan the list of numbers on the phone records. It took a minute to pick out Jessie's phone number from the others. After twenty minutes, Jackson had found five phone numbers that had connected with her—either in or out—at least ten times in the last billing cycle. He circled two more numbers that appeared five and seven times each.

Starting with the most frequent contact—twelve outgoing and fourteen incoming connections—he punched the number into LEDS, the law enforcement data system. The phone line was registered to Joanne Clarke and was part of a cluster of three numbers, all of which had cell phone prefixes. Nicole Clarke was one of Jessie's friends, and Joanne was probably Nicole's mother and the one who paid the phone bill. He opened his electronic note file, added the name and the number of calls, then moved back to the records.

Three of the other frequently called numbers belonged to Angel Strickland, Ruth Greiner, and Katrice Jahn. Angel Strickland was one of the girls he'd interviewed, and Ruth Greiner was the mother of Rachel Greiner, the third member of Jessie's clique. The name Katrice Jahn was new to him.

But she was probably the mother of Tyler Jahn, the surfer boy from the Teen Talk group. He plugged the address into the database just to check. Katrice was listed at 3460 Potter Street, which was in the Kincaid neighborhood.

Jackson sipped his cold coffee from that morning and punched the next number into the database. This one had eleven total calls and a 206 area code, which Jackson recognized as Seattle, Washington. The computer came up with Paul Davenport, Jessie's father. Jackson had met the man once, two years ago at a soccer game. Had he moved to Seattle? Even so, with a cell phone, Paul Davenport could be calling Jessie from anywhere. Schakowski was already tracking him down, and a father's calls to his daughter didn't trigger Jackson's suspicion.

He kept moving down the list. A local number with only seven connections belonged to George Miller, the first name in the group that sparked Jackson's interest. A classmate? A boyfriend? He ran him through a second database.

Miller lived on Friendly Street, worked for the county as a building inspector, and had three kids. One was a four-teen-year-old boy named Greg Miller who attended Kincaid Middle School. The boy had been picked up for shoplifting in a convenience store when he was twelve. As Jackson made a note to interview Greg Miller, he realized that the kid was also one of the Bible study group. He wondered if Evans had interviewed him yet.

Jackson punched in the last number he'd circled, which also had a 513 cell phone prefix. A moment later, a familiar name came up: Miles R. Fieldstone.

The mayor again? A tingle went up Jackson's spine.

He quickly scanned for the address associated with the number: 27575 Blanton Heights. Yep, that was the mayor. Jackson glanced back at the printout. The calls were evenly split both ways, four incoming, three outgoing. Now the hairs on the back of his neck were standing at attention.

Why would the head of the city chat on the phone with a thirteen-year-old girl seven times in thirty days?

To arrange get-togethers at the apartment he rented near her school—right next to where her body was found.

A surge of adrenaline rushed through his torso, and Jackson bolted out of his chair. Now he had a suspect with a direct link to the victim.

But that charged feeling—like a bloodhound that has picked up the fox's scent—was overshadowed by a more sobering thought. Fieldstone was the mayor. He played golf with the chief of police. This would not go down easy.

‹ **13** ›

NICOLE SAT IN THE BACK of her fifth period class, waiting for Mr. Abrams to show. She hated math, especially negative integers, and she really wanted to leave. She was having trouble concentrating. Around her, the unsupervised kids buzzed with animated conversations, lewd laughter, and occasional bursts of music from forbidden iPods.

Next to her, a loud sharp thump burst through the noise. Nicole turned to see Pat Kelly's math book on the floor. One row over, David Turner laughed like the idiot that he was. Nicole was not amused. Pat was a small, moon-faced boy with thin, white grandpa hair who had no friends and got picked on all the time.

Without a word, Pat retrieved his book and placed it back on his desk.

Moments later, David knocked it on the floor again. A few kids laughed. Most did not even notice. What a jerk, Nicole thought. She wanted to get up and punch him in the chest. Or at least, tell him off. But of course, that would focus everyone's attention on her. They would probably even make fun of her for being a nerd.

Pat picked up his book, still not looking at David or showing any expression, and set it back on his desk. This time, he kept his hands on top of it.

Good, Nicole thought. Now it would be over and she could stop worrying about Pat and–

Thunk. The book was back on the floor.

Without thinking, without realizing she was even going

to do it, Nicole yelled at David across two rows of desks, "Leave him alone!"

The room went silent. Every pair of eyes stared directly at her. Nicole grabbed her backpack and fled.

She ran down the open breezeway, flip-flops squawking, and ducked into the school's computer center. Only a few kids were in the room, and the supervisor was nowhere in sight. Where were all the teachers?

Nicole picked a PC in the corner, dropped her heavy pack on the floor, and wished she could just disappear. A year ago, her life had been happy and simple. Now she and her friends were fornicating like crazy, Jessie was dead, and she had just screamed at another student in front of the whole math class. She didn't care what David thought of her, but she did like to have more control of herself than that.

Nicole closed her eyes and tried to pray, but she became so filled with guilt, she couldn't continue. Why should God help her? She had been self-involved and unconcerned with His feelings for a long time.

Nicole tried again. This time she prayed for Jessie. She prayed that God would welcome Jessie into heaven and keep her safe for eternity. But the prayer gave her little comfort. Nicole could not visualize what the afterlife looked like. She could not believe that Jessie was really gone. Nicole kept seeing Jessie's body in a dumpster and imagining the horrible things that her friend had suffered before she died. Why had God let that happen?

One thought kept coming back to her. What if God didn't just let it happen, but actually made it happen? Nicole could not let go of the idea that God had punished Jessie as a warning to all of them. That He had picked Jessie out of the group to make an example of because she had gone too far. Fornication was one level of sin, adultery was another.

Nicole knew what she had to do. She thanked God for sparing her life, then logged into her Hotmail account. Without even checking her messages, she opened an outgoing message box and typed in two addresses: angelface@ hotmail.com, racyg@gmail.com.

> *Rachel and Angel*
> *I'm sorry I've been avoiding you guys. I'm not mad or anything. I'm just pretty freaked out about Jessie. I don't think I'm coming back to Teen Talk. I'm not sure the sex is OK anymore, and I don't like living the lie. I have a lot on my mind, and I need some time to figure things out. Don't take it personally. You're still my friends. Love Nic*

Nicole quickly pressed send before she could change her mind.

As soon as the message disappeared, she regretted it. She should have told them in person and reassured Rachel and Angel and the guys that the secret was safe with her. Just because she planned to stop going to the meetings didn't mean she would tell anyone about their activities. But she had been thinking lately that telling someone, maybe even her parents, about the sex would make her feel better. She loved her parents deeply and hated keeping this secret. But she also hated the idea of hurting them with the truth. They said they wanted her to always be honest with them, but they couldn't handle the truth about Teen Talk. They would be devastated. Nicole didn't know what to do.

To distract herself from the jumble of thoughts, she opened her e-mail. Tyler Jahn wanted to know if she wanted to hang out with him at the dance this Friday night. Nicole hit reply and told him her parents wouldn't let her go. The rest was junk mail, so she clicked on her favorite blog by a guy named Jimmy in Hawaii who surfed and painted and talked about spirituality. But today the words just swam in front of her.

She kept thinking about Teen Talk and how it had started so innocently, or at least, so easily. One day last March, Angel had announced at the start of a meeting that she had a surprise. "I found this tape in my dad's study," she'd said with a strange little laugh. Dad was Reverend Strickland, the First Bible Baptist preacher, and the tape was a porno film with group sex. The Teen Talk kids had been transfixed, intensely curious to witness the activity their parents were so intent on suppressing. And, as Greg Miller had commented, "If the Reverend watches, it must not be a sin."

At first, Nicole had been disturbed by the close-ups, the slapping of flesh on flesh. But she had also been fascinated, then eventually, very turned on. Everyone had been turned on. And there was no stopping a roomful of teenage hormones. Only Jessie and Greg had gone all the way that first time. But after a few more meetings, during which they viewed more of the Reverend's collection, everyone hooked up. Once Nicole let her body relax and feel what it was supposed to feel, the sex had been great. Finally, she understood what the obsession was all about.

The small group of kids had sworn—on their lives, with a mingling of blood from pricked fingers—to never tell anyone about the sex. Katie Jackson had stopped coming to Teen Talk soon after, but she swore she would keep their secret.

"Nicole?" Mrs. Greeley was suddenly standing over her, trying to get her attention. Nicole quickly shut down the website.

"Yes?"

"Why aren't you in class? This isn't your free period."

"Sorry, I forgot my homework and didn't want to be called on."

The technology teacher shook her head. "You'd better get going."

Nicole picked up her backpack and shuffled out. But she

didn't head for math. There was no way she was interrupting that class again. Besides, she was still confused and unable to concentrate. She wished she had a rational adult she could talk to about sex and God and why a person could not have both.

Thursday, October 21, 1:16 p.m.
KERA DROVE FROM the Mongolian Grill directly to Kincaid Middle School. Traffic was light and she was happy to be out and about in the warm afternoon. There would not be many more days like this. They were already shorter and darker and the cold weather was coming.

She had called Kincaid's principal, Andrew Taber, this morning, and he'd reluctantly agreed to give her twenty minutes of his time this afternoon. He was leaving tomorrow to attend a conference, and apparently he didn't want this meeting waiting for him when he got back. Kera was always surprised at how uncomfortable the subject of teen sex and birth control made people.

As Kera walked across the south Eugene campus, a crisp wind carried the smell of damp grass and triggered a nostalgic, back-to-school memory—new clothes, fresh books, and the anticipation that exciting things were about to happen. The feeling stayed with her as she crossed the narrow lawn and entered the front office. Young people were everywhere. Waiting in chairs, standing in the short hallway. Two female students were even behind the reception counter assisting other students. Kera waited her turn until one of the young assistants pointed her "down the hallway and to the left."

Taber's office was small and cluttered, with only one narrow vertical window. The view, which could not be enjoyed from where the principal was seated, was of a dull gray building on the other side of a walkway. Kera wondered how much he was paid to spend his days in such a claustrophobic environment. It made her appreciate her job.

Taber was her height and a little stocky. His hair brushed his coat collar, and his glasses had minimalist frames. A liberal, she thought, pleased. The principal shook her hand as they exchanged names and pleasantries.

Kera took a seat.

"What can I help you with?" His tone was abrupt and wary.

"I'd like to know about your sex education curriculum and perhaps recommend some supplementary reference material." Taber didn't respond, so Kera plunged forward. "Planned Parenthood is sponsoring an outreach program that involves young people acting as mentors and educators for other young people. These programs have been very successful in Europe, and we hope to duplicate that success with the support of local schools."

"We don't have a sex education curriculum anymore," Taber said. He took off his glasses and cleaned them on his sleeve as he talked. "Historically, Oregon has had a progressive attitude about young people's ability to think for themselves. That is why our state allows Planned Parenthood to dispense birth control to minors without parental consent. But in many schools, Kincaid included, sex education has come under pressure from the Conservative Culture Alliance." Taber sighed. "Between the CCA and budget cuts, we had to cut sex ed from the curriculum."

Kera was distressed that she had not been aware of this. Had it happened recently? "The high schools are still teaching it, aren't they?"

"Sort of." Taber telegraphed that their meeting was over. "I don't think there's anything I can do to assist you."

"Can I put up some flyers?"

Taber pushed his hands through his hair. "I'd rather you didn't. As much as I want our students to have access to information, I don't relish the idea of getting the CCA stirred up again."

"Can you recommend some student hangouts nearby?"

He smiled, and Kera realized he was amused by her determination.

"There's Sam's Pizza on Patterson Street."

As Kera jotted it down, Taber stood to see her out. "Even though I am unable to assist your efforts, Ms. Kollmorgan, I do appreciate them. I truly hope your peer program is successful."

"Thanks, me too."

Kera headed back through the throng of kids in the front office, who had been joined by some parents. Outside, the day was bright and crisp—her favorite weather—but a sense of emotional weariness seeped into her soul. After nearly an eighty-year struggle, beginning with Margaret Sanger and others like her, women were still battling the same puritanical forces for reproductive freedom that their grandmothers had fought. Kera wondered if they would ever prevail.

As she moved toward the parking lot, a group of yellow buses pulled up in front of the school. Kera waited for a safer moment to cross the parking lot. After a moment, a soft voice on her right said, "Excuse me."

Kera turned to see a nervous young girl trying to get her attention. She was slender, with long dark hair and a tiny upturned nose. Her outfit of black Capri pants and short pink blouse looked almost retro. Kera thought she seemed familiar.

"Hello."

The girl leaned in close and whispered, "You're from Planned Parenthood, aren't you?"

"Yes." Kera recognized her voice from the phone call yesterday. "Are you Nicole?"

The girl looked startled for a second, then asked, "Are you the one who had Jessie's phone?" Just then, the school's buzzer rang. Moments later, the walkway was swarming with middle school kids.

Kera leaned down and said softly, "Would you like to continue this conversation?"

"Yes, but not here." Nicole's eye's darted around.

"We can talk in my car."

"What kind is it? I'll follow you out there."

"It's a white Saturn parked in the upper lot. See you in a minute." Kera quickly stepped between two big yellow buses and headed across the parking lot. It amused her that Nicole didn't want to be seen with her. Was she worried that another student might recognize Kera from the clinic? Or was she embarrassed by Kera's purple blazer? You never knew. Kids were particular about clothes and acquaintances.

Kera found herself hurrying. She was quite curious about what Nicole had to say, especially after the girl's emotional outburst on the phone yesterday. Once she was in the car, the minutes ticked, and she thought Nicole might have changed her mind. Then suddenly, she was there, sliding into the seat next to her.

Kera waited for the girl to speak. Experience had taught her that was the best way to prime a ready pump. Finally, Nicole asked, "Do you believe in God?"

Kera had not expected this subject. She treaded lightly. "I used to believe there was a higher power, a purpose in our existence, but I'm not sure anymore."

"How come?"

"People keep dying. It's hard to find purpose in that."

Nicole nodded. "I believe in God, but I don't believe everything they say in church. I don't understand why dancing and sex are supposedly sins."

"A lot of people don't believe that they are."

"But are they honest about it?" Nicole twisted in her seat to scan the parking lot. "Or do they just go ahead and do whatever they want, but then keep quiet about it around other church people?"

Kera felt unprepared for this conversation. She was much more comfortable talking about sex than about religion. She gave it her most diplomatic effort. "Most people try to find a church that supports their personal beliefs. The Unitarian Church, where I used to attend, is open-minded about sex and dancing and all kinds of things."

"My parents would never let me go there."

"You'll have more choices when you get older. In the meantime, you can try to make the best of it."

Nicole twisted nervously at her hair. "I hate lying to my parents, but I can't tell them the truth without hurting them. And I don't want to get my friends into big trouble." Her eyes went wide with despair. "I don't know what to do."

Kera's heart went out to the girl. "Can I assume we're talking about sex?" And not just any sex, Kera thought, remembering the chat room conversation she'd read.

Nicole nodded.

"It's a tough situation to be in." Kera chose her words carefully. "I can't tell you what is right for you. But there might be some middle ground. One option is to simply stop the activity and not say anything to your parents. You can also ask your friends not to tell you about their sexual experiences. That way you have nothing to hide from anyone. Unless you're worried about your friends. Are they engaged in risky sexual behavior?"

"No." Nicole looked away, then back. "Sometimes." Tears suddenly welled up in her eyes. "I loved Jessie. And I think God killed her as a punishment."

A loud rapping on the window startled both of them. On Nicole's side of the car, a young boy had his faced pressed against the glass and was making monkey gestures with his mouth. Nicole shook her head and waved him off. As she watched him walk away, someone or something else caught her eye. The girl's expression instantly changed from grief to fear. Kera tried to zero in on who she was looking at, but the area in front of the school was still crawling with buses, students, and teachers. It was impossible to tell who she had seen.

"I'd better go. Thanks for talking to me." Nicole was already on the move.

"Nicole, wait." Kera reached over and touched her lightly on the arm. "I don't believe that God punishes people for having sex. Jessie may have gotten involved with the wrong person. If you know who he is, you should tell the police. Or tell me and I'll pass it along."

"I don't know." Nicole jumped from the car. "See you."

AS RUTH WAITED to speak with the vice-principal about Rachel's attendance record—her teachers had messed it up again—she was startled to see Kera Kollmorgan walk out of Andrew Taber's office. Her heart missed a beat. What was the abortionist-whore from Planned Parenthood doing at her daughter's school? She'd better not be spreading her promiscuous propaganda here, Ruth thought, or she is in for the fight of her life.

Ruth quickly abandoned her quest and followed Kollmorgan outside. Under different circumstances, she would have gladly confronted the whore right then and there. But considering her campaign against the clinic—Kollmorgan in particular—Ruth thought it best not to get too close. But still, it was important to keep an eye on Kollmorgan. So Ruth watched and waited from a distance. Rachel and Caleb were probably waiting in the car, but they would survive a few minutes of inconvenience.

Ruth's breath caught in her throat as she saw Nicole Clarke walk up to Kollmorgan and speak to her. What was Nicole doing? Did she know the abortionist? How and why? Ruth watched as the two talked briefly. Then Kollmorgan walked off, leaving Nicole standing there. Ruth let out a sigh of relief. Perhaps it meant nothing. Maybe Nicole was just being friendly, offering directions or something.

Ruth hurried to the end of the sidewalk so she could see around the buses and into the parking lot. In the upper section, the abortionist-whore climbed into her little SUV but didn't start the engine. The woman leaned back like someone who was planning to wait. Ruth glanced back at Nicole, who was now talking to a boy Ruth didn't know. The boy stood close, stroking Nicole's beautiful hair. Ruth was dismayed that the teacher standing nearby didn't intervene. Why did they allow such inappropriate behavior at school?

Ruth glanced back to the upper parking lot. Kollmorgan was still waiting for something or someone. Ruth turned her attention back to Nicole just in time to see the boy give the girl a full body hug. Ruth's jaw ached with tension. Then Nicole pulled away and darted out through the buses. She crossed the lower lot and headed into the upper parking area. One of the buses roared to life and pulled out, obscuring Ruth's view. As soon as it passed, she darted across the driveway, causing the next bus in line to brake hard to avoid hitting her.

Ruth didn't care. She had to see where Nicole was headed. The girl stepped out from behind a row of cars, then quickly walked up to Kollmorgan's SUV and slipped in.

Oh no. Shooting pains filled her stomach. How dare that harlot come to the school to brainwash one of God's children. Ruth desperately wanted to dash up to the car and drag Nicole away. But she couldn't. Approaching Kollmorgan face to face while she was targeting her would be dangerous. Ruth had no intention of getting caught and arrested. The greater good would be served by keeping her distance.

But only for the moment. Ruth planned to deliver swift and righteous justice to the abortionist. Jesus had been very clear about that. Ruth knew the passage by heart:

Whoever causes one of these little ones who believe in me to sin, it would be better for him to have a great millstone hung around his neck and to be drowned in the depths of the sea. Woe to the world because of things that cause sin! Such things must come, but woe to the one through which they come!

Yes, Kollmorgan would suffer for this.

Ruth couldn't take her eyes off the car. What were they talking about? How did Nicole even know the woman? Ruth dug in her purse for an Ativan and put it under her tongue to dissolve. She had to settle herself down. On the way to her car, Ruth prayed for Nicole. Keep her mind pure, dear Lord. Don't let her be influenced by the abortionist-whore.

"Hey mom." Ruth looked up to see her daughter hurrying in her direction. "What are you doing?"

"Just stretching my legs while I wait." Ruth wanted to give Rachel a hug, but she knew better than to do so when they were at school. Rachel would only make a face and squirm away.

Her daughter glanced over at Kollmorgan's car where Nicole and the abortionist were still engaged in conversation. "You were watching Nicole," Rachel accused.

"I just wondered who she was talking to."

Rachel shrugged. "I have no idea who that is."

"I'm worried about Nicole," Ruth said. "I want you to stay close to her. Don't let her forget that she is God's child."

"Of course. She's my friend."

Ruth took the opportunity to remind her daughter that there was guidance in scripture for almost everything. "You know what Jesus said about friends: Greater love has no one than this, that he lay down his life for his friends."

‹ 14 ›

JACKSON LEFT A message with the district attorney, asking Victor Slonecker for a meeting ASAP. Then he contacted McCray, Evans, and Schakowski and called them in for a task force update. Schak was already in the building. While still talking to him, Jackson looked up and saw his partner walking toward him, cell phone pressed against his ear. They both hung up.

"You have something. I can see it on your face." Schak pulled up a chair. "What is it?"

"I'd better wait until everyone is here. In the meantime, I need you to contact the preacher or secretary or whoever at First Bible Baptist and get a list of everyone who attends church there. We need it right now. Ask them to fax it. If they can't, go pick it up."

"I'm on it."

Schakowski hustled over to his own desk. Jackson closed his eyes and tried to work through a plan. Should he have a conversation with Fieldstone and give the mayor a chance to explain his phone calls to Jessie and proximity to the girl's dead body? Or would that simply give their new suspect an opportunity to cover his tracks and lawyer up? Jackson wished he had at least one piece of physical evidence. It would be so much easier to make the right move.

The apartment. They needed to search the mayor's Oakwood apartment immediately. Jackson began to write up the paperwork. Did he have enough to justify a search warrant? Probably not. He needed the district attorney's counsel and clout on this one. This was the biggest fish he'd ever had on his line, and he couldn't afford to take one wrong step.

He pushed the search warrant aside and called the state medical examiner's office. Debbie answered.

"It's Officer Jackson. Are any of the Davenport labs back yet?"

"Let me check."

He drummed the desktop with his pen and sipped his cold coffee. In a minute, she was back. "I know it's you, but protocol says you have to give me the case number before I can tell you anything."

Jackson shuffled through his paperwork, found the code, and rattled it off.

"Thanks." She paused as if to consult the paperwork. "We only have a preliminary report. There was no semen in the vagina, but there were traces of vinegar."

"Say that again."

"Vinegar. It's a common ingredient in vaginal douches."

"So our suspect washed away his trace evidence?"

"Only from the vagina. There was semen in the anus and two hairs in her pubic area that do not belong to the victim. We'll have a DNA profile for both the semen and the hair sometime in the next few days. Then we'll compare it to the body standard you brought in this morning."

"Anything else?"

"Her last meal was a nutrition bar, heavy on the soy protein."

"What about cause of death?"

"Nothing more definitive yet. Ainsworth is still looking at lung tissue."

"Thanks. Tell her to call me the minute she knows for sure."

"She will."

Jackson hung up. He had to keep his mind open and wait for evidence. Grady was still in the picture. Those pubic hairs could be his. Maybe Fieldstone was Jessie's uncle or godfather, thus explaining the calls. And the proximity of the apartment could be a coincidence. Both quite possible. Jackson shook his head. Un-fucking likely. He left a second message with Slonecker, letting the DA know about the task force meeting.

Seconds later, his desk phone rang.

"This is Sophie Speranza with the Willamette News. I understand you're investigating the death of Jessie Davenport. Do you have any leads?"

This was the reporter's second call. The seasoned television newscasters had been calling the department's spokesperson, knowing that no one else in the department would talk to them, but Sophie was young and ambitious and looking to break the story.

"We're following up on several leads," he said finally.

"Is it the work of a psychopath? Should parents be concerned about the safety of their young daughters?"

"It's too early in the investigation to draw any conclusions. But parents should always be concerned about the safety of their children."

"Is the autopsy report completed? Do you know the cause of death?"

"Not yet. I have to go."

Jackson arrived in the conference room early, so he could update the case board, which still looked pretty thin. The sky had turned dark with clouds, so he turned on all the overhead lights. By 3:45, the other three detectives had rolled in. Evans was the only one who didn't have dark circles under her eyes or the glassy stare of the sleep deprived. Jackson studied her face for traces of heavy makeup but didn't see any.

"What's your secret, Evans? Why do you look so fresh?"

"Provigil." She smiled. "And thanks for noticing."

"What's that?"

"It's a prescription drug. It was developed for narcolepsy, but of course, it will keep anyone awake. The military gives it to pilots and special forces on long missions to keep them alert."

"And your doctor just wrote you a prescription for it?" Schak was skeptical of all drugs and most medical procedures.

"Yep. She likes to keep me happy."

Jackson could have used one of the pills, but he would never ask her in front of the others. "What have you got to report?"

"Mrs. Davenport seems a little schizophrenic. On the one hand, she's grieving for the loss of her daughter. Yet"—Evans made a face—"I don't think she liked Jessie all that much."

"How so?"

"Weird little criticisms kept popping up. Jessie's bad taste in color choices for clothes. Jessie's inability to be honest about her feelings." Evans consulted her notes. "And, at one point, she said with some disgust, 'Jessie likes to flirt with older men.'"

"Did she mention anyone in particular?"

"I asked her that, and she rushed into a discussion of Jessie's father."

Jackson turned to McCray, who looked as if he had aged overnight. "What did you find out about Paul Davenport?" Jackson wasn't ready to talk about the mayor yet. He wanted someone to come up with a different suspect.

"Well, for starters, he didn't know his daughter was dead." McCray took his glasses off and rubbed his eyes. "Apparently his ex-wife didn't bother to call him and tell him. Davenport became distraught when he heard about Jessie and had to get off the phone. I mean he cried like I have never heard a man cry before. I called him back an hour later. He said he was at work all day Tuesday. Two other employees at McFarland Insurance confirmed his alibi. He also says he does not know of any boyfriend. But he's driving down from Seattle tonight, so you can interview him yourself tomorrow."

Jackson put a small check next to Paul Davenport's name on the board. "How long will he be here?"

"I don't know. Probably until after the funeral service."

"Thanks, Ed. After this you ought to go home and get some rest."

"I'm okay."

The door opened and the district attorney rushed in. Slonecker had thick black hair and eyes so dark his pupils disappeared, making him seem imposing even though he was only five foot ten. His charcoal pinstripe suit and maroon tie looked expensive and gave the impression of a successful, confident man on his way up. Jackson expected him to be the state attorney general some day.

"Thanks for coming." Jackson shook his hand, not sure why. He didn't need to schmooze. He and Slonecker had worked well together in the past.

"You made it sound important."

"It is. I think we have a second suspect."

The other detectives looked up expectantly.

"Unit five of the Oakwood Apartments is rented by Mariska Harrison, who is Mayor Fieldstone's assistant. The apartment is for the mayor, as a place to take breaks occasionally during his long workday." Jackson paused to let that soak in, then continued. "The mayor also placed four calls to Jessie's cell phone in the last month and received three from her."

"Shit." Slonecker and Evans said it simultaneously.

The fax machine on the other side of the wall started a noisy printout.

"That's probably for me." Schak popped up and ran to retrieve it.

"Have you talked to Miles yet?" the DA wanted to know.

Jackson cringed. Slonecker was on a first-name basis with the mayor. "I wanted to confer with you first."

"You have to give him a chance to explain," Slonecker said. "This could all be harmless coincidence."

"If he's innocent, an interview will clear him. No harm done." Jackson gave a small shrug for effect. "But if he's our man, an interview will tip him off, give him a chance to clean up after himself and talk to a lawyer."

Schakowski rushed back into the room and thrust a paper printout at Jackson. "Fieldstone's on the list of people who attend First Bible Baptist."

"It's probably where he met her," Jackson said.

"And could innocently explain the phone calls between Miles and the girl," Slonecker offered.

"I'm still hoping for some physical evidence."

"What does the autopsy say?"

Jackson fought to keep his frustration in check. "No signs of rape. No semen in the vagina, likely washed away by a vinegar douche, but semen in the anus. Death by asphyxiation, probably intentional, but no bruising and no signs of struggle, except some binding marks on her wrists. All together, it looks like a homicide, but Ainsworth won't give me a homicide ruling, yet. I'm still waiting for DNA analysis on trace evidence. Meanwhile, we need a search warrant for body standards from the mayor."

Slonecker snorted. "You won't get one. Not for the mayor. Not with what little you've got."

Jackson handed him the paperwork he'd prepared before the meeting. "Then we need a warrant to search the apartment. I think Cranston will sign it if he knows you support it. Fortunately, judges here are elected, not appointed."

Slonecker looked over the form. "This is pretty broad. I'd like to rework it."

"We don't have time," Jackson argued. "I talked with Harrison, Fieldstone's assistant, last night. I'm sure she told the mayor that she told me about the apartment. He could be there right now destroying evidence."

"Hey," Evans cut in. "I didn't finish my report earlier. I've got something else." She glanced at her notes. "Randi Arnell, one of the Oakwood tenants I had to get back to, recognized Jessie's photo. She says she saw Jessie outside apartment number five a couple weeks ago. She couldn't pin down the day, but she knew for sure it was in the afternoon around 3:30 because she was going out to meet her kid at the bus stop."

They all stared at her.

"Then we'd better search it," Slonecker said. He didn't look happy. He slid the warrant into his briefcase. "I'll call you as soon as I have a signature. We'll meet at the apartment." He looked at Jackson. "You handled this well. Thank you."

"It could still get ugly."

Slonecker snapped his briefcase shut. "That's inevitable. But for now, not a word about the mayor gets to the media. Not a hint." He made eye contact with everyone, individually.

"Not a chance," Jackson promised.

After Slonecker left, the energy in the room intensified.

"Fieldstone. I don't believe it," Evans said. "I met him at a community policing meeting. He seemed like a decent guy—for a Republican with serious political aspirations."

"What about prints?" McCray asked. "Did we get anything from Jessie's clothes or backpack?"

"Good question. Why don't you go over to the print lab and find out?" Fingerprints and photographs were the only evidence they had the technology to process onsite. "Even if they don't have anything yet, run the mayor through the database and see if he's on file anywhere. Who knows? Maybe he has some petty conviction from when he was nineteen and his prints are available for comparison."

After McCray left, Jackson said, "Let's get over to Fieldstone's apartment now and wait for Slonecker's call."

Thursday, October 21, 3:47 p.m.
KERA DROVE TO THE CLINIC, her mood as dark as the sky had become. As she crossed the parking lot, she could feel the negative ions in the air and goosebumps popped up on her arms. A storm was rolling in.

Once she was back at work, she didn't have time to brood about her failure at the middle school. Time flew by in a rush of walk-in appointments, calls to clients about their lab results—including one to a twenty-year-old woman who had tested positive for AIDS—and a protracted search for a missing chart. She stayed an extra hour, re-filing charts to make up for some of the time she had been out at the school that afternoon. The filing was fairly mindless work, and it gave her time to think about the design and wording of the flyers she planned to post around Kincaid.

Her instinct was to be direct, something along the lines of "Are You Sexually Active?" as a headline. But now that she knew she was up against the Conservative Culture Alliance, she would have to be more careful. Still, she found it difficult to talk about sex without actually mentioning sex. Euphemisms were not her style. Maybe she needed a focus group of young people to consult.

When she finished the filing, Kera grabbed her purse and headed across the lobby toward the front door. She could feel a cold wind whistling in around the plywood covering the front window area. As she glanced over at the damage, her eyes caught sight of a small brown package under the chair near the reception desk.

She froze.

No one was in or near the chair, but a young Hispanic woman was seated against the opposite wall. A small boy sang quietly to himself as he played with a puzzle on the floor near her.

What if it's a bomb?

Kera's heart rate picked up. For a moment, her body relived the powerful tremor that had shaken the building on Tuesday.

Panic raced through her system. She fought to keep herself from running out the door. There were clients and staff members to alert and protect. Kera moved quickly to the reception desk.

"Roselyn." Her tone was sharper than she intended.

"Yes?"

"There's a small brown box sitting under one of the chairs in the lobby. Was a client seated there recently?"

"Uhhh." Roselyn's eyes danced with emotion as she processed the information and what it could mean. "I don't think so. Besides those two," she nodded toward the woman and child, "there's only one client in the building. She came in with those two and now she's back with Julie."

Kera's mind skittered around as she tried to determine the appropriate steps to take. Her instinct was to call the police and clear everyone out of the building. But if the package belonged to a client—and was likely harmless—there was no need to freak everyone out.

"Where is the security guard?"

"He went home at 5:30," Roselyn responded.

Some security. Kera walked over to the pretty, dark-skinned woman and calmly asked, "Is that your package?"

The woman looked blank, then said with a Spanish accent, "No English."

Great. Kera smiled, pointed at the package, and asked, "Is that yours?" She hoped the tone of the question would convey its meaning.

It did. The woman shook her head.

"Gracias." Kera hurried back to the receptionist. "What's the name of the client with Julie?"

Roselyn clicked a few computer keys, then said, "Eva Rios."

"I'm going to go ask her if she left anything in the lobby." Kera spoke slowly and deliberately. "Meanwhile, call the police and quietly alert them to our situation. Stay on the phone with them until I get back."

"Do you think it's a bomb?" Roselyn whispered.

Deep breath. Friendly smile. "Probably not. We're just playing it safe."

Kera moved quickly to exam room two. She knocked, and before Julie could respond, Kera said, "This is important. I must speak to Eva right away."

In a moment, Julie opened the door a few inches. "What's going on?"

"Suspicious package in the lobby. I need to know if it belongs to Eva."

The nurse's eyes widened in alarm, and she turned back to her client, whom Kera could not see, and said quietly, "Did you leave anything in the lobby?"

Kera heard a young woman say "No." She reached through the open door, grabbed Julie's arm, and squeezed. "Get out of the building as quickly as you can. Take your client and go out the back door."

Kera raced toward the lab area. Two staff members—both female college students—were hunched over some paperwork.

"Leave the building immediately. Go out the back door." Kera did not stay to explain, and the women, responding to her tone, did not hesitate or call after her with questions.

She made a hurried sweep of the clinic, finding only two other staff members. Both Andrea and Sheila were gone for the day, so there was no one to report to, no one else to manage the emergency.

Charging back up the hall to the front of the building, Kera hoped like hell she was handling this correctly. Roselyn was still on the phone, as she had directed. Kera took it from her and spoke quickly. "The package does not belong to anyone who is currently in the building. I'm getting everyone out now."

"Good. A bomb squad is already on the way."

Kera hung up and turned to Roselyn. "Please tell the woman in the lobby, in Spanish, that she has to leave. Tell her Eva is already outside."

Roselyn started to move around the counter, but Kera stopped her. "Tell her from here, then go out the back door. I don't want you anywhere near that package."

Roselyn spoke loudly in Spanish. The woman didn't move. Finally, the receptionist yelled, "Vamos."

The client grabbed her child and swore softly.

Just then a loud boom reverberated through the lobby.

15

Kera jumped, and Roselyn screamed. But it was only thunder. The lobby, still intact, soon flashed with lightning. A moment later rain pounded the roof. The storm was in full velocity.

The women looked at each other, then ran for the back door. They would take their chances with the weather.

Kera waited in her car for the police, rain pounding the roof and keeping her on edge. She had sent everyone else home and moved her car to the street. It was a small package, but that didn't mean it couldn't blow the whole building. The police bomb unit arrived and told her she should leave. After they went inside, she drove to KFC, picked up some chicken, and came back.

The squad members were now in the parking lot, and the rain had let up some. From her spot on the street, Kera watched them blast the package with a water canon. Nothing happened. Relief washed over her. It had not been a bomb. For a few minutes, she watched the officers examine the debris. Curiosity drove her out of her car and into the rain. She jogged up to an officer, still wearing his protective gear, and asked him, "So what was it?"

He smiled. "We think it contained Girl Scout cookies."

Kera laughed out loud for the first time in days.

When she got home, Kera did fifty minutes on her elliptical cross trainer to burn off the stress and the fried chicken. After a shower, she settled into her daily online routine. She checked her e-mail: nothing from Daniel, but one from her mother, who had forwarded a petition for the federal legalization of medical marijuana. It made Kera smile.

She'd spent the first twelve years of her life in a commune fifty miles north of Redding, California. Her parents—Mariah and Keith Demaris—had been hippies before it was popular to be hippies. In the early sixties, they'd left college in San Francisco and joined a group living off the land upstate. Her mother wrote political essays while her father made handcrafted cedar chests. They each earned a little money for their efforts, but otherwise lived off the vegetables, goats, and chickens raised in the commune.

Kera had been born at home a few years later. At the age of three, her family had made a hurried, worried trip to the hospital in Redding for the birth of her sister Janine. It was the first time Kera had seen the city. She was happy to leave it and return home. Her childhood had been simple, quiet, and happy, and she hadn't known what she was missing until her parents left the commune when she was twelve. They never talked about it, but Kera suspected her father had had an affair that caused a lot of turmoil in the community and in their family. But the marriage had survived, and her mother had become an activist for every hungry child, mistreated woman, and abused animal. And Mariah Demaris was still going strong.

Kera added her name to the petition, forwarded it to a few like-minded friends, and went back to her browser in search of her favorite breaking news site. More explosions in Iraq, but no new hostages.

The news could not hold her attention. Too much was happening in her own little corner of the world, and Kera couldn't pull her mind away from it. Today's episode only served to remind her that the clinic bomber was still out there, probably plotting his next attack. Jessie's killer had not been apprehended either. For a moment, Kera wondered if they were the same person. But that seemed unlikely. In law enforcement terms, they probably had very different profiles, very different motives and methods.

Surfing mindlessly without really absorbing what was on the screen in front of her, Kera soon found herself at girlsjustwanttohavefun.com where last night she'd read the chat room exchange between *blowgirl_jd*, *perfectass*, and *freakjob37*. Before logging in, Kera gave some thought to her reasons for coming back to the site. To a certain extent, it was research for her teen outreach program. On another level, it was personal. Both Jessie and Nicole had contacted her outside of the clinic. Kera took that as a sign that both girls had wanted or needed something from her personally.

On the surface, they had sought her advice. But did they also want her permission? Forgiveness? Maybe they didn't even know. But they had drawn her in, and now she felt compelled to follow through. And, she admitted to herself, she was very curious about this group of girls.

Logging in as *blowgirl_jd* gave Kera a twinge of the creeps. But she believed she was acting in Jessie's best interest. It was very possible that Jessie's sexual activity—particularly, her "guy on the side"—was connected to her death and that some of the information on the website might help find the killer.

Kera wanted to tell Detective Jackson about the website, but she couldn't decide where exactly the boundaries of client confidentiality fell in this strange case. She had discovered the website on her own, independent of her job at Planned Parenthood. But some—maybe all—of these girls were clinic clients, and ultimately, their visits to the clinic had led Kera to this site. Yet, she countered, it was Jessie's personal e-mail to her that had given Kera the screen name to get in.

Kera made up her mind. She would read through some more message boards, then call the detective.

First, she skimmed through a Dirty Gossip session. These chatters had different user names than those on the Sex Talk page, and the conversation was only dirty in the sense of mud slinging rather than sex. Kera didn't remember her junior high classmates ever being that cruel—to anyone. Sure, they had talked about each other behind each other's backs, but they had said things like "She wears that pink sweater all the time; doesn't she own anything else?"

But never in any school or work setting—even in the most primitive foreign countries—had she ever heard one female call another female a "donkey sucking whore." Yet that was how these thirteen- and fourteen-year-old girls talked about each other. It was sad.

Kera moved to the Sex Talk page but wasn't sure how much more she could stomach. Very quickly, she stumbled into a conversation that had taken place yesterday.

freakjob37: I still can't believe JD is dead. And why was that policeman asking us questions instead of trying to find the killer?

racyG: It sucks. I know. A cop came to our house too. But of course, my mother, paranoid supreme queen, didn't let him in. When is JD's funeral? Are we going?

freakjob37: It's Sunday afternoon, and of course we're going."

racyG: Should we go out cruising afterward? While our parents are at their monthly sex club meeting? BTW: Why are they so obsessed with faggots fucking? And fornication? No wonder we're all such perverts.

freakjob37: Has anyone talked to NC lately? I saw her after school today with one of the nurses from Planned Parenthood. What is that about?

lipservice: No idea.

racyG: Maybe she's pregnant.

freakjob37: Don't say that. Not about one of us. Remember our pact. No one ever tells no matter what.

The phone rang and Kera jumped. She received so few calls now that she was alone in the house—and no longer heard from telemarketers, thanks to the national "no call" list. She let it ring again while her nerves settled back down, then picked up. "Hello." After a moment, she heard a click. The other party had hung up. They must have realized they had a wrong number when they heard her voice.

Kera went to the kitchen and made herself a cup of tea. Then changed her mind and poured a glass of white wine from a bottle that had been in her refrigerator since late summer. Back at the computer desk, she read a few more of the Girl2Girl chat pages but didn't learn anything new. What she did know for certain was that these girls were horny, uninhibited, critical of outsiders, and careful to only use initials when referring to each other. Based on her list from the clinic, she was pretty sure she knew who most of them were, but they did not seem to know the identity of Jessie's "guy on the side."

Kera picked up her cell phone to call Jackson. It was time to point him in the direction of the Kincaid sex club. But that was all she could do. She would not give him any of the names from her list. Then it hit her again. His daughter was probably a member of the club, or at least she had been. Kera set the phone back down, unsure if it was the right thing to do.

Thursday, October 21, 4:12 p.m.
JACKSON AND EVANS rode together in his Impala. Schakowski said he'd meet them at the complex in fifteen minutes. Thunder boomed in the sky, and a sudden rain pounded the car as they drove. Jackson hoped they wouldn't have to wait long for Slonecker.

After a few minutes on the road, Evans said, "The mayor, wow. Isn't he campaigning as a moral majority type? Do you really think he killed her?"

"Maybe. But don't forget about Oscar Grady. McCray will track every move he's made in the last two weeks."

"But with Fieldstone, if the working theory is that they had a sexual relationship, why kill her?" Evans asked.

"Maybe she threatened to end it. Or to tell someone. Or blackmail him."

"I buy that." Evans nodded. "With his political career at stake, he could be driven to murder. But why take the risk of screwing her in the first place?" She looked at Jackson as if she expected him, as a man, to know.

He shook his head. "I don't understand the attraction to young girls. I prefer padding and mileage myself."

Evans laughed. "I hope you never said that to your wife."

Jackson didn't respond.

"No offense."

"None taken."

He made a right on Hilyard, and they rode in silence for a minute.

"Are you all right? You've been pretty quiet during this investigation."

Jackson wasn't sure if he should share his concerns. He didn't want to get pulled off the case. He decided to trust Evans. "I'm worried about my daughter. She used to be friends with Jessie."

"Maybe that's why they stopped being friends. Jessie went in a direction Katie didn't like."

"Maybe. But why won't she talk about it?"

"For the same reason cops don't rat on each other. It's a code of honor."

The Oakwood, opposite the Regency Apartments on the next block, was a smaller, newer building with fresh pale-mint paint. Set back from the street and tucked in among a cluster of overgrown maples and firs, it offered its tenants a certain seclusion. Jackson figured privacy was one of reasons the mayor had chosen it. The location was also within walking distance of Kincaid Middle School and a five-minute drive, bus ride, or bike ride from city hall—a convenient place for Jessie and Fieldstone to meet in the afternoons.

Jackson drove around to the back of the building, which was adjacent to the basketball court and dumpster where the body had been found. The lot had driving access to the alley and the dumpster. He parked at the end in the space for unit eight. From that vantage point, they still had a view of the door to unit five, which was on the ground floor on the opposite end. The building had four apartments on two levels, with stairs at each end. A maroon Vanagon kept the Impala mostly out of sight from the driveway.

Jackson studied the door to unit five, which was tucked under the stairs and shaded by a giant maple tree. He could see why the mayor had chosen it. A person could pull up in front and quickly slip inside without being seen.

He and Evans sat, waiting and listening to the rain. Jackson made a quick call to Renee's sister asking her to have Katie stay over one more night. She agreed.

"Thanks, Jan. You're a life saver. I'll make it up to both of you."

Jackson hung up and tried not to feel guilty. These kinds of cases happened for him only a few times a year. Most of the murders he dealt with had obvious suspects. Drug deals gone bad. Abusive ex-husbands.

"Who's Jan?" Evans asked casually, as though they had that kind of relationship.

"Renee's sister." Jackson surprised himself by giving Evans more information than she asked for. "She's been amazing. She talked Renee out of fighting for custody of Katie."

"How are you going to make it up to them?" Evans asked, referring to his promise.

Jackson scowled. "I don't know. Any ideas?"

"A gift certificate to a day spa."

He would never have thought of it in a million years. "Good idea. Thanks." He decided that talking to people about personal stuff could be okay sometimes.

A large woman in a wool poncho, trailing two kids, came home to unit seven.

"Who's that?"

"Windsong Mathews." Evans checked her notes. "No arrests. No convictions. She works at ShelterCare, the outfit that finds housing for the mentally ill."

A moment later, a thin, long-haired guy in his late twenties departed from unit three upstairs.

"That's Louis Frank, the tenant with the drug and theft convictions," Evans said. "I talked to his girlfriend this morning. She claims he's staying clean, working hard, and never hurt anybody in his life. Not physically, anyway."

The rain abruptly stopped and silence filled the car between them. Jackson checked his watch: 5:15. Where was Slonecker? He rolled down his window. The air smelled of wet warm asphalt.

A few minutes later, a gray older model Mercedes pulled into the parking slot in front of unit five.

"Shit. That's the mayor." Jackson sat up and reached for his cell phone. "Get out there and stall him."

"How the hell…" Evans was out of the car and running for the building.

He hoped she would think of something. Jackson pressed speed-dial, followed by the seven pad. A moment later, Slonecker answered.

"Where are you?" Jackson asked.

"I'm on the way," Slonecker said. "I've got the paper, and I'll be there in ten minutes."

"Fieldstone just showed up at the apartment. Call him and tell him you have a court order to keep him out."

"But I don't."

"We can't let him in there before we search it. I'll arrest him if I have to."

"Don't do that. Just stand in front of his door and question him like you would any other tenant. I'll be there in a few minutes."

Jackson was already out of the Impala and moving toward the building. Evans had managed to get between Fieldstone and his apartment door, and the two were engaged in a spirited discussion.

"I told you. I've just arrived. I haven't seen Mrs. Mayfield's children." The mayor's tone was clipped, bordering on nasty. With his dark-chocolate suit and matching leather briefcase, he looked out of place in this working class neighborhood. His hair and skin were both golden brown, and he looked younger than his forty-six years. In fact, Jackson thought Fieldstone looked like he could have just stepped out of a cologne advertisement.

"That's not what your neighbor implied, sir." Evans kept up the stall.

Jackson moved into the mix and placed himself a step behind Evans, directly in front of the dark green door.

"What's going on?" Fieldstone set down his briefcase and folded his arms across his chest.

"A young girl was found dead in that dumpster." Jackson pointed across the alley. Fieldstone didn't turn. "We've questioned everyone in the neighborhood except you because you were never here, until now. So we need to ask you a few questions. Did your assistant tell you any of this?"

"She did." Fieldstone looked around uncomfortably. "Can we please go inside? This is awkward and potentially embarrassing for me."

"I understand, sir. And I apologize for the inconvenience. This is all routine. We'll go inside in a moment. But first, Officer Evans will retrieve a photo from my car and show it to you."

Evans headed toward the car, taking her sweet time. The mayor watched her ass for a moment, then looked back at Jackson with distress. "We need to do this some other time. I have to get back to a meeting soon."

Jackson asked, "Where were you on Tuesday, October 19, between 2 and 6 p.m.?"

Fieldstone looked him right in the eye. "Most likely in conferences, but I'll have to consult my schedule. I've had a busy week." The mayor suddenly lurched forward. "I'm going inside."

Jackson stood his ground. Their faces were less than a foot apart. Up close, Jackson could see that Fieldstone's skin was mottled with sun damage.

"Let's wait for Officer Evans."

"I'm not going to answer any questions." Fieldstone stepped back and pulled a cell phone from his suit pocket. "I'm calling my lawyer." Then he turned away and spoke for a moment in a hushed tone. Jackson suspected he was leaving a message.

Evans came back with Jessie's photo and held it out for Fieldstone. "Do you recognize this girl?"

The mayor glanced at it casually. "She looks familiar. I think I've seen her in church."

"Look at it again. I want you to be sure," Jackson said.

"Let's go inside."

Schakowski strolled up at that moment. "Good evening, Mayor."

Fieldstone rolled his eyes. "This is starting to feel like harassment. I'm not answering any questions without my lawyer."

"You're free to leave," Jackson said. "But I expect you to come in for questioning tomorrow morning at 9 a.m. sharp. If you're not there, I'll issue a warrant for your arrest."

"I'll check my schedule." The mayor walked toward his car. Then he turned and stared back at his apartment as the three detectives made no move to leave.

The day was losing its light, and the four of them stood in the eerie shadow of a nearby maple tree. Jackson willed Fieldstone to get in his car and go.

Headlights entered the parking lot, and Slonecker's black sedan pulled in behind Jackson's Impala. As the DA climbed out, Jackson watched Fieldstone recoil from the full implication of the prosecutor's presence. Then the mayor pulled himself together and stepped around the front of his Mercedes to meet Slonecker head on.

"What's this about, Victor?"

"We have a search warrant for your apartment." Slonecker held up the paperwork. "I'm sorry, Miles, but in the course of the investigation your name kept coming up. If you cooperate, we should be able to clear you as a suspect very quickly. Please let the detectives into your residence so they can do their job."

"Not until my lawyer gets here."

"That's not how it works." Slonecker turned to Schakowski. "Go get the manager and his pass key." The DA turned back to the mayor. "Are you sure you want to go on record as uncooperative?"

Fieldstone strode to the door, unlocked it, and threw it open. "Go for it. I have nothing to hide."

16

From the entry, the apartment appeared immaculately clean but sparse, with pale gray Berber carpet and mahogany toned Italian leather furniture. While Evans operated the video camera, Jackson and Schakowski pulled up couch cushions and searched the entertainment center's many compartments. An eclectic collection of videotapes included Winged Migration, the Matrix trilogy, and some standard porn. A few of the tapes had handwritten labels, which made Jackson think the mayor may have filmed his sexual adventures.

As he began to bag the entire stack of videos to take back to the department, he heard Fieldstone—still standing in the foyer—complaining to Slonecker about it. The DA assured the mayor that everything that wasn't booked as evidence would be returned to him. Jackson and Schakowski moved into the kitchen, where the refrigerator was well stocked, but the cabinets were essentially bare. The mayor had a preference for lime-flavored Smirnoff, Gorgonzola cheese, kiwi fruit, and smoked salmon, all of which he kept chilled. The two detectives headed for the bedroom where Evans was shooting footage of the room's layout.

"Anything of interest?" Jackson asked as she waved them in.

"Not on the surface."

A king-sized bed took up a large portion of the space. While Schak opened dresser drawers, Jackson focused on the bed, recalling the "cotton-like fibers" Ainsworth had found in Jessie's nose. He gently gathered the light blue sheets one at a time into separate plastic bags, careful not to shake loose any evidence. He was conscious of the camera following his movements, knowing that a judge or jury might see this tape some day. The sheets were critical. If they could find a hair or a drop of saliva that placed Jessie in the apartment—particularly, in the bed—their case was over the top.

Schak called out "condoms," and Evans moved over to document the evidence collection on film. Jackson stepped over and glanced in the drawer, which also contained a large jar of Vaseline, a tube of KY jelly, an assortment of multicolored handkerchiefs, and a prescription bottle of little blue pills.

"He's ready for anything," Schak muttered.

Jackson went to the end of the bed and lifted the mattress to look under it. Nothing. So far, he was disappointed. He had hoped to find something big and obvious—like an item of Jessie's clothing—that they could use to pry a confession from Fieldstone.

Schak moved to the closet, so Jackson went into the connecting bathroom. Evans followed. Apparently, she thought the bathroom was a better bet than the closet. She was right. Near the sink, Jackson found a small round container of Peach Blossom Lip Balm that didn't look like it belonged to the mayor. He placed it in a pre-labeled brown bag and said a little prayer that Jessie's saliva would be present in the goo.

The medicine cabinet was mostly empty except for shaving cream, a few disposable razors, and a bottle of aspirin. There was nothing under the sink except some cleaning supplies. The empty trash receptacle was also a disappointment. Jackson had hoped to find an empty douche bottle that would match the vinegar trace inside Jessie.

Next, he looked in the shower: Head and Shoulders shampoo—which a young girl would never use—and bone dry walls. No one had showered lately. He checked in the back of the toilet tank out of habit from his days on the vice team. Nothing. Evans took the camera back into the bedroom.

Jackson was about to follow, then he stopped and backed up. The bathroom door was open against an interior bathroom wall. Jackson closed the door and was rewarded with a navy blue bathrobe hanging from a hook on the door's backside. He slipped his gloved hands into the robe's pockets for a quick check. A pair of orange-colored bikini briefs were balled up in the left pocket.

"Evans."

She came back on the fly and filmed him bagging the panties. Jackson would have liked to arrest Fieldstone and hold him in custody, but he couldn't, not yet. Not without charging him. Now that Fieldstone had called his lawyer, they would be lucky to get the mayor alone in a room for questioning. But if the DNA results connected Jessie to this room, he could charge Fieldstone and argue for no bail. Unfortunately, even if Jackson drove the evidence to Portland himself, it could still take up to a week to process DNA comparisons. Maybe he could get the mayor to go on record with a provable lie.

Jackson headed for the living room. Fieldstone paced, while Slonecker slouched in a fat leather chair. Jackson approached the mayor and pulled the panties out of the evidence bag. "Who do these belong to?"

Fieldstone shrugged. "I'm not sure."

"Is that your blue bathrobe on the back of the bathroom door?"

"Yes."

"We found the panties in the pocket. So I assume you have seen them before."

"Assume what you like. I'm not answering any more questions without my lawyer."

From the chair, Slonecker signaled Jackson to back off.

The detectives spent another thirty minutes going through the apartment again, then left the mayor alone in his love nest. Schak agreed to post a stakeout and tail Fieldstone if he left. Jackson promised to have a patrol unit relieve him in a few hours. They all needed some sleep.

As Jackson and Evans drove back to the department with their load of evidence, his cell phone rang.

"Detective Jackson? It's Kera Kollmorgan."

Her smooth, sexy voice startled him. "Hello. What can I do for you?"

She hesitated. "I discovered something that might be relevant to your investigation."

"Tell me about it." Jackson slowed down, so he could focus on the conversation.

"I found a website where I think Jessie's friends gossip in chat rooms. They use screen names and initials, so it's not definite."

"What's the URL?"

"Girls just want to have fun dot com. All one word."

Jackson repeated it back and signaled Evans to write it down.

"What makes you think it's relevant to the investigation?"

"I'm not sure." Kera sounded embarrassed, and he regretted his businesslike tone. In a moment she said, "There was nothing that directly related to her death, but because of the sexual content, I thought you might want to know about it."

"I appreciate that. I'll look into it. Thanks, Kera."

He pocketed the flip phone and turned left on 8th Street. Evans looked at him intently. "Who was that?"

"A nurse from Planned Parenthood. She says that website has a chat room where Jessie's friends talk about sex."

"How do you suppose she knows that?" Evans arched her eyebrows.

"That's a good question. But you can bet, she'll never tell. Planned Parenthood is very protective of its clients."

As they pulled into the lower-level parking lot at city hall, Evans said, "You called her Kera."

"So?"

"You never call anyone by their first name. Except your wife and daughter."

Thursday, October 21, 7:23 p.m.

RUTH PULLED ONION and hamburger out of the refrigerator with the intention of making meatloaf. But five minutes later she was still standing at the counter with nothing accomplished. She could not stop thinking about Kollmorgan, the abortionist, talking alone with Nicole.

"Mom? When are we going to eat?" Caleb whined at her from the kitchen doorway.

"Soon, honey."

"Can I have a snack?"

"No. But you can start on your homework."

Caleb disappeared and Ruth got busy on the onion. But her mind was a whirl and her nerve endings were firing overtime. It took every ounce of control she had to resist calling the Clarkes and speaking with both Nicole and Joanne immediately. Nicole clearly needed some counseling, and Joanne deserved to know that the devil was after her daughter. But Ruth had to be careful how much she said about Kollmorgan—even to other church members.

Her first order of business was to teach the abortionist-whore that coming after one of the faithful was a very bad idea. *Vengeance is mine.* Ruth took the biblical sentiment to heart and tried to form a lesson that would be swift and effective. But she couldn't afford to raise suspicion among either the police or church members. Because she was not finished with God's work. He wanted her to close the abortion clinic, and she intended to complete that mission.

Ruth chopped and planned. As usual, the cat smelled raw meat and rubbed against her legs. Ruth ignored it. How far should she go to punish Kollmorgan? How many more lives should the abortionist be allowed to ruin?

"Ruth, calm down before you cut yourself." Sam, her husband, placed a gentle hand on her shoulder. She hadn't heard him come into the kitchen. Ruth put her knife down and opened her arms for a hug.

Sam obliged. "What's wrong, honey?"

"I'm upset about Jessie. And I'm worried about the other girls in Teen Talk."

Sam pulled back. "Do you think a killer is targeting our girls?"

"I don't know. It was just a thought. I worry too much."

He touched her chin. "Then you're not praying enough. Leave it to God, Ruth. He'll take care."

"You're right."

Later, during dinner, Ruth came up with the perfect plan. The only uncertainty was the quantity of powder. Too much ricin, and Kollmorgan would die. But that would be up to God. Only He had the moral authority to give and take life.

‹ 17 ›

FIELDSTONE SHOWED UP for questioning the next morning with not one, but two lawyers. His personal attorney, Aaron Park, was a tax and probate man who was not qualified to handle a criminal investigation. So the mayor had called in Roger Barnsworth, a defense attorney who specialized in sexual charges. Barnsworth was a large black man with a shaved head and wide smile. Jackson had encountered him in court before and knew that he was good with juries. He tried not to hate him just because he was a defense attorney.

They stood in the detectives' work space and introduced themselves, shaking hands politely as if they were about to start a business meeting. On the surface, police work had become very cordial. In the trenches, passions still raged.

"I'm sorry Mr. Fieldstone, but I can only allow one lawyer into the room with you," Jackson said. He noticed that Fieldstone didn't look quite as dapper today. He'd lost a little sleep and some of his sun-kissed glow.

Park took off. The rest of them entered the interview room, including McCray, whose role was to throw in a little spice now and then to keep the suspect off guard. The ten-by-twelve room felt like a padded phone booth after the four of them had squeezed in. But Jackson, having slept for five hours the night before, felt refreshed and ready to nail this guy.

He set a tape recorder in the middle of the table, turned it on, and stated the date and the names of the participants. There was no wall camera recording the interview. No opaque observational window. Such amenities weren't in the budget when Eugene's city hall was built fifty years ago, and proportionally, law enforcement's budget was even smaller now. It fact, the DA's office was so understaffed, they no longer prosecuted about three hundred types of minor crimes, including shoplifting, forgery, and breaking-and-entering.

Jackson got right down to business. "Where were you on Tuesday, October 19, between 3 and 5 p.m.?"

The mayor was calm and confident. He'd had all night to prepare for the questioning. "I was in a meeting with a lobbyist group until 3:30, then I went out for a walk around the block. It was a nice afternoon. After that, I was in my office until I left for a dinner meeting at 5:30."

"Who did you meet with?"

"Members of the Conservative Culture Alliance. They're upset about the county's decision to issue marriage licenses to same sex couples." Always the politician.

"Give me the name of someone at the meeting who can vouch for when it ended."

"My assistant, Mariska Harrison."

"Who else?" Jackson was not impressed.

Fieldstone turned to his lawyer. "Do I have to give him a name? It was a private meeting."

Jackson cut in. "I need an impartial witness. And I'd like to point out that a solid alibi can only help you."

"Sam Greiner," Fieldstone offered.

"Thank you." Jackson jotted it down, thinking he'd seen the name recently. "Mayor, this will be a really long morning if you don't cooperate. We'd like to clear you of involvement as quickly as possible."

Nobody believed that.

"Did anyone see you during your walk?"

"I'm sure they did. I don't recall anyone specifically."

McCray jumped in. "But you recall that it was a nice day?"

"Yes. That's what made me think to go outside."

"What time did you get back?"

"Around 4:20, I think."

"Did you look at your watch?" McCray pressed. "I mean, you're a busy man. You must look at your watch quite regularly."

"I don't remember."

"After your walk, did anyone see you while you were in your office?" Jackson asked.

The mayor pretended to think about it. "I don't think so."

"What did you do during that time?"

"Read, studied, prepared for my dinner meeting."

Jackson decided it was time to mix it up. "Whose panties were in the pocket of your bathrobe?"

Fieldstone's face went blank, like a man trying to lie without giving it away. "A prostitute's."

The response threw Jackson off a little. The mayor had clearly thought this through. "What's her name?"

"Heather. We didn't exchange last names."

"How often does she come to your apartment?"

"She was there once. On Monday evening."

"Where can I find this woman?"

The mayor shrugged. "I have no idea. I met her in the bar at the Hilton."

Jackson was suddenly a little nervous about the DNA results on the orange panties. What if they didn't belong to Jessie? The mayor could have screwed a hundred different women in that apartment. And how much time should his team waste trying to track down a prostitute who probably didn't exist?

"How many women have been in your pleasure pad?"

"Don't answer that." Barnsworth jumped in and suddenly decided to earn his fee.

"Does your wife know about the prostitute?"

Barnsworth stood. "We're done here."

"Mayor Fieldstone isn't," Jackson said.

McCray suddenly produced a photo of Jessie taken during her autopsy and shoved it across the table at Fieldstone. "How well do you know this girl?"

The mayor leaned back away from the photo. He seemed to struggle for control. After a long moment, he said, "I told you. She goes to my church."

"You weren't that sure yesterday."

No response.

"Do you know her by name?" Jackson needed the mayor to make a statement that they could later prove to be a lie. Then they would have leverage.

"I believe her name is Jessie."

"Do you know her last name?"

"I can't think of it at the moment."

"Have you seen or spoken to Jessie outside of church?"

"I may have seen her at a church function that was held somewhere other than church property." Fieldstone's voice stayed calm, but his eyes were jittery.

Jackson kept trying. "Have you ever seen Jessie or spoken to her at any functions that were unrelated to your church?"

A slight hesitation. "No."

"Does that mean you consider sex a religious experience?" Jackson asked.

"We're done," Barnsworth stood to leave. Fieldstone followed suit.

"Not yet." Jackson stood up too, so he could look his suspect in the eye. "Mayor Fieldstone, what did you and Jessie talk about so frequently on the phone?"

Fieldstone lost a little more color from his face, and Barnsworth looked stunned. "Don't answer that."

"Do you admit making four phone calls to Jessie Davenport?"

"My client isn't answering any more questions." Barnsworth grabbed the mayor's elbow and pushed him toward the door. "Good day, detectives."

"We may want your client back in here very soon for more questions," Jackson warned. "Don't make any travel plans."

"I'm giving a speech at the Republican party headquarters in Portland tomorrow." The mayor tried to demonstrate that he was still in charge of his own schedule.

"Plan on coming right back. Thanks for your time."

After they left, McCray said, "He doesn't have an alibi for the time of Jessie's death."

Jackson shrugged. "But he has money and politically connected friends. Just wait. He'll produce someone who saw him taking a walk."

By 10:35 a.m., Jackson was on Interstate 5, heading once again for the medical examiner's office in Portland. His critical cargo today was a pair of orange panties, a tiny container of lip gloss, and a set of high-quality blue sheets. He hadn't yet received the DNA results from the trace evidence collected during the autopsy, so he had no illusions about getting the new samples processed in a hurry. For all of technology's advances, lack of funding still kept criminal investigations moving at a glacial pace.

Fifteen minutes into the trip, Judy Davenport called him on his cell phone.

"What's going on? Have you found Jessie's killer yet?" Her distress was palpable.

"We have a solid lead. That's all I can tell you right now."

"But how did she die? I want to know. Did she suffer?"

Poor woman. Jackson felt bad that he hadn't called her

after the autopsy. "Jessie didn't suffer. She was suffocated, but there were no bruises."

"Thank God."

Jackson shifted the phone to his other hand, so he could pass a line of slow moving trucks. "Mrs. Davenport, did you know that your daughter was sexually active?"

A pause. "I don't believe it."

"If you know who she was having sex with, I'd appreciate it if you'd tell me."

"Jessie was a good girl. You just find her killer." And she hung up.

Jackson sighed. Some parents never got over the denial, even when confronted with the evidence. He'd seen it time and again, and it was bad for the child.

The sun popped in and out of the clouds as he drove, and Jackson kept putting his sunglasses on and taking them off. A Led Zeppelin CD kept him company for the first half of the trip, then his thoughts turned to Kera Kollmorgan. Jackson suspected that she knew more about Jessie than she was telling. Last night, he'd visited the website she mentioned but had been unable to access any of the chat rooms because he didn't have the right user name. But clearly, Kera had been able to get in. He needed more information from her. And he suspected that, with the right pressure, she would help him. Because he believed that's what she really wanted to do.

Working his cell phone keys with thick fingers while squinting at the tiny print in the display screen, Jackson scrolled back through his incoming calls until he found Kera's call from last night. Then he pressed OK and send. If he had witnessed a civilian doing that while driving, he would have written them a ticket for failure to maintain control of the vehicle.

Kera's lovely voice asked him to please leave a message.

"It's Detective Jackson. I couldn't access that website you

gave me last night, so I'd like to discuss it with you. I'll buy you dinner while we talk. Call me at 729-8154."

A few minutes later, he called Katie, but she was in class and didn't answer. He left a message saying he'd be home late and suggesting the two of them do lunch and a movie that weekend. The call left him feeling frustrated and guilty.

As much as he loved his daughter, what he really wanted to do this weekend was start collecting the parts he needed to build a trike. He'd fixated on the idea for crafting a three-wheeled motorcycle fifteen years ago when he was a patrol cop. He'd stopped a man who was driving one for speeding on Beltline. The Volkswagen–Harley combination rig with its fat tires and chopper front end had intrigued him so much he had asked a dozen questions and never ticketed the man. Jackson had walked away with the idea that one day, he would build one for himself. Over the years, he had visited trike websites and drawn a few designs, but life had gotten in the way of his actually building it. But taking care of Renee and Katie was no longer eating up all his free time, so he thought he could finally make it happen. Next weekend, he promised himself.

In the state medical examiner's office, Jackson checked in the new evidence with Debbie and asked her to prioritize it, then met briefly with Ainsworth. She was ready with a manila envelope containing the full autopsy and lab reports.

"I ruled it a homicide," she said, handing him the paperwork. It was only the second time Jackson had ever seen her without a surgical-style hair covering, and it surprised him to see that she had gone completely gray. Jackson reflexively touched his own hair, which had begun to sprout some silver at the temples. His life was flying by and there was so much he hadn't done yet.

"I found cotton fibers in her lungs, which could indicate

a struggle to breathe."

"Anything special about the fabric?"

"Not really. Six-hundred-count baby blue cotton sheets, available in every Bed, Bath and Beyond."

"I brought in some sheets to compare the fibers to."

"You have a suspect." She looked pleased.

"Circumstantial only. I still need a physical connection."

"Then you're not going to like this." Ainsworth scowled behind her big glasses. "The pubic hair DNA does not match the semen deposit."

Jackson processed the information. "You're saying she had sex with two unknown and different men before she died?"

Ainsworth gave him a small smile. "Although the semen deposit was fresh, the hair could have been there for a day or so."

The information was a curve ball—Jessie was having sex with more than one partner. Fieldstone and Grady? Had Jessie been obsessed with older men? The mayor was still his prime suspect, because, so far, McCray had not established a physical link between Grady and Jessie. But a second lover, no matter who, would make it harder to convict Fieldstone for the killing.

"There's more."

"Yes?"

"She had hydrocodone in her bloodstream. It's a prescription pain reliever. An opioid that's often used recreationally."

Jackson sensed that Jessie's pain had been emotional. "What else?" He prepared himself for more bad news.

"She was pregnant."

It shouldn't have stunned him, but it did. He still thought of Jessie as a kid. "How far along?"

"Four to six weeks. She probably didn't know."

"Could she have known?"

Ainsworth shrugged. "It's possible. But a lot of girls that young don't have regular periods or don't keep track of their periods, so they don't even suspect they're pregnant until they start to show or their breasts start to swell."

"If she knew and she told him, it would be a motive for killing her."

"It wouldn't be the first time."

Jackson leaned back in his chair and let it soak in. The hodgepodge of evidence couldn't be sorted out until he had Grady's DNA results and a DNA sample from the mayor. But this report didn't give him anything new that he could take to Cranston that would convince the judge to sign a warrant demanding that the mayor submit to a DNA swab. Unless one of the other task force members came up with something today from their interviews with Fieldstone's family, friends, and neighbors.

"I brought in panties and lip gloss today, both found in the suspect's apartment. How soon can I get a DNA comparison to the victim?"

"Three days is a best-case scenario. We had to cut two lab positions this spring when the bond measure failed." Ainsworth sounded weary. Jackson sympathized, yet he had more evidence that needed immediate attention.

"I brought in some bed sheets too. If they match the fibers found in Jessie's nose and lungs, I should be able to get a search warrant for a DNA sample from the suspect. Once we have that, we'll have a standard to compare the hair and semen to." It was a lot of tenuous connections, but it was all he had. "Any chance of getting the sheets processed today?"

"We'll try. That's all I can promise."

"Thanks."

Friday, October 22, 12:05 p.m.

ON HER LUNCH BREAK, Kera walked around the block—soaking up some weak autumn sun—and checked her cell phone messages. First, her sister Janine asked her to come to Bend for the weekend, which she was seriously considering. She could use an out-of-town break. It had been an intense week.

The next message was from Detective Jackson, asking to meet with her. And buy her dinner. Kera's stomach fluttered with a twinge of excitement. She stopped in the middle of the sidewalk and laughed at herself. How lonely she must be, to look forward to meeting with a police officer who was conducting an investigation. Kera vowed to get out more often with her friends.

She called the number Jackson had given and left a message. "I'm free to meet with you this evening, but I'm not sure that I have any more information to share. Dinner sounds good, but there's no reason for you to buy. Either way, I'll be home by six."

Did that sound casual? She hoped so.

Kera arrived home an hour early. Clients were starting to come back into the clinic, but it still wasn't as busy as usual. And Sheila was cutting staff hours to help pay for the security she'd hired. Kera parked her Saturn, then walked back out to her mailbox on the street. She hadn't checked it in days, and the metal box was stuffed to capacity.

Kera hauled the pile into the house and dumped it on the kitchen table. A pale pink envelope caught her attention. Curious, she scooped it up and looked for the sender's name. In the return address corner, the initials NC were scrawled in fat cursive letters with an exaggerated flourish. The recipient line contained only her first name, Kera, also done in cursive, followed by her address in small block print. Overall, the effect seemed childlike.

Kera tore the envelope open and extracted a matching pink card with a simple "Thank You" printed on the front. A lovely fruit scent wafted from the card. Instinctively, she lifted it closer to her nose and sniffed. It was a melon and cucumber blend, like the body wash she used.

Inside, the message was handwritten in the same small block lettering, except for the signature, which repeated the cursive flourish:

Kera,
Thanks for spending time with me. It means a lot to me.
NC

It had to be Nicole, she thought. What a sweet and surprising gesture. Most adults never bothered with thank-you cards, and it never occurred to Kera that a teenager would. In fact, it struck her as a little peculiar that Nicole had penned and mailed the note so quickly. Kera had only talked with her yesterday.

She set the envelope down, grabbed a Diet Dr Pepper, then sorted through the rest of the mail. A plain white envelope caught her eye. This one contained no return name or address, only a sticker in one corner that said God is Love. This will be amusing, Kera thought, running the letter opener along the seal. Some church group either wanted her money or her soul.

Dear Sinner,
Planned Parenthood is the work of the devil and you are
his pawn. You must repent your sins and stop murdering
unborn babies. It is the worst transgression against God.
Teaching God's children to fornicate freely is the second
worst transgression. You must stop or God will punish
you. This is a promise. And God does not break His prom-
ises.
— God's Messenger

Kera dropped the letter and jumped up from the table.
The anti-abortion bomber–crackpot was targeting her personally. Her heart pounded wildly, and Kera began to pace.
The clinic had received piles of hate mail over the years, but
it had never come to her home before. If the bomber knew
her address, then he knew where she lived. A nerve in the
pocket of her thumb began to twitch, and Kera put her soda
back into the refrigerator. She had to stop drinking so much
caffeine. She went back to the table and stared at the letter.

She started to pick up the envelope to examine it more
thoroughly, then thought better of it. If it had fingerprints,
she didn't want to ruin them. She retrieved some latex
gloves from the bathroom and slid them on, something she
did twenty times a day in the clinic, then carefully picked up
the envelope again. She started to feel a little lightheaded.

The postage mark was local. The stamp sported the popular blue-heron-in-flight image. Her full name and address
had been printed from a word processing program. It looked
like Times New Roman or Minion font, about twelve point.
It matched the font in the letter. Very standard stuff, available on any computer.

Out of curiosity, Kera picked up the pink envelope. The
stamp was also from the Blue Heron series. But there was no
postage mark, no sign that it had been processed through
the US postal system. That was very odd, indeed. Nicole—
or someone—had put it directly into her mailbox. How and

why would Nicole learn her home address?

Kera told herself that it was coincidence that the two letters had the same stamp. It was a popular stamp choice in Oregon. She had a book of Blues in her desk drawer. If the same person had sent both, why had one been mailed and one delivered directly?

Kera's chest tightened, and she fought to take a deep breath. Don't panic, she told herself. They're just letters. They can't hurt you. But her heart knew better. In the recent past, letters had caused her a lot of pain. Kera grabbed her cell phone and pressed redial. Jackson's voicemail picked up.

"It's Kera again. I received some letters in the mail today that I think you should see." Her chest began to burn. Was she having a heart attack? "Or maybe I should call Detective Quince..."

All of sudden, Kera felt as if the oxygen had been sucked out of her body. She tried to speak, but could only make shallow grunting noises. The room began to spin, and she grabbed for a kitchen chair.

‹ **19** ›

JACKSON SHUT HIS phone off while he met with Sergeant Lammers. She despised interruptions and had once tossed Casaway's cell phone out the window after the detective had taken one too many calls in the confinement of the car they were riding in.

A thirty-year police veteran, Lammers had no patience for small talk either.

"You called the meeting, Jackson," she said, seconds after he stepped into her office. "It's your show." She was six feet of fleshy muscle and political power, and even sitting down, she could be intimidating.

"I thought you should know that our top suspect in the death of Jessie Davenport, you know, the girl found in the dumpster..."

"I know who she is."

"...is Mayor Fieldstone."

"No." Her poker face went slack. "Tell me it's circumstantial."

"So far, it is. He rents a secret apartment five hundred feet from where the body was found. He talked on the phone to Jessie seven times in the last month. And another tenant saw the girl outside his unit."

"So they know each other." No high-ranking city employee wanted to jump to conclusions about the mayor.

"We searched his apartment yesterday and collected fiber evidence and some female panties. I hope to get a warrant for a DNA sample soon."

"You should have informed me sooner."

"I've been driving back and forth to Portland, taking evidence to the lab." Jackson knew he was late with this conversation, but he'd been so damn busy.

"Who else have you looked at?" Lammers was obviously worried about a lawsuit. Police departments in Oregon had been sued recently for not investigating enough suspects.

"We're investigating a sex offender named Oscar Grady. He lives about four blocks from where the body was found and has a penchant for young girls. The state lab is comparing his DNA to the trace evidence now. I should have results soon."

"Don't move on the mayor until you get Grady's labs. If there's no match with Grady, then get a warrant to swab Fieldstone." She leaned back with her arms folded across her chest. "Fieldstone is very well liked by a lot of powerful Republicans who want to see him elected to the Senate. That group includes the chief of police. So tread carefully."

"I will."

On the way back to his desk, Jackson turned his phone on and checked his messages. He had missed a return call from Katie, asking if she could stay over at Emily's and a call from Kera agreeing to meet him for dinner. He checked his watch: 5:27. According to her message, Kera wouldn't be home for another half an hour.

He played his last message. It was Kera again, and she sounded upset about some letters she'd received. Then suddenly her voice cut off, and he thought he heard some choking sounds. Then the recording stopped.

Jackson felt his pulse quicken. Was she in trouble? His gut instinct said yes, but his intellect told him he was overreacting. Her phone call had simply been interrupted by something or someone. Cell phones were notorious for cutting out.

He dialed her number, but she didn't answer. It didn't

mean anything, he told himself. She could be in the shower. Or whatever. He plugged her phone number into LEDS, noted her address, then shut his computer off. He had planned to meet her soon anyway, so he might as well drive over there and check.

Before he reached his car on the lower level, Jackson ran into Schak coming up the stairs.

"Did something break for us?" he asked. "You're moving like a man with a mission."

"I'm late for a meeting." Jackson stopped mid-step. "Did you get anything interesting on Fieldstone today?"

Schak shook his head. "Everybody loves the guy. Including his good-looking wife. When are we scheduled to meet again?"

"Not until Monday, unless you hear from me sooner. I've gotta run."

Waiting for a left turn light at 18th and Chambers, he called Kera's cell phone again. Still no answer. Jackson made the turn and headed up the hill. It was Friday at 5:40, and the traffic was thick and slow. Jackson felt his blood pressure rise. He was tempted to use his siren. He unbuttoned his jacket and took off his seat belt instead.

By the time he reached Kera's place at the top of McLean, he could smell his own sweat. Jackson parked next to her Saturn in the driveway and rushed to the front door. He rang the bell, counted to five, and followed with a loud knock. No response.

He tried the doorknob, which turned easily. Her car was in the driveway and her front door was unlocked, so he figured she had to be home. Jackson pushed the door open and called out, "Kera. Are you here?"

No answer. His heart thumped against his chest. Had something happened to her?

Jackson drew his Sig Sauer and pushed inside. The living

room was empty. He moved cautiously through the dining room into the kitchen. Kera was on the floor behind a chair. Her eyes were open, but vacant, and her hands clutched at her chest.

He holstered his weapon and reached for his cell phone, using speed dial to call the emergency dispatch center on the other end of Chambers. "This is Detective Jackson. I need an ambulance at 3245 McLean. The victim is conscious but seriously ill. Hold on for a moment."

Jackson knelt down on the floor. "Kera, can you hear me?"

"Yes." Her voice was barely a whisper, and her face was turning a bluish color.

"What happened? Are you injured?"

"My lungs. The letters." She grimaced with the pain of speaking.

He spoke to the dispatcher again. "This is a possible poisoning. Have the ambulance meet me in the Bi-Mart parking lot at 18th and Chambers."

Jackson jumped up and scanned the table. White latex gloves lay next to a couple of envelopes, one business-sized and white, the other square and pink.

He started yanking open kitchen drawers. "Do you have ziplock bags?"

She tried to speak, but her voice erupted in violent coughing.

Jackson located a couple of freezer bags in a drawer near the refrigerator, then quickly pulled on the too-small latex gloves. He didn't have time to go out to his car for his own. He shoved each letter into a separate plastic bag, then crammed the evidence into his jacket pockets. The hospital would need to know what poisoning they were dealing with.

Jackson lifted Kera off the floor, but struggled to keep her up. She was tall and muscular and probably weighed a hundred and fifty pounds.

"I can walk if you help me," she whispered against his neck.

He lowered her feet to the ground, and moved his arm around her waist.

Half dragging, half carrying her, Jackson maneuvered Kera out of the house and down the walkway. Midpoint in the driveway, she had another coughing fit and her knees buckled. Jackson scooped her up and did a staggered run to his Impala. He folded Kera into the back seat, and she promptly fell over on her side.

Jackson climbed in the driver's side, fired up the engine and raced down the hill toward town. He hoped he wouldn't encounter one of the deer that were famous for darting out of the trees at dusk on Chambers. He was still breathing hard when he hit his first stoplight at 24th. He cursed the traffic for being there and himself for being so out of shape. Jackson turned on his siren, something he almost never had cause for, and cleared the intersection.

As he pulled into the Bi-Mart parking lot, he heard Kera vomiting in the back seat. The sour-acid stench made his stomach heave. Jackson bounded out of the car and opened the back door. Grabbing Kera around her knees, he dragged her from the car and eased her onto the ground, rolling her up on her side in case she vomited again. Her breath was shallow and ragged, and there was no pink left in her face. "Hang in there, Kera. Help is coming."

He racked his brain to remember his first aid training. But for poisoning, as long as she was breathing, there wasn't much he could do. The paramedics would soon give her oxygen, then the emergency room doctors would probably give her charcoal to absorb whatever was in her system. No, that was for ingested substances. If it came from the envelopes, the poison was probably in a powder form and she had inhaled it. He had no idea how to help her.

He reached for his pockets to make sure the envelopes were still there.

What had they used? Anthrax? Man, he hoped not. The hospital lab would test the envelopes. If they discovered which agent she had been attacked with soon enough, they could save her. Jackson squatted next to Kera and stroked her hair. Then he closed his eyes and pleaded with God to save her.

A moment later, he heard the siren.

20

Friday, October 22, 7:17 p.m.

Jackson paced the waiting area of Northwest McKenzie's trauma center, unsoothed by the lush plants and neutral colors. It had only been ten minutes—too soon to ask the nurse at the intake desk if there was news about Kera's condition. He called Katie and was relieved to hear her answer the phone.

"Hi Dad. How's the case going?"

"Better now. I should be home this weekend."

"I'm glad. I miss you."

Jackson was surprised by how much he needed to hear that. "I miss you too. Are you feeling abandoned?"

Katie laughed. "Are you serious? You call me all the time." She hesitated. "Mom called me today."

"How is she?"

"She says she's going into rehab."

He'd heard that before. "That's good news. I'm sorry to cut this short, but I've got to make another call. Will you put Emily's mom on the phone for a second."

"Why?"

"I just need to talk to her."

"You're checking up on me. To see if I'm really at Emily's." The friendly daughter was gone, replaced by the petulant teen. "You don't trust me all of a sudden."

"Just do it, okay. I love you. See you tomorrow."

Better get used to it, he thought after he was off the phone. I'm not going to let you become Jessie.

Next, he called Quince and told him about Kera's letters.

It seemed likely that the clinic bomber had also orchestrated the attack on Kera, and the sooner Quince examined the evidence, the better chance of stopping him before the next round.

"Do you know anything about Kera's family?" Jackson asked.

"Not really," Quince said. "Except that she lives alone."

"Look into it, will you? They need to know she's in the hospital."

After a half hour of pacing, a male nurse in his mid-forties approached Jackson. "Are you the officer who brought Kera Kollmorgan in?"

"Is she okay?"

"We just got word from the lab," the guy in the blue scrubs said. "There was ricin powder on the pink card. It's a deadly poison derived from castor beans, but fortunately, inhaling it is less toxic to the system than swallowing it."

He's stalling, Jackson thought. "Is she going to be all right?"

"We don't know yet. There is no antidote. All we can do is treat the symptoms." The nurse's tone was detached; he could have been talking about a lunch order.

"What are you actually doing for her?"

"Fluid keeps building in her lungs, so we're keeping them drained. We're also giving her oxygen. But her blood pressure is still dropping."

"How long do the symptoms last? When will you know?"

"It depends on how much she inhaled and how healthy her immune system is." His pudgy face betrayed no emotion. "You should contact her family."

"We're trying."

The nurse turned and went back through the solid swinging doors. For a split second, Jackson glimpsed a group of medical professionals all in drab blue scrubs, surrounding a trauma table. The scene was surprisingly quiet. Then the doors closed, and he was alone in the hallway again.

Fifteen minutes later, Quince showed up.

"How is she?" The vice detective was in his mid-thirties, but with his blond hair and thick smooth skin, he looked twenty-two. It had worked against him as a patrol cop, and the physical confrontations he'd had with offenders had almost kept him from making detective.

"Hanging in there. There was ricin on one of the letters, and there's no antidote for it. If she's healthy, she'll make it."

"She seemed healthy to me." Quince said it with a straight face, but they both knew what he meant. "Where are the letters?" Quince asked

"In the lab on the fourth floor." Jackson knew that Quince could figure it out on his own, but he might as well give him a head start. "The envelope that contained the poisoned thank-you card does not have a postmark. So it was probably hand delivered to Kollmorgan's mailbox. So I'd start by dusting the box for prints and asking her neighbors if they saw anything."

"Why do you think the bomber is targeting Kollmorgan?"

"I don't know." Weariness hit Jackson like a wave, threatening to knock him down. "But we'd better warn the other Planned Parenthood employees not to open any suspicious mail."

"I made the calls on the way over. Yesterday, I sent a full report to the FBI. An agent from the Portland office is coming down to meet with me tomorrow."

Quince started to leave, but Jackson called after him. "Did you find any of Kera's family?"

"I've got a dispatcher working on it. She'll call the hospital as soon as she has anything."

"Thanks." Jackson sank into a couch. He had things to do, but he didn't feel right about leaving the hospital until Kera's family showed up—or until he knew she was going to make it.

At 8:26, he got a call from Debbie in the state lab. "You're working late," he commented.

"I need the overtime pay, and you need the lab results." She paused. "Ready?"

"Sure." Jackson got the feeling that this would be good.

"The sheets you brought in this morning match the fibers we found in Jessie's nose and lungs."

He felt his chest muscles loosen. Finally. He had a piece of physical evidence connecting one of his suspects to the victim. "It is an exclusive match?"

Debbie let out a little sigh. "No. This type of sheet is somewhat common. And so far, I haven't spotted any ir-regularities that would prove the threads came from the ex-act same batch. But the upside is that the nose fibers may very well have come from those sheets. It rules them in, not out."

"Any DNA evidence on the sheets? Saliva or vaginal dis-charge?"

"We found a spot with a significant amount of saliva. We're running a DNA comparison to the victim, but it'll take another day."

"Thanks Debbie. And thanks for working late to do the sheets."

"No problem."

Jackson hated to leave the hospital without knowing if Kera would pull through, but getting a DNA sample from the mayor was urgent business. Sergeant Lammers had said to wait for Grady's results, but now that he had a fiber match, it was a whole new scenario. Impulsively, he strode over to the double doors and pushed through. The nurse who had spoken to him earlier looked up. "How is she?" Jackson demanded.

"The same. We'll let you know if it changes."

The night sky brightened with stars as Jackson drove out from under the lights of the city and climbed Lorane Highway. He had already been to Judge Cranston's home for a signature on the search warrant, and he was starting to feel optimistic that Jessie would get justice for what had been done to her. He phoned Slonecker. The fact that it was late on a Friday night didn't matter. Not to him, the judge, or the DA. There was no time clock in their world.

"Slone, it's Jackson. The bed sheets we took from Fieldstone's apartment match the fibers in Jessie's nose. I'm on my way to his home now with a warrant."

"Don't blow this," the DA warned. "I want him to volunteer the sample. If we arrest him, and it leaks to the press, and then his swab doesn't match, there will be hell to pay. The Republicans will punish you if you tarnish their golden boy."

Shit. This was why Jackson hated politics. "What if Fieldstone refuses to cooperate? What if he decides to run instead of give us a body standard?"

"You'll do the right thing."

Jackson approached the mayor's Blanton Heights home with some trepidation. If he was wrong about this, his job was on the line. The mayor headed the committee that hired—and could fire—Jackson's boss, the chief of police. Ultimately, if Fieldstone held on to his position, he could pressure the right people and force Jackson out. If it got ugly enough, he could even lose his pension.

Jackson stood in the driveway, feeling dwarfed by the money surrounding him. Five years ago, this area had been a forest. Now it was a meadow sprouting three-thousand-square-foot homes, some with tennis courts and swimming pools. In addition to being mayor, Fieldstone owned a thriving construction business, and he had probably paid for his McMansion with the profit made from doing business with his neighbors.

Jackson squared his shoulders and strode up to the front door. Janice Fieldstone answered his knock. She was a soft, pretty woman in her late forties, who tried to look young by keeping her hair very blond and long. But her voice had the tight control of someone who has been drinking and is trying to hide it. Jackson knew the charade well.

"What can I do for you, Officer?"

"I need to speak with Mayor Fieldstone."

"He's not here."

"Where can I find him?"

She was suddenly concerned. "Why do you want to see him?"

"It's police business. But it will only take a minute."

She hesitated, then shrugged. "He's having drinks with some out-of-state visitors at the Statesmen. It's a private club downtown on Oak Street, at the top of the US Bank building."

"I know it. Thanks."

In an effort to be discreet, Jackson called Fieldstone from the building's lobby. The mayor did not appreciate the courtesy. "What do you want now?" he blurted.

Jackson resisted the urge to be sarcastic. "I have a search warrant for your DNA. Are you coming out to the lobby or am I coming in?"

"Why can't this wait until tomorrow? I'm in the middle of an important meeting."

"This will only take a moment."

"Fine. I'll be out in a minute."

Jackson checked his watch: 9:02. He glanced over at the host–bouncer, who, despite his age, moved with the muscular grace of a dancer. "I'll give him five minutes, then I'm going in."

"I won't stop you, sir, but I'd rather not have a scene. This is an exclusive club, and our members expect privacy and decorum."

Decorum was a pretty highbrow concept for a man who had probably raped and killed a child, Jackson thought.

Seven minutes later, the mayor had failed to show. Jackson pushed past the gatekeeper and entered the club. The lighting was so subdued, he felt like going back to his car for a flashlight. Wouldn't the members love that? A long bar lined the wall to the left, and attractive look-alike blonds in plunging white shirts poured drinks for the town's elite. High-backed booths and partitions created a host of private meeting places, most of which were occupied by men in suits. Most members gave him only a cursory glance. The mayor was not among them.

But there was more to the club. Swinging doors led into a room with pool tables. Three private nooks with low-slung couches were carved into the left side of the room. Jackson could feel anxiety building in his chest as he realized that Fieldstone had fled. He ran down a short hallway that opened into a kitchen. The small dinner crew was cleaning up.

"Where's the back door?"

A waiter pointed past the dishwashing room. Jackson ran for it, but he knew he was too late. The back exit led out to the parking lot, where there was no movement in the dark, no car doors slamming, no engines starting. The mayor had given him the slip.

Damn. How far would he go? Jackson wondered. Would he leave town? Or was he simply stalling to avoid giving a DNA sample? Jackson decided not to take any chances. Back in his car, he called in an attempt-to-locate request, which would go out over all local law enforcement radios. Then he notified the police units in the Eugene and Portland airports. Politics be damned. Fieldstone wasn't getting away.

21

Jackson raced across town, running stoplights in the deserted streets. He reached Blanton Heights in less than ten minutes and parked his Impala across from the mayor's home. He didn't see Fieldstone's Mercedes, but it was probably tucked away in the roomy three-car garage. He suspected the mayor was in the house now, packing his bags, and would come out on the run at any moment. Jackson had handcuffs in his jacket pocket just in case. He sat for a couple of minutes, trying to decide if he should call Slonecker and let him know what was going down. He decided against it.

Moments later, a car came up the dark road and turned into Fieldstone's driveway. Jackson was out of the car and running across the street before the mayor could get his garage door open. He pounded on the car window.

"Fieldstone!"

The mayor shut off his engine and stepped out. "I have nothing to say. My lawyer and I will come in tomorrow morning to review your search warrant."

"I'd rather not wait." Jackson stood between the suspect and the walkway. "You can come with me now, voluntarily, or I'll cuff you and take you in. Your call."

Jackson held out his warrant for the mayor to see. There was no way he could read it in the dark, but Jackson didn't want the DNA analysis to be tossed out of court later because the search warrant hadn't been properly served.

The mayor didn't even bother to glance at the paper. "This is harassment, and I intend to sue the department."

You and everybody else, Jackson thought. "Let's go."

"I will come in with my lawyer in the morning." The mayor spoke slowly, as if Jackson were either deaf or stupid.

"I trusted you once this evening, and you evaded me. I'm not making that mistake again."

"I went to discuss the matter with my lawyer. I have that right."

"You lied, then ran. Let's go." Jackson pulled out the handcuffs.

The mayor must have thought Jackson was bluffing, because he turned and started to walk away. Jackson had him cuffed and pinned against the Mercedes in six seconds flat.

"Your career is over," Fieldstone threatened with an ugly laugh.

"Yours too."

When they pulled into the parking lot below city hall, Jackson considered uncuffing Fieldstone, then rejected the idea as an unnecessary courtesy. He wouldn't do it for anyone else, and until he had a DNA sample, why take the chance? At ten in the evening, the parking garage was nearly empty and the surrounding city was eerily quiet. Fieldstone had not spoken on the way and stayed silent as he walked up the concrete stairs in front of Jackson. They crossed the open area and veered to the right toward police headquarters. Suddenly, two figures were running toward them in the dim light.

Instinctively, Jackson reached for his Sig Sauer.

Then a bright flash went off.

Shit. A photographer.

"Can I get a statement, Detective Jackson?"

And a reporter. Sophie Speranza from the Willamette News was suddenly in his face. Damn, she was tenacious.

The mayor tried to veer away from the pair, but Jackson held firm to his elbow and pushed past the two. Another flash went off, and Fieldstone swore under his breath.

"What are the charges?" Speranza called after them.

They rushed into the department's foyer, and the desk clerk buzzed them in without any verbal exchange. She had probably seen the photographer's flash. Or maybe it was the look on Jackson's face.

They moved past the administrative desks and down the narrow hallway into the detective area in back. Jackson's pulse would not slow down. This DNA swab should have been so simple, and now it was so screwed up. The crowded room was lifeless except for Pete Casaway, a vice detective. Casaway looked up, nodded, then went back to his reading. Jackson led Fieldstone into the interrogation room they had occupied that morning.

"Have a seat. I'll be back."

From a central cabinet, he retrieved a cotton swab and a small brown bag with a white label, then stopped by Casaway's desk.

"Videotape a cheek swab for me?"

"Sure. Was that the mayor?"

"Yep. That's why I need the video."

"Is he your suspect in the Jessie homicide?"

"Lucky me, huh?"

Back in the interrogation room, Jackson said to Fieldstone, "We plan to film this. Would you like us to take the cuffs off and tell the camera you're offering it voluntarily? Or leave them on and have you be labeled as an uncooperative suspect?"

The mayor gave it some thought. He must have figured his best bet for getting the DNA suppressed would result from being uncooperative now. "You do not have my permission to take my DNA," he said with a certain smugness.

So the cuffs stayed.

Casaway filmed while Jackson displayed the warrant, took a cheek swab, and placed the swab in the evidence bag.

"Thanks, Casaway." Jackson uncuffed the mayor and said, "You're free to leave. If you'd like, I'll take you home."

"I'll pass."

Jackson escorted Fieldstone out of the building. He heard the mayor making a call as he walked away. Jackson went to his desk and sat for a moment to calm himself. His heart had been pounding since the photographer's flash. It was one thing to bring the mayor into the department in handcuffs. It was another to have the scene photographed and displayed on the front page of the newspaper.

How had Speranza known Jackson would be bringing in a VIP tonight?

Oh shit. It was the attempt to locate bulletin he'd issued earlier. Crime-beat reporters often monitored police frequencies. Oh shit. Slonecker would be royally pissed. Lammers would be equally livid. Jackson felt a little queasy. If he was wrong about the mayor, his career was over.

And if not Detective Jackson, who would he be?

22

Saturday, October 23, 6:49 a.m.
KERA TRIED TO open her eyes, but they would not cooperate. They only fluttered, letting in tiny flashes of light at
the bottom of her vision. She could hear people's voices, but
she couldn't wake up enough to see them or find out what
they wanted. One of them kept saying her name.

"Kera? Kera? Can you hear me, Kera?"

Finally, her eyes stayed open long enough to focus on the
face next to her bed. It belonged to a woman with flawless
bronze skin and shiny black hair. She was wearing a yellow
nursing scrub.

"Do you know where you are, Kera?"

She became aware of tubes in her nostrils. "Why am I in
the hospital?"

"You were very sick for a while, but you're going to be
okay. We're giving you oxygen."

"What happened?" Pain seared her throat as she spoke.
Kera remembered sitting at her kitchen table and coughing
violently.

"You inhaled ricin powder. It looks like someone deliberately poisoned you. I'm Sheri, by the way." The nurse smiled
brightly, revealing a mouthful of beautiful white teeth.

Oh yeah. The letter from the crackpot. Kera remembered
opening her mail, and she vaguely recalled seeing Jackson in
her kitchen. After that, it was a blur of motion and sickness.

Kera pushed herself into an upright position, making herself a little dizzy. "I have to warn the other staff members."

The nurse looked startled. "You should lie back down."

"This is important."

"I'm sure the police are taking care of it. In fact, the police are out there now, wanting to speak to you. I told them you weren't ready."

Was it Jackson? "I'll see him. In fact, would you please put my bed into a sitting position and remove the oxygen tube?"

"I'll sit you up, but I'm sure the doctor will want the tube to stay."

As Sheri elevated her bed, Kera pulled off the tape holding the tiny tube in place.

"Please don't do that," Sheri protested, but she made no move to stop her.

"I'll be fine," Kera said, relieved to have the tube out. "The more I move around, the faster I'll get better. Trust me. I'm a nurse."

Sheri let out a little snort. "Only doctors make worse patients." She appraised Kera for a moment, then said, "I'll go get your visitors."

It wasn't Jackson. Michael Quince, the boyish looking detective who had taken over the bomb investigation, came in followed by another man in a dark suit. An older man with thick glasses and deep furrows around his eyes. They stood at the end of her bed, each with a notebook in hand.

"Hi Kera," Quince said. "This is Agent Daren Fouts. He's with the Federal Bureau of Investigation. Are you okay to answer some questions?"

She wanted information first. "Were any of the other staff members poisoned? Have you warned them?" Her voice was hoarse and weak, and she didn't sound like herself.

The detective smiled, making himself look about twelve. Especially compared with the somber Agent Fouts.

"The rest of the staff is fine," he reported. "Two others

received a threatening letter, but no poison. The ricin you inhaled came from the pink thank-you card signed NC. Do you know who that is?"

Kera hesitated. She didn't believe Nicole had done this. "Yesterday, I talked with Nicole Clarke, a young girl at Kincaid Middle School. But I don't believe she would poison me."

"Why not?" Fouts spoke up.

"She has no motive. She barely knows me."

They both jotted something down in their little black notebooks.

"What did you talk about?" Quince asked.

"It was personal. I can't tell you."

Quince frowned. "How can we rule her out as a suspect if we don't know what her relationship is to you?"

"We don't really have a relationship. I happened to be at Kincaid school yesterday. Or the day before." Kera was suddenly confused. "What day and time is it?"

"It's around 7 a.m., Saturday morning. Please continue." Quince moved in closer, so he could hear her better. Fouts stayed put.

"I was at the school on Thursday. Nicole approached me and asked if we could talk." Kera's voice faded out, sounding like a hoarse whisper. "We went to my car and chatted for about ten minutes about personal stuff. That's it."

"Did anyone see you talking to her?"

"I don't know. It's certainly possible."

"Why would someone poison you and not the other clinic workers?" Fouts suddenly took the lead.

"I don't know." Kera's head hurt and she wanted them to go away.

"Do you perform abortions?" Fouts asked.

"No. They're done by a doctor, who provides the service on a contract basis. Sometimes I assist, though."

Agent Fouts scratched his jaw. "Someone tried to kill you.

Are you sure you don't want to tell us what you and Nicole Clarke talked about?"

Had someone meant to kill her? Kera hadn't really considered the idea that she could have died. "You'll have to ask Nicole."

"I will. I suspect she knows more about this than you think she does."

"I doubt it." Kera was tired of the questions and didn't believe there was anything she could say that would help them. "I need to rest, please."

"I hope you get well soon," Quince gave her another smile on his way out.

After they were gone, Kera tried to remember what she knew about ricin poisoning. It seemed that the toxin shut down the production of some type of protein on a cellular level, causing cells to die. The only recourse was to flush it from the system. Ingesting ricin was much worse than inhaling it though, because eating it damaged the digestive system. People who recovered from ingested ricin poisoning often had bowel trouble for the rest of their lives. Kera was grateful she wouldn't face that. Her lungs might never be good enough to run a marathon, but she would recover.

Suddenly, she felt dizzy and weak. Kera put her bed back down to rest for a while. Was she marked for execution now? Abortion clinic staff members in other states wore bullet-proof vests every time they left the house—and carried concealed weapons. Could she live like that or should she give up her job? Either choice seemed unacceptable.

Saturday, October 23, 6:35 a.m.
RUTH ROLLED out of bed, put on a pot of coffee, and while it brewed, called Northwest McKenzie Hospital.

"My sister, Kera Kollmorgan, was brought into the hospital last night. How is she doing?"

While the receptionist transferred her to a nurse, Ruth pulled out flour and sugar from the cupboard. Her family was attending a prayer breakfast this morning, and she had signed up to bring the pancake batter. In a minute, a nurse came on and informed her that Kollmorgan had been moved out of intensive care and was recovering in room 213.

So the abortionist-whore had survived. Ruth had not necessarily intended for her to die, but she had accepted that it might happen. God must have His reasons, she thought.

She thought about the bomb in the back of the laundry room closet. She was anxious to place it inside the clinic. But they had a security guard now, so she would have to be more careful this time. She had bought a long-haired wig and some oversized sunglasses to disguise herself for the drop. But still, she worried. It would be better if the bomb were on a timer. Could she craft a timer? And if she could, would it be possible to target Kollmorgan's office inside the clinic?

Ruth whipped up a large batch of buttermilk pancake batter with a hint of maple, then stepped outside for the paper. She rarely read the liberal rag, but Sam liked to keep track of what the politicians and godless groups were up to. Back in the house, she poured herself a cup of coffee, then sat down at the kitchen table to enjoy the morning brew. The paper lay folded in front of her, and the front-page photo caught her eye. She opened the paper to reveal a portrait-size photo of Mayor Fieldstone in handcuffs with a detective in the background behind him.

Ruth let out a little yelp.

The mayor was a member of First Bible Baptist and a CCA supporter. He was their main advocate inside local government. They had hoped to see him elected to the Senate soon. He was supposed to help CCA accomplish its goals. What in God's name had he done? Ruth anxiously read the story, which was substantially smaller than the picture.

Mayor Miles Fieldstone was brought into police head-quarters in handcuffs late Friday evening. Making the arrest was Detective Wade Jackson, head of the investigation in the death of thirteen-year-old Jessie Davenport, whose body was found Tuesday in a dumpster. Jackson would not comment on Fieldstone's arrest, but Judy Davenport, the victim's mother, says the police told her that her daughter was suffocated and that they have a solid lead. Davenport also confirmed that Jessie and Mayor Fieldstone knew each other from attendance at the First Bible Baptist Church on 18th and Garfield in Eugene.

Ruth had to stop reading. How irresponsible! She could not believe the paper would print such trash. They practically accused the mayor of killing Jessie. With one irresponsible story, they had probably ruined his chances of getting elected to the Senate. Evangelical Christians across Oregon had been counting on Fieldstone to represent their interests in Congress. Ruth wanted to slap that reporter silly.

And why did she have to mention the church? Any opportunity to make Evangelicals look bad. The media were willing tools in the war against Christians. Maybe the newspaper needed a little shake up too. Make them think twice about printing such propaganda.

Saturday, October 23, 7:45 a.m.

THE ALARM BLASTED Jackson out of a fitful sleep. He had lain awake for hours the night before, his brain scampering from one worry to another. He'd mishandled Fieldstone and would suffer the fallout from that. He might even be pulled off the case. And if the mayor's DNA didn't match, he could kiss his job goodbye.

Then there was Kera Kollmorgan in the hospital fighting for her life, while her attacker was still out there, most likely preparing for a new assault. Jackson felt helpless to protect the clinic workers. And he could not stop thinking about Katie and Jessie. How much did they have in common? The idea that his little girl may have had a sexual encounter made him ill, and he refused to believe it. Katie and Jessie had gone their separate ways.

Jackson showered, grabbed his keys and his evidence bag, and stepped out into the early morning mist. The Saturday paper was a little damp, but the mayor's twelve-by-twelve photo was unaffected. Jackson's image in the background was a little blurry, but the tension in his face was unmistakable. Ah Jesus. This would get ugly.

Jackson read the story in the car and cursed Sophie Speranza for her recklessness. If the case ever came to trial, the mayor would probably be granted a change of venue because this story would poison the jury pool.

He tossed the paper in the back seat and hit the road, buying coffee and breakfast at McDonalds on the way. He hoped like hell it would be his last trip to Portland for this case.

‹ 23 ›

The lab did not have good news for him.

"There was no saliva in the lip gloss to test," Debbie reported. "And the vaginal discharge in the orange panties does not match Jessie Davenport."

Damn. Jackson tried not to feel disappointed. He knew better than to count on the evidence to support his theories. The evidence spoke for itself. "What about the saliva in the sheets?"

"We're still processing that."

"Thanks, Debbie." The woman looked exhausted, and he knew she was working over the weekend to expedite this case. He handed her the brown evidence bag. "This new swab is critical. Please compare it to both the semen and the pubic hair. And I need the analysis immediately. I put myself out on a limb for this one."

She signed Fieldstone's saliva into record keeping.

Jackson's cell phone rang three times on the trip back to Eugene, but he didn't pick up. Instead, he played the messages. First, Owen Warner, the chief of police, left a message that opened with "What the hell is going on?" Then, Sophie Speranza called and said she wanted to "chat with him about the mayor." That would be a cold day in hell. And last, McCray said he needed to talk to Jackson right away.

He decided to call McCray before talking to the chief. If there was an update on Oscar Grady, he needed to know.

"It's Jackson. What's the word on Grady?"

"He killed himself last night."

"Oh shit." Guilt stabbed him in the stomach. "Please tell me he left a confession. Poured out his guilt on paper." Jackson forced himself to focus on the road.

"He didn't. He left a note saying the police had cost him his job and his girlfriend and ruined his life."

The knife twisted in his gut.

McCray's voice got quiet. "I feel like shit. Do we have Grady's DNA results yet? I'd feel less like shit if I knew he was guilty."

"Not yet. I'll let you know as soon as we do. You were just doing your job, McCray. We're seeking justice for a murdered young girl." Jackson was trying to make himself feel better too.

"I know. But what if he had rehabilitated himself? How can guys like Grady ever build new lives if we keep tearing them down?"

"I'm not sure there's a better way," Jackson said. "Did he have a family?"

"His mother lives in Cottage Grove."

"No kids though?"

"No."

"Let's wait for the DNA. Take the weekend off. Try to get some rest."

"Okay."

After hanging up, Jackson replayed his interrogations of Grady. Had he crossed the line? Had he pushed an unstable man too far? It hadn't seemed that way at the time. But he had instructed McCray to "pick his life apart." And clearly, they had done just that. Jackson couldn't shake loose of the guilt.

But this case wasn't over. And he had to stay focused. The chief was probably going to tear him apart, and he needed every piece of supporting information he could gather. Jackson pressed the accelerator and tried to break free from a clump of weekend traffic. Then he dialed Judy Davenport and asked if she would meet with him this morning.

"Not right now," she said. "I'm getting ready for a prayer breakfast at the church." She sounded distracted, as if she were in the middle of something.

"I'll meet you afterward."

"Call me back." And she hung up.

Jackson arrived in Eugene in time to catch the crowd at the First Bible Baptist spilling out of the red-brick church. It was a massive building surrounded by a parking lot that took up an entire city block.

This morning's faithful, a small group compared with a regular Sunday service, hurried for their cars. Rain pelted them as they ran, wetting their bright, crisp church-going clothes. Fieldstone did not appear to be among those praying over bacon and eggs this morning. Had the mayor lost his faith? Or his appetite?

Jackson watched a group of young girls, Jessie's age, trot down the wide front steps. They were dressed demurely in pink, white, and floral combinations. Jackson wondered if one of them had left some orange panties at the mayor's pleasure pad.

Judy Davenport was one of the last to leave, flanked on both sides by elderly women, each with a firm grip on her elbows. Dressed in mourners' black, Davenport kept her head down to avoid the onslaught of rain. Jackson jumped out of his car and followed her to a blue Toyota. Several church-goers gazed in open curiosity.

"Mrs. Davenport, can we talk for a moment?"

She seemed surprised, but not upset to see him. "Sure. Let's sit in the car."

"Did you see the newspaper this morning?" Jackson asked as he dug out his notebook.

"Do you really think Mayor Fieldstone killed Jessie?"

"He is only one suspect. I wish I could tell you more, but I have to wait for the lab results."

"But why would he kill her? I don't understand." She seemed genuinely confused.

"We are pretty sure he was having sex with her. Did you know they had a relationship?"

"Not that kind of relationship." Mrs. Davenport's eyes darted around at the church people in the parking lot. "But I saw him talking to her a few times."

"Where?"

"Here, in church. And once at a fundraiser at the fairgrounds."

"Did you ever suspect anything?"

"No!"

"Did you know Fieldstone personally? Were you friends?"

Davenport's hands twisted in her lap. "He made a point of being nice to me." She hesitated for a long moment. Jackson resisted the urge to prompt her. Finally she said, "He gave me money once."

"How much? And what did he say when he offered it?" This was unexpected.

"He offered me fifteen hundred dollars so I could pay off Jessie's braces. I wondered how he knew I needed the money."

"Is there anything else I should know?"

Judy Davenport shook her head and began to cry.

Jackson squeezed her hand. "Thank you."

As he stepped out of the car, he noticed Trina Waterman, a reporter with KRSL, setting up in the parking lot for interviews with two churchgoers.

Oh shit. Not now. Jackson could not get back to his car without passing right by her. But he had no choice, he had a meeting with the chief of police in twenty minutes.

The reporter noticed him as he approached and signaled

her cameraman to swing his camera around. Jackson smiled, nodded, and kept walking.

"Officer Jackson, is Miles Fieldstone your only suspect in this case?"

"I can't tell you that." He kept moving.

"What motive have you established? Were he and Jessie sexually involved?" Waterman called out her question from about five feet away. The two church women who were preening for their turn in front of the camera looked horrified.

"It's too early to speculate. We're waiting for lab results." Jackson kept moving.

Waterman was behind him now and Jackson resisted the urge to run. But he suspected that her other potential interviewees had taken off. That was the gamble in going for the bigger fish.

Saturday, October 23, 11:46 a.m.

ON THE RIDE home from the prayer breakfast, Nicole and Rachel sat in the back seat of the Clarkes' Ford Astro and didn't talk much—not in the presence of Nicole's parents. Rachel had come up to Nicole after the meal and asked to spend the afternoon together.

"I'm sad about Jessie too," Rachel whispered in her ear as she hugged Nicole. "And I can't bear to lose you as a friend right now." Feeling guilty about not seeing Rachel for the past few days, Nicole agreed to have her over.

As they pulled into the driveway of their Potter Street home, Nicole noticed a blue sedan parked on the street. The men who climbed out were both wearing dark suits and carrying small notebooks. A sense of dread invaded Nicole's stomach as she and her family climbed out of the van. The men looked like cops, and she knew this would be bad. Her parents, who were still arguing about when they'd taken the van in for a tune-up, hadn't noticed the men approaching.

"Mr. and Mrs. Clarke?"

They both spun around. "Yes?"

"I'm Detective Michael Quince, Eugene Police. And this is Agent Daren Fouts with the FBI. We'd like to speak to your daughter Nicole for a few minutes."

Her parents looked at each other, terrified. Rachel gave Nicole a wild-eyed look that meant "Don't you dare tell them anything." Nicole felt her face flush and her heart flutter. Was this about Jessie? Why did the FBI want to talk to her?

"About what?" Her mother was always the first to react, leaving her dad looking a little slow.

"We'd prefer to let Nicole discuss that with you afterward." Detective Quince's voice was soft and soothing, and Nicole was a little less scared. The other man hadn't said a word yet.

Her mother turned to her. "Nicole, do you know what this is about?"

"No."

"We'd like to be present when you talk to her." Her dad finally spoke up.

The FBI agent stepped forward. "We're investigating a very serious incident. It may, or may not, involve your daughter. Either way, it's imperative that we speak to Nicole alone."

Her parents looked at each other and communicated in that silent language adults speak with their eyes. While they all stood there, the sky began to spit moisture. Finally, her mom said, "Come inside and I'll make you some coffee. You can talk in the sunroom."

Nicole had mixed feelings about being alone with the cops. Depending on what they wanted to talk about, her parents could either be a protection or a nightmare. She wished Rachel could stay with them. Rachel had nerves of steel. But her mom had invited her friend into the kitchen to make lunch. Rachel rolled her eyes and went along. Now Nicole, Detective Quince, and Agent Fouts were seated in the sunroom, surrounded by plants, watching the rain drizzle down the glass.

"How well do you know Kera Kollmorgan?" Quince asked.

"Who?"

"Kera Kollmorgan. She's a nurse at Planned Parenthood."

"I don't know her." She didn't, not really.

"You've never met her?" The detective's expression said he did not believe her.

"No. Why would I know her?" Nicole asked God to forgive her lies. But how could she admit she knew Kera without starting down that whole road?

"I think you do." Quince paused. "Do you own any pink stationary?"

"No. Why?"

Fouts leaned forward. "Why did you poison her?"

"What?" Panic tapdanced on her heart.

"Somebody sent Kera Kollmorgan a thank-you card laced with ricin," Agent Fouts said. "She almost died."

"I don't even know what that is!" Nicole struggled not to cry.

"The card was signed NC," Fouts said.

"I'm not the only person in the world with those initials." It was almost a shout. Nicole hoped her parents hadn't heard.

"You talked to Kera the day before she received the card."

Nicole realized she was trapped. Kera had told the cops about their conversation. Her parents would find out she had been to Planned Parenthood! Her legs began to shake. Quince moved over and sat next to her on the couch.

"Tell me about it, Nicole," he said in a quiet voice. "You'll feel better if you do."

"I did talk to Kera. I was upset about Jessie's death, and I needed to talk to someone. And she was there at my school."

"So you already knew her?"

Nicole sucked in a big gulp of air. "I recognized her from the clinic. I went there once with Jessie, just to keep her company. Please don't tell my parents. Their very religious. They'll freak."

"Did anyone else see you talking to Kera?" Fouts again.

"No. Uh. Actually, yes. A friend of mine. A guy."

"What's his name?"

"It doesn't matter." Nicole wished she could cut out her own tongue. "He just came up to the car when I was talking to Kera and flirted with me. He doesn't know her, and he wouldn't hurt her." The sobs she held back threatened to choke her. "I swear to you in God's name, I didn't send any poison to Kera. Please don't tell my parents that I know somebody at Planned Parenthood."

"Tell me the boy's name," Fouts pressed.

"Trevor Harvick." Wow, was he going to be pissed at her when the FBI showed up at his house.

Detective Quince took over again. "Do you know anyone who would want to cause you trouble?"

"No. It must be some other NC."

"Do you know anyone who would want to hurt both Jessie Davenport and Kera Kollmorgan?"

"No. None of this makes any sense."

Detective Quince stood and handed her a business card. "Please call me if you think of anything that might relate to this incident." Agent Fouts hesitated, then got up as well.

"What are you going to tell my parents?" Nicole spoke directly to Quince.

"That we talked about Jessie."

"Thank you." Nicole cried with relief.

AS THEY WALKED away from the Clarkes' home, Agent Fouts asked, "Who is Jessie Davenport?"

Quince hesitated. "She's a fourteen-year-old girl who was murdered last Tuesday."

"What makes you think her death is related to the attacks on the Planned Parenthood clinic and its staff?" Fouts frowned. "And why didn't you tell me about her?"

Quince felt compelled to play it down. "I don't think they are related. But it occurred to me to ask Nicole because she is a friend of Jessie's and her initials came up in the ricin card. It was just a long shot."

"You still believe in coincidences?" They had reached the car, and Fouts stared at him over the top as they stood by the doors.

Quince was quiet as they climbed into Fouts' sedan. Then he asked, "In your experience, has an anti-abortion fanatic ever turned out to be a sexual predator as well?"

Fouts gave it some thought. "No. But I intend to investigate the possibility. Who's handling the Davenport case?"

"Detective Jackson."

"I'll set up a meeting."

Saturday, October 23, 1:05 p.m.
FOR THE CHIEF OF POLICE and the district attorney to come into the department on a Saturday afternoon was an occasion so special that it could only result in someone being fired or arrested. Jackson was keenly aware of this as he walked into the chief's office.

Slonecker was already there, standing at the window. As usual, he had too much energy to sit and wait. The chief was behind his desk, his squat muscular body looking out of place in a tailored gray suit. He had a salt and pepper flattop, a crooked nose, and wild eyebrows in need of a trim. It was the first time Jackson had seen either man without a tie.

Jackson realized he didn't know the chief well enough to make any predictions about how this conversation would go. Owen Warner had been imported from Texas a year ago—pissing off the entire department, who had hoped one of their own, Captain Tillager, would end up with the position.

"Officer Jackson." Chief Warner stood to greet him. But he was not a tall man, and this put him at a disadvantage to both Jackson and Slonecker. He motioned everyone to sit.

"I had a very unpleasant conversation with the mayor this morning. He wants you off this case. He threatened to sue the department." Warner's fleshy face turned pink as he talked. "You want to tell me what the hell is going on?"

"He's our main suspect, sir, in the murder of Jessie Davenport. He has an apartment near where her body was found, he spoke with her on the phone seven times last month. The fibers in her nose match–"

Warner cut him off. "I know all that. I want to know why you brought him into the department in handcuffs and how the hell that photo ended up on the front page."

"He also gave Mrs. Davenport fifteen hundred dollars."

"What?" Slonecker turned to stare. "When did you learn this?"

"A half hour ago."

Warner slapped his desktop. "More circumstantial bullshit. I want to know why you went out of your way to turn this investigation into a PR nightmare."

Jackson kept his voice deadpan as he described his call to Fieldstone offering the mayor a chance to come in voluntarily for a DNA swab. He detailed the mayor's uncooperative behavior, both at the club and later at his home. "I believe he was, and is, a flight risk, sir. I had no other choice."

"And the press? Did you call the fucking newspaper?"

"No sir." Jackson fought to keep his cool. The question was on par with accusing him of taking bribes. "The reporter must have been monitoring our radio frequency and heard my attempt-to-locate request. Then she and a photographer ambushed me at the department. I am sorry it happened. But I can't say I would do anything differently if I had to do it again."

"I would," Slonecker interjected. "This whole case could get suppressed."

"I had a search warrant for DNA. It'll hold."

There was a long silence while Warner stroked his chin.

"How sure are you that the mayor's DNA will match the trace evidence found on the victim?" he asked finally.

Doubt squeezed Jackson's bowels. How sure was he? The victim had sex with two different men in the hours before she died, one of whom may have been a known sex offender. The orange panties found in the mayor's apartment did not belong to Jessie. The 600-thread blue cotton fibers were somewhat common.

"I believe the mayor was screwing this girl. She got pregnant. He got scared and killed her to save his career." Jackson paused and the chief jumped in.

"Even if Fieldstone was having an affair with the girl— and I'm not saying he was—that doesn't mean he killed her. What about the sex offender you brought in?"

"He killed himself last night."

"Sounds like a guilty man to me." Warner seemed unaware of his own hypocrisy.

"Oscar Grady's DNA results aren't back yet."

"When will we know?" Warner impatiently drummed the desk.

"Maybe today. Or Monday."

The chief nodded. "If Grady matches the trace evidence, close the case out. Hold a press conference and exonerate Fieldstone."

Jackson was so angry he was afraid to speak. "What if the mayor's DNA is a match?"

"We'll cross that bridge if we come to it." Warner stood, indicating the meeting was over. "If it doesn't match, I want your resignation."

‹ 25 ›

Saturday, October 23, 1:28 p.m.

Jackson felt stunned—as if he'd just been assaulted. The chief seemed willing to protect the mayor, no matter what the evidence said. Would he be forced to pin a murder on a dead man, so Fieldstone could save his career? Jackson was as disturbed by that possibility as he was about the prospect of losing his job.

As he walked to his car, his phone rang.

"Wade, it's me." Only his ex-wife called him Wade.

Jackson braced himself. "Hello, Renee."

"That was quite a splash you made on the front page today. Looks like this one could be a career-boosting case."

He laughed out loud. "Not likely. What can I do for you?"

"Did Katie tell you I'm in rehab?"

"Yep."

"I haven't had a drink in three days. I think you should let my daughter come visit me."

He knew this question would surface, but he still didn't have a good answer. "What does your sponsor think of the idea?"

"She thinks it would be good for me."

"But will it be good for Katie? I think it's too soon to get her hopes up. Why don't you give it a month?"

"You're so self-righteous."

Jackson didn't respond.

"I will get sober. And you will have to let her see me."

"I hope so. I mean that, Renee. I hope you make it.

Thanks for the call."

Jackson hung up. He climbed into his car, locked the door, and laid his head back against the seat. He was so tired. He felt like he could sleep for twenty-four hours. Logistically, this case had not been that difficult, but emotionally, it had sucked the life out of him. And it was far from wrapped up.

He sat up, put on his seat belt, and started the engine.

He couldn't rest yet. He had people to see.

Twenty minutes later, he was stepping off the elevator on the third floor of the downtown hospital. Kera was in a small beige-walled room, separated from a snoring old man by only a beige plastic curtain. She was upright and reading a copy of Newsweek. Her face was pale and her braid was a mess, but her eyes lit up when she smiled at him. He felt a load of tension melt away. Thank God, she was going to recover.

"Detective Jackson, I owe you one. If you hadn't showed up when you did, I might not have made it."

"Happy to be of service."

"Sorry about vomiting in the back of your car." Kera made a face.

"I've been treated worse."

Jackson scooted the chair closer to her bed and sat. "How are you feeling? You look great for someone who was near death last night. What's the prognosis?"

"Possibly some impaired lung function. They say I'm lucky, that I could have died." She grinned, and he noticed her dimples for the first time. "But I say, a truly lucky person wouldn't have someone trying to kill them."

"Any long-term problems?"

"Minor brain damage." She laughed. "Kidding. But I do feel a little sluggish, like my brain isn't really clicking like it should."

"It's the hospital environment. It's not a good place to be."

"Careful. I'm a nurse, remember? I've worked in hospitals."

Jackson cringed a little. "I just meant that you'll feel better when you get home."

"Damn straight. And I'm leaving in the morning with or without their permission."

"Do you have a ride? I could pick you up."

"Thanks, but a friend from the clinic already volunteered. The whole gang came in to see me today." Her smile faded. "They're pretty upset. Sheila and Andrea also got letters from God's Messenger."

"Detective Quince is investigating. And he called in the FBI."

"I know. They came to see me this morning."

Jackson remembered the initials on the pink card. "Do you know anyone with the initials NC?"

Kera smiled. "Quince asked me that too. The only person I could think of was Nicole Clarke, but I don't believe she had anything to do with this."

"Nicole Clarke? Friend of Jessie Davenport?" She was one of the Teen Talk group he'd interviewed.

"Yes. Why?"

"It's odd that her name would come up in both cases. How do you know her?"

"When I was at Kincaid the other day, she approached me and wanted to talk. That's all I can say."

Jackson tried to weave this new information into his Jessie-and-the-mayor scenario, but it didn't fit. How would an anti-abortion extremist be connected to a pedophile?

Kera looked worried. "What is it, Jackson? Do you know something about Nicole that I should know?"

He touched her hand lightly. "No. I was thinking about Jessie's funeral service. It's tomorrow afternoon at the First

Bible Baptist Church."

"Do you plan to go?"

"It's standard procedure. Killers often come to their victim's service."

"Do you have any idea who the killer is?"

"Did you see the paper this morning?"

She frowned. "I missed it. Do you have someone in custody?"

Jackson leaned in and spoke softly. "I'm waiting for DNA results, but I think Miles Fieldstone was sexually involved with Jessie. If so, he may be our killer."

She choked on her sip of water. "The mayor? Are you serious?"

Jackson put his finger to his lips. "I am serious. But you can't repeat that to anyone." It wasn't like him to talk about his cases with civilians, but after the front-page photo this morning, everyone in Lane County was talking about whether the mayor killed Jessie. Jackson felt like he had nothing left to lose with this one. If he was right, Fieldstone's career was toast anyway. If the mayor was clean, then Jackson was out of a job.

Kera suddenly closed her eyes and grimaced. Jackson jumped up.

"Are you okay? Should I get a nurse?"

She opened her eyes. "I'm fine. But I get these searing pains in my head every once in a while."

"What does your doctor say about that?"

"Be patient. They'll eventually go away."

"I should let you rest."

"Thanks for coming. I appreciate the company."

"When you're feeling better, I'll buy you that dinner I promised."

"Deal."

Jackson didn't want to let go of her hand. "See you soon."

On the way to pick up Katie, Jackson caught himself humming. It surprised him. The only time he hummed was when he was in his shop tinkering with the engine on his midnight blue, 1969 Pontiac GTO or while spreading bark mulch around the edge of his neatly mowed yard. Kera, he thought, smiling. What little he knew about her, he liked very much. He looked forward to their dinner together, which now seemed much like a date.

Katie bounded out of Emily's house before Jackson reached the door. He tried to give her a tight hug, but her bulging backpack got in his way. She gave him a quick squeeze, then wiggled free.

"It's only been a couple days, Dad."

"I'm just happy to see you."

They both climbed into his Impala.

"It stinks in here," Katie announced immediately.

"Sorry. Roll your window down a bit."

"It's too cold."

Jackson noticed she was wearing a tank top—with little bra straps showing—but nothing over it.

"Where's your coat?"

She turned away and he knew she was making a face. "I don't need one. Where are we going to lunch?"

"Your choice."

They ended up at Kowloons, eating spicy noodles and deep-fried shrimp. Jackson chowed down like a wilderness survivor—he'd missed many meals in the last four days—but Katie picked at everything. She wasn't skinny like most of her friends, and he knew she worried about it. He thought she looked fine, but he had learned not to make food-weight-body comments, even positive ones. Katie either got upset or shut down. And Jackson had something very important to talk to her about. He needed her to be open and friendly when he brought it up.

They talked about school ("boring"), soccer ("okay, but not as fun as she thought it would be"), and staying at Aunt Jan's ("fun, but too crowded after a while").

"When mom gets out of rehab, will you guys get back together?" she asked suddenly.

He hadn't seen that question coming. "Is that what she's saying?"

Katie squirmed in her seat. "Sort of."

"It's not that simple. My feelings for her have changed."

"If she stops drinking, could I go live with her?" Katie looked out the window at the millpond. "I mean, if I wanted to." She looked back at him. "Not that I do."

Jackson tried to smile, but he knew the effort was weak. He finished chewing his bite of shrimp but found it hard to swallow. "I don't know. We'll see if she gets sober."

His phone rang and Jackson looked at the number. It was the ME's office in Portland. "I have to take this, honey."

"That's okay. I need to go to the bathroom anyway." Katie scooted off.

"Detective Jackson? It's Debbie. I have the results on the first body standard you brought in."

"Don't keep me in suspense."

"It doesn't match the semen or the pubic hair found on Jessie."

The news hit him hard. Oscar Grady had not been involved with Jessie. Jackson had pushed an innocent man to suicide. Maybe not innocent, but not guilty of this murder.

"Detective?"

"Thanks, Debbie. Overnight me the report, okay?"

Jackson pushed his plate away. In a minute, Katie came back. Then the waitress brought a to-go box, poured more tea, and left. Jackson decided it was time to ask the question. It seemed even more important now.

"Why did you and Jessie stop being friends?"

Katie let out a groan. "I don't want to talk about it."

"Why not?"

"Because it was a long time ago. It's over. Forget it."

"What's over?"

"We stopped getting along, okay? Why are you trying to make something out of it now?" She slumped back against the booth and crossed her arms in front of her chest. Next, she would shut down or walk away.

"I'm asking now because Jessie was sexually active, with more than one person. And you used to be her best friend. Do you know who she was having sex with?"

Katie's eyes darted around the restaurant. "Will you please not talk to me about this right here?"

Jackson reached for his wallet. "Will you please just answer the question?"

"I can't." She scooted out of the booth. "I don't know what you're talking about."

Jackson watched his daughter through the giant windows as she hurried out to the Impala, only to find it locked. He watched her stamp her little foot and slump against the car. She was so young, and so worldly at the same time. He paid the bill, tipped the waitress, and strolled out to the car. Katie gave him a look to let him know she didn't like to be kept waiting.

When they were rolling down the road, he asked casually, "Have you had a sexual experience?"

"No!" She shouted in her best "Are you crazy?" voice. But she didn't look at him. And Jackson had taken his eyes off the road to watch her reaction. He decided he believed her.

He turned his attention to the street again and took a right on Coburg Road. "Do you want to attend her memorial service with me tomorrow?"

She chewed her pinkie nail. "No."

"Why not?"

"I don't like that church."

Jackson wanted to probe, but Katie was staring out the window, and he knew he had pushed far enough for now.

When they readed home, a dark blue sedan was parked on the street in front of the house. Jackson sent Katie inside as the car's driver got out and strode up the driveway. The man wore a dark blue suit and thick glasses. He looked about sixty and walked with a slight favor to his right leg.

"Detective Jackson? I'm Agent Daren Fouts with the Federal Bureau of Investigation."

Jackson smiled and shook the outstretched hand. Inwardly, he cringed. He had occasionally asked the FBI for help, but when they came to you, it meant they wanted to take over a case. "What can I do for you?"

"I'd like to discuss the Davenport homicide."

"What's your interest?" Jackson wanted desperately to sit down, but he wasn't going to invite Fouts into his home. He resented the fact that the agent had shown up here without calling.

"I think Davenport's death may be related to the attacks on the clinic and Kollmorgan," Fouts said.

"How so?"

"Nicole Clarke is one link. She's a friend of Jessie's, and her initials were on the ricin card."

"The initials NC were on the card. They could mean anything."

Fouts nodded. "Still, we're both trolling in the same pool of suspects—the Baptist church members—so I'd like to see the information your team has gathered."

"We're happy to share it. Why don't you join our task force meeting Monday morning?" Jackson took a step toward the house.

"I'd rather have the information right now." Fouts looked

irritated, his brows bunched up in the middle.

Jackson set his black bag on the roof of the car and dug out his case file. "Here's a list of church members. And you should also know that I'm likely to arrest someone for the homicide very soon. So this theory of overlap may be moot."

"Is your suspect a church member?"

"Yes. But he's also Eugene's mayor. And I don't think he had anything to do with bombing the clinic or poisoning Kera Kollmorgan."

"Hmm." Fouts seemed disappointed. "I think I'll talk to him anyway."

"No. Not yet. I'm very close to making an arrest. I don't want to spook him."

Fouts was unmoved. "I need to rule him out if he's not involved with the clinic attacks."

"This is my case. My suspect." Jackson heard his voice get loud, but was too tired to care. "I'm just asking you to back off Fieldstone for now. There are plenty of other church members to look at."

Fouts was silent for a moment. "What time is the meeting on Monday?"

"Ten sharp. See you then." Jackson walked away.

Sunday, October 24, 6:05 a.m.

WHEN A YOUNG blond nurse named Isaac roused her to take her pulse and blood pressure, Kera felt as if she had hardly slept. The hospital had been a cacophony of night sounds: squeaky wheels, muted conversations, doors opening and closing. She could not wait to leave. How did anyone get any rest here?

She put up with the unnecessary medical attention because Isaac was sweet and there was no point in taking out her ill humor on him. But she also requested that he bring her clothes.

"I don't think you're scheduled to leave this morning." He was soft spoken and polite too.

"Then this will be an unscheduled exit."

"I'll get your clothes, but I'm sure a doctor will want to see you first."

"He'd better hurry then." She smiled to let him know she had no hard feelings for him.

Kera stayed long enough to have a weak cup of coffee, an unsalted soft-boiled egg, and tasteless toast. None of it was satisfying, but she needed something to go on. Her doctor, whom she had not seen since the day before, never made it to her room to give her any parting advice.

She called Andrea, then got dressed and headed to the nurses' station. When the floor supervisor couldn't talk her out of leaving, Kera agreed to sign a paper saying she had checked out against medical advice.

Kera started to leave, then turned back. "Can you find out how Rebecca Dunn is doing?"

After a minute on the phone, the nurse said, "I'm sorry. She died yesterday."

Kera's throat, sore from the intubation tube, closed up completely. She walked away, biting back tears. On legs that felt like lead, she dragged herself to the elevator, each breath a sting to her injured lungs.

In the parking lot, a cold wind charged her weary body with a little surge of fresh energy. Damn, it was good to be outside. Patches of blue sky peeked out through the clouds, and Kera was grateful to be alive to see it.

After sleeping for a few hours at home, she woke with cottonmouth and a groggy brain. Aspirin, water, and strong coffee revived her enough to think she could go out. Kera dressed in black slacks and a black turtleneck. It would be more appropriate to wear a dress to Jessie's funeral, but she wasn't in the mood to totter around on heels.

Halfway down the hill on Chambers, her legs started to shake and she almost turned the car back. The thought of sitting through a memorial service so soon after Nathan's terrified her. So much grief concentrated in one room could tear a person to pieces.

Yet Kera felt compelled to go, even though she didn't really understand why. Was it regret that she hadn't been able to help Jessie? Sometimes she thought that if she had only said something different—something better—to Jessie that day in the clinic, or in the e-mail later, that her young client might have made a different choice and not met up with the man who had ultimately killed her. But that wasn't really rational. Jessie's fate was a complex tapestry of many choices and many circumstances, and Kera knew she had been only one small thread in the weave.

The red brick of the First Bible Baptist Church glinted in the harsh afternoon sunlight. Puddles from yesterday's rain were still evident in the parking lot, and a few black-clad mourners made their way up the front stairs. Kera moved slowly through the lot and into the church without directly encountering anyone. Apprehension gnawed at her stomach the moment she saw the church, and now that she was inside, she felt trapped. It was more than just the dark, windowless interior. A religious crackpot had just tried to kill her, so it was reasonable to be a little frightened of the faithful.

But in this case, the crowd—and its many witnesses—probably made her safe. The lobby was filled with men in dark suits, and a small group of elderly women stood near the double doors. Bits of conversation buzzed in her ears as Kera passed through the foyer into the main sanctuary.

...can't be true...I've know him for years...Judy hasn't been to church in weeks, but Jessie was here...where has Paul been while this was....

The spaciousness of the main sanctuary surprised her. So did the turnout. The chairs—in a semi-circle of tiered seating—were mosty full and faced a red-carpeted stage below. A pink and white casket stood in the center surrounded by a dozen floral arrangements.

Women and children were clustered in groups, quietly talking, praying, and crying. Kera glanced left and saw Jackson standing in a back corner of the room. His eyes moved slowly through the crowd, but his expression didn't change. She wondered if his daughter had come. If Katie was involved in the sex club, then she had most likely known Jessie well.

Kera decided it would be inappropriate to approach Jackson under the circumstances, so she took a seat in the opposite back pew, near the center and the exit doors. Kera always sat near an exit if she could, but today it felt more important than ever. A group of young girls around Jessie's age were seated two rows in front of her. Did any of them go by the screen names *perfectass* or *freakjob* she wondered? From the back, the girl on the left, with the long silky dark hair, could have been Nicole.

RUTH HAD JUST turned around to ask Joanne if she planned to attend the CCA meeting that evening, when the abortionist-whore waltzed into the church as if she owned the place. Her heart missed a beat and she stopped mid-sentence. It was all Ruth could do to keep from rushing up there and dragging the woman out by her hair. How dare she violate the sanctity of God's house! What was she doing here? First, she had propagandized Nicole at the school, and now she was here at Jessie's funeral.

Had she known Jessie?

For a moment, Ruth was confused. How would Kollmorgan know both Nicole and Jessie? What was going on? Then her head cleared. The abortionist did not know Jessie. Or Nicole. She was here looking for converts. She was an opportunistic vulture who sought out young girls to become advocates for her way of life. Ruth knew all about Planned Parenthood's teen outreach program. The way they used other teenagers to teach their peers about promiscuity.

She would put a stop to it immediately. The ricin had apparently been too subtle. Ruth made up her mind. The next bomb would be just for Kollmorgan.

"Ruth? What's wrong?" Joanne twisted her head around to see who Ruth was looking at.

Ruth leaned back over the pew, and Joanne met her halfway so Ruth could whisper in her ear. "See that woman in back? With the long reddish-brown hair?" They both stared. "Her name's Kera Kollmorgan. She's with Planned Parenthood."

Joanne looked at her with disbelief. "Why is she here?"

"She's recruiting."

"In church? At a funeral service?" Joanne's voice was no longer a whisper.

Ruth shook her head. "Kids are vulnerable when they're grieving."

Just then, Nicole got up from her seat, scooted into the aisle, and headed toward the back of the room.

NICOLE HURRIED UP the aisle, wishing she had gone to the bathroom sooner. The service was about to start, she could tell, because all the men were moving into the sanctuary. But she couldn't wait. Then she saw Kera, sitting in the back row, looking gorgeous and out-of-place in her snug turtleneck. What was she doing here? Nicole tried to look away, but Kera saw her, smiled, and lifted her hand in a small gesture of "hello."

Nicole was mortified. Angel and Rachel could be watching. Even worse, her mother could be watching. Nicole regretted talking to Kera that day at school. It had made her feel better at the time, but the feeling hadn't lasted. Her guilt had resurfaced as soon as stepped into her home and spent five minutes with her mother. Then the cops had come to her house and accused her of poisoning Kera. Nicole had been a nervous wreck ever since. She was glad to see that Kera was okay, but she prayed the nurse wouldn't try to talk to her here.

Nicole moved through the foyer and trotted downstairs to the restrooms, her intestines feeling like a pot of soup that was about to boil over. She desperately wished she could move forward in time a few years, past all the conflict and hypocrisy, to a point in her life where she could just be herself without any pressure from anyone.

Yesterday after the cops left, if Rachel hadn't been there to stop her, she might have lost it and told her parents everything. Of course, she was glad she hadn't. Her parents controlled her life so much already. If they knew the truth about Teen Talk, they would take away her cell phone and never let her out of the house by herself again. Nicole thought she might kill herself if it came to that. But she hated living the lie. She was trapped between two unacceptable situations and didn't know how to escape.

As she was leaving the bathroom, she heard the music start and she hurried upstairs. As she neared the top, Nicole heard her mother's voice—the familiar shrill whisper she used when things weren't going her way.

KERA FELT LIGHTHEADED. This woman—with her high forehead, tightly wrapped hair, and bulging eyes—was so vehement that her voice felt like a stick jabbing Kera in the chest. Kera had no idea who she was.

"How dare you come here to God's house. And at such a time, a memorial service for a child." A fine spray of spit flew from the woman's mouth, and her breath smelled like stale coffee and garlic. "You're immoral and disgusting."

Kera was too stunned to speak. As she struggled to draw air into her lungs, the woman's eyes tried to burn holes through her face. Finally, Kera said, "I'm here to pay my respects to Jessie."

"Respect? What do you know about respect? Just get out. And stay away from Nicole."

Ah. Nicole's mother. Kera tried to pull together an intelligent response, but her brain just wouldn't work. Dizziness overwhelmed her. She decided to skip the service and go home to lie down. As she turned, her knees went weak. As they were about to buckle, a strong arm went around her shoulders and held her up. She knew it was Jackson before looking up. His sea-breeze deodorant was becoming a comforting smell. He didn't speak until they were outside.

"You looked like you were going to pass out," he said. "Was it her breath?"

"The combination of garlic and self-righteousness can be overwhelming." Kera started to laugh, which made it even harder to breathe.

"You probably shouldn't be out wandering around just yet."

"You're probably right." She took several deep breaths, and the fog cleared a little.

"I think I should drive you home." Jackson was staring at her intently, as if looking for signs of something.

"I'm all right. But thanks."

"I'll follow you. If you start to feel compromised in any way, just pull over. I'll get you home."

"Thanks." Kera typically didn't like being fussed over, but the events of the last week had left her feeling vulnerable. And right now, she felt physically weak. It had been foolish to come here.

Sunday, October 24, 3:20 p.m.
JACKSON FOLLOWED KERA out of the parking lot, glad for the excuse to leave the service early. Although he had been to almost as many funerals as autopsies, he never became immune to a family's grief. Even the riffraff who were killed over bad drug deals had people who cared about them and depended on them for emotional support—and it was disturbing to witness their pain.

By the large turnout of mourners, it was clear that Jessie had been well loved, and the weeping would soon begin. His main objective in attending the service had been to see if the mayor would show and to scan the crowd for any known sex offenders. But he hadn't seen any. And after his front-page photo, Fieldstone was not likely to make any public appearances.

He tailed Kera home without incident. She got out of her car and turned to wave and smile at him. Jackson could have waved and driven on, but he didn't. He parked on the street and joined Kera in the driveway, where she waited and watched him approach.

"Feeling any better?"

"Not really. I shouldn't have gone out."

"Have you eaten anything lately?"

She laughed, a sound he had come to enjoy. "It always irritates me when people say they're so busy they forgot to eat," she said. "But I have not thought about food today. And that is very unusual for me."

Jackson reached for her elbow and steered her toward the house. "I'm not much of a cook, but if you've got some basics, I can come up with something."

KERA ENJOYED WATCHING Jackson scrounge through her kitchen and lament her lack of food supplies. It felt good to have someone here, in her home, complaining about something. He finally found a chicken breast in the freezer, which he thawed in the microwave, seasoned with parmesan cheese and garlic, and pan fried. While it was cooking, he nuked a can of cream of broccoli soup.

"Are you sure you won't eat too?" she asked. "I feel guilty about letting you cook for me."

"I just had lunch with my daughter, and I plan to go home and have dinner with her too. I haven't seen much of her since this case started, and she's probably feeling like an orphan."

"Her mother's not around?"

"Her mother is an alcoholic who can't be trusted with a child. That's why we're getting divorced." His kept his eye on the sizzling chicken as he talked, and Kera couldn't see his expression.

"That must have been a difficult marriage."

He laughed. "In the dictionary, next to 'difficult' is a picture of Renee." He turned to look at her. "So what happened to your marriage?" He gestured toward her left hand. "I notice that you used to wear a ring."

"You want the long version or the Cliff Notes?"

"You decide. I'm a good listener." The microwave timer went off and Jackson moved to take out the soup.

Kera plunged forward, feeling, for the first time, a little distance from the events. "In essence, when our son moved out, we lost our mutual focus, the thing that we had in common, and so we drifted apart. Then Nathan was killed in Iraq, and we both went a little crazy. Now Daniel's over in Iraq trying to get himself killed or find a new purpose in life. Either way, I'm not part of his plans."

He stood motionless and met her eyes. "I'm so sorry about your son."

"Thank you."

"And now you're dealing with the end of a marriage. Are you all right with that?"

"I don't know." Kera had avoided thinking about it, but now she made herself put it into words. "I'm a little scared. I'm a little lonely. But it also feels like a chance to start over, to build something new and better." She laughed. "If someone doesn't kill me first."

Jackson shut off the stove and sat down across from her. "You need to get a perimeter alarm system installed. And I'll arrange to have patrol units drive by here regularly for a while."

He reached over and grabbed her hands. A little surge of pleasure pulsed through her torso.

"And take down your mailbox," he insisted. "Rent a post office box instead, in another name."

"Good ideas. All of them."

They stayed like that for a moment, hands together, eyes locked, then Kera pulled away. "That chicken smells great. Is it done?"

"Yep."

He brought the food to her and she ate ravenously. Jackson drank a cup of coffee and watched her chew. Kera didn't care. For some reason, he didn't make her feel self-conscious. About halfway through her meal, Jackson's phone rang. He took the call, and moments later, an intense look of relief flooded his face.

"Thanks, Debbie. You're my hero." He snapped the phone shut and grinned. "I have to go."

"That must be good news."

"It is."

IF IT HAD BEEN anybody but Miles Fieldstone, Jackson would have made the arrest without hesitation. But this one called for him to cover his ass at every step. So as he drove away from Kera's, he called Chief Warner at home and interrupted his dinner.

"This better be good news, Jackson." Warner sounded like he'd had a beer or two.

"It's good news for Jessie." Jackson paused but the chief was silent. So he continued, "The DNA results are in. Grady, the now-dead sex offender, does not match. Fieldstone does. The mayor's pubic hair was found on Jessie's body. I intend to arrest him for rape and murder."

"No. Hold off on the murder charge."

Jackson had to unclench his teeth to speak. "I'd like to remind you that Jessie was suffocated and that the fibers in her nose and lungs match the mayor's sheets."

"It's not a 'match.' I've read the reports. Those fibers could have come from a hundred other sets of sheets in this town."

Since when did the chief read lab reports?

"Listen, Jackson. You don't know Miles the way I do. He's a good man. I don't believe he murdered that girl. And if you file a murder charge, people will never forget it, even if he proves himself innocent."

"It's the DA's decision."

"Slonecker will do the right thing."

"I believe he will, sir."

Jackson hung up. And had to resist the urge to throw the phone. Without the murder charge, a judge might not even set bail. Fieldstone would be walking around free while they tried to build a murder case against him.

He dialed Slonecker's number. Would the DA support him in defiance of the chief?

‹ 27 ›

Sunday, October 24, 8:35 p.m.

The mayor was watching a medical drama on television when his slightly drunk and worried wife escorted Jackson into their family room. The city's leader and Republican senate hopeful wore white sweat pants, a blue T-shirt, and red plaid slippers. Patriotic, but not cool for a trip to jail, Jackson thought.

"Miles Fieldstone."

The mayor looked up and his face tightened into a mask of controlled fury. "What now?"

Jackson held up his paperwork. "You're under arrest for the rape and murder of Jessie Davenport."

Through tight teeth, Fieldstone stood and said, "You're making a mistake."

"Turn around, please. I have to cuff you." Jackson checked his watch: 8:36.

"Can I get some things together?"

"That won't be necessary. They don't allow any personal items in jail." Jackson was suddenly worried that his suspect might try something. He was done being pleasant. "Let's go."

"Can I call my lawyer?"

"You can make that call when you're booked into the jail. Or your wife can do it now. Turn around."

The mayor complied. Janice Fieldstone started to cry as she watched the cuffs go on. Jackson let the man walk himself out to the Impala without a hand on his arm—a last moment of dignity.

He brought the mayor into the department for questioning before booking him into the jail. Now that he had physical evidence connecting Fieldstone to Jessie, Jackson half hoped to get the mayor to unburden himself. In trial, a confession was worth a ton of circumstantial connections. Jackson put his suspect in the small interrogation room with the ugly pink walls and let him sit for twenty minutes while he had a cup of coffee and called Evans, McCray, and Schakowski with the news. They were all coming in to have a celebratory drink later.

When he sat down across the table, Jackson tried to make eye contact, but the mayor wouldn't cooperate. Fieldstone's face had thinned some in the last week, and he had the dark under-eye circles of the sleep deprived. Jackson turned on the recorder and established the time, the date, and the participants. Then he launched into a new round of questioning.

"Your pubic hair was found in Jessie's genital area. So we know you had sex with her. Did you rape her?"

"I'm not talking without my lawyer."

"You could do yourself a lot of good right now by explaining your side of it. Everybody who saw the paper yesterday thinks you raped and killed that girl. And they don't even know about the physical evidence yet."

The mayor met Jackson's eyes long enough to say, "My lawyer has already filed the papers to sue you, the city, and the newspaper for that photo. You're going to lose both of the nickels you've accumulated."

"And you're going away for rape. And murder too. Unless you can explain what happened. Maybe negotiate a deal."

"I have nothing to say."

Jackson remembered Fieldstone was a lawyer. But that didn't mean the man was without emotion.

"You cared about Jessie didn't you?"

No response. Fieldstone stared off at the wall.

"I knew her." Jackson offered. "She was my daughter's best friend. The two of them hung out together at our house. I can see how a guy could be attracted to her. She knew how to make people feel special." The words coming out of his mouth revolted him, but Jackson needed to reach inside this guy and make some connection. He had to establish empathy before he could get a confession.

The mayor wasn't buying it.

Jackson tried a new tactic. Sometimes if you gave a killer an out, a way to minimize his crime, the suspect would grab onto it like a lifeline.

"I figure you probably didn't mean to kill her. Maybe she threatened to break it off or tell her mother. You got scared, threatened her, things got out of hand."

The mayor grunted. "You're wasting your time."

Jackson wasn't ready to give up. "The physical evidence will just keep coming. The lab found carpet fibers on Jessie's shoes. They're being compared to your carpet right now. And if Jessie drooled on your sheets, we'll know that soon too. You had sex with the girl, in your apartment, a stone's throw from where she was found dead. Any jury will convict you."

"A jury isn't likely to hear about any of it because of the way you handled the case." Fieldstone sounded more tired than smug.

Jackson took a long shot with speculative information. "When they hear that her baby's DNA matches yours, they'll give you the death penalty."

The mayor's eyes went wide. He tried to hide his reaction, but Jackson could tell he was stunned. Had Fieldstone not known about the pregnancy?

"Is that why you killed her? She wanted to keep the baby?"

Fieldstone closed his eyes and put his head down on the

table. After that, he did not look up or respond in any way. Jackson was disappointed but not surprised. This case would probably go the distance and take years to resolve in court, especially with all the political maneuvering. But their work on the case and the evidence his team had collected would stand the test of time.

Sunday, October 24, 6:23 p.m.
RUTH COULD FEEL her heart pounding in her fingertips and knew her blood pressure was off the charts. She'd been distressed since she'd seen Kera Kollmorgan at Jessie's service this afternoon and couldn't think about anything else. She'd warmed up frozen pizza and canned corn for dinner, of all the shameful things, because she was shaking too badly to fix a decent meal. Now Sam was preparing for their trip to Portland for the monthly CCA meeting.

"Sam, I'm too upset to go," she said, as he poured a thermos of decaf. "I think I'll stay home and pray."

He gave her a look. "Ruth, just take one of your anxiety pills. That's what they're for. The doctor said you won't get addicted if you only take them every once in a while."

Ruth hesitated, then decided it would be good to get her blood pressure down. She took the prescription bottle out of the cupboard above the sink and swallowed one of the tiny white tablets. She felt better just knowing it would kick in soon. Reverend John Strickland and his wife Eva would be here in a few minutes to pick them up in the church van. Then they would stop for Joanne and Steve Clarke. Judy and Paul Davenport used to ride with them to the CCA meetings too, before they divorced. Ruth felt guilty that she hadn't been to see Judy since Jessie's passing.

"Rachel, Caleb," she called the kids into the kitchen. The TV went mute, then moments later they were seated at the table looking a little bored. Her children had heard it a few times already, but Ruth gave them her standard lecture.

"We'll be gone until midnight. I expect you to behave the same when we're not here as when we are. God is watching you, and I will know if you break the rules. Do your homework, don't leave the house, and don't let anyone in. Don't test us. You know the consequences."

The first half of the trip was a little tense for Ruth. The group talked briefly about Jessie's death, then moved on to CCA business. Their new project was a voter initiative aimed at changing the state law that allowed minors to get an abortion without telling their parents. It was Ruth's idea, and she knew it would be a tough battle. The language of the TV commercials supporting the initiative would have to be carefully crafted. Ruth suggested hiring a marketing firm. Reverend Strickland objected. He was seated in front of her and made a point to turn and give Ruth a disapproving look. She was not concerned. Only God could judge her, and He thought she was doing fine.

Then the conversation shifted, and Eva began to chatter about her daughter and how nerve-racking it was teaching Angel to drive now that the girl had her learner's permit. About that time, Ruth's Ativan kicked in and she was able to tune out the others and focus on her personal objectives.

In simple terms: Kera Kollmorgan had to be stopped. She could not be allowed to continue her ruthless recruitment of Christian kids. First at the school, then at church—the woman's audacity knew no limits. The poisoning incident apparently hadn't convinced the abortionist-whore to back off. What else could Ruth do? It was time to send Kollmorgan to the fires of hell where she belonged.

Monday, October 25, 8:30 a.m.

KERA SLEPT LATE, ate a big breakfast of scrambled eggs and yogurt, then, with the phone book in front of her, called alarm installation companies until she found one that could come out the next day. She made an appointment for Tuesday morning at 10:15. Sheila had told her to take off all the time she needed, and Kera figured she would take at least a day or two. She told herself that her body needed time to heal, but in truth, she was a little afraid to step out her front door.

Later she checked her phone messages. There were three from her sister who lived over the mountains in Bend. On her last two messages, Janine sounded a little panicked that Kera had not returned her calls, but Kera didn't think Janine knew about the ricin incident. The hospital staff had not found her relatives, and once she was conscious, Kera had instructed them not to look. Her family worried about her enough already. But she called Janine back to reassure her sister that everything was fine.

But Janine had heard about the bomb and was not reassured. "Please get out of that clinic. As a skilled nurse, you can work anywhere." This was her family's consistent theme. Every time they saw abortion clinic violence on TV, they called her and begged her to find a new position.

"I'm not letting one fanatic drive me away from a job I love. What if everyone at the clinic quit? Where would kids and poor women go for birth control?"

"Let someone else do it for a while. You've paid your dues."

"We've hired a security guard. And the FBI is investigating. I'll be okay." That's what she kept telling herself. "But as long as we're talking about this, I want to let you know that I'm changing my will to make you my beneficiary and executor."

"Why are you telling me this?" Janine's voice pitched even higher.

"I'm just taking care of business. Daniel isn't coming back from Iraq, and I believe our marriage is over, so if anything happens to me, you have to take charge."

"I don't want to hear this."

"Relax. It's just me being anal. I'm not going to die."

While Kera was checking online news sites, the alarm company called and said they couldn't be out until Thursday. When she tried to explain the urgency of her situation, they suggested she hire a bodyguard. Kera thanked the man in a less-than-gracious tone and hung up. She grabbed the phone book, thinking she would start over, but now she had one of those blinding headaches, so she went back to bed instead.

Monday, October 25, 8:45 a.m.
FIELDSTONE'S ARRAIGNMENT was held in a small courtroom inside the Lane County jail. There were no spectators, no family supporters, just a few harried public defenders and five inmates in dark green prison garb that looked just like nursing scrubs: no buttons, no zippers, no strings.

Fieldstone, with his good looks, tanned skin, and full set of teeth, stood out from the other prisoners, most of whom had never seen a dentist. Roger Barnsworth, Fieldstone's silk-clad attorney, looked out of place among the more modestly dressed public defenders. Next to Barnsworth sat a younger man in a business suit. His cropped blond hair and square jaw gave him a no-nonsense appearance.

Jackson caught himself staring. Who was this guy? And why was he at Fieldstone's arraignment?

He soon found out. When the proceeding opened, Barnsworth stood up and said, "I move to dismiss all charges, Your Honor."

"On what grounds?" Judge Morrison looked liked a salt-and-pepper version of Val Kilmer.

"We have an eye witness who places my client a mile from the scene of the crime during the one-hour window for the time of death."

Jackson groaned. It was partially audible, and Barnsworth glanced his way.

"Please come forward for a conference."

Barnsworth and Slonecker both approached the judge, who was seated about five feet from the front bench. There were no tables in the tiny room. During the three-minute discussion, Barnsworth gestured at the crew-cut man twice. Jackson concluded that he was the witness.

When the lawyers returned to their seats in the benches, Judge Morrison said, "Motion denied. On the matter of bail–"

Barnsworth stood again. "I move for nominal bail. My client has no criminal record and an exemplary history of public service."

Morrison didn't hesitate. "These are serious charges. Motion denied. Bail is set at five hundred thousand dollars. The preliminary hearing is scheduled for one o'clock, November 29. Next case."

The witness had come out of nowhere, and Jackson felt his case get shaky. They would need much more than a pubic hair to convict Fieldstone of murder. A lot of wealthy people wanted the mayor to beat the charges, so raising the fifty thousand needed for a bond would be easy. Fieldstone would be out of jail by late afternoon, free to destroy evidence and bribe more witnesses.

A few minutes before 10 a.m., Slonecker showed up in the conference room with a load of coffee and pastry from Full City. The task force was already there, but Agent Fouts had not made an appearance. While they nibbled on coffee cake, Slonecker launched into a speech about documenting the relationship between Fieldstone and Jessie.

"I want witnesses. People who saw them together." The DA rubbed his hands as he talked. "We have enough physical evidence to convince a jury the mayor had sex with Jessie right before her death. But now that he has a witness—even a bogus one—our challenge is to convince the jury that no one but the mayor could have killed her and dumped her in the trash."

Jackson was pleased with Slonecker's passion. The DA had been lukewarm about filing the murder charge, especially knowing that the chief of police was opposed to it. But Fieldstone's phony witness seemed to have lit a fire under him. Before Jackson could say anything, Agent Fouts walked in.

"I apologize for being late," he said without sounding sorry. "I had an unexpected call from my supervisor this morning."

Jackson introduced everyone, then turned to Fouts. "Miles Fieldstone has been charged with rape and murder in the Jessie Davenport case. He's currently in custody."

"I'd like to interrogate him about the bombing and ricin incidents."

Jackson hesitated, then thought, maybe a little more fear would be good for Fieldstone. "If that's what you want to do."

"It is." Fouts pulled his lips back in what was supposed to be a smile. "I also need access to all your case notes."

"Of course. Everyone, hand your notes to McCray, who will photocopy them for Agent Fouts."

With obvious skepticism, Slonecker asked, "You think the mayor bombed the Planned Parenthood Clinic?"

Fouts scowled. "I didn't say that. I'm just trying to be thorough." The agent's phone rang and he stepped out of the room to take the call. McCray followed with the paperwork.

Slonecker said, "Where were we?"

"You were talking about witnesses," Evans reminded him.

"Right. I want you guys to re-canvass the area around the dumpster. I want someone who saw the mayor that afternoon."

Just then, the door swung open and Robert Zapata, from the missing persons office, charged into the conference room. "Excuse me, I'm sorry for interrupting. But I have a case that might interest you." Zapata's mustached face was unusually flustered.

Jackson instantly got an oh shit vibe. "Tell us."

"Nicole Clarke left her home last night sometime between 6 and 10 p.m. and did not return. Her parents are hysterical because of what happened to Jessie Davenport. Apparently, the two girls were friends. This is why I'm telling you."

The oh shit feeling slid into Jackson's bowels and squeezed. "Are her parents here now?"

Zapata nodded. "They're pretty upset. They called dispatch last night and a patrol officer went to the house and took statements. But there were no signs of struggle, the girl is fourteen, and her parents admitted that she'd been out late on a previous occasion. So Officer Parsons sent out an Amber Alert and told the Clarkes that was all he could do, and if they hadn't heard from her by this morning, they should come in and fill out a missing persons report. Now they're here, and they want to know why we haven't called out the National Guard."

Jackson stood up and took a deep breath. "I'll go talk to them."

The Clarkes were both pencil thin, with pinched faces, dull brown hair, and big glasses. They could have been brother and sister. Except Mrs. Clarke also had a long forehead with a deep crease from years of scowling. Zapata had put them in the soft brown interview room, and they huddled close together on the big leather couch. Joanne's pink sweater was the only bright thing about the couple. But her eyes were swollen with tears just waiting to overflow.

Jackson introduced himself and sat down across from them. Zapata sat in a chair off to the side with his notes in hand. Neither parent moved to shake Jackson's hand. They just nodded.

Before Jackson could speak, Joanne blurted out, "Why isn't anybody looking for my daughter?"

"An Amber Alert went out last night, and search and rescue teams will get involved now. But I need to ask you some questions before I can investigate."

"We've been through this twice now," Steve Clarke spoke up.

"I know. I'm sorry. Tell me again. Were you home last night?"

"No. We went to a meeting in Portland. A Conservative Culture Alliance meeting." Mr. Clarke tugged at his tie. Jackson realized he was probably still wearing his Sunday church clothes. "We left the house around six o'clock. Nicole was home by herself."

Mrs. Clarke cut in. "Nicole's fourteen and a half and very responsible."

"When did you get home?"

"Just before midnight." Joanne took the lead again. She leaned forward, as if she could will Jackson into doing something with the force of her physical presence. "We go the first Sunday of every month, and we've never had a problem before. Nicole wouldn't just take off. Something terrible has happened, I just know it."

"I assume you've called all her friends?"

"Of course. We called last night and again this morning. We called every place she could possibly be."

"Do you have a picture of her with you?"

"We gave one to Officer Parsons and one to Officer Zapata."

Robert opened his file folder and handed the five-by-seven photo to Jackson. The picture didn't do Nicole justice, Jackson thought. She had seemed quite pretty that day in the school office with her orange blouse and shiny dark hair.

"Let's notify the local media that she's missing. Get her picture out to the public."

The Clarkes perked up at the idea, but Jackson was not optimistic.

‹ 29 ›

TRAVIS WALTERS and Jeremy Carson left school at noon in Travis' 95 Toyota Corolla and headed up Willamette Street. Their destination was Edgewood Park near the base of Spencer Butte. It was at the edge of the city limits, in a large wooded area between two new upscale housing developments. They had an hour for their lunch break, the sun was shining, and they intended to enjoy their free time. On the way, they rocked with Kid Rock, and Jeremy rolled a joint from a small bag of pot he'd swiped from his cousin. Jeremy started to light the joint, but Travis protested.

"Not in the car. My parents will smell it." Travis had only had his license for three months, and he didn't want to lose it yet.

"Pussy."

"Shut up."

Once they reached the park, they took off on foot for a place known as Party Rock. It was a massive granite outcropping that overlooked a small shaded valley covered with ferns. The view wasn't that great, but they had the place to themselves and a bright blue sky to sit under.

They smoked the joint without much discussion. Afterward they talked about a girl they both liked, then had a contest to see who could throw a rock the farthest. Travis won by a good thirty feet.

"Who's the pussy now?" he gloated.

Jeremy flipped him off, then demonstrated his ability to

stand on his hands for three minutes. Travis was impressed every time he saw the display.

Travis checked his watch. It was 1:25 and they had already missed half of fifth period. "Oh crap. We gotta go. I can't miss algebra again or Peterson will call my parents."

"And then you'll get grounded?" His friend used one of his annoying voices.

"That's right."

Travis started down the trail back to the parking area. Then wham! Jeremy shoved him off the path and onto the slope. He landed face-first in a bed of ferns.

"Fucker!" Travis yelled, spitting greenery out of his mouth.

Jeremy laughed like a donkey.

Travis put his hands out to push himself up and encountered something strange with his right fingers. It was smooth and cool and a little squishy. He clambered to his feet and stepped down the slope to investigate.

It was a leg. A bare human leg.

"Holy shit. Check this out."

Jeremy trotted down as Travis pushed some ferns aside for a better look.

"It's a girl."

"She's naked." Jeremy said.

"She's dead." Travis added.

"Are you sure?"

"Her skin is cold. I accidentally touched it."

"Jesus. This is creepy." Jeremy stepped toward the body. "Let's roll her over and look at her tits."

Travis pulled him away. "Don't touch her, you retard."

"Check this out," Jeremy said, reaching down through a clump of ferns next to the body. He came up with a cell phone. "I'll bet it's hers." He grinned. "Was hers. Now it's mine."

"That's sick, even for you." Travis just wanted to get out

of there. "Let's go. We have to tell the police."

"No way. I'm not talking to the police. I'm too stoned."

"I'll call them when we get back into town."

Monday, October 25, 2:07 p.m.

JACKSON GOT THE call as he waited to meet with Sergeant Lammers to discuss Nicole's disappearance. The dispatcher tried to sound detached, but her voice was shaky. "We just got a call about a body in Edgewood Park," she said. "The dead person is reportedly a young female."

The city had never had back-to-back homicides of young girls. Jackson felt a little shaky too.

"Any ID on the caller?"

"He wouldn't identify himself, and the call came from a cell phone with a blocked caller ID. He sounded like a high school kid. Maybe a little scared. Maybe a little high."

"What exactly did he say about the location of the body?"

She hesitated, as if to read her notes. "It's on the right side of the trail near Party Rock. That's a place where–"

"I've heard of it. You know the drill: Get the ME and the DA's office out there ASAP."

Jackson left a message with Lammers, then went in search of his task force team. His afternoon coffee burned in his stomach. What in the hell was going on? If the body was indeed Nicole Clarke, then his theory that the mayor had killed his teenage girlfriend because she was pregnant might be shot to hell. He could be dealing with his first serial killer. Was Agent Fouts on the right track?

Schakowski and McCray had gone out to re-canvass the neighborhood around Jessie's crime scene, but Evans was at her desk.

"We've got another one," he announced.

"Another what?" She looked up, not understanding.

"A body in Edgewood Park. Another young girl."

"Shit." Evans was up and moving as she swore. They left the building without speaking again. By the time they hit the parking lot, they were moving at a run.

"Fieldstone was in custody last night," Evans said, as Jackson punched the Impala out into the street.

"He may have an accomplice."

Evans gave him a look. "That would be unusual."

"But not unheard of." Jackson suddenly felt defensive about his push to nail Fieldstone. The evidence had led him to a viable suspect, and he wasn't ready to toss that out. But if a girl had been killed while the mayor was in custody...

Shit.

On that Monday afternoon in late October, there was only one car in Edgewood's unpaved parking lot—a faded red Toyota Celica—and its owners were nowhere in sight. Jackson had drunk an occasional beer on Party Rock during his senior year at Spencer High. And he'd been up here once since, during his third year as a patrol officer, in response to a 911 call about a stabbing. They had arrested the remorseful drunk without incident.

Jackson grabbed his black bag from the floor of the back seat as Evans climbed out of the car. Before taking off, he called Sergeant Lammers again. This time she picked up, and he requested a canine unit. She respected his need for speed and refrained from asking too many questions. "Full report before the day is over," she concluded.

Jackson hustled to catch up with Evans, who had already crossed the clearing and was standing at the head of the trail. As they hiked uphill, the cool damp pine smell brought back memories of camping trips to Silver Lake with his father and brother. Jackson missed those moments of stillness and crisp air. Why hadn't be been camping in the last ten years? Oh yeah. His daughter hated to be away from her blow dryer and cell phone, even for a weekend, and Renee hated the outdoors. He had one of those rare moments when he wished he'd had a son. It came and went before he had a chance to feel guilty.

The trail was not a government-maintained hiking venue, so it was kept clear only by foot traffic. There were plenty of deep gouges in the dirt, and in places, fir boughs had to be pushed aside to pass. But overall, the path was well worn and clear of debris, except for the occasional cigarette butt. The distance to the rock was less than half a mile, so he kept looking down the slope side as he walked.

In a few minutes, he spotted a place where the ferns and other foliage had been trampled. From the trail, he could see patches of naked flesh among the greenery.

"There she is."

Jackson hesitated before moving down for a closer look at the body. There was an opportunity—at this moment—to look around the whole area before it was overrun with investigative personnel and search dogs.

"Let's look at the trail for a minute first," he said to Evans without looking back. He started down the path again. Immediately, a pattern emerged in the dirt under his feet.

"This is interesting."

Jackson stepped to the side of the trail, squatted down, and began to take pictures. Two faint, parallel lines ran lengthwise along the trail, stopping and starting between the footprints.

"It looks as if something has been dragged," Evans said.

"Or someone." Had the marks been made by the heels of the dead girl as she was dragged from further up the trail?

Keeping to the side so that they wouldn't smudge the parallel marks, he and Evans moved down the path. Along the way, Jackson stopped to pull on latex gloves, then bagged and tagged a cigarette butt. It looked as if it had been exposed to the elements for some time, but it would be foolish to ignore it on that assumption.

As the trail reached the wide flat area that merged into the rock outcropping, Jackson took more photos of the drag marks. They were more distinct here but had still been smudged in places by shoe prints. The marks faded as the dirt turned to rock.

"Those look like skater shoe marks," Evans commented.

"Probably the kid who called it in."

The outcropping was about thirty feet wide and fairly flat. A pocket in the gray and red rock contained the remnants of a freshly smoked joint and several not-so-fresh cigarette butts. Evans took notes, while Jackson put each of the evidence pieces into its own small brown bag.

"I'm surprised there are no empty alcohol containers," Evans said with genuine surprise. "I thought kids came up here to drink."

"There's probably enough empty cans and bottles in the brush below to keep a transient happy for life." Jackson wondered what else was down there in the brush. A murder weapon? The girl's clothes? He would leave that search for the canine unit.

"Let's go look at the body."

To preserve the footprints so the evidence tech could make casts, they kept to the side of the trail by stepping in the foliage. Evans expressed gratitude that the recent rain hadn't turned the area into a mud slough. Jackson wondered about the killer's activities. Why had he dragged the body back down the trail instead of dumping it off the rock? Because there was less chance of it being seen here?

When he spotted the pale flesh among the green, Jackson took three long strides down the slope, being careful not to step on exposed dirt and leave footprints. He kept his feet on the short ferns that had already been flattened by the killer, the victim, and/or the person who had found her. Or had the killer called in the body himself? A psycho might do that as part of the game. Evans followed him, taking giant steps to stay in the same areas.

The girl was face down, nude, and unbruised. A couple of small scratches on her back and legs looked postmortem, probably made when she was dragged or rolled down the slope. Jackson snapped a few photos. Her long dark hair was bunched around her head but was surprisingly free of twigs or leaves. He took a close-up shot of her heels, which were darkened with dirt, supporting his theory that someone had held her by the armpits and dragged her along the path.

Jackson gently rolled the body onto its side. Nicole's dark brown eyes stared up at him. He tried to remember what she had looked like that day in the school office, before death distorted her pretty face. Nicole had been grieving for Jessie and nervous about talking to him.

Now she'd been dead long enough for blood to pool in her face, giving her skin a purplish tint. A spider had chewed its way across her left cheek, leaving a series of nasty red bumps. And maggots were feeding in her ears. Jackson pressed a gloved finger against her face. When he pulled away, the color didn't change. The lividity told him three things: Nicole had been killed out here at least six hours ago, and had been left lying on her face soon after her death.

After a moment, he said, "She looks like Jessie did, naked but with no obvious abrasions or trauma."

"It's odd, isn't it?" Evans mused.

He knew what she meant. The girls' unmarred bodies didn't seem to be the handiwork of a sexual predator, but what else would explain their deaths? The fact that the two girls were friends indicated that the killer identified his victims through the school or church and probably knew both girls, at least superficially.

Jackson thanked God that Katie no longer hung out with that group. But that did not mean she was safe. She would not be safe until this sicko was in permanent custody. Jackson could feel a stress headache coming on. Was he completely wrong about the mayor? Had Fieldstone screwed Jessie but not killed her? None of it fit together.

He heard voices coming, so he gently lowered Nicole back to her face down position and moved up the embankment to the trail. Evans stayed with the body.

Sergeant Brian Riggs came down the path leading a German shepard. Jackson had worked with Riggs before, sometimes cooperatively, sometimes not. They shook hands.

"This is Daisy," Riggs said, scratching the dog's head. "So what's the situation here?"

"We have a dead girl, most likely a homicide victim. I need you to search the area for her clothes or anything that may have been left by her killer." The dog whined with impatience.

About then, a young female evidence tech, dressed in dark blue coveralls, came up the path followed by the county ME. Gunderson, who had processed Jessie's body at the scene, asked Jackson, "Do we have a serial killer?"

"Maybe."

Gunderson glanced at Jackson's gloved hands. "Did you touch the body?"

"I rolled her up on her side to see if I recognized her."

Gunderson gave him a look. "And?"

"I believe it's Nicole Clarke, our missing person. I need the time of death ASAP. I need to know if she was killed before or after I arrested Fieldstone."

"I'll do what I can."

Gunderson and Riggs moved down to where the girl lay. The evidence tech introduced herself as Jasmine Parker, then began to make casts of the shoe prints on the path.

Jackson thought about Nicole's parents, anxious and upset and waiting to hear something—anything. Jackson believed it was his responsibility to tell them, but he didn't want to leave the scene or make them wait until he returned. He called Zapata and asked him to break the news to her parents. Ultimately, the Clarkes would have to look at the body and confirm that it was Nicole. He could not imagine how horrific that moment would be. Jackson hoped God would spare him from ever having to go through that. Then he felt guilty for the thought. He didn't deserve any special treatment.

After a minute, Riggs came back up with Daisy, who was straining on her leash, anxious to follow a scent. Then the two were off toward the rock outcropping. Jackson moved down the slope, so he could listen to Gunderson as he examined the body.

"She's still in full rigor mortis," the ME was saying as he lifted her limbs. "So she's been dead at least twelve hours, but less than thirty." He looked up at Jackson. "So that means sometime between 9:30 yesterday morning and 3:30 this morning."

"Her parents saw her at six o'clock last night," Jackson said.

"So that narrows it down even further." Gunderson shoved a long thermometer into the girl's rectum. After a moment, he said. "Body temp is sixty-one, only five degrees warmer than the air, so she's had about twenty-one hours to cool, give or take an hour on either side."

Jackson calculated the time in his head.

"Between 7:30 and 9:30 last night." Gunderson said it out loud a moment before Jackson reached the same conclusion.

Jackson groaned. "I arrested Fieldstone at 8:36. And this park is only a ten-minute drive from his house on Blanton Heights. So he could have done it and been home by the time I showed up to arrest him."

"Don't get worked up yet," Gunderson said. "I'm not done. Some of these bugs crawling out of her nose might narrow the time down even further."

"Was she raped?"

"I don't see any bruising or tearing or signs of semen."

That seemed consistent with Jessie's death, but inconsistent for a serial killer. But not unheard of. Some psychopaths were impotent, which was part of the insecurity that drove them to kill. Now that Jackson knew Nicole could have died before Fieldstone was in custody, his theory pingponged back to the mayor. Fieldstone could have been screwing Nicole too. If she had seen him on the evening news and questioned him about Jessie's death, the mayor may have killed her to keep her quiet.

Jackson would ask the state lab to compare Nicole's DNA with the secretions on the orange panties found in the mayor's love nest. But in the meantime, he and his team would look at serial killer profiles and widen their investigation of sexual predators. The investigation was suddenly an open field again.

"This is interesting." Gunderson said suddenly.

Jackson stepped closer, as Evans said, "What?"

"A tiny piece of thin white plastic is caught in her earring. And there's a light crease in the skin on her throat." Gunderson looked up. "She may have been suffocated with a plastic bag that was held tightly around her neck."

"A second suffocation," Jackson said.

"Same method, but different material," Evans noted. "So he uses whatever is handy."

Gunderson grunted in response, then they were all quiet for a moment. The ME took several close-up photos of Nicole's neck and ear, then bagged some of the insects crawling out of the girl's ears.

Jackson turned away from the sight. For the first time, he thought about leaving this line of work. He could get a job as an investigator with the DA's office. He would never again have to look at the lifeless body of a young person—while his own daughter fended for herself. If he had been forced to choose at that moment—here with the dead girl or home with his daughter—he would have taken off his shield and walked away.

A wave of anxiety rolled through him. Was Katie in danger? Should he hire a bodyguard for her?

As they processed the scene, the bright afternoon gave way to a dark sky, and the wind whipped their jackets. In the distance, Jackson could hear the dog's excited barking.

A few minutes later, Riggs and Daisy came down the trail from Party Rock. Riggs carried a bulging white plastic bag—similar to the ones offered in grocery and retail stores.

"We found her clothes," Riggs called out.

Gunderson and his assistant were in the process of getting Nicole into a body bag to carry her out. They both looked up.

Jackson yelled, "Careful with that plastic bag, it may be the murder weapon."

Riggs was wearing latex gloves and had a good grip on one corner. He shrugged and said, "Okay."

Jackson pulled out a large brown paper sack from his shoulder bag and took possession of the evidence, putting the plastic bag full of clothes into the larger paper bag. "Anything of the killer's?"

"Not yet."

"What all is in there?"

"Jeans, T-shirt, panties, rubber sandals."

"Any personal stuff? Cell phone or purse?"

"Nope."

"Let's keep looking then."

As Gunderson and the technician carried the body up the embankment, Jim Trang, an assistant DA, showed up, and Riggs went back to his search. Jackson brought the ADA up to speed on the new homicide.

If Nicole had died before the mayor was taken into custody, they could file a murder charge and get his bail revoked.

But if she died while Fieldstone was in jail, a good defense attorney would use the second murder to claim there was a viable, alternative suspect for the first.

And probably win him an acquittal.

‹ 30 ›

Monday, October 25, 6:43 p.m.

RUTH AND RACHEL were in the kitchen cleaning up after a pork roast dinner when the phone rang. "It's either solicitors or someone from the church," Ruth said before picking it up. "No one else uses our land-line anymore." She greeted the caller cheerfully. "Hello. This is the Greiners."

"Ruth, it's Eva. I have some very bad news."

Ruth felt her blood pressure surge. "What is it?"

"Nicole Clarke is dead. They found her body this afternoon. Joanne and Steve are completely distraught, of course, so a group of us are going over to pray with them."

"Oh dear Lord."

Rachel was suddenly at her elbow asking, "What's going on?"

Ruth waved her daughter away and focused on getting information from Eva. "How did she die?"

"I'm not sure. They found her in Edgewood Park." Eva paused and Ruth heard her fighting back sobs. "She's been missing since last night. But, of course, you knew that. They called everyone they could think of when she didn't come home."

Ruth had not known Nicole was missing. Had Joanne called here last night? Ruth had taken a second Ativan in the middle of the CCA meeting, and things were a little blurry after that. She must have slept on the way home.

"I'll be over in a little while. Joanne must be out of her mind."

When Ruth hung up the phone, her daughter grabbed her arm. "Tell me what's happening."

"Sweetie, let's sit down."

Rachel's hand tightened on her arm. "Just tell me."

Ruth led her to a seat at the dining room table. After a deep breath she said, "Nicole is dead. They found her in the park."

"What?" Her daughter looked confused, as if the information didn't make sense. Ruth could sympathize.

"I don't have any more detail than that. Except that she's been missing since last night." Ruth put her hand on Rachel's shoulder even though Rachel didn't like to be touched. "Did Joanne call here last night looking for her?"

Rachel nodded. "You were asleep. She wanted to know if I had seen Nicole, but I hadn't." Rachel started to cry. "I didn't think anything was really wrong. I can't believe she's dead."

Ruth hugged her daughter, but after a moment, Rachel pushed her away. "First Jessie, now Nicole. What's going on, Mom? Is it a serial killer? Am I next?"

"Don't say that, honey. God will keep you safe. Let's go over to the Clarkes and pray with them. They need all the support they can get."

"Where's Dad?"

"He's teaching a Bible class. But go get Caleb. I don't want to leave him home alone."

On the drive over, Ruth's thoughts turned to Kera Kollmorgan. She had seen the abortionist-whore talking to Nicole at school last Thursday. And earlier last week, Ruth thought she'd seen Jessie at the Planned Parenthood clinic, where Kollmorgan worked. Coincidence? Ruth didn't think so. But was Kollmorgan a killer?

Of course she was! She murdered babies for a living. But why would she kill young girls? Was she a psycho? A lesbian rapist serial killer? Or was she working with some sick guy? Ruth had read about couples who kidnapped, raped, and tortured young girls. Maybe Kollmorgan was part of a demented team.

"Mom!"

Ruth looked up to see a car stopped directly in front of her. She slammed on the brakes.

"Jesus! Pay attention," Rachel snapped at her from the passenger's seat.

Ruth backhanded her daughter hard. But Rachel had seen it coming and pulled away. The blow glanced off. "Don't ever take the Lord's name in vain or speak to me in that tone. We will deal with this when we get home."

Rachel scrunched herself against the door and faced out the window. Caleb had the good sense to keep his head in his Game Boy. Ruth was so fed up with her daughter's attitude. Kids today had no idea how easy their life was with their computers and cell phones and no younger siblings to care for. So little was expected of them, and they were so ungrateful. The discipline she and Sam administered to their kids was nothing compared to the beatings Ruth had received from her mother for the smallest offenses.

Ruth pulled into the small shopping center on 30th Avenue and parked in front of the Sweet Deal bakery. The kids waited in the car while she picked out a coffee cake for the prayer group. An offering of food would excuse her for leaving early. After an hour, she would take the kids home, drop them off, then do some reconnaissance for where she would plant the bomb that would stop Kera Kollmorgan once and for all.

Monday, October 25, 6:01 p.m.

STILL TIRED FROM her poisoning ordeal, Kera lay down on the couch after dinner to watch the news. National news was more of the same: the war in Iraq, government corruption, the mid-term elections. But the local news caught her attention. KRSL's Trina Waterman led off with "And now we bring you the latest in Eugene's crime wave."

First Waterman recapped the clinic bombing, including an update that Rebecca Dunn had died as a result of her injuries, then reported that the FBI was working the case. The anchorwoman followed up with a second story:

And in yet another bizarre incident, a Planned Parenthood staff member was poisoned with deadly ricin through her personal mail. She was rushed to the emergency room where she almost died. The victim is still recovering and has not returned to work at the clinic. Other Planned Parenthood staff members also received threatening letters signed "God's Messenger."

A source at Planned Parenthood says they receive religious letters quite frequently, but the poisoning incident is the first of its kind. The clinic has added a security guard and says the FBI will screen all its mail for a while.

And in another case, this morning Mayor Miles Fieldstone was arraigned on charges of statutory rape and murder in connection with the death of fourteen-year-old Jessie Davenport. Jessie, who had recently been a client at Planned Parenthood, was found in a dumpster last Tuesday with the cause of death reported as suffocation. Mayor Fieldstone was not available for comment.

Kera did not hear the rest of the report. She was too upset that someone had told the media about Jessie's visit to the clinic. Who would do that? And why? And what would that breech of confidence do to the trust Planned Parenthood had built up with the community's young people?

And the ricin incident. Someone at the hospital must have talked to a reporter. Kera didn't care much that her personal drama had been made public, but these stories would hurt the clinic's business. Their clients were already scared. If enough people stayed away, the parent foundation would have to close the clinic.

Kera went to the kitchen and poured a glass of wine, then took it to her computer desk. She could not even look at news sites. Her thoughts kept swirling around her own small reality—the bomb, the poison, the deaths of Jessie and Rebecca. Right now, her whole existence seemed to be about survival. The fact that she was still alive while others around her were dying left her with a fair amount of guilt. Her life was no more valuable than others. And yet she would fight for it with everything she had.

Instinctively, Kera ended up on the girlsjustwanttohavefun.com site. She hadn't planned to go back there; she didn't want that much detail about these girls' sex lives. But she couldn't shake the idea that somewhere in all that detail was a clue to who had killed Jessie.

After landing on the wild-colored main page, Kera clicked open Sex Talk, found nothing new, then opened the Dirty Gossip link. She scrolled down through some talk between *socccerstar* and *tigertoo* about a girl named Dana who had supposedly, while high on meth, had sex with her stepbrother, then was sent away to a reform camp somewhere in the woods of California. If it was true, Kera felt sorry for Dana. Those correction camps could be brutal.

After a discussion about a life-skills homework assignment, the page ended. Kera clicked through two more subpages—Disgusting Guys and Hot Guys—without finding any postings from the sex club members: *racyG*, *perfectass*, *freakjob37*, or *lipservice*. Annoyed by the content and frustrated by her lack of progress, Kera almost gave up. Then it occurred to her that each of the chat rooms had its own list of users who could access it. She decided to check the Parties page.

A chat was in progress about a party that was happening after the dance that Friday night. The discussion was about who they could get to buy beer. A chatter named jellybean said her brother might. Then a new posting popped up:

lipservice: You are not going to believe this but Nicole Clarke is dead. My mom just got a call from her prayer group asking her to pray for the Clarkes because of what happened to Nicole. This is so freaky.

The news hit Kera like a punch in the gut. As she sat there, stunned, follow-up postings appeared on screen.

jahnboy: So what happened to her?
lipservice: I don't really know. They found her at Party Rock. My mom thinks it must be a serial killer.
jellybean: That is so sad. And scary. Especially for us girls at Kincaid.
jahnboy: Should we cancel the party?

Kera's hands began to shake and she pushed away from the computer. Nicole had reached out to her for guidance. Just as Jessie had. Now they were both dead, gone from this life forever. What in the hell was going on? Who was targeting these girls?

Kera took a long drink of wine, then wandered aimlessly through the house. Was the girls' communication with her somehow a trigger for their deaths? Or was it a coincidence? The girls had both come into Planned Parenthood recently. Kera thought about the psychopath who was targeting her for her work at the clinic. Could it be the same person? Did the killer think the girls were sinners who deserved to die? And how did it fit with Jackson's theory about the mayor?

Kera ended up on the back deck, breathing in the cool night air. Then, impulsively, she called Jackson's cell phone. He didn't answer, so she left him a brief message. "Jackson, it's Kera. I heard about Nicole. And I'm worried. I need to talk to you."

Kera went back to her desk and checked the messages on the chat site to see if she could learn more. The conversation was still going but it was mostly speculative *…was she naked like Jessie? Was she raped?* Then a new joiner to the chat room said his brother's friend, a guy named Travis Walters, claimed to have discovered the body when he and another guy were up at Party Rock getting high.

Kera shut the machine down and went in search of something to read. She had to distract herself. She found an unread copy of Mother Jones in the stack of mail on her dining room table and settled into a chair in the family room.

Moments later, she heard a thump near her front door.

The sound startled her and she almost spilled her wine. Her brain jumped immediately to the psycho stalker who had sent her poison. Kera's heart began to pound. She ran to the kitchen and grabbed a container of mace from a drawer near the stove. She kept it on hand to take with her when she went for walks by herself.

Mace gripped tightly in her fist, Kera moved cautiously toward the door. She had locked it, hadn't she? Of course she had. She was being extremely careful about that now. She cursed the alarm service company for postponing her installation.

Footsteps sounded right outside the front door.

31

Monday, October 25, 4:35 p.m.
AFTER LEAVING Edgewood Park, Jackson dropped Evans off at the department so she could pick up her own car. While he was in city hall, he stopped at his desk to check his phone and e-mail messages and to call the state ME. The receptionist said Hillary Ainsworth was busy, but Jackson insisted on speaking to her right away.

After a long wait, Ainsworth came to the phone and said, "This better be important, Jackson. I was in the middle of a teaching autopsy, and we were looking at a very interesting liver."

"I have another young girl coming your way tonight. We may be dealing with a serial killer, and the attacks were less than a week apart."

"Oh dear. Not another Green River type, I hope." She was referring to a notorious killer who had victimized prostitutes in the Portland–Vancouver area for decades before they caught him.

"The deaths aren't as violent as those cases, but this one is targeting a much smaller circle of victims. My daughter used to be in that circle. I need you to do the autopsy first thing in the morning."

"Are you too close to this one, Jackson? Do you need to take yourself off the case?" Ainsworth threw it out as a casual observation. Jackson didn't sense any real concern from her.

"I'm fine." It had not occurred to him to tell his superiors about Katie's past friendship with the victims. Telling them now would only serve as a setback to the investigation. "I'll be there by eight sharp with the victim's clothes, which were found separately from the body. Can we do the autopsy then?"

She let out a deep sigh. "I'll change the schedule."

Jackson stopped at home to pick up Katie. He intended to take her to her Aunt Jan's again. This would be another long night for him, and he didn't want his daughter to be alone. He stepped into the house, called out "Katie," then checked the answering machine. As he skipped through the telemarketing messages, he called out to his daughter again.

When she didn't respond, he shut off the answering machine and headed for her room. But Katie wasn't there. Had she made plans that he'd forgotten about?

Her blue denim backpack was on the floor. Katie never went anywhere without her backpack.

An icy knot filled his stomach. Where the hell was she?

Jackson ran down the hall and into the kitchen, looking for a note. A sauce pan that had cooked macaroni and cheese was soaking in the sink, but no note was on the table.

Where in the hell was his daughter?

Jackson ran for the answering machine and pushed play. Any second he would have an answer, he told himself. He skipped through a message from his credit card company and a message from his brother, who he hadn't spoken to in four months. Nothing from Katie. He checked his cell phone. No message there either.

Where would she go? Emily's? What was the girl's last name and did he have her number?

Jackson's heart pounded like a set of cylinders on a V-twin Harley. The thought that he had been pushing away suddenly slammed its way in. What if she had been taken? Kidnapped, raped, and killed by the maniac who was preying on her old circle of friends?

"No!" His shout echoed in the empty house. He pressed speed dial and called Renee's sister.

"This is Jackson. Have you seen Katie?"

"Not today. Why? What's wrong?" Jan caught his contagious panic.

"She's not here. Her backpack is here, but Katie isn't here."

"Did you check with your neighbors? Katie's been talking about a litter of puppies–"

Jackson ran for the front door just as Katie burst in.

"Hi Dad. I had dinner without you. Have you seen the Finkler's puppies yet?"

Jackson snapped the phone shut without saying goodbye. He grabbed Katie in a hug that must have been painful for her. After a moment, she wiggled to get free.

"Are you okay?" she asked.

"Yes and no." Jackson took a deep breath. "I didn't know where you were. It scared me. Please, don't ever leave the house again without leaving a note or calling me."

She rolled her eyes. "I was just next door. I didn't think you'd be home until later."

"Humor me. In a few minutes, you'll understand why. Now, please back a bag. I need to take you over to Aunt Jan's."

He told her about Nicole, and Katie burst into tears. The guilt ripped him apart. She needed him to be there, and all he could give her was a hug and a promise that this was an unusual situation, that their lives would be back to normal very soon.

But it was a promise he might not be able to keep. For the first time, he seriously doubted his ability to be a good detective and a single father at the same time. Tonight's scare had brought that home.

On the way to the Clarkes' house, Jackson called Schakowski and asked him to track down the ID of the person who had reported finding the body. If it had been a land-line phone, the owner and address would have come up on the dispatcher's monitor. But cell phones were not in the system yet.

Vehicles clustered around the Clarke house on both sides of Potter Street, and Jackson had to settle for a spot about three homes away. Evans was parked nearby and waiting for him. The sun had begun to set and the sky threatened rain. Jackson could smell it in the metallic quality of the air. Their Indian summer was over.

"Mourners gathered already?" Evans commented as they walked toward the two-story home. "This could make our job difficult."

"Or save us a lot of time. Why don't you start on the neighbors?"

"Gladly." Evans kept moving up the street.

The walkway to the Greiners' house was lined with short black yard lamps that lit up as he moved toward the wide front steps. Two fake ceramic fawns were nestled under a Boxwood hedge near the tall concrete porch. Jackson rang the doorbell and braced himself for more grief. At least he hadn't been the one to break the news this time.

Joanne Clarke opened the door, shook her head, then silently waved him in. Beyond the foyer, the spacious high-ceilinged living room was filled with·people, most in their thirties and forties, with a few teenagers sitting together on the pale beige carpet. Jackson's entrance drew a series of glances from the group, some surprised, others angry. But most of the supporters quickly returned to their prayers. Only one of the men continued to stare, then stood and walked toward him. He was at least six-two and heavyset with a drinker's nose and thick straight eyebrows.

Jackson took out his notebook and pen. He preferred not to shake hands with anyone he had to question in connection with a crime.

The man's expression was animated. "I'm Reverend John Strickland, of the First Bible Baptist Church." His energy telegraphed confidence—an assertive man who was used to being in charge. "This is a private prayer session. Among good Christian people. You have no business here, and I'd like you to leave."

Jackson stepped forward into Strickland's personal space. "Detective Jackson, of the Eugene Police. The sooner you and your members cooperate with our investigation, the faster we can find this killer."

Strickland's eyes wavered, then he stepped aside. "Please make it quick."

Jackson nodded and turned back to Joanne Clarke, who hovered near him, twisting her hands in a white-knuckled grip. Jackson touched her arm lightly. "Can we go somewhere private and talk?"

They moved through a large kitchen with an island counter in the center and into the family room on the other side. A group of young children were playing video games in front of a wide-screen TV. The kids didn't even look up as Jackson and Mrs. Clarke stepped into a small office at the back of the house.

Their conversation was brief. Mrs. Clarke's story hadn't changed. She and her husband had left Nicole at home alone and driven to Portland with a church group. When they returned around midnight, Nicole was gone.

"Why do you keep asking me this?" she wanted to know. "How does it help you find my daughter's killer?"

"Every piece of information could be important. For example, I need to know exactly what Nicole had in her possession when she left the house. Backpack? Purse? Cell phone?"

"Her school backpack is in her bedroom. And she never carried a purse. Just a cell phone and a tiny little compact case with her house key and a tube of lip gloss."

"What does the compact look like?" Jackson asked, as he made a note to track down the cell phone.

"It's lavender with silver beading."

"Any jackets or sweaters missing?"

She shook her head.

"Thanks for your patience. Is your husband here? I need to talk with him again too."

She nodded. "I'll go get him."

Jackson filled out his notes while he waited. In a few minutes, Steve Clarke appeared, looking even more gaunt than he had that morning. His eyes were swollen, and he was still wearing the same shirt and jacket. But the tie had come off. He also stuck to his story and griped about having to tell it again.

Jackson ignored the complaints. "Who else drove to Portland with you? Are any of them here now?"

"Why is that important?" Clarke jumped up from the chair. "Are you checking out our story? Are we suspects?"

"I'm just doing my job. Please be patient and answer my questions."

Clarke made a groaning noise. "Sam and Ruth Greiner and John and Eva Strickland. Ruth, John and Eva are here now."

"Not Sam Greiner?" Jackson jotted down the names.

"I haven't seen him."

"What did Nicole do yesterday before you left for the meeting?"

Clarke pressed his hands to his forehead. "We went over this with Officer Zapata. We all attended Jessie's memorial service, then we had dinner with Nicole, then left for the meeting when the Greiners picked us up."

"Did Nicole have a boyfriend?"

Steve Clarke lost his patience. "No! She's fourteen."

"No offense intended. I'm just trying to figure out who she might have left the house with."

"She didn't leave voluntarily. Unless she was tricked. Nicole followed the rules."

"Okay." Jackson had questioned too many stunned parents to put much stock in that conviction. "Thanks. I'll talk with you again later." He walked Steve Clarke back to the kitchen, where a group of people had gathered around a large coffee cake.

"Any of your carpoolers here?"

Clarke pointed out Ruth Greiner and Eva Strickland.

His conversations with those who had driven to the CCA meeting confirmed the Clarkes' account of the evening and gave him nothing new. He decided to chat with their daughters, who seem to have been unsupervised while their parents were in Portland. He called Angel Strickland back to the little office. He would have recognized her as Eva's daughter even if he had not met her before; they had the same reddish-blond hair and sprinkling of freckles. He remembered that Angel had seemed shy the first time he questioned her, and she had trouble making eye contact again today. In a quiet voice, she told him that she'd sat with Nicole at Jessie's service but hadn't seen or talked to her since.

The interview was cut short by her parents, who stepped in and announced they were leaving and taking their daughter. Angel looked relieved.

Jackson's interview with Rachel Greiner was not much more productive. "Did you speak with Nicole last night?" he asked. "Call her to chat while your parents were gone?"

The girl's steel-blue eyes fluttered with impatience. "No."

"Did she tell you about any plans she'd made?"

"No." Rachel pushed back a loose strand of hair. The rest

of her ash blond mane was pulled tight into a spiky bun on the back of her head.

"Do you have any idea where she might have gone?"

"Not really."

"Did Nicole have a boyfriend?"

Rachel made a face, but every other part of her body remained still. "In case you haven't noticed, this is a religious group. We're not allowed to date."

"Are any of the boys from Teen Talk here tonight?"

"Greg Miller."

"Send him in here, please."

The interview with Miller was disappointing. The boy— an average-size kid with a pleasant face—gave monosyllabic responses and shook his head a lot.

"When was the last time you spoke to Nicole?"

Shrug. "Friday?"

"Have you had sex with either Jessie or Nicole?"

Another shake of the head.

"Do you know why anyone would want to harm either Jessie or Nicole?"

A little distress finally crept into his eyes. "No, man. They were both great."

"Have you seen Tyler Jahn or Adam Walsh today?"

Another shrug. "I saw Adam at school, but Tyler hasn't been around for a few days."

"Any idea why?"

"No."

"Have either of them been acting strangely in the past week?" Jackson wondered if the killer had been right in front of him all along—one of the boys in the Teen Talk circle.

"No."

Evans stepped into the room and Jackson told Miller he could go.

"Anything?" Evans asked after the kid had left.

"Not really. How about you?"

"Nada. Although no one was home at the house to the immediate left, and one woman across the street kept saying she doesn't keep track of her neighbors. Which makes me think she does. I'll go back to both again in the morning."

Jackson checked his watch: 9:17. "Let's go examine Nicole's clothes and write up some search warrants. I'll meet you at the department."

Out in the car, Jackson checked his cell phone for messages. There was one from his mother in Salem, who was just saying "Hi" and one from Kera. She sounded upset, so he decided to stop in and see her briefly.

KERA HAD THE mace in one hand and her cell phone in the other when the doorbell rang. Would a psycho ring the doorbell? From about twelve feet away, she called out, "Who is it?"

"Jackson."

Her shoulders slumped forward, and Kera smiled at her own paranoia. She slipped the mace in her pocket and hurried to open the door. The sight of Jackson standing there gave her a sense of peace that she hadn't felt in weeks.

"Officer Jackson. Thanks for coming."

"You sounded upset. Is everything okay?"

"Not really. Please come in." Kera stepped back and locked the door after he came through it.

"Would you like some wine or coffee?"

"Coffee sounds good."

Jackson followed her into the kitchen, where Kera started a small pot.

"So how did you hear about Nicole?" he asked. "I don't even think the news media has wind of it yet." Jackson sat at her small kitchen table, looking particularly handsome in a tan blazer. She could feel him watching her even when she wasn't looking at him.

"I went to that chat room that I told you about, where some Kincaid students post messages. And someone said their mother's prayer hotline had called with the news about Nicole."

"Any buzz I should know about?"

"Just that some boys may have found her when they were up at Party Rock smoking dope. One of the guys is Travis Walters."

"Good to know." Jackson jotted the name down. "I still need to check out that website. Do you have a password or user name?"

Kera felt her cheeks get warm. "I use Jessie's. I'll write it down for you." As she jotted down the website's URL and the *blowgirl* ID, Kera asked, "Can you tell me what happened to Nicole?"

He hesitated. "Completely confidential? Just like the way you protect your clients' information?"

"Of course."

"It looks like she was suffocated. At first glance, the scenario seems very similar to Jessie's death."

"Does that mean the mayor is a psychopath? It seems so hard to believe."

Jackson rubbed his temples as Kera poured him a cup of coffee.

"I can't figure how all this fits together," he said after a long moment. "Fieldstone may have been in custody at the time of the murder. But maybe not. He may have an accomplice. Or it could be a copycat killing. Or maybe the mayor is a child rapist but not a murderer, and a serial killer is out there, preying on girls who attend my daughter's school."

Kera sat next to him and sipped her wine. She would need it to sleep tonight. "I've been thinking about all this too, and I had a strange idea earlier."

He looked surprised and a little eager. "Tell me."

"What if the murders are connected to the crackpot who bombed the clinic and poisoned me?"

A dark look flashed in Jackson's eyes. "How so?"

"Jessie and Nicole both contacted me." Kera's scattered thoughts about the converging events finally came together. "What if the bomber, while targeting the clinic—and specifically me—zeroed in on Jessie and Nicole? What if he is a moralistic executioner type who punishes people he judges to be sinners?"

Jackson looked somewhat alarmed. "The FBI agent working the clinic bombing case has a theory along those same lines."

Kera chewed her lip. "But I can't figure why the poisoned card was signed NC."

"This just keeps getting weirder." Jackson scowled, and Kera noticed he was starting to get a furrow between his brows that gave his face even more character. Finally he said, "Both victims' families attend the First Bible Baptist Church. And both girls belonged to a religious youth group. It could be somebody from the church."

"And the letter to me was signed God's Messenger."

"I was so sure it was the mayor." Jackson pushed his hands through his hair. "And it still could be. He goes to the same church. But I just don't see him as the clinic bomber. I feel like I need to start all over with this investigation."

"Will this psycho target another young girl? Or should I be worried about my own safety?"

Jackson grabbed her hands and held them in his own. "Can you get out of town for a while? Maybe take a leave of absence?"

"I could. But I won't. I don't run from things."

"I knew you would say that." He let go and reluctantly stood to leave. "You need a perimeter alarm."

"I made an appointment to have one installed, but they

can't be here until Thursday."

"You should carry mace with you at all times."

Kera laughed and pulled the little canister from her pocket. "I had some in my hand when I answered the door."

"Excellent. Other safety basics." Jackson used his fingers to tick off his points. "Stay in groups of people, stay in well lighted places, and vary your route to work but always take busy streets."

They were standing six inches apart. Kera could feel the warmth of his body and the lingering scent of his deodorant. "You sound like my mother." She smiled. "Except for the part about varying my route to work. She advocates for consistency."

Jackson pulled back and gave her a serious look. "Consistent patterns are how killers and rapists target their victims. Mixing it up is important right now."

"Okay. I can do that."

Kera walked him to the front door. He opened it, then turned. She thought he was going to give her one more piece of safety advice, but instead, he leaned in and kissed her forehead.

"Take care of yourself. The world needs people like you."

Monday, October 25, 9:06 p.m.

ON THE DRIVE HOME, Ruth had second thoughts about leaving the kids alone, but Sam showed up a few minutes after they walked in the door.

"Where have you been?" Ruth asked out of habit when they were alone in the kitchen. She was too preoccupied at the moment to feel any real concern.

"At a meeting with supporters," Sam said, opening a cupboard. "Businessmen with deep pockets who want to fund our Moral Marriage campaign."

"That sounds promising." Ruth kissed him lightly on the

cheek. "I have to run out to the store. Need anything?"

"Mothers Taffy cookies."

Ruth laughed. "I knew you would say that."

She grabbed a light jacket and headed out.

Ruth stopped at Safeway and bought the cookies and some chocolate soymilk, so she wouldn't forget them later and walk in the house empty-handed. The drive up to Kollmorgan's took only six minutes, despite the climb. As she passed the address, she realized the house was within walking distance of her own home.

Ruth was also struck by the obvious value of the home. Not to mention the view Kollmorgan must have from her backyard. Was her husband a lawyer? Or a plastic surgeon?

Ruth made a U-turn at the next intersection, then circled back and parked across the street, one house down. There weren't many street lights up here, but the homes all had porch and yard lights, so she had just enough illumination to assess the situation's tactical possibilities. Kollmorgan's front yard was narrow, and a tall brick wall snugged up tight against the building on either side, keeping the backyard private. Except for the front door, most of the points of entry were on the other side of the brick barrier. Not good. But there was no sign or sound of a dog anywhere nearby. That made up for the lack of access.

Ruth quietly opened her car door and slid out. She scurried across the narrow curving street, then moved down the sidewalk and stood in the shadows at the edge of Kollmorgan's property. The abortionist's little white SUV was parked in the driveway, despite having an oversized garage. Another unexpected bonus. This would be so simple.

Just as Ruth turned to leave, Kollmorgan's front door opened. Her heart fluttered in panic as she backtracked. As she darted up the sidewalk, Ruth glanced back at the house. A familiar man stood near the doorway, then leaned in and kissed Kollmorgan. Ruth ducked behind a van parked on the street, then peeked back.

The man moving toward the sidewalk was Detective Jackson! The cop who had just questioned her and the other CCA members right in the middle of a prayer session and made them feel like criminals. Now he was kissing the killer! Ruth's fists balled in anger, and she could feel blood swooshing in her ears. Who would Kollmorgan seduce next? She was the devil!

Ruth decided she must act immediately. The Bible said so. The revenger of blood himself shall slay the murderer: when he meeteth him, he shall slay him. She would target the car tomorrow night.

32

Tuesday, October 26, 7:05 a.m.

AFTER A SHORT NIGHT'S SLEEP, Jackson was in his car, gulping coffee and making the familiar drive to Portland. The morning was dark and wet, and he was in an agitated mood. This second murder was turning his brain into a pretzel. Fortunately, traffic was light, the Impala had cruise control, and he was able to let his thoughts percolate.

So far, all he knew was that Nicole Clarke had disappeared from her house Sunday evening while her parents were gone, then turned up dead—suffocated—the next day, five miles away in a city park. If Jessie had not died under similar circumstances a week earlier, Nicole's parents would have been Jackson's primary suspects. But not only did Joanne and Steve Clarke have alibis for the time of her disappearance, he also had no gut reason to believe they were involved in her death.

Of course, they were still suspects. Everyone was.

Last night, driving home around 2 a.m., it had occurred to Jackson that the core group of Bible Baptist Church members might be involved in a conspiracy to cover up the girls' sexually motivated murders to protect one of their own. Even though in the fresh energy of the morning he realized the idea was unlikely—one born of frustration and exhaustion—he would not dismiss it. The Clarkes' alibis came from other church members, and Jackson had left Evans a message, asking her to verify that all of them had actually been at the meeting.

The light rain turned into a steady downpour, so Jackson

turned his wipers up a notch, then passed a semi tractor-trailer that was kicking up a wall of water. Once he was out front, alone on the road again, his thoughts returned to the two murders.

The idea that the killer and the clinic bomber could be the same person now intrigued him. If this person saw himself as God's avenger, perhaps he had moved beyond saving fetuses to killing girls whom he believed to be promiscuous and offensive to God. And if the avenger had been following Jessie and saw her leaving the mayor's apartment, he may have killed her for her sins.

But where had he done the deed? Jackson wondered. In the parking lot? In a car? So why hadn't anyone at the apartment complex seen something? And what about the sheet fibers in Jessie's nose? Then there was Nicole. How did she fit in? Was she also having sex with Fieldstone? Did the orange panties belong to her?

Oh shit. A new scenario hit Jackson like a slap to the head. His foot came off the accelerator, and the cruise control kicked off.

What if the mayor's wife had killed both girls out of jealousy and revenge?

Jealousy was right up there with greed, lust, and revenge as a motive for murder.

He needed to interview Janice Fieldstone ASAP. And he would assign either Schakowski or McCray to check out her activities for the days of both homicides. Jackson could not believe that he hadn't thought of the scorned wife before now. In retrospect, it seemed that he might have zoomed in on the mayor too quickly and ignored other possibilities. Jackson was not happy with his performance. Homicide investigators could not afford to be sloppy.

Jackson felt a familiar tightening of his chest, accompanied by a little burst of pain. He hoped it was just stress.

Tuesday, October 26, 7:52 a.m.

RUTH PULLED UP in front of Kincaid Middle School, and Caleb hopped out of the car. "Bye mom."

Ruth willed Rachel, who was in the back seat, to follow suit without discussion. Her daughter didn't move. "Rachel, you're pushing my limits. You are going to school. Now get out."

"Have some compassion. Two of my best friends just died. I really don't want to be here today."

Ruth turned and gave her a stern look. "I know you're sad, but you must pray for strength. Your other friends need comfort too."

Rachel started to say something, then thought better of it. But she couldn't resist slamming the car door just little. Ruth wondered if she should let Rachel get away with it. Her daughter was grieving. Ruth had all day to decide about that, but for right now she had more important things to focus on. She needed to hurry home and get cracking on her timer while the house was empty and before her volunteer shift at the hospital started.

Ruth drove too fast on the way home, and she prayed she wouldn't get a ticket. She was wound up and anxious to get this phase over with. Other faithful Christians had ended the lives of abortionists, and Ruth admired their passion and courage in doing God's work. But many of them had paid the price. She had no intention of getting caught. She couldn't do the Lord's work from a jail cell.

Ruth hurried into the house and locked the door behind her. She stopped in the laundry room to pick up her new supplies, which she had purchased at the 24-hour Wal-Mart the night before. She carried everything to Sam's office, the only room inside the house that had a lock. The idea of making a timer would have been intimidating to her a few months ago. But once she had connected with her mentor Josiah Stahl, Ruth had seen new possibilities for herself. And watching her first bomb detonate had been empowering. She could be God's instrument here on earth. She could make things happen now.

Ruth, who had never even changed a flat tire, had been called on by God to keep fornicators from making their babies pay for their mistakes. The ease with which she picked up skills and adapted to her secret war tactics sometimes still surprised her.

She had easily located on the Internet the instructions she needed for making a bomb, then confirmed them with a phone call to Josiah. That such information was so readily available was handy for her, but also horribly frightening. Anyone could learn how to create high-impact explosives and then do a devastating amount of damage. That information in the hands of terrorists or anarchists could be deadly on a massive scale. If her work in saving God's little ones weren't so important, Ruth would start lobbying for laws to control what was allowed on the Internet.

From the bottom of Sam's bookshelf, Ruth picked up a copy of *The Feminine Mystique*—something her husband had never, and would never, look at—and pulled out her instructions. She had printed them from a website called Ka-Boom!

First and always, she pulled on plastic gloves. Next she pried the backing from the cheap digital watch, then disconnected the alarm buzzer. The alarm itself would be set to serve as the timer. But first, she used a soldering gun to connect wire leads to the timing device inside the watch.

The phone on Sam's desk rang, startling her. Ruth jumped and accidentally pulled the lead wire loose. "Damn." She picked up the phone. "Hello. This is the Greiners."

"Ruth, it's Eva Strickland. How are you?"

"I'm good, Eva. But I'm in the middle of something. Can

I call you back?"

"It's important." Eva's tone dropped to indicate how serious.

Ruth tried not to be annoyed. "What is it?"

"I found a condom under a seat in the minivan."

"Oh dear. What do you think that means?" Ruth looked at her unfinished timer and willed herself to be patient.

"I think John is having an affair."

"Oh no. Perhaps there's another explanation."

"Like what?"

"I don't know. Have you talked to him?"

"Not yet. Do you think I should? Or should I try to keep track of his coming and going for a while?"

"You mean spy."

"Yeah. Why not?"

"Deception isn't good for a marriage," Ruth counseled. "You should talk to John. Get it out in the open and pray about it."

"You're right. Thanks Ruth. I know you're in the middle of something, so I'll let you go."

"Take care, Eva. I'll pray for you, too."

Ruth hung up the phone and asked God to help Eva and John through their difficulties. God couldn't do it by Himself though. Eva needed to keep a better eye on both her husband and her daughter. Calling her Angel didn't make her one. Ruth remembered to thank the Lord for Sam and his faithfulness to her.

Then she moved back to her task at hand. After resoldering the wire lead, she grabbed the twelve-volt battery and started to work on the primer that would connect the timer to the pipe bomb. This stuff was easy if you took it step by step. The scary part would be attaching it to Kollmorgan's car. But with a little duct tape and the cover of darkness, all she had to do was slide under the car and tape a little package under the driver's seat. Rigging the bomb to the ignition would be more effective but Ruth didn't have those skills, nor the time to acquire them. This could not wait. Kollmorgan was too dangerous. And God's vengeance must be swift.

Ruth decided she would go out this evening on foot around 2 a.m. The abortionist's house was within walking distance, and if anyone saw her or if Sam woke up, she could always claim she was out walking off her insomnia.

The timer alarm would be set for 8 p.m. sharp the following evening. Ruth planned to slip out of Wednesday night Bible study and call Kollmorgan from the pay phone across the street from the church. She would call at exactly 7:56, giving the target four minutes to grab her purse and get into her car. Ruth would pretend to be a pregnant teenager, desperately in need of help. She would beg the abortionist to come rescue her right away. Kollmorgan would not be able to resist such a plea. She would rush to her car and race out the driveway.

And it would be the last thing she ever did.

< **33** >

Tuesday, October 26, 9:46 a.m.
NICOLE'S SMALL PALE nakedness against the stainless steel table, illuminated under harsh halogen bulbs, gave Jackson a sense of *deja vu*. He had experienced this same scene less than a week ago, and it was not any easier this time.

Ainsworth's slow, methodical examination made him impatient. He wanted information now. He wanted to be back in Eugene, interviewing Janice Fieldstone and looking at Nicole's phone records.

"No signs of rape," the ME said after an examination of Nicole's pubic area. "But she's no virgin either. This girl has had vaginal and anal intercourse and shows faint scarring where I believe she was treated with liquid nitrogen sometime in the past month or so."

"For genital warts?"

"Most likely."

"So she and Jessie shared a sexual partner."

"Possibly." Ainsworth never made assumptions.

"But she was not sexually assaulted at the time of her death?"

"No."

"Any trace evidence?"

"None in her pubic area. But there's a small scratch on her hip that could have been made from someone pulling off her pants." The ME used a magnifier for a closer look. "There's a tiny piece of fiber stuck in the scratch. We'll compare it to her clothes."

She placed the fiber, which Jackson could not see, in an evidence tray and continued her examination, moving slowly up and down the body. "She has an odd scar on her right shin, possibly made from a dull razor used while shaving her legs."

Jackson's irritation escalated. "Can we look at her nose and lungs? I need to know if she was suffocated.

Ainsworth looked over her glasses at him but didn't respond. She began to examine Nicole's head and neck. She used tweezers to extract the piece of white plastic from Nicole's earring. "Did Gunderson see this?"

"He thinks she was suffocated with the plastic bag her clothes were in."

"Lab analysis will tell us if it's the same material. But I'd say it's a pretty good guess. This mark across her neck was made from pressure, and this bruise looks like it could have come from a thumb."

Jackson had not noticed a bruise yesterday, but now Nicole's whole face had a reddish tint. "Is the color in her face consistent with suffocation?"

"More likely strangulation. The blood vessels are slightly occluded from the pressure that was placed on her neck."

"Was she moved after she was killed?"

"If so, not far. The lividity is all on the front side."

"Any tissue under her nails? Did she fight her attacker?"

Ainsworth looked over her glasses at him again. "Patience. I'm not there yet."

But when she examined Nicole's hands, no trace evidence was obvious. The ME took scrapings from under the painted nails anyway. She also took scrapings from the girl's heels, which were dark with dirt. The internal exam revealed that Nicole had eaten chicken and broccoli about an hour before her death—which had most likely occurred before Fieldstone was arrested—that she had a small amount of scarring from anal sex, and that she had died from asphyxiation.

Ainsworth declared the death a homicide, then emptied the bladder so the lab could test the urine for drugs, poisons, and other chemicals.

"Please compare her DNA with the secretions on the orange panties."

"So is Mayor Fieldstone still your prime suspect?" The ME looked genuinely puzzled. "Do you think he's psychotic or killing these girls to keep them from talking about the sexual activity?"

"I honestly don't know."

Ainsworth also ran a comb over Nicole's clothes while Jackson was there. From the girl's dark purple T-shirt, she picked up an eight-inch blond hair that clearly had not come from Nicole's brownish-black waist-length mane.

Jackson's first thought was Janice Fieldstone.

"This shirt has some short hairs as well," the ME mumbled. "Possibly feline." Jackson did not remember seeing a cat at the Clarkes' or the Fieldstones.'

Ainsworth noted a barely visible smear in the crotch of the pink panties. "Looks like menstrual blood," she commented. "We'll analyze it for DNA."

"You'll check for a pregnancy too?"

"Of course. But I have a budget meeting this morning, so the trace work will have to wait until this afternoon or tomorrow, unless someone else can get to it first."

"Thanks for doing the autopsy right away." Jackson made a mental note to send Ainsworth some flowers. "Call me as soon as you have anything to report."

"We always do."

He raced back to Eugene, pushing eighty most of the way without seeing a single state sheriff. A task force meeting was set up for 11 a.m., and Schakowski, McCray, Evans—and Fouts—were already in the conference room when Jackson rushed in ten minutes late. The detectives were relaxed, drinking coffee, and joking about an internal investigation into prostitutes' complaints of sexual harassment by patrol cops. Jackson was not in the mood for sexual humor.

"Sorry to be late. I just got back from Nicole's autopsy." He turned to Evans. "Is Slonecker coming?"

"He said he'd try."

Jackson looked at the dry-erase board with Jessie's information still up there. "This is a first for us," he said to the group. "Two homicides, less than a week apart, with similar victims, possibly—or probably—committed by the same person."

Fouts spoke up. "Agent Morales will be joining this investigation today or tomorrow. I think we need the manpower."

Jackson noticed the assumption of authority and ignored it. He turned to McCray. "Will you update the board as I talk?"

"Sure." McCray moved toward the wall with a sluggishness that suggested he might be in pain.

Jackson summed up the new case, using his hands to track his points. "This is what we know about Nicole's disappearance: She was last seen at home around 6 p.m. She exited her house sometime after that without any sign of struggle.

"This is what we know about her death: She was suffocated, most likely with a plastic bag placed over her head and held tightly around her neck. The murder most likely took place in the city park where she was found. She was not sexually assaulted. And there is no evidence of consensual sex immediately prior to her death. Most of this is consistent with the facts of Jessie's death."

"Except the sex part," Schakowski commented. "Jessie had sex with two different men before she died. Was Nicole a virgin? Or just not active on the day of her death?"

His tone rattled Jackson and made him feel defensive of

the girls. "She was sexually active. And there's an indication that she had been recently treated for genital warts, so she may have shared a sex partner with Jessie."

"The mayor?" Fouts asked.

"We don't know yet."

Slonecker quietly stepped into the room and sat down. "Please continue." He looked energized and confident. But Jackson knew that the coming media frenzy and public pressure to bring justice to two slain teenage girls would soon change that.

"If the mayor was sexually molesting both girls—and we won't know that until the DNA testing is done—he may have killed them to keep them quiet about his pedophilia," Jackson said. "Or we could be dealing with a sociopath who kills for pleasure. Or a religious nutcase with a need to punish," Jackson paused. "Or a scorned wife seeking to eliminate her husband's little mistresses."

"I never even thought about the wife," Schakowski mumbled.

"It hit me a little late too." He met Schak's eyes. "I'd like you to follow up with Janice Fieldstone. Arrange for her to come in for questioning. We'll interview her together and try to pin down her whereabouts for each of the homicide time frames. Try to get a search warrant for her cell phone records. Get a photo of her car. We'll show it to Nicole's neighbors, to see if they remember seeing it the night she disappeared."

"I'll lead the interrogation when she comes in," Fouts said.

Jackson refused to be baited into a turf war.

"Be very discretionary in how you handle this," Slonecker warned. "Mayor Fieldstone has already decided to sue us, and Janice Fieldstone is well known and respected by many in this community, myself included."

Jackson didn't care about the politics, only the task at

hand. "McCray and Evans, I want you to work the religious avenger theory. Run background checks and profile scans on everyone who attends the First Bible Baptist Church, then start on the local CCA group, which includes a wide network of churches."

Fouts spoke up again. "I've already run those checks, and I'll get copies to you. And I've got the agency drawing up profiles for the bomber and the killer. We'll see if there's any overlap."

"Excellent." Jackson turned to Evans. "Did you get back to Nicole's neighbors this morning?"

She brushed her short auburn hair out of her eyes, which still looked lively despite the grueling effort of the last week. "I tried," she reported. "Neither of the parties I wanted to talk to were home."

"Keep on it. If someone picked Nicole up and drove away, I want to know." He looked up at the board with Jessie and Nicole's data listed side by side. "I'll follow up on the serial killer angle and hit CODIS again." He looked at Fouts. "I assume you're still focused on the bombing?"

"I still believe it's connected to the murders," Fouts responded. "Especially considering the lack of sexual assault or any kind of violence to the victims."

"The lack of sexual violence also fits the theory that Mrs. Fieldstone may have killed them," Evans commented.

Fouts looked skeptical. "Maybe."

Schak said, "I think the mayor is our best suspect."

McCray spoke up for the first time. "But if Fieldstone killed Nicole only to keep her quiet—and didn't have sex with her first—why did he take her clothes off?"

Jackson had wondered about that also. "Maybe to throw us off. To make it look like a serial killer or sexual predator." He closed his notebook. "We have a lot of work to do. Keep me posted if anything interesting comes up, and we'll meet again tomorrow, same time."

"Speaking of interesting," Schak said as they headed down to the parking lot. "The number of the phone used to call in the tip on the body is registered to Steve Clarke."

"What?" Jackson stopped dead in his tracks.

"That was my first reaction." Schak gestured at the look on Jackson's face. "But then I thought that it might be Nicole's phone and was left by her body. Maybe the boys who found her picked it up and used it to call us."

"I'll check that out." Jackson made a mental note to find the boy Kera had mentioned. The name was in his case-book.

He headed for his desk, but before he had a chance to sit down, his phone rang with the short tone of an inside line. Jackson picked up. Sergeant Lammers said, "Detective Jackson. We have a press conference scheduled this afternoon. And by 'we,' I mean you and Officer Anderson. Two-thirty, right out in front of the department."

"It's too early in this second case," Jackson countered. "There's nothing I can share with the press."

"We have to give them something. The TV reporters have made the religious connection between the murdered girls, and now they're interviewing church members who claim the girls were targeted because they're Christian. The speculation is running rampant. We need to look like we're in charge here."

"What can I tell them?"

"That's your call."

"Thanks." It came out a little more sarcasticly than he intended.

He checked his watch: 1:15. He had an hour or so before the press conference and plenty to do. Jackson took a long drink of cold coffee, then logged on to CODIS, the national crime database, and entered the details of the new homicide. A search for a match spit out the same three crimes the system had produced when he plugged in Jessie's death. None of them were anywhere near Oregon, and none looked promising.

Jackson leaned back in his chair, closed his eyes and let his mind go blank. Something had been nagging at him for days—a lead he had forgotten to follow up on. He had learned that trying to force his brain didn't work. He had to let it rest, then the missing detail would pop up soon after. And in this case, the information could mean life or death for another young girl.

But he couldn't keep his mind clear. The press conference was looming, and he had to prepare for it. After scanning his notes and jotting down the few details he would give out, Jackson headed for the men's room to comb his hair. There wasn't much he could do about the dark circles under his eyes or his failure to shave this morning.

The sight of the big cameras filled Jackson with dread. He didn't know how Jim Anderson, the department's spokesperson, met with the press week after week, year after year. Jackson would have developed bleeding ulcers after a month. It'll be fine, he told himself. All he had to do was stay calm, say very little, refuse to commit to anything, and reassure everyone that both homicides would be resolved soon.

No problem.

Anderson started by making a short statement praising the dedication and long hours put in by the team working on the homicides. Then he turned the microphone over to Jackson, whose prepared statement was succinct:

The long hours are paying off. We have filed charges in the death of Jessie Davenport and are pursuing several leads in Nicole Clarke's homicide. We believe we'll resolve both of these cases soon and bring justice to the victims. I have time for just a few questions.

Jackson pointed to Trina Waterman because he recognized her, and she seemed reasonable.

"Did you file a murder charge against Mayor Fieldstone?" she asked.

"Yes."

"So if Mayor Fieldstone has been charged with murdering Jessie Davenport, does that mean he probably killed Nicole Clarke too?

"Not necessarily." Jackson chose his words carefully. "The two deaths are similar in many ways, but the physical evidence does not yet support the idea that they were committed by the same person. So we're waiting for more lab results before we jump to any conclusions."

A reporter named Scott Kippler from KTAV jumped in without waiting to be called on. "Wasn't the mayor in jail when Nicole was killed?"

Where did he get that information?

"Nicole's time of death has a two-hour zone. The mayor was in jail for only part of that time."

A woman TV reporter whose name he could not remember asked, "Is it possible the murders were committed by a serial killer targeting young Christian girls?"

"We're looking into the possibility that it could be a serial killer," Jackson responded. "But the physical evidence doesn't support that theory."

"Was Nicole pregnant too?" Trina Waterman again.

The question rattled him. Where were they getting these details?

"Not according to her autopsy." He decided he was through. "That's all the time I have." Jackson handed the microphone back to Officer Anderson and started to walk away.

Then the voice of Sophie Speranza called after him. "Officer Jackson. Is the bombing of the Planned Parenthood clinic and the ricin attack on one of its staff related to the deaths of Jessie and Nicole? Were they both patients at the clinic?"

Jackson wanted to keep walking. This was the one question he hoped no one would ask. But he couldn't leave the question hanging like that for the reporters to twist into assumed information. Kera would be disappointed if he did.

So he turned back and said, "As yet, we have no reason to believe that the bombing incident is related to the murders. And Planned Parenthood does not release the names of its clients. Good day."

Sophie kept asking questions, but Jackson moved away.

He felt violated. Someone was leaking information to the press. He could not believe that a member of his task force would do that. But who else? Slonecker? Fouts?

Also hard to believe.

How could he proceed if he couldn't trust his team?

Wednesday, October 27, 1:35 a.m.

RUTH LAY IN bed watching the clock's red digital display. She had drunk two cups of regular coffee late in the afternoon so that she would still be awake at this hour. Sam had been asleep for an hour or so, most of it spent snoring. But he had recently rolled over on his other side, and the ruckus had come to an end. Ruth figured he was now in a deep sleep that would hold him until daylight, when he got up to relieve his bladder.

It was time to go.

She eased out of bed and tiptoed over to her dresser. She slipped on matching dark blue fleece sweat pants and sweat shirt over her pajamas and moved into the hall. She heard a muffled thump from Rachel's room. Ruth froze. Was Rachel still awake? Ruth waited silently for a few minutes but didn't hear any other sounds. Her daughter had probably just rolled over and bumped her nightstand.

Ruth grabbed her tennis shoes, then went to the laundry room for a miniature flashlight, a roll of duct tape, and the explosive device. The device and the tape went into the kangaroo pocket of her sweatshirt, and the flashlight she kept in hand. A wool cap from the front closet concealed her hair. Ruth slipped her house key into her left shoe, then quietly closed and locked the door behind her. She wanted her family to be safe while she was gone.

She moved at a fast clip up 27th Street. The sky was black with clouds, and the thin sliver of a moon gave off little light. Ruth prayed as she walked, first thanking God for covering the city with darkness while she carried out her mission, then asking that He continue to guide and protect her until she was back home. Ruth drew comfort from a passage in Leviticus and recited it as she walked: *Wherefore ye shall do my statutes, and keep my judgments, and do them; and ye shall dwell in the land in safety.*

Eight minutes later, she cut down Friendly Street to 28th, then continued west. Ruth had yet to see a single car on the street, and only one dog had barked from a dumpy home on the corner of Olive. Another five blocks and she veered left on McLean and began the climb. Ruth was surprised by how quickly her heart rate escalated. Even though she rarely exercised, she treated her body like it was the Lord's temple, and she had thought she was pretty healthy.

Soon her lungs begged her to stop and rest, but Ruth pushed on. By the time Kollmorgan's home came into view, her face was sweating, and she could feel her feet swelling in her shoes. She slowed down to calm her heart and promised God that she'd take better care of herself in the future.

The road was quiet and the homes were dark, but the yard lights kept her from feeling secure and anonymous. Ruth pulled the stocking cap down, leaving just enough room to see out from under it. Her strategy was to keep moving, to act like she belonged, and to never hesitate or look around. At the edge of Kollmorgan's property, Ruth veered right and cut across the narrow grass to the white Saturn. She dropped to her knees, rolled over flat on her back, and shimmied under the car.

The smell of gas and oil made her a little nauseous, but Ruth stayed on task. She turned on the flashlight and located a flat spot on the chassis under the driver's side of the vehicle, then quickly shut the light back off. Without it, her visibility was limited, but a light under a car in the middle of the night would raise a red flag if anyone saw it.

With clammy hands, Ruth pulled the pipe bomb and the duct tape from her pocket. She laid the bomb on her chest while she ripped two eight-inch pieces of tape from the roll. Her heart pounded frantically under the weight of the device. Keep me safe, Lord, she prayed. Ruth set the tape down on the cement beside her while she dried her sweaty hands on the sides of her pants.

She took a deep breath to calm herself, then felt with her hands for the flat spot. Still working in near darkness, she positioned the bomb in place with her left hand and used her right hand to tape each end of the cylinder. She tried to be careful not to cover the timing device. Was that enough tape? Would it hold until this evening? Ruth tore off another strip and ripped it lengthwise down the middle, using half of it to secure the center of the cylinder.

As soon as the last strip was in place, Ruth felt panicked and anxious to get out from under the claustrophobia of the car. She shoved the tape and the flashlight into her center pocket and scooted on her backside until she cleared the edge of the vehicle. Relief washed over her. She'd done it. And the entire process had taken only a few minutes. Ruth scrambled to her feet, then allowed herself one quick look around. She saw no one, and the neighboring homes were still dark. She trotted toward the sidewalk.

A light flicked on in the three-story home across the street. Ruth turned her face away, and she thought she heard a door open. Her heart skipped a beat. Do not fear, she soothed herself. In the shadows, with the stocking cap pulled low, no one would be able to identify her. She was God's Messenger. He would watch over her.

She picked up speed as she moved downhill, turning off McLean Street at the next intersection, just in case Kollmorgan's neighbor had seen her and called the police. As she jogged toward home, Ruth felt herself smiling. She liked this work and hoped God would have more of it for her.

Wednesday, October 27, 7:15 a.m.

JACKSON PICKED UP Katie from her aunt's and drove her to school. It wasn't much time, but it gave them twenty minutes together and let his daughter know that she was never far from his mind. She seemed to appreciate the gesture. She also hit him up for some cash. For teenagers, sometimes all you could be was either an emotional touchstone or a dependable resource.

As he was driving away from Kincaid Middle School, he received a call on his cell phone. Jackson pulled into a Dairy Mart to take it. The morning traffic around the schools—soccer moms in giant SUVs—was too crazy to allow him to operate a vehicle and a phone at the same time.

"It's Debbie in the ME's office."

"Great. What have you got for me?"

He heard her pull in a heavy breath, so he braced himself. "The blond hair from Nicole's clothes doesn't match any of the trace evidence from Jessie's body. Nicole's DNA does not match the secretion from the orange panties found in the mayor's apartment. And none of the DNA from either crime scene has produced a hit on CODIS."

Jackson pressed his teeth together to keep from shouting obscenities.

"I'm sorry." Debbie's sympathy was genuine. After a moment of silence, she said, "I have more lab results if you're ready."

"Give 'em to me."

"Nicole had lorazepam in her blood and bladder."

"What is that?"

"A tranquilizer."

"Like for anxiety?"

"Exactly. Only it's not typically prescribed for children. Especially at that high a dosage. You'll have to ask her parents or doctor if she was taking it."

"Anything else?"

"The entomology report confirms that she died between 7:30 and 9:00 on Sunday night. Oh, and some of the hair on Nicole's clothes is feline."

"Huh." Not one fucking bit of help, he thought. This second murder was so baffling. Nothing added up. "Thanks. Send copies of all the labs."

"Wait. There's a final report on the Davenport lab work. The DNA of the fetus, a boy, is so closely matched to the sample submitted by Miles Fieldstone that if this were a paternity case, he'd be paying child support."

Yes! "Thanks Deb. Thanks for working overtime to get it all done. How can I make it up to you?"

"You can buy me lunch sometime."

"Will do."

Now, they had Fieldstone on motive. If only he could figure out how Nicole fit into the picture. Jackson decided it was time to find Travis Walters, the kid Kera said had bragged online about finding Nicole's body. He figured Travis probably had Nicole's phone.

Jackson was also waiting for Schak to call him with a time to interview Janice Fieldstone. The news about Jessie being pregnant with her husband's baby might be just the leverage that would push the mayor's wife into a confession.

As Jackson pulled into the parking lot at Spencer High School, vivid memories flashed in his brain. Friday night basketball games in front of an intense crowd, skipping class with Joe and Eric on warm spring afternoons, pining after Melissa Johnson until he was sick with lust. Twenty years had passed, but some images from his teen years had never lost their edge the way memories from last week often did.

Out of habit, Jackson took it all in—the boys in the low rider Honda Civic with the illegal running lights under the car, the loner in front of the office defiantly smoking a cigarette on school property, the group of girls—all with tanning salon bellies on display. Teenagers had always been rule breakers, but many kids today were fearless in a way that past generations had not been. It made his job more difficult.

In the front office, he was greeted by a cheerful student helper, who quickly turned to an adult when Jackson identified himself.

"How can I help you, sir?" This woman didn't fit the school secretary mold. She was in her late twenties, built like a rock climber, and had a man's haircut. But the smile was still a friendly–wary combination.

"I'm looking for Travis Walters."

"Let me look up his schedule."

After a moment, she said, "He's in Life Skills with Mrs. Olsen right now. Kristy, would you please take the detective there?"

The school had been given a new coat of pukey purple paint sometime in the ensuing years, but not much else had changed. Twenty heads turned as he stepped into the classroom and asked for Travis. An attractive young man with a buzzed head and baggy jeans tentatively approached him. He had dark eyes and full lips and could have belonged to any number of ethnic groups. Jackson held open the door and followed him out. The whispers of curious classmates cut off as the door closed.

"Let's go to my car and talk."

"About what?"

"I'll let you know when we get there."

When they were in the Impala, Jackson locked the doors just for effect. "Travis, we know you and a friend found Nicole Clarke's body in Edgewood Park. You bragged about it on the Internet. We know you used her phone to call it in. Unless you want me to think you also killed her, you'd better tell me what really happened."

Travis took two full seconds to make up his mind.

Then he shrugged and said: "Nothing happened. We went up to the park to hang out. Jeremy pushed me off the trail. You know, goofing around. And I accidentally touched her body."

"Who's Jeremy?"

"Jeremy Carson."

"Who drove?"

"I did." The kid yawned.

"Did you know Nicole?"

"No."

"Did you kill her?"

"No!"

"Then you won't mind giving me a DNA swab?" Jackson reached back over the seat for his black bag.

"No way. You're not putting me into the system. Not without a warrant." Travis laughed at the absurdity of the suggestion.

Jackson tried not to get mad. Kids were so much more savvy about the law and about their rights than they used to be. "What did you do with her phone?"

A slight hesitation. "Jeremy has it. I told him to leave it, but he doesn't listen." Travis rolled his eyes. Apparently, being Jeremy's friend wasn't easy.

"Where can I find him?"

Travis shrugged. "He's not in school today. You can check at home, but he's not there much."

"Where else would he be?"

"Jason's, maybe. Or the skate park."

"Let's go find him. I need that phone today."

‹ **35** ›

Wednesday, October 27, 9:05 a.m.

KERA'S INTERNAL DEBATE about whether she should go to work went on through most of the morning. She even dressed in business-casual clothes and made a lunch. But she didn't go. Physically, she felt capable—not good yet— just functional. But she could not make herself leave the house. Finally, just to put an end to her mental ping pong, she called Sheila and told her she was staying home. Sheila was so nice about it that Kera was able to shed some of her guilt.

After mentally working through her anxiety, Kera realized that what she feared was that God's Messenger would breach the sanctuary of her home while she was gone. Once inside, he could inject poison into almost anything in her kitchen. And the horror of the ricin trauma was kept fresh by every painful breath. So until she had a secure alarm system, she could not leave herself that vulnerable. Emotionally, it felt cowardly. Intellectually, it seemed reasonable.

Because she wasn't going out, Kera felt compelled to be productive at home. She spent some time cleaning, then made several phone calls. She arranged to rent a storage space and hired movers to haul Daniel's stuff out this weekend. He had called the night before and made it clear they had no future together. It had been an awkward and painful conversation, but now she knew for sure. It was time to move forward. A second call to Security First netted her a promise that they would be out "tomorrow before nine" to install her alarm system.

Fresh-brewed coffee in hand, Kera sat down at her computer and used Safari to get online. She scanned MSNBC—no breaking news—then went directly to the girlsjustwanttohavefun website. It was time to get involved. This group of kids needed a safe sex intervention, and this website presented an opportunity for her to contact them directly, but anonymously. Kera logged in using Jessie's ID and opened the chat page labeled Dirty Gossip, which—no surprise—always seemed to have the most traffic. But this morning, there was no activity; its users were probably in class.

Calling herself *safe_sex_fiend*, Kera took a few minutes to compose and post a brief note.

Are you having sex? Good for you. Are you using condoms? No? Then it's time for a visit to Planned Parenthood. You could already have a sexually transmitted disease. Or be pregnant and not know it. Planned Parenthood will safeguard your privacy and provide reproductive healthcare services, regardless of your age or ability to pay. Make the appointment now. Or just come in when you can. (The clinic is on Commerce St., across from CourtSports.) Your friends (and partners) are counting on you.

Kera reread the message several times, made a few minor edits, then hit post. She was curious to see if anyone would respond directly, or if the group would even find her post worthy of discussion. But even if they didn't chat about it, at least some of them would read the message and maybe give it some thought. Kera checked other news sites, but clicked back to the sex club page every five minutes. So far, no one had responded. She decided to get away from the computer for a while and give it some time.

In the kitchen, she poured herself another cup of coffee and promised that she would use her elliptical machine this afternoon to burn off the caffeine.

The pile of unopened mail on the kitchen table beckoned her. It was unsightly and needed to be dealt with, in spite of her fear. Kera donned latex gloves and a fabric particle mask that covered her mouth and nose. She kept the masks on hand to use while mowing the lawn or cleaning the oven. Today, she hoped it would keep her safe from any contaminants that might come through the post office. This mail is harmless, she told herself. All of it had come either before or on the same day as the poisoned letter. Everything since then was still sitting out there in her mailbox, which was probably crammed to capacity.

Kera wrote checks to the utility company, her dentist, and Disabled Veterans of America. The solid white envelope with the feminine handwriting addressed to Nathan, she saved for last. The postmark was Salem, the state capital about sixty miles north of Eugene. She made herself open the envelope.

Kera's hands shook as she read the last communication to her son.

Dear Nathan

I know you thought you'd probably never hear from me again. What's that saying? Ships that pass in the night. But circumstances have changed. I found out this morning that I'm pregnant. And it's your baby. There hasn't been anyone else.

Kera stopped reading. She stared at the plain white paper with the short, handwritten note, which was now gripped tightly in both hands. It took a moment for the information to process. Nathan had a child. She had a grandchild. Joy filled her heart, expanding out from her chest until her entire body felt almost weightless. She still had a family.

Kera focused on the rest of the words.

I'm sorry. I didn't mean for this to happen. I didn't want this. In fact, I'm thinking of having an abortion. But I couldn't just do it without letting you know. I know this

*is the last thing you need right now, being in the middle
of a war and all, but I thought you had a right to know.
If I don't hear from you within a month, I'm going ahead
with it. I can't wait any longer than that.
Again. I'm sorry. I hope you're doing okay. Be safe.
Danette*

Panic clutched at Kera's chest and snatched back her moment of happiness. What if it was too late? Danette may
have already had the abortion. Kera searched frantically for
a date. There was none on the letter, but the postmark on
the envelope said October 10. Why had she let the letter sit
so long? She had to find this young woman, to let her know
that she wanted this baby. She would offer to help Danette
financially—and emotionally—in any way that she could.
She could even offer to adopt the baby.

As Kera reached for the phone book, tears rolled down
her cheeks. She did not know if she was happy or sad or
simply overcome. Ultimately, whether this child was born
or not was not her decision, no matter how painful that
seemed.

Ohh, but to have a grandchild....

Wednesday, October 27, 10:55 a.m.
JACKSON RUSHED through the department, only nod-
ding at Alicia behind the desk, even though she was always friendly to him. He had chased after Jeremy Carson
all morning and had nothing to show for it. And the task
force was meeting at eleven o'clock and he didn't want to
be late again. Schakowski and McCray walked up just as he
approached the conference room.

Schak clasped him on the shoulder and said, "You look
like shit, Jackson. The bags under your eyes are too big for
carry-on. Put in for some time off when this is a done deal,
okay?"

"Thanks, Mom. I'll do that." Jackson was suddenly aware

that his jacket was wrinkled and that people had noticed he was only shaving every other day.

Agent Fouts and a younger dark-haired man with a thick torso sat in the chairs. Fouts introduced the new guy as Agent Miguel Morales.

"Agent Morales is here to help me conduct extensive interviews with the members of the First Bible Baptist Church and the Conservative Culture Alliance. Our focus is to find the bomber and the perpetrator of the ricin attack. But we'll sit in on these task force meetings for the homicides to gather background information and stay in the loop. Even though Mayor Fieldstone is not a likely candidate for the bombing, there's still plenty of overlap in these cases."

Jackson nodded and resisted the urge to smile. Fouts must have interrogated Fieldstone and come away disappointed. But the FBI agent seemed to be hanging on to the theory that the bomber and the murderer were the same person, or at least connected. Jackson asked, "Have you found anything in your investigation that we should know about?"

"I got a look at Jessie Davenport's medical record this morning. She never had an abortion. So that's not likely the link between the cases."

Evans waltzed in looking bright-eyed and sharply dressed in a cobalt blue blazer. Jackson made up his mind to call his doctor for a prescription of that energy drug.

"Good morning." She glanced around at the men. "Did you start without me?"

"No. But let's get moving. I want this to be brief. You start, Evans. What do you have to report?"

Without checking her notes, she said, "I finally talked to someone in the house across the street from the Clarkes. Guy named Ian Marcowitz. He said he took the trash out on Sunday night sometime between 6 and 7 p.m. and saw a minivan parked in the Clarkes' driveway." She stopped and cocked her head at Jackson. "What are you looking at?"

"Nothing. Continue." Her energy made the rest of them look like zombies.

"He says the Clarkes drive a minivan, but this one wasn't theirs. He claims it was bigger. And maybe maroon. But it was getting dark, and he's not good with color." Evans made air quotes around the last phrase.

"Any idea of the make or model?"

Evans shook her head. "He says he's not good with cars either." More air quotes.

"So, a color-blind man saw a minivan in the driveway. Great. I bet everyone in that fricking church drives a mini-van."

Evans stared at Jackson. "Did you just say 'fricking church'?"

"Sorry."

She laughed. "You didn't insult me, you surprised me." She continued her report: "I've got a call into the DMV to get the make and model of every car registered to everyone connected with these homicides."

"I'd like a copy of that report when you get it," Fouts interjected.

"Of course." Evans glanced over at Jackson. "Are you okay?"

"I feel like a blind man swinging at a piñata on this one. I know the goods are right there in front of us, but I just can't hit it."

"I know what you mean." Schak tapped his notebook. "Fieldstone's wife checked herself into a private mental health clinic in Eastern Oregon on Monday. Which means she could have killed Nicole Sunday night, then had a little breakdown. But the clinic director won't let me talk to her without a court order."

Damn. Jackson's frustration jolted up a notch. Except for the trace evidence, the wife looked good for both homicides. "Find out what she drives and push the paperwork for the court order to see her."

"Anything else?" Jackson asked

McCray spoke up. "I did a background check on Field-stone's eyewitness like you asked me to. He's been investigated for fraud twice. So his credibility is crap."

"Thanks. I needed to hear that." Jackson threw in his bad news. "Nicole's lab results are mystifying. None of the trace evidence matches the DNA in Jessie's death. It's like we're dealing with a whole new perpetrator. Which knocks down all of our current scenarios."

"A copycat crime?" McCray offered.

"Or an opportunistic crime." Jackson checked his notes from Debbie's call. "Another thing. There was cat hair on Nicole's clothes. But the Clarkes don't have a cat. Anyone remember a cat in any of the homes you've visited?"

Evans laughed. "I have a cat. So do several of the tenants in the Regency Apartments. As does Ian Marcowitz, the Clarkes' neighbor who saw the van in the driveway."

"Maybe the neighbor is trying to throw us off. Get back over there. Get a sample of that cat hair." Jackson had been feeling a sense of urgency all morning. Now his chest tightened in a painful grip. "Any other cats?"

Schak shook his head. "Do the mayor and his wife have a cat?"

"Good question." Jackson made a note in his casebook. "I'll find out. I need to talk to him again anyway. As it turns out, he is the father of Jessie's baby."

Evans slapped her notebook. "That makes the statutory rape charge a slam dunk."

"And ruins his lawsuit." Schak made a face that showed he was not above gloating.

Jackson wasn't ready to celebrate. There was still something going on in these cases that he had not yet wrapped his head around. Something big still loomed out there. He looked at his team. "Evans, go back to the Clarkes' neighbors. Schak and McCray, you guys get back to the church people, looking for cats. And maroon minivans. Call me with anything significant."

Jackson dreaded this next moment. "At the press conference yesterday it became obvious that someone is leaking details of these cases to the media. I find it hard to believe that it is anybody in this room, yet who else has the information?"

The group was silent. Evans and Schakowski each gave him a hairy eye, but McCray just looked tired. Jackson couldn't read either Fouts or Morales.

"Any ideas how information might be getting out there? Anybody sharing their discoveries with another detective or officer?"

"No." Schak was the only one to respond verbally. McCray and Evans shook their heads.

"I shouldn't have to say this. Be careful with your notes. Do not talk to anyone about these cases. Do not sabotage our efforts. These young girls deserve justice."

As he stepped out of the conference room, the front desk officer informed Jackson that the chief was looking for him. Jackson's stomach reacted with a sharp pain. This would not be good.

He stepped into the corner office and could feel the chill in the air. Warner did not get up or display any expression. "Have a seat, Jackson, but don't get comfortable. This won't take long."

Oh shit.

"In simple language, I'm pulling you off these homicides," Warner deadpanned. "Schak will take the lead, and you will go back into the rotation."

36

Jackson's heart missed a beat. "May I ask why, sir?"

"Don't play dumb with me." Warner scowled. "Your press conference yesterday set off a media frenzy about Fieldstone. You sabotaged his career. And I specifically instructed you not to. It's insubordination, and it's grounds for dismissal."

Jackson swallowed hard. "Slonecker filed the charges, sir. Sergeant Lammers instructed me to hold a press conference. I couldn't lie. The arraignment records are open to the public."

"You could have played down the mayor's charges." Warner shook his head in disgust. "And you should not have told the media that Jessie was pregnant. I no longer trust you to handle these cases."

"I didn't tell them, sir. I don't know where they got that information." Jackson started to feel desperate. "I'm about to make a breakthrough. Pulling me right now is a mistake."

"Bullshit. And don't tell me I'm making a mistake or I'll put you on leave of absence too."

Jackson couldn't accept the idea that he would have to step down. It was not in his nature to give up or let go. "I just got the lab results on Jessie Davenport's fetus. The DNA matches Fieldstone. She was pregnant with his child."

The chief was silent. Jackson said a little prayer.

"Shit." Warner was at a loss for words.

"Give me some more time," Jackson implored.

"Stay away from the mayor."

Jackson could not promise that, so he said, "Thank you, sir," and quickly walked out.

Jackson headed straight to the skate park near the Amazon ball fields. His stomach was growling, but food would have to wait. Nicole's phone records had not come through yet, and he wanted to know who she had talked to the night she was killed. His gut told him that Janice Fieldstone may have called.

He had stopped by the park this morning with Travis Walters, Jeremy's friend and conspirator, but Jeremy had not been around. Afterward, they'd stopped by Jeremy's house and picked up a photo of him, so Jackson could find Jeremy later on his own.

And there he was, hanging out at the four-foot cement outer wall, gesturing wildly to another boy in the telling of some story. Jeremy was five-six, lean but sinewy, and his curly dark hair was cut close to his scalp. He had an infectious grin, even for a cop coming his way while he skipped school.

He hitched up his jeans as he spoke. "Are you looking for me?"

"Jeremy Carson?"

"Yea." He nodded. "What's up?"

"Let's take a short walk."

About half way across the lawn, Jeremy announced, "This is far enough. I'm not getting in your car."

Jackson lost his patience and yelled. "You smell like weed. That's probable cause to search and arrest you. But I don't give a shit about stoners because I'm trying to find a killer. So give me the dead girl's phone right now. Don't waste any more of my time being cute."

Jeremy gave him an all-teeth grin. "You could have just asked nicely." He produced the phone from deep in a pocket on the left leg of his cargo pants. "I only made a couple calls."

Jackson pulled on gloves from his bag before taking it. "Did you kill Nicole?" He watched the boy's eyes.

"No way. I never even met her, and I had no reason to hurt her."

"I want a DNA sample. Will you come into the department tomorrow and give one?"

Jeremy shrugged, unsure. "Uhh. Okay. If it will clear me."

"Great. Thanks."

Jackson headed back to his car. Homicide statistics said that the person who reported finding the body was often the perpetrator. But those were typically domestic situations, among family members. Instinct told him that Travis and Jeremy were just stoners who stumbled on a dead girl and had the momentary respectability to call it in.

Back in the Impala, he flipped open the phone and hit the Menu key, then pressed the Calls selection. From that menu, he selected Incoming, the second-line choice. A list of eight calls showed on the small screen with more available through scrolling. The top number—the most recent call—looked familiar. Jackson down-scrolled to the number and clicked OK. The screen lit up with Rachel Greiner across the top, with the phone number repeated on the second line. The third line of type contained the time and date: 6:22p Sun Oct. 24.

Rachel had lied to him when she said she hadn't talked to Nicole on Sunday night. But why? Who was she protecting? He would have to get back to her about that.

Jackson scanned the list of recent calls but didn't see Janice Fieldstone's number. He was disappointed but not ready to give up. It was time for another talk with the mayor.

37

Wednesday, October 27, 3:05 p.m.

A young woman in her early twenties opened the door, and Jackson could see that she was Fieldstone's daughter. She had the same dark eyes and glowing skin. She scowled at Jackson but let him in.

"How is Mrs. Fieldstone?" Jackson tried to disarm a potentially hostile situation.

"She cracked up. I thought you knew." The young woman walked him back to the den.

"Dad, your favorite cop is here to see you again."

Fieldstone was staring at a home remodeling show. He looked up at Jackson and shook his head, then gestured for him to come sit on the couch. Jackson sat. Fieldstone muted the TV but didn't turn it off.

"Good afternoon, Detective Jackson." The mayor spoke the words carefully but couldn't mask his whiskey-sour breath.

"Mr. Fieldstone." Jackson nodded. "Do you have a few minutes to talk?"

"Sure. I'm on vacation. I've got lots of time."

Jackson reached in his shoulder bag for his recorder. "Do you mind if I tape? It's so much easier than taking notes."

Fieldstone shrugged, so Jackson started the mini-cassette. "We have all the lab results now. They don't look good for you."

"I imagine not."

Jackson glanced at the door, where the daughter stood in

the opening. "Please close the door," he said. She looked at her father with disgust, then sharply pulled it shut.

Jackson spoke gently. He was here to sympathize, to nudge. If Janice Fieldstone had killed the girls, the mayor probably knew about it. And probably felt somewhat responsible. "We know you had sex with Jessie right before she died. You left body hair on her pubis. And she was suffocated with a sheet that matches the sheets in your apartment. You'll get a life sentence unless you tell me what really happened. Start with when your wife stopped into the apartment and caught you with Jessie."

The mayor looked startled. "What are you talking about?"

"Your wife. She killed the girls didn't she? Jealousy can be a powerful emotion."

Fieldstone emphatically shook his head.

"Tell me what happened."

The mayor's handsome face was distorted with alcohol and despair. His eyes watered copiously. He stood slowly and headed for the mini-bar in the corner of the room. Fieldstone came back with a tumbler full of ice and what looked like whiskey.

"My wife had nothing to do with this."

"The baby was yours," Jackson threw out. "I got the DNA test this morning. A son."

Fieldstone hurled the full tumbler across the room. It missed the TV and broke against the wall. His daughter, who must have been right outside the door, burst in. She looked at her father, then at the mess of glass and booze, then at Jackson.

"Get out," she yelled at Jackson. It was both a command and a plea.

"No, you get out." The mayor shouted back, his voice hoarse and pathetic. The daughter backed away. Jackson was upset by the distraction. He thought the mayor had been on the verge of talking.

Jackson said nothing while Fieldstone poured himself another drink. But the mayor didn't return to the couch. Instead he paced the room, pausing in front of the windows that faced the lush backyard and the forest beyond.

"I could have been a senator," he said finally. "But I was weak and lonely. Does that seem strange to you? To be married and lonely?" He turned back to Jackson, clearly needing some empathy.

Jackson didn't have to fake it. "I was married and lonely for a long time. It's like being in a box with the only exit leading to more loneliness, and a big dose of stress and guilt."

Fieldstone gave a little laugh. "I found another exit. It cured my loneliness, but it also led to stress and guilt."

"Tell me about Jessie. She must have been quite a girl."

Fieldstone hesitated for a moment, then—looking for redemption—began his story.

He had noticed Jessie the summer before at the First Bible Baptist's annual potluck picnic, held at Armitage Park on the McKenzie River. She was blond and pretty and tall for her age. Jessie reminded him of his wife, Janice, when she was young, whom he had met in high school and married soon after. He couldn't believe Jessie was only thirteen and a half. The way she moved and smiled and spoke was beyond her years. She was confident and friendly, complimenting Fieldstone on his softball skills. When they were alone together at the beverage coolers, she flirted with him, flicking her perfectly straight hair off her shoulders and smiling coyly.

Fieldstone had been flattered. He was used to being flirted with—it came with his job and his good looks—but that a girl so young would find someone his age attractive appealed to his vanity and his fear of aging.

"She came on to me," Fieldstone said emphatically. "From that first day. She touched me in church. She rubbed against me at a garage-sale fundraiser. She teased me for months, and I resisted. Oh, I enjoyed it. I had not experienced that kind of sexual anticipation in a long time." Fieldstone smiled dryly. "The curse of man."

The apartment, he swore, was meant only as a place to escape to during long workdays and for his parents to use when they came to town. But then one time, at a prayer breakfast, Jessie had expressed a need for a place to get away from her mother. Fieldstone had invited her to his apartment. They had agreed to meet there after school, a safe place where she could talk about her problems.

The talking hadn't lasted long. Jessie had her tongue in his ear within five minutes of walking in the door, he claimed. Thirty minutes later, Fieldstone was naked, spent, and stunned at what he had just done. But Jessie's obvious sexual experience mitigated his guilt. He had not taken her virginity. Or even been asked politely if he wanted to tango.

"I know this sounds like blaming the victim, but believe me, that girl was a sexual force. She was the aggressor. At least at first." Fieldstone sucked down the remains of his drink. "I got hooked though. In fact," he looked at Jackson with guileless eyes, "I fell in love with her."

Jackson's thoughts went immediately to the orange panties he'd found in the mayor's robe in the apartment bathroom. They didn't belong to Jessie or Nicole. Were they Janice Fieldstone's or was the mayor a serial cheat? Jackson kept his thoughts to himself and let the man continue. He hoped the mayor would get to Jessie's death before the tape reached the end and needed to be flipped over. Fieldstone had probably forgotten that he was being recorded, and Jackson didn't want to remind him.

Their sex play had become experimental. Fieldstone wanted to try everything his prudish Christian wife wouldn't do, and Jessie was game. They were both into bondage, with Jessie being the one who liked to be tied up. Toward the end, though, Jessie had started showing up at their Tuesday trysts high on Vicodin. Fieldstone had mixed feelings about her recreational drug use. It made her sexually more pliable, but he missed the spark in her eyes and the sharp banter they had exchanged.

Yeah, Jackson thought, *You were in it for the conversation.*

The mayor continued his story. The last time they were together, Jessie had been high again. But Fieldstone hadn't realized just how much she'd taken. He had tied her to the bed, face down as usual. He wanted to have anal sex, but Jessie said no, and that surprised him. She said she was too sore. And he realized that she'd been with someone else. Maybe even that day.

"At first, the idea of it bothered me," Fieldstone admitted. "But I let it go. After all, I was still giving it to my wife every once in a while. And Jessie and I never talked about fidelity to each other."

So they'd had vaginal sex, with Jessie face down on the bed, a pillow under her hips. Fieldstone had been excited, strangely turned on by thinking about another guy with his dick in her ass. He'd taken a Viagra earlier, so the encounter had gone on for a long time, maybe forty minutes. He remembered pushing on her shoulders, maybe even the back of her head. He remembered that she became kind of quiet, which was unusual for her. But he was caught up in his own passion and didn't stop until he climaxed.

"Afterward, I said her name. I worried that she hadn't had her usual noisy orgasm." He closed his eyes at the memory. "She didn't respond. I slapped her ass playfully, and she didn't even flinch. Then I got scared."

"I untied Jessie and rolled her over on her back. Her eyes

were open, but vacant. I grabbed her face and shouted at her to wake up. But it was too late." Fieldstone choked back a sob. "I felt for a pulse, but she didn't have one."

"She must have passed out from the Vicodin while we were screwing," he said, his voice wrecked with alcohol, grief, and shame. "Somehow, her air must have been cut off. The sheet was bunched up around her face, and maybe I held her too hard. I don't know. I didn't mean to hurt her." Fieldstone began to sob. "I was devastated. I loved her."

"Tell me what happened next."

The mayor wiped his face with his bathrobe sleeve and tried to control himself. "At first I couldn't even think straight. I held her in my arms and cried."

But when the mayor's brain did kick in, it went into self-preservation mode. He had a career to think about. He could do a lot of good in the world as a politician. Nothing would be served by his spending twenty years in prison, he rationalized. So he douched her vagina to rinse his sperm out and combed her pubic area to eliminate his hair. Then he stuffed her body into one garbage bag, and her clothes and backpack into another.

Fieldstone had pulled on a baseball cap and sunglasses—which he often wore when coming and going from the apartment—and went out to the parking lot to turn his car around. With the trunk backed up next to the front door, he carried the bags out to the car and dumped her in. He knew it would have been better to wait until dark, but he had a city council meeting that he could not miss. And other people had keys to the apartment: his assistant Mariska, the apartment manager, and his parents. Leaving her body there for six hours was a risk he couldn't take.

He thought he would take her out of town and dump her from a deserted road, but his phone rang. It was his assistant. He knew he had to answer the phone to give himself an alibi. Mariska wanted to know why he hadn't made it back to the office. He told her he was on his way. After hanging up, he'd become nauseous. The idea of Jessie, dead in his trunk, made him want to vomit. So he'd simply crossed the alley and shoved her in the dumpster. Then he'd driven down the alley, tossed her clothes in a trash can, and returned to work.

"I loved her. It was an accident." Fieldstone looked relieved to have it off his chest. He also looked smashed. "I want to make a deal. I'll plead to a lesser charge."

"What about Nicole Clarke?"

"I never touched her. I'm not sure I ever even spoke to her. I swear to you on my mother's life, I had nothing to do with her death."

"Let's get you some coffee, then we'll go talk to the DA."

Later, as they drove downtown, a haunting question plagued Jackson: So who killed Nicole?

38

Wednesday, October 27, 3:35 p.m.

ACCORDING TO THE return address information, Danette's last name was Blake, and Kera had called every Blake in the Salem phone book. She'd taken her cell phone and the white pages out to the back deck just to get out of the house, but after about twenty minutes, the rain and wind had kicked up and, even under the patio umbrella, she'd ended up wet. So she'd come back inside and put on a Tracy Chapman CD, thinking it would soothe her. She had never been indoors continuously for three days. It was making her stir crazy, and she was running out of fresh food. Thank god, the alarm people were coming in the morning.

Kera made twenty-six calls, leaving fourteen messages and speaking to ten people who claimed they had never heard of Danette. While waiting for return calls—that would not likely come—she tried an online search, plugging Danette's name into Google. A Danette Blake was president of Windhover University in Montana, but she was fifty-six years old. No other solid hits. Kera came up empty-handed from a search of Yahoo's online white pages too.

She was not discouraged. She would keep trying the fourteen numbers where she had left messages until she talked to each of them. As a last resort, she might try calling her friend Cher at the Planned Parenthood branch in Salem, just to see if an abortion was scheduled, or had been performed, for Danette Blake. But that would be a desperate call, and she probably wouldn't go through with it. It wasn't fair to ask Cher for that information.

As she took out the Chapman CD, which had made her sad instead of soothed, her cell phone rang. Kera checked the number displayed but didn't recognize it. It was a local number, so she knew it wasn't a telemarketer.

"Hello?"

"Is this Kera?"

"Yes."

"This is Rachel. I was a friend of Jessie's. I need to talk to you."

"Okay. When?"

"Can you meet me now at Starbuck's on 28th and Willamette?"

"I can't. Not today." Kera felt guilty for putting her off. But she really did not want to leave the house until she had an alarm system installed.

"This is pretty important." Rachel sounded a little desperate. "I know you care about what happens to us. That's why you posted that safe sex message on our website."

Kera hesitated, not ready to give up the anonymity of her message. "Why don't you come here? I have the time to see you, I just don't feel well enough to leave the house."

"Hmm. Okay. I guess that could work. I'll come by tonight around seven."

Kera gave her the address, and they hung up. Rachel had sounded scared. Was it about the sex club? Or was she afraid of whoever had killed Jessie and Nicole?

She would soon find out.

Wednesday, October 27, 5:42 p.m.

JACKSON DROPPED OFF the mayor at the DA's office, where Fieldstone's lawyer and Slonecker waited to meet with him. Jackson could have stayed, but his input wasn't really needed or welcome at this point. In truth, the plea bargain negotiations were hard for him to stomach. In exchange for saving the city some time and money in court, criminals were given light sentences. With the current funding crisis, it was the new justice.

Jackson wanted no part of this one. Although Fieldstone's story was believable on some levels, there was no one to dispute his version of the events. The mayor may very well be a grieving pedophile who had accidentally killed his young lover—or he could be a cold-blooded murderer who was also a good storyteller and actor. On some level, Jackson was glad a jury would be spared the difficulty of making that call.

The rain finally let up on the drive home. Jackson planned to have dinner with Katie, then maybe go back to work for a while. Or maybe he would stay home and read through his case notes, thinking about how Fieldstone's confession dramatically changed the scenario of Nicole's death. The mayor claimed he never touched Nicole, and the trace evidence supported that claim. If everything Fieldstone said was true—a huge hypothetical—then the motive for Nicole's murder could be different than anything they'd speculated about so far. No serial killer, no religious avenger, no jealous wife. He had to go back to the basics: greed, lust, fear, revenge, love, and hate.

The wind had blown a new layer of leaves over his lawn, and Jackson vowed to rake this weekend. He also hoped to clean out the shop and make room for his trike project. He smiled just looking at the garage and visualizing the activity.

The smell of Italian sausage, garlic, and basil greeted him at the front door. Katie was cooking spaghetti. He stepped into the kitchen and gave her a hug.

"Gun," she said, stepping back.

"Sorry." Jackson took his jacket and his Sig Sauer into the bedroom. He never worried that his daughter would follow in his career footsteps.

While Katie boiled angel hair pasta, Jackson heated up

some canned green beans in the microwave. "Is that garlic bread I smell in the oven?"

"Yep."

"Bonus on your allowance this month. I'm so hungry. I feel like I haven't eaten much this last week."

"You look like you've lost weight." She grinned, and they both burst out laughing. It was a family code they used to distract Renee when she was on a drunken rant, typically about getting old.

"Thanks." Jackson kissed her forehead. "For cooking too."

After dinner, they cleaned up together, and Katie gave him a detailed account of a field trip she'd taken to the state capitol that day. Then Jackson's cell phone rang. He glanced over to where it lay on the dining room table. It could be one of the team.

"Go ahead." Katie dismissed him with a casual wave.

Jackson picked up on the third ring.

"It's Evans. The fax from the DMV just came in. The Stricklands own a maroon minivan and a white Dodge extension van that seats twelve."

"Interesting." Jackson moved out of the kitchen and out of his daughter's line of hearing. "I picked up Nicole's cell phone today from one of the boys who found her. And Nicole's last call came from Rachel Greiner at 6:22 Sunday evening. But when I questioned Rachel, she said she hadn't talked to Nicole since the memorial service that afternoon."

Jackson stepped into his bedroom and closed the door.

"So?" Evans said. "Kids lie just because they're afraid. I'm more concerned about the possibility that one of the Strickland's vehicles was parked in Nicole's driveway before she disappeared. What if the Reverend is a pervert?"

"He was in Portland at the CCA meeting, right? You

checked with other members?"

"He and his wife were both there."

"Hmm. Who else lives in the home besides Angel?" Jackson asked.

"No one. They have an eighteen-year-old son in college in Portland."

So who drove the minivan? Angel was too young, wasn't she? And why would she and Rachel both lie about talking to Nicole? The detail that had been bothering him for days—the thing he had failed to follow through on—suddenly came back in a rush. Twice, Kera had mentioned a website to him. What had she said? A chat room where Jessie's friends discussed their sexual activity. Kera had called it a sex club.

"Evans, I'm going to check out something online. I'll get back to you."

"Anything I should do in the meantime?"

"Get something to eat. We're probably going back to work tonight."

Wednesday, October 27, 6:45 p.m.

RACHEL HEARD her parents' car leave the driveway and leaped out of bed. She had complained of a stomachache as soon as she got home from school, then had spent the evening in bed to get out of attending Bible study with her family. Caleb had stopped in and tried to call her bluff—because of course, he still had to go—but she ignored him, and he went away. Caleb would never rat her out. Just as she had never told her parents about the time she'd caught him sneaking out of the house in the middle of the night. She and Caleb annoyed each other, but they had both suffered too many beatings with a belt—among other things—to give each other up.

Rachel pulled on a sweatshirt and Sketchers and grabbed her cell phone. And talk about sneaking around in the middle of the night, what was her crazy mother up to now? Rachel had heard her go out the night before around one-thirty in the morning, then return about an hour later. And she hadn't taken the car.

Rachel dialed Angel, who took a moment to answer.

"Are you on your way?"

"Yes. But you shouldn't call me when I'm driving." Angel laughed nervously. "I almost hit the mailbox backing out of the driveway. I really hate backing up. But I have to practice so I can pass the driver's test."

"Shut up and drive." Rachel hung up. Angel only had her learner's permit, and she was a pretty bad driver so far, but it was the only way they could get around by themselves. And they had so few opportunities.

Rachel hurried to the kitchen and used a chair to retrieve her mother's Ativan prescription from the cupboard above the sink. She shook five of the tiny white tablets into her palm, then slid them into an empty trial-sized Midol container. The Ativan prescription bottle was still pretty full, so her mother probably wouldn't notice that any were gone. Rachel hoped she would not have to use them. But it was important to be prepared.

Angel gave a little beep of the horn when she pulled into the driveway, and Rachel cringed. Angel was sweet, but stupid. It made Rachel miss Jessie. That girl had been fun and smart. She had figured the angles on everything. Jessie was the one who had found the Stricklands' hiding place for spare car keys. Jessie had also convinced Angel they could get away with taking the minivan out when their parents were at the CCA meeting in Portland. Jessie had been very persuasive. And boatloads of fun. Rachel missed her immensely. The mayor was a rotten son-of-a-bitch for killing her.

She grabbed her cell phone and headed out. Was she forgetting anything?

Outside, the sun had dropped below the horizon, and she was glad for the twilight. They were much less likely to be noticed. Especially with Angel driving. Rachel jogged to the van and jumped in. It still smelled of sour milk.

"Why don't you clean this carpet?"

Angel rolled her eyes, then asked, "Are you sure we have to do this?"

"Let's go. We only have an hour and a half."

Angel sighed, then put the vehicle in reverse. She backed out of the driveway in jerky fits and starts, and Rachel prayed the neighbors weren't watching. This was almost over. They just had to stay cool, and everything would smooth out in time. She still had another three and a half years before she could escape her parents' house, but she would survive. As she had so far.

None of this would be necessary if Jessie hadn't been killed. Rachel still couldn't believe it. "I miss Jessie," she said when they were rolling down 27th Street.

"Me too. I dream about her all the time." After a moment, Angel said, "I miss Nicole too."

"I know. But she's in heaven with Jesus now. She's happy. And we'll see her again some day." Angel was still pretty emotional about what they'd had to do to protect the club's secret, so Rachel changed the subject. "Do you have a soccer game this weekend?"

Angel shrugged. "Yeah." They pulled into the left lane, and Angel started to make the turn on Olive.

"No!"

Angel slammed the brakes and Rachel lurched forward in her seat. They were stopped in the middle of the intersection, and the traffic whizzed by on both sides. Angel looked frightened. Rachel had just kept her from turning straight into a jacked-up truck.

"You have to wait for the green turn arrow," Rachel explained, again. "Or wait for a break in traffic. You'd better take driver's ed."

"My mother says I have to pay for it myself, and it's two hundred and fifty dollars."

"You can go after this car. Get ready."

Angel successfully negotiated the turn, and they traveled two blocks on Olive without mishap. Then they turned right on 29th Street and headed south.

"What are we going to say?" Angel asked with a little whine.

"Don't worry. Just follow my lead." Rachel reached out to reassure Angel. "We're just trying to find out what she knows and whether she plans to say anything. I think that's all it will come to."

"Why are you so sure Kera knows about the Teen Talk meetings?" Angel sounded distressed again.

Rachel was losing her patience. "She posted on our website. That means she read our messages where we talked about the sex. And we didn't hold back. Plus, I told you, I saw Nicole talking to her at school last Thursday. Kollmorgan also has access to our files at Planned Parenthood. She knows everything except how loud we are when we come."

Angel giggled. "You're loud. I'm not."

"Turn left up here. That's her street."

Angel veered left on McLean and they started up the hill.

"You know I feel bad about Nicole, but she was going to ruin our lives with her big mouth." Rachel fought the sickness in her stomach. "And we have to make sure Kollmorgan doesn't say anything either. Do you have any idea what would happen to me if my parents found out?"

"I know, Rachel. I've seen the welts." Angel's voice was barely audible.

"They would beat me every day for a month. They would ground me for a year, except for church and school. They might even pull me out of Kincaid, so they could home-school me." Rachel paused as that sank in. She would rather die than spend all day, every day with her mother. "The next few years of my life would become a living hell."

"My parents would send me away to one of those camps," Angel said. "They've threatened me with it enough times." Angel turned to her. "Maybe we should disband Teen Talk, at least for a while."

"Watch the road." Rachel shook her head. "We will, but not yet. It would look suspicious. Let's see how this goes. I think it's going to be okay."

Angel nodded, and Rachel hoped that turned out to be true. She didn't want to hurt anyone else, but sometimes you had to take action against a few individuals to protect a larger group. Her mother had taught her that, both as a direct lesson, and by example.

Rachel knew about the pipe bombs. She'd seen the materials in the laundry room, and she'd read some of her mother's e-mails to Josiah, the CCA member who had bombed some clinics in Portland. She'd also seen the news report about the girl who had died because of the bomb at the clinic. And her mother, the most religious person Rachel could imagine, had made it happen. Her mother did it to save the babies, the unborn souls. She could understand that.

Rachel hoped God would forgive her, but she just wanted to save herself.

39

Wednesday, October 27, 6:47 p.m.

JACKSON BOOTED UP his home computer, which was on a desk in the spare bedroom. The room functioned as a storage space for everything they didn't know what else to do with. It was a cramped and cluttered arrangement, but not much different from his workspace in the department, so it didn't bother him. While Windows loaded, he thumbed back through his notebook looking for the reference to the website Kera had mentioned.

The notation was in Kera's handwriting, in purple felt-tip with a confident, loopy flair: girlsjustwanttohavefun and below that, *blowgirl_jd*.

Jackson typed the URL into his browser. A bizarre scenario was taking shape in his brain, but he was having trouble accepting it. He hoped that a look at this site would ease his mind and allow him to reject his suspicions. The site loaded and overwhelmed him with its day-glo colors. His stomach sank just reading the chat room heads: Disgusting Guys, Hot Guys, Dirty Gossip, Sex Talk, and Parties. Instinctively, he opened Sex Talk and logged in using Jessie's screen name.

The current page displayed a recent chat about Jessie and Nicole's deaths and the possibility of a serial killer stalking the group of friends, but it had nothing about sex. Jackson found a link to the previous week's postings and opened it. The screen names added weight to the sick feeling in his stomach: *perfectass, freakjob, lipservice*. Who were these girls? And good God, had Katie ever been one of them?

Jackson scanned through the postings, mesmerized and repulsed at the same time. Then he came across a most disturbing exchange.

freakjob37: My dad has a new video called Candy Strippers. It's really hot. Lots of butt sex.

blowgirl_jd: Cool. I like it up the ass, I mean, if I'm ready for it. And no worries about pregnancy.

perfectass: Despite my screen name, I'm not that crazy about anal encounters, but neither is TJ so we'll hook and let you guys do the nasty stuff.

blowgirl_jd: Like you can get through a "meeting" only doing one guy. Hah!

freakjob37: I think it's time for little miss *perfectass* to start doing girls too.

perfectass: I'm working up to it. I made out with RG last time. The guys got really hard for that session.

Jackson pushed his chair back from the computer, needing distance from the words and images. He felt as if he'd just walked into a children's orgy. Tremors shot up his legs and he felt as if he might throw up. These were eighth-grade girls! Girls his daughter used to hang out with.

At least, that's what everything pointed to. *Blowgirl_jd* was clearly Jessie, and RG must be Rachel Greiner. So the other chatters could be Nicole and Angel. All these girls belonged to religious families. God-fearing people who would be shocked and devastated to learn about their children's behavior.

A dozen questions competed for his attention. When and where had this group sex taken place? Where were the parents? How could they not know? Did they know? Were the parents involved too? The dark scenario, in which Nicole had been killed to keep a secret, took form and breathed on its own.

Jackson stood, legs trembling, and stepped out into the hall. "Katie!"

His daughter came quickly, her expression frightened. She had never heard him sound like that before: Anguish, fear, and anger all rolled into one roar.

"What is it?" Katie was wearing a Winnie the Pooh T-shirt, and her face was plump with baby fat.

"Tell me about the sex club."

"What are you talking about?"

"Don't bullshit me. I've been to the website. I've read the chats about group sex." Jackson heard the sounds coming out of his mouth but did not recognize the thinness of his own voice. "I know Jessie and Nicole and Angel were all involved. They used to be your friends. Were you in the club?"

They stood in the hallway, where all their confrontations seemed to take place, and a great silence engulfed them. It stretched out until Jackson thought his blood vessels would all burst in a simultaneous pop.

"I can't talk about it. I promised I would never tell anyone." Katie's voice was high-pitched and ready to cry. "I took a blood oath."

Jackson's chest tightened in a painful squeeze. He vowed to see his doctor again soon. "Nicole may have been killed because she threatened to break that promise. You're protecting the wrong people."

"It's not a serial killer?" Now she looked confused.

"No."

"Then who?"

"I'm trying to figure that out. Now tell me!"

"What do you want to know?" she said finally.

"Everything." Jackson realized that wasn't true. He didn't want to know the details, especially if his daughter had participated. He didn't want to know the name of the boy or boys who had penetrated her. If he didn't know them, he couldn't kill them. He couldn't find them and beat them senseless with his bare hands.

Jackson shook his head. "No. Not everything. But I need to know some names. I need to know if any of the parents participated. And where it took place."

"Ehww." She made a horrified face. "No parents. Just kids. And it happened during Teen Talk, after school on Tuesdays at Angel's house." She hesitated again, then finally rattled off the names in one long breath. "It's who you think it is: Angel, Jessie, Nicole, and Rachel. Plus Greg Miller, Tyler Jahn, and Adam Walsh."

Jackson had heard all those names at the beginning of his investigation. He had just never connected the Bible study and the sexual activity.

His silence must have worried Katie, because she began to cry. "I quit the group, you know. After the first couple of times. I didn't like it. And I lost all my friends. Don't be mad at me."

Jackson knew he should comfort her, that he should stay and talk. But he couldn't. Not yet. He was glad he needed to leave. "I'm not angry." That was bull. He started over. "Scratch that. I am angry. You lied to me. Again and again. There's a lot more we need to talk about. But I have to go back to work right now. I need to find Nicole's killer."

Jackson moved toward his bedroom to get his jacket and weapon. At the door, he turned back to Katie, who was sitting in the hall crying. "I'd like to trust you to stay home by yourself while I'm working tonight, but I can't. So pack a bag, you're going to Aunt Jan's. But this case will be over soon, and we will talk."

Seven minutes later, they were headed out into the damp darkness.

Jackson knew he had to stop thinking about Katie and focus on this case. Rachel had called Nicole on the night of her death and then lied about it to him. Angel's parents owned a vehicle that matched the description of the one that had been seen in Nicole's driveway the night of her death. Had Rachel and Angel worked together? Jackson thought they must have had help from one of the boys in the club. He couldn't imagine either Angel or Rachel putting a plastic bag over Nicole's head and holding it until she died. Teenage girls didn't commit murder.

Yes they did, he reminded himself. Last summer, two girls in Bend—one fourteen, one fifteen—had murdered the fourteen-year-old's brother. Bludgeoned him over the head and took his iPod and the fifty dollars in his wallet. And a fifteen-year-old girl in Klamath Falls had killed her mother a few years ago, then took off in the family car. And that was just in Oregon. Adolescent girl violence had increased dramatically all across the country. Psychologists said it was because females' roles were changing. Jackson thought it was because all kids in America grew up overexposed and desensitized to violence.

He started the Impala and looked over at his daughter, who was staring at her hands. She was a good kid. They would get through this.

Jackson decided to start at the Stricklands. But first he would call out the team. They would help him round up all the Teen Talk participants and bring them into the department. They would play one against the other until they had the story.

Wednesday, October 27, 6:30 p.m.
KERA WAS JUST getting out of the shower after completing fifty minutes on her elliptical machine. The exercise had not only taken the edge off her tension, it had worn her out. She thought she might sleep well tonight. Or at least better than she had lately.

While she was getting dressed, her cell phone rang. She grabbed it from the bed where she'd left it. "Hello."

"This is Margaret Blake. You left me a message asking if I knew Danette Blake. Can I ask what this is about?"

Kera assumed this had to be the young woman's mother. "Danette sent a letter to my son." She paused, wanting to glide over this part. "But he died, and so I opened the letter, in case it was important. I just wanted to let Danette know."

"Give me your son's name and I'll tell her."

"I'd rather tell her myself. If you don't want to give me Danette's contact information, I understand. But please pass my number along to her. I'd really like to speak with her. I have some information that she should have."

Margaret was silent for a moment. "Okay. I'll give her your number, but she may not call."

Kera gave her the number and said, "Please tell her this is important."

Kera thought about Margaret as she pulled on socks and padded into the den to boot up her computer. She understood the woman's hesitation. A mother protecting her child. She wondered if Margaret knew about her daughter's pregnancy. If she did, was she in support of the abortion? Would she be angry at Kera for butting in? Decisions about parenthood could be heartbreakers from the beginning.

As soon as she opened the Internet, her front doorbell rang. Kera jumped at the sound. Who was out there? She started toward the back bedroom, where she could see the front porch from the window, then stopped halfway down the hall. Rachel Greiner had called and said she wanted to come by this evening. Kera hurried back to the living room. She was curious about what Rachel had to say. She wondered if Rachel knew something about Jessie and Nicole's deaths, something she felt she couldn't tell the police but maybe would tell her.

As a precaution, Kera peeked through the keyhole. Two young girls stood in front of her door, the taller one glancing about nervously. Kera opened the door. "Rachel?"

40

7:03 p.m.

"Hi Kera." The girl smiled, but her pool-water blue eyes were solemn. She was five-three or so, slender and striking, but not necessarily pretty. Rachel gestured toward the girl standing slightly behind her. "This is my friend, Angel."

"It's nice to meet both of you. Come in." Kera stepped back and let the girls pass. Angel glanced over at her shyly. Kera remembered from the files that Angel was fifteen. She was meatier and taller than Rachel, but her strawberry blond hair and freckled cheeks made her seem younger. They both wore pullover sweatshirts and factory-faded jeans and smelled like grape gum. Kera locked the door out of habit.

"Would you like something to drink?" Kera asked as she directed them into the living room. "I have Diet Dr Pepper and coffee. And I think I have pineapple juice in the freezer."

"Dr. Pepper's good," Rachel said, and Angel nodded.

As the girls took a seat on the leather couch, Kera went to fetch the sodas. She stopped in the archway between the rooms, and turned back. Angel and Rachel had their heads together.

"Do you want it in a glass with ice? Or straight up in the can?

"The can is fine." Again, Rachel answered for both of them. Clearly, she was in charge of their friendship. Kera wondered if Rachel was also the leader of the whole sex club group.

Kera pulled her last three cans of DP from the fridge and

grabbed an unopened sleeve of low-fat Ritz crackers from the cupboard. She brought everything back to the living room and took a seat in the matching leather chair across from the couch.

There was a moment of silence followed by the sound of three pop cans opening. Angel giggled.

Kera decided to skip the small talk. "You said you wanted to speak with me about Jessie."

Rachel nodded and said, "We're upset about what happened to her. And we thought you might know something."

"Why would you think that?"

Rachel leaned forward. "Because you know her screen name. And you used it to post on our website. How do you know Jessie's screen name?"

The question took Kera by surprise. She had not expected the other club members to identify her as the author of the "safe sex" posting. And it never occurred to her that anyone would confront her directly about it. She was torn about how to respond. Jessie was dead and these girls had been her friends. Kera wanted to put them at ease if she could. But she still had to protect Jessie's confidence. She took a drink of soda while she formed an answer.

"Jessie sent me an e-mail. And after she died, I used her hotmail name to access the websites she had frequented. My goal was to learn something about her. I hope I haven't offended you. I meant well."

"Did you read the message boards?" Rachel kept her hands in her lap, each a small closed fist.

"I glanced at them."

"Why?"

So far, Angel hadn't said a word.

"I was upset about Jessie's death. I thought there might be information that could shed some light on it."

"Did you learn anything useful? Were you surprised by

the sex stuff?"

"Not really." Kera struggled to get inside Rachel's head and figure out what was driving this discussion. "As you probably know, I work for Planned Parenthood. I don't make judgments about people's sex lives."

"I suppose you were able to figure out who everyone is." Rachel's diction was perfect, and deadpan.

Yet Kera sensed hostility from her, so she avoided a direct response. "Identities are not important. I just want the group to practice safe sex. To use birth control and to come in for STD screenings."

"Those discussions were private," Rachel said. "You had no business reading them." She had the uncanny ability to sit perfectly still and focus on the person she was talking to. Kera found it discomforting. Angel, on the other hand, squirmed incessantly. They were an odd pair.

"You're right. I'm sorry." Kera decided it was time for them to go. Rachel was clearly not concerned about Jessie. And for some reason, she had not even mentioned Nicole's murder. She was mostly angry that Kera had accessed the club's website. Kera stood. "I'm not sure we're accomplishing anything here. But feel free to come see me at the clinic any time."

7:16 p.m.

THE BITCH. She was trying to make them leave. Right after lying about not knowing the names of the kids in the sex club. Rachel decided that Kera Kollmorgan could not be trusted.

"Can we stay a while longer, please?" Rachel smiled. "We have important questions. And we can't ask our parents."

"I don't think your parents would want you to be here," Kollmorgan said. "And I'm not comfortable giving you advice outside the clinic." She brushed her long hair back and glanced at the door.

The nurse not only knew who the sex club members were, she also knew their parents. This was bad news. "Will you get me a glass of water please?" Rachel asked in her polite church voice. "My throat hurts and this soda is making it worse."

Kollmorgan stood for a moment, staring at her. Rachel tried to look sad. Then Kollmorgan said "Sure" and headed for the kitchen.

As soon she was out of the room, Rachel lunged across the small space between the furniture grouping and snatched up Kollmorgan's Dr. Pepper can. She quickly dropped in all five Ativan tablets, which had been pressed in the pocket of her hand. She had only given Nicole three, but Kollmorgan was a big woman. Rachel covered the hole in the top of the can with her thumb and gave it a quick shake. The tablets, she had learned, dissolved almost instantly when they came into contact with liquid. Rachel wiped the can with her sleeve to smear her prints, set it down on the end table, and bolted back to the couch.

"What are you doing?" Angel whispered.

"The same routine we did with Nicole," Rachel whispered back. She heard the water shut off in the kitchen.

"You said we wouldn't have to do this." Angel sounded distressed. But she'd been that way for days, and Rachel ignored her.

"She knows too much, and I don't trust her. Now be quiet, she's coming."

As Kollmorgan came back into the room with a glass of ice water, Rachel looked up and smiled. "Thank you."

7:17 p.m.

JACKSON WAS GRATEFUL for speed dial. It allowed him to call Schak, Evans, and McCray while racing up Willamette Street in the dark with only one hand on the wheel. Sometimes cops were the most dangerous drivers on the

road. His first call had been to the dispatch center to retrieve an address for John Strickland: 3260 Donald. It was a
beautiful upscale neighborhood with a wide street, mature
oak and cherry trees, and large homes with perfectly mani-
cured front yards. Jackson did not see or appreciate any of
this in his present frame of mind, but he had noticed it two
days earlier when he'd driven up to Edgewood Park, where
Nicole's body waited.

The Strickland's two-story home was near the top and set
back from the road a little farther than others. Lights were
on, but there were no vehicles in the driveway. Still, they
could have been tucked into the oversized two-car garage.
As he trotted up to the front door, Jackson sensed no movement or sound from inside the house. He had the sinking
feeling that no one was home.

Repeated ringing of the doorbell and loud knocking confirmed that. Under the porch light, he opened his notebook
and searched for the Stricklands' phone number. He didn't
find it.

Jackson ran to his Impala and backed out into the street,
squealing his tires. Dispatch would probably get a complaint
from one of the neighbors about the disturbance. He called
Evans and she picked up immediately.

"What's happening?" she asked.

"No one is home at the Stricklands'. Any luck at the
Greiners'?"

"I'm not there yet. I'm coming in from Barger Drive.
Where are you headed now?"

"I think I'll swing by the church. If you find Rachel at
home, call me. I want to be there when you question her."

"Will do."

Jackson resisted the urge to call Schak and McCray; they
were probably also still en route to their assigned Teen Talk
homes. Schak lived in Springfield and McCray lived in the

River Road area, so they had even farther to drive than Evans. Jackson eased up on the gas and forced himself to breathe deeply. This was just another step in the investigation. If his theory was sound, it seemed unlikely that anyone else was in danger. Once they picked up the kids, it was simply a matter of pressing until one of them cracked. He veered left at Willamette and headed for 18th Street and the First Bible Baptist Church.

41

7:23 p.m.

KERA DECIDED TO LET them stay for a while. Rachel's anger seemed to have dissipated, and Angel's green eyes flickered with stress. The older girl still hadn't spoken, but now she kept glancing at Kera and looking away. While Rachel talked about the frustrations of having religious parents, Angel helped herself to a handful of crackers and munched them down as though it were a task she had to complete quickly. Kera wondered if she might be high on something.

"My parents are obsessed," Rachel said, her voice showing emotion for the first time. "Teen sex, gay sex, unmarried sex. They want to stop everybody. It's because they believe the Bible says sex is for procreation only. And my younger brother is eleven, so apparently they haven't done it in a long time. I guess they figure nobody else should have any fun either."

Kera was amused by her perception and thought Rachel might be right, but she wouldn't criticize the girl's parents.

"My parents have sex," Angel said suddenly. "I can hear them sometimes. And my dad has a bunch of porno tapes, so he must like to watch people fornicate."

Kera didn't know what to say. She took a long a drink of soda. It seemed a little bitter on the back of her tongue. She thought the soft drink must be reacting with the garlic chicken she'd had for dinner. After a moment she said, "Most people discover that it's best not to think too much about their parents' sex lives."

Rachel laughed, a short harsh sound. "Good advice." She leaned forward more intently now. "What did you and Nicole talk about?"

"That's confidential. But I think you know she shared some of your concerns."

"You mean about what would happen to her if she got caught?" Rachel's eyes held the flicker of anger again.

Kera felt her forehead pucker into a frown, then forced her face to relax. "Is that what you're worried about, Rachel?"

"Of course." Her expression turned mean. "My parents like to punish sinners."

Kera got goose bumps on her arms. Was this poor girl abused? She felt a lump rise in her throat, so she gulped another drink of soda to wash it down. The taste was worse this time. She pushed it aside.

"I hope this isn't out of line," she said, "but do they abuse you? I can give you the name of a lawyer who can help."

Rachel closed her eyes and shook her head. "I don't need a lawyer."

"They beat her," Angel said softly.

"Shut up, Angel."

Fear crept into Kera's bones. Rachel was an abused and angry young girl, but she was not here for help. Kera rose, anxious to terminate the conversation and get them out of her home. For a moment, she felt a little light headed and had to steady herself. "Let me get you the phone numbers of people and agencies you can call to report your situation."

Kera started to head for the Rolodex in her office, but Rachel's screech stopped her cold. "I don't want you to report my situation. I want you to stay out of my business!"

Kera turned back, feeling frightened and spacey at the same time. "It's your choice. Will you excuse me, please? I don't feel well." Kera took a step toward the front door, hoping the girls would get up and follow.

They didn't move.

She stood there for a moment, then felt like she had to sit back down. Her brain was mushy, and her legs felt as if she had just run five miles. Had she overdone it on the elliptical machine? Kera staggered back to her chair and flopped into it. What was wrong with her?

Rachel and Angel just sat there watching her, as if waiting for something.

And then the fear she had felt earlier took shape, and its newly formed fingers circled her heart. These girls had drugged her drink. They were here to harm her. Dear God, why?

Kera struggled to make sense of it, but her brain worked slowly. Rachel was clearly angry that Kera had been on the website and knew about the sex club. But what was she afraid of? That Kera would tell her abusive parents?

Now, even her heartbeat felt slow. Kera looked around for her cell phone. She needed to call for help. She needed Jackson.

"What did you put in my soda?" The words came out in a slog of syllables.

"Just something to help you relax." Rachel smiled, and Kera felt a chill run up her spine.

"Why?"

"It's easier this way."

Rachel's casual confidence sent shocks of panic through Kera's torso. Rachel and Angel had done this before. The adrenaline surging in her veins cleared her brain enough to make the connection that these girls may have killed both Jessie and Nicole to keep them from talking about the sex club's activities. And now they planned to kill her too.

She had to get out, to make a run for it before the drug immobilized her completely.

7:35 p.m.
RUTH HAD JUST checked her watch when Detective Jack-

son burst into the small sanctuary in the church basement and interrupted the women's Bible study. They were reading First Corinthians Chapter 11, about women's roles in church and why their heads should be covered.

Ruth glanced back at him. With his dark suit, eyebrow scar, and short-cropped hair, Jackson looked like an FBI agent. But his insistence on harassing church people gave Ruth little confidence that he would ever find who killed Jessie and Nicole.

"Excuse me," he called from the back of the room. "I'd like to speak with Ruth Greiner and Eva Strickland, please." Some of worshippers turned to look at the detective. Most glanced at Ruth and Eva. Ruth felt a great wave of anger travel from her heart to her head, where it threatened to burst out. She had plans! She had to make that phone call to Kollmorgan in exactly twenty-one minutes. For Kollmorgan to die, she had to be in or near her car at eight o'clock.

But Ruth rose calmly, ignored the glances from her friends, and moved to the top of the sanctuary where Jackson stood, hands on hips, waiting.

"Where are Rachel and Angel?" he asked, not bothering with pleasantries.

"Rachel's home with a stomachache," Ruth answered, letting her irritation show. "Let's step out into the vestibule."

As they moved through the door, all eyes on their backs, Jackson said, "She's not home. My partner was just there." The detective turned to Eva. "No one is home at your place either."

Ruth's rage pulsed in her temples, causing little flashes of light under her eyelids. Rachel was in so much trouble. Why wouldn't that girl learn? Ruth needed an Ativan. Eva looked at her with panicked eyes. Neither said a word.

"Do you have any idea where your daughters are?" Jackson demanded. "I need to talk to them right now."

"What is this about?" Eva gripped her Bible for support.

"It's a homicide investigation. Where are they?"

Ruth really didn't like this man. "I'm not sure. Perhaps they're with a mutual friend."

"Who?"

Ruth started to say "Nicole," but sadly, that couldn't be true. "I don't know. They've lost two of their close friends recently. They're still grieving."

Eva's face crumpled. "What if they've been abducted? Like Nicole and Jessie? Oh my God. I should have never let Angel stay home by herself."

The detective touched Eva's arm. "I don't think they've been abducted. In fact, I think the girls may have taken your minivan. It's not in the driveway."

Eva gasped. "They wouldn't. Angel only has a learner's permit."

"Help me out here," Jackson pleaded. "Where would they be?"

"Wherever it is," Ruth said dryly, "I imagine they plan to get home before we do. So be patient, detective, they'll show up soon." And get their butts beaten, Ruth thought. "Now, if you'll excuse me, I have a Bible study waiting for me."

Ruth walked down the hall toward the restroom instead. The pale green walls and pink floral trim annoyed her. She preferred subtle, neutral tones. Ruth stepped into a stall and checked her watch: 7:45. She had ten minutes. She pulled a small pill bottle out of the zipped compartment in her purse and shook a tiny Ativan tablet into her hand. She put the pill under her tongue to dissolve directly into her bloodstream. She needed to be calm for this next phase of the operation. And she needed to be calm later, when she confronted Rachel about this nonsense, whatever it was.

Ruth left the bathroom, moving purposefully. She trotted up the stairs to the main lobby. Detective Jackson was nowhere in sight. Excellent. She pushed out the double doors and hurried down the wide front steps. Halfway across the parking lot, she picked up her pace. She could see the bright lights of the 7-Eleven store across the street. The two quarters she needed for the call were in her hand, and the number was in her head: 342-5597. She mentally searched the Bible for strength from God's words and found them in Matthew Chapter 18:

Whoever causes one of these little ones who believe in me to sin, it would be better for him to have a great millstone hung around his neck and to be drowned in the depths of the sea.

Blown to smithereens would work just as well.

42

7:45 p.m.

JACKSON SAT IN HIS Impala in the church parking lot making phone calls. The first was to Evans. "Stay at the Greiners' house. Ruth Greiner says Rachel will come home before Bible study is over."

"They're out joy riding in the Stricklands' van while their parents are in church?"

"So it seems. Stay in touch."

Jackson called the other team members: Schak had picked up Greg Miller and was headed down to the department, and McCray was currently at the Jahn home. "Find Adam Walsh too, if you can," Jackson said. "Evans and I will be there as soon as we locate the girls."

Where could they be? Jackson wondered, as he started the car. He hated the idea of just sitting in front of the Stricklands' waiting for Angel to come home. He wanted to keep moving. The fact that the girls were together somewhere right this moment, and no one knew exactly where, gave him a bad feeling. He was starting to think they may have acted alone to kill Nicole and make it look similar to Jessie's death. Maybe Greg, Tyler, and Adam were just horny adolescents, not killers. But if that was the case, was anyone else in danger?

He pulled out of the church parking lot and turned left onto a quiet 18th Street. Then it occurred to him that the only other person who knew about the sex club was Kera. Jackson glanced over at the 7-Eleven parking lot out of habit. The convenience stores were famous for drug deals. He noticed a short woman standing at the pay phone. It was Ruth Greiner. How odd, he thought. Jackson almost circled back to see what she was up to, then decided the growing panic in his gut was more important.

Kera not only knew about the sex club, she had access to the girls' clinic records. She knew about the VD, the birth control, and possible pregnancies. And both Jessie and Nicole had contacted her. That might make Angel and Rachel very nervous.

Jackson decided to stop by Kera's and check on her again.

7:47 p.m.

KERA THOUGHT HER best chance of getting outside and away was to throw the girls off guard. If she had not been drugged, she would have simply plowed right through them if they had tried to stop her. She'd grown up playing football with the boys in the commune and had taken self-defense classes in college. But the drug not only made her mind mushy, it made her muscles weak and her reactions slow. She didn't know if she could run. She thought it must be a tranquilizer similar to what was used in the ER to calm hysterical and violent patients.

"Why did you kill Jessie and Nicole?" Kera struggled with each word.

"We didn't kill Jessie," Rachel said, rather defensively. "The mayor did. Don't you read the paper?"

"But why Nicole?" Kera asked.

Rachel shook her head. "Nicole was mixed up and unhappy. Let's just say she laid down her life for her friends." Rachel turned to Angel. "Get a bag from the kitchen. We have to make it look like the others. Hurry."

A bag? They were going to suffocate her? Kera felt sick. With blurry vision, she watched Angel as she ran into the kitchen. Now, she told herself. Now or never.

With every bit of strength she could muster, Kera propelled herself out of the chair and toward the front door. She staggered across the living room like a blurry-eyed drunk, knowing the way from memory. Out of the corner of her eye, she saw Rachel jump up and come after her. Kera tried to keep moving, but her legs buckled. She stumbled, caught herself, and lunged for the front door, landing on her knees.

It was locked. Shit!

Mean hands tangled in her hair and yanked her back. The pain was intense, but she was too drugged to scream. She swung wildly with her elbows but caught nothing but air.

"You don't need to do this," she mumbled. "Your secret's safe."

She tried to pull away, but the pain in her scalp brought tears to her eyes. Another pair of hands cinched down in her hair. Her head was spinning, and she thought she would vomit. It enraged her that they had attacked her from behind. Kera wanted to see their faces, to force them to look her in the eye.

She twisted and yanked and tried to turn herself around so she could use her arms to swing at them, but she only managed to lose a few clumps of hair. Rachel was standing on the backs of her calves. Kera heard a crinkling plastic sound, then a bag came down over her head. The loss of air sent a new wave of adrenaline rushing through her torso. In one great push, she lunged to her feet.

At that moment, Kera's cell phone rang. Perched on the half wall in the foyer, about a foot from where she fought for her life, it played a short crappy version of Free Bird by Lynyrd Skynyrd. The sound was so startling, they all froze for a split second. Kera seized the moment to grab the top of the plastic bag and yank it off her head. As she lunged for the doorknob, Rachel leaped on her back. Kera ignored the weight and tried to unlock the door. Rachel had one arm around her eyes and the other arm around her neck, pressing into her throat.

Kera knew the door handle well, and even without her sight, she managed to unlock it and pull it open. Before she could scream for help, Rachel's hand was over her mouth.

"Dammit Angel, help me," Rachel yelled at her friend.

Kera tried to bite her hand but couldn't get at it.

On weak legs, she staggered out the door, down the three steps, and onto the wet lawn. Rachel still clung to her back like an angry child. Kera's brain kept attempting to shut down, and she thought it was only a matter of moments before she would pass out.

She lurched forward across the grass, each step threatening to bring her down. Her head swam, and her eyes kept closing. She stepped on a sprinkler, lost her footing, and stumbled to her knees. The sudden pitch downward sent Rachel flying off. Through blurry vision, Kera saw the girl land near the driveway, about three feet from her car. Rachel cried out in pain as she hit the cement.

Without the girl's weight, Kera was able to climb to her feet. Holding her head in her hands—because it felt as if it might fall off—she staggered diagonally across the lawn, moving away from Rachel. As she reached the edge of the sidewalk, she glanced back. Angel stood in the doorway, illuminated by the porch light, her eyes darting from Rachel to Kera. Rachel was in the shadows by Kera's Saturn. The girl was struggling to stand up.

Just as Kera started to turn away, her Saturn exploded.

In a nanosecond, the passenger door blew off and smashed into Rachel. The windows shattered and scattered into a hundred flying pieces, and a bright orange fireball blew straight up into the air. Before Kera had a chance to cover her face, the blast knocked her to the ground. A chunk of metal landed on her leg, and right before she lost consciousness, she sensed that her ears were bleeding.

43

8:04 p.m.

UP AHEAD, in the curve of the road, Jackson watched a middle-aged couple dash across McLean Street. To his left, an old woman stood on her front lawn in her pajamas, staring up the road toward Kera's house. What in the hell was going on?

As he cruised to a stop in front of Kera's home, Jackson scanned the scene and tried to take it all in. A young girl sat in the middle of the yard, rocking and wailing. Parts of Kera's vehicle were scattered in a fifteen-foot radius while the remains of the frame smoldered in a shattered heap in the driveway. One of the car's doors was splayed on the lawn, still intact, with a leg sticking out from under it. A woman lay on the sidewalk about twenty feet from the explosion.

The couple who had run across the street went in different directions. The man rushed to the girl on the lawn, and the woman moved to the prone figure on the sidewalk. Instinctively, Jackson reached for his radio. "Dispatch, this is Detective Jackson. There's been an explosion at 3245 McLean. Several people are injured."

"Medics and patrol units are already on the way. A neighbor called it in two minutes ago."

"Great. Call Detective Quince and Agent Fouts and get them out here ASAP."

He shut off the Impala and jumped out. Without making a conscious decision to do so, he moved toward the woman on the sidewalk. The long braid told him it was Kera. The neighbor woman pushed a chunk of metal off Kera's leg, revealing purple warm up pants. Her feet had black socks and no shoes. The questions flashed in his brain in split second intervals. Had she been in the yard when the bomb went off? Why had she gone outside in her socks?

"Is she breathing?" Jackson yelled, moving to kneel down on Kera's other side.

"I don't know." The neighbor looked up at him, her face pinched with concern. "I don't see any blood, though."

Fear hit him like a sneaker wave. It knocked him down and sucked him under for a moment. Jackson fought desperately to control the emotions that gripped him. He swallowed hard before he could speak. "Kera! Can you hear me? Kera!"

She opened her eyes. They fluttered, then closed again.

She was alive! He leaned over her face and listened for breath sounds. Ragged but steady.

"She's breathing."

Then he saw Kera's lips moving. No sound came out, but she was trying to talk. Jackson put his ear next to her mouth. At first, it sounded like "uh," then he realized she was saying "drug."

Oh shit. "I think she's saying she's been drugged," he told the neighbor. "We have to make sure the paramedics know that. She probably needs her stomach pumped. If she starts to vomit, roll her on her side. Stay with her and talk to her until the ambulance arrives."

Jackson would never forgive himself for not protecting her better. Where were the patrol units he'd assigned to cruise by? Jackson forced himself to push to his feet and move away from Kera to check on the others. He had to sidestep twisted debris to get to the young girl in the middle of the yard. It was Angel Strickland. She looked older than he remembered from two nights ago when he'd questioned her. Her face was streaked with mascara, and she was clearly distraught. But physically, she seemed uninjured. The male half of the neighbor couple was on his knees with his arm around Angel telling her that everything would be okay. Jackson sincerely doubted that.

Angel looked up at Jackson and burst into a fresh round of tears. Through them she sputtered, "The car exploded and killed Rachel. I told her we shouldn't have come here."

Jackson looked over at the body under the now-detached car door. He could see Rachel's head, her hair in the same spiky bun as the last time he saw her. Only now, one side of her face was unrecognizable, and the blood flowed freely down her sweatshirt. He moved over to her, squatted, and checked for a pulse. She was as dead as she looked.

Jackson had never been at a crime scene like this. For the first time in his career as a detective, he was unsure of himself. It was important to hear Angel's story before her parents or a lawyer had a chance to coach her. But more important, he needed to be at Kera's side.

He rushed back to where she lay, unconscious. As he kneeled next to her, he heard the wail of sirens coming up 29th Street. Thank God. "Hang in there, Kera."

Jackson would not let them put Angel in the ambulance with Kera. "No. This one doesn't ride with her," he directed the two male paramedics carrying Angel. "Put the girl in the other wagon."

To the female medic attending to Kera, he said, "She's been drugged, so let the ER doctors know to pump her stomach."

Jackson insisted on riding with Angel.

"She's in shock, sir," the young paramedic argued. "She's not getting away. I'm giving her a mild sedative and a glucose IV."

"She's under arrest and I'm staying with her."

The paramedic shrugged and stepped aside.

As they barreled down Chambers, siren wailing occasionally, Jackson leaned in to speak with Angel, who was stretched out on a mobile gurney. Her face was streaked with tears and she had dark smudges on her forehead, but she seemed calm. The sedative had apparently kicked in.

"Did you and Rachel set the bomb at Kera's?"

The paramedic gave him a look, but didn't say anything.

"No." Her blond head moved slowly from side to side. "I don't know anything about the bomb."

"Why did you go to Kera's house?"

"To talk."

"What did you give Kera?"

"I don't know. Rachel did it." Angel's voice was so soft, Jackson had to move his head next to hers.

"Why?"

"It's easier that way."

Jackson felt a shiver of dread. "What's easier?"

The paramedic watched them both, eyes bouncing back and forth.

"Nicole was easier," Angel whispered. "After Rachel put the bag over her head, she just stopped breathing. Kera fought back."

Jackson had to take a moment—after envisioning Kera with a plastic bag over her face, drugged and fighting for her life. He was glad the paramedic had heard Angel's confession. They might need his testimony.

"Why did you and Rachel kill Nicole?"

"She was going to tell her parents about the sex. And they would have told our parents."

"Why did you try to kill Kera?"

"I didn't." Angel suddenly reached out and grabbed his arm. "I didn't do it. Rachel was the one. That's why God let her get blown up."

The paramedic said, "You should let her rest." But his voice lacked conviction. He was hanging on their every word.

Jackson started to ask another question, but the ambulance's siren wailed loudly for three long seconds. They were in the downtown area now and only minutes from the hospital.

"Do you know who set the bomb?"

Angel shook her head and fresh tears rolled from her eyes. "Am I going to jail?"

"You'll probably get sent to a juvenile detention facility."

"That's okay." She pressed her lips together. "I can't go home."

Jackson circled the hospital lobby again and again as he waited for news about Kera. At times, his brain worked frantically as he tried to figure out who had set the two bombs and whether they were connected to Rachel and Angel in any way. Then his mind would shut down and all he could think of was Kera. Please God, let Kera be okay.

Finally, a young doctor came out to tell him that Kera was awake and asking for him. His heart surged with joy and relief.

"Jackson." She gave him a weak smile from her half-reclining position in the hospital bed. Her voice was a little hoarse, and she had an IV in her arm, but she looked fine. Really fine.

"I'm so sorry, Kera. I should have protected you better. We—the public safety department—should have protected you better. I did not anticipate a personal car bomb."

"It's not just the bomb." Kera leaned forward. "Rachel and Angel tried to kill me. The same way they killed Nicole to keep her quiet about the sex club."

"I know. I talked with Angel on the way here. She says it was all Rachel."

Kera shook her head. "Rachel was definitely the aggressor, but Angel grabbed me by the hair while Rachel pulled a plastic bag over my face."

"That must have been horrifying."

Kera closed her eyes. "You have to find the bomber. I can't take much more of this."

"We will." Jackson said it because Kera needed to hear it. But in his heart, he was afraid to make that promise.

‹ **44** ›

Friday, October 29, 2:37 p.m.
RUTH WOKE FROM A NAP, drank a glass of water to wet her dry mouth and throat, then got back in bed and began to pray again. All she had done for two days was pray and sleep and read the Bible. The Ativan kept her from physically jumping out of her skin, but her mind was in turmoil. Rachel's death was a pain unlike any she had ever known. The fact that her own bomb had killed her daughter instead of the abortionist was more than Ruth thought she could bear. She had begged God again and again for understanding. She had prayed for the strength to bear this burden and to accept that it might be one of God's mysteries that she was not meant to understand.

Then the rumors started. Church members began to say that Rachel had killed Nicole and tried to kill Kollmorgan to hide Teen Talk's dirty secrets. The gossipers said the kids in Teen Talk had not been studying the Bible at all, but instead had been fornicating in an unspeakable sexual orgy week after week. Ruth learned that her daughter had been the worst kind of sinner.

Ruth reached for her Bible and began to read from the book of Genesis. When she came to the passage where God asks Abraham to sacrifice Isaac, Ruth stopped. And then, in a moment of enlightenment, God opened her mind and it all became clear. Demonstrating His infinite wisdom and justice, God had used Ruth's bomb to punish Rachel—and to test Ruth's faith.

And Ruth vowed not to fail that test.

She prayed for guidance. She prayed for God to make His will known to her. And in another moment of pure clarity, He did. God wanted her to stay committed to the mission. For Rachel's death to mean anything, Ruth had to find the strength to continue God's work.

The day before, in a moment of grief and rage, she had almost thrown away her bomb-making materials. But something had stopped her. God had stopped her. Because He wanted her to complete the mission.

Maybe not immediately. But in time.

Friday, October 29, 3:05 p.m.
JACKSON HAD TAKEN the day off and driven to Portland with Katie. They had spent three hours at Lloyd Center—a gigantic shopping mall with an ice rink—and now they were driving to HarborView House to see Renee. As much as Jackson hated shopping malls, he knew he would enjoy the visit with Renee even less. But Katie was thrilled by all of it. It was great to see her smile. She'd been sullen and contrite and weepy for days.

They'd already had a long talk yesterday about how truth and trust went together and how she would have to earn back his trust, step by step. They still needed to have another serious conversation. Jackson was nervous.

"Katie. We have to talk about sex."

Long sigh.

He tried to catch her eye.

"Are you sure?" she whined. "Mom and I can have this conversation instead, you know."

"This happened on my watch. I have to set things straight."

Another long sigh. "Not that much happened."

"Did you have unprotected sex?"

"No. I'm not stupid."

Jackson refrained from direct comment. "I'd still like you

to be tested for AIDS."

"Not necessary, but okay, if it will make you feel better."

Jackson rounded the corner at the top of the hill and pulled off into a viewing area. The city and the river stretched out below them.

"Katie. I want you to know how I feel about this. Look at me."

She grudgingly turned her head.

"Sex between two young people who care about each other is okay. But when I say young, I mean nineteen or twenty. Sex is an emotional experience that most people your age are not ready to handle, especially young women."

"Why especially women?"

"Because you have different hormones. I can't explain it as well as I'd like to, but the bottom line is that you can get hurt. Emotionally and physically. And I can't stand the thought of you being hurt."

"Okay." Her voice was uncharacteristically quiet.

He wasn't finished. "And by the way. Birth control isn't foolproof. Your mother was taking the pill when she got pregnant with you. So until you're sure you can handle taking care of a baby, you'd better skip the sex."

"I was an accident?"

"Most people are."

He started the car and headed back up the hill. "You're still the best thing that ever happened to me though. I love you, kid."

When they reached HarborView, Jackson decided to let Katie go in by herself for a while.

"One more thing," he said, as she got out of the car. "I have a date next weekend with a woman named Kera. So if your mother starts talking about the two of us getting back together, don't get your hopes up."

"Shit." Katie rolled her eyes.

"That's fifty cents off your allowance. Now get going."

‹ **45** ›

Jackson and Slonecker met for lunch at the Lucky Noodle across from the 5th Street Public Market. Jackson liked the atmosphere as much as the food. It was dark and quiet with private booths and lots of greenery. Feeling indulgent, he ordered phad thai and a side of hot-and-sour soup. He'd lost eight pounds in the last two weeks just from being too busy to eat or sleep much.

"We've decided to leave Angel in the juvenile system," Slonecker said, as his soup arrived. "There's not much support for trying her as an adult."

Jackson was relieved. He didn't think Angel deserved to be thrown away. She was messed up, no doubt. But she was still a kid. And she seemed sincerely remorseful. He believed that if Angel had never known Rachel, she would never have hurt anyone.

Angel had also described in detail the punishments Rachel had endured from her parents, and Jackson had called Child Services Division. They had promised to investigate for the sake of the other child in the Greiner house.

"Will Angel be free at eighteen?" Jackson asked.

"Oh no." The DA scowled. "She'll be incarcerated until she's twenty-five." He shook his head. "Or maybe not. You never know who the shrinks will turn out."

"What kind of deal did you make with the mayor?" Jackson asked, not sure he wanted to know.

"He'll plead to statutory rape and aggravated manslaughter. Seven years; out in five."

"Five years for three lives. Pretty fucking light."

"Three lives?" Slonecker was puzzled.

"Jessie, her baby, and Oscar Grady, the sex offender who killed himself after I interrogated him."

"That was unfortunate. But it wasn't your fault. Or Fieldstone's. Grady must have had a guilty conscience. And it was only a matter of time before he re-offended."

"He already had," Jackson said. "Casaway investigated him for me. Grady had been sexually abusing the fourteen-year-old daughter of one of his roommates."

Jackson took a long drink of coffee. "And I can't prove this, but I think Casaway was the leak. McCray finally admitted that he'd left all our case notes in the photocopy machine while he used the restroom. He says he saw Casaway in the hall when he came out. And later, when I talked with Casaway about Oscar Grady, I realized he had more information about the homicides than he should have. But it's only suspicion."

The waiter brought their food and they both dug in. Halfway through the meal, Jackson's cell phone rang, and he answered it. Slonecker didn't seem to mind.

It was Debbie from the medical examiner's office in Portland. "Hey Jackson. I have some interesting news."

"Tell me."

"Detective Quince found some cat hairs in the cracks of the driveway under the car that exploded. He sent them here for testing. I remembered that Nicole's clothes had cat hair present too. So I compared the samples just for kicks. It's the same cat."

"The exact same cat? As in a DNA match?"

"Yep. A white long-hair."

"You're amazing, Debbie. I owe you more than lunch. Thank you, thank you."

Jackson relayed the news to Slonecker. The DA swallowed a big bite of angel hair pasta and shrimp before saying, "Do we know whose cat it is?"

"The Greiners'." Jackson knew about the big white cat because Schak had reported it at their task force meeting this morning when they met to wrap things up.

Slonecker vocalized what they were both thinking. "So one of the Greiners left cat hair in Kollmorgan's driveway when they planted the bomb under her car."

"The apple doesn't fall far from the tree," Jackson said. "My money's on Ruth to be God's Messenger. Schak said she was squirrelly when he questioned her about Jessie."

Slonecker pulled out his cell phone. "Let's get a search warrant and get over there this afternoon and find out."

Monday, November 1, 2:46 p.m.
AS SOON AS RUTH saw the two men in suits at her front door, she began to pray. She knew why they were here, so she did not bother to read the search warrant they offered.

Ruth had moved the potassium nitrate and metal cylinders out of the laundry room and into a back shed, but still, after an hour, they found them. God's answer to her prayers was that she should go to jail. So when they cuffed her, she did not protest. She hoped to be out of the house before Caleb got home. She didn't want him to see her like this.

As they led her to their car, the clouds opened and the sun poured through. Ruth had another moment of clarity. God still wanted her to fulfill her mission. From a prison cell, she could write letters to the faithful everywhere. She knew there were others like her, those who were willing to defy man's law to do God's work. She just had to find them. And teach them how.

Monday, November 1, 1:15 p.m.
KERA TOOK A SEAT at a table in the corner of Max's, a little restaurant near Oregon State University in Corvallis, a college town about thirty miles north of Eugene. The lunch

crowd was thinning out, and the place smelled of fried meat and potatoes. Kera ordered black coffee and stared out the window where more storm clouds gathered. Hope and fear gnawed on her nerves in equal portions. Despite everything she had been through—and still faced—all she could think about was Nathan's baby.

Danette would be here soon. The young woman had called her Sunday—after the longest four-day wait of Kera's life—and agreed to meet her. Kera promised herself that she would not be pushy or needy. She would simply make her offer and let it go. Life was too short and too unpredictable for regrets or what-ifs. And this baby was a gift she had never expected. And perhaps did not deserve.

When Danette entered the restaurant, Kera knew intuitively who she was. The young woman was five-eight, with curly auburn hair that she wore loosely around her shoulders. She had a wide, expressive face that needed no makeup. Arched eyebrows and full lips made her naturally attractive. Kera watched Danette move toward her. She wondered if the young woman would realize, as she had, that they looked like each other.

"Kera?"

"Yes." She stood and they shook hands, a formal gesture that felt awkward in the situation.

"Nathan looks like you," Danette said, as she sat down.

Kera smiled. "How did you meet him?"

"At a party." Danette laughed. "Where else?"

Danette took a moment to order a glass of orange juice from their waitress, then continued. "I was in Eugene for the weekend visiting friends. Nathan and I hit it off." She shrugged. "We saw each other on weekends for a while, then he told me he was shipping out to Iraq in three days."

"August 3rd." Kera would never forget the day.

"I was so upset." Danette shook her head. "I was pissed that he hadn't told me up front and pissed that the first guy

I really liked was going off to get killed." As soon as she said it, Danette looked horrified. Her hand flew to her mouth. "I am so sorry. That was completely insensitive."

"It's okay." Kera knew their encounter would be an emotional challenge, and she had steeled herself for it. "When did you find out you were pregnant?"

"About a month ago. I'd written to Nathan once and never heard back from him. I figured I was just a pre-deployment fling. I didn't blame him for that." Danette paused and seemed introspective. "I never expected him to respond to my second letter either. I think I wrote it mostly to ease my own conscience. To tell myself that I had tried to let him know about the baby and give him a voice in the decision."

Kera figured this was the right moment. "I can't speak for Nathan. If he had lived, I don't know what he would have wanted. This decision would have been difficult for him too." Tears came to her eyes and Kera fought to stay in control. "But as the child's grandparent, I would like the chance to know and love this person." Kera reached out and touched Danette's hand. "If you choose to keep the baby, I will help you in any way I can. You can even stay in my home if you'd like. I'm willing to adopt the baby once it's born if you don't feel ready to be a parent." Kera met her eyes. "I'm a good person, and I'd be a good mother to your child."

Danette smiled sadly. "I know. Nathan thought the world of you. That's partly why I liked him so much."

There was a long moment of silence.

Finally, Kera forced herself to say, "But there is no pressure from me. It's your decision. And I will support it, whatever you choose."

"I appreciate that." Danette took a long drink of her juice and seemed far away for a moment. "This is so hard. I want to finish college and get a job teaching math to seventh graders. I get so scared when I think about having this baby." Now Danette fought back tears. "And I get so sad when I think about aborting it. But your offer changes things. I will seriously consider it. That's all I can promise right now. Let me think about it."

"Of course."

Kera closed her eyes and mentally let go of her desire to affect and control this situation. She felt herself relax for the first time in weeks. She sipped her coffee—it was fresh ground the way she liked it—and thought that her life and her future would be good with or without this grandchild. She had to believe that.